*He was both
a vampire and
a playboy . . .
and impossible
to resist.*

*"I've never bitten a mortal.
And I've never bitten for food.
So you can relax.
You're completely safe."*

Instead of feeling reassured, Abby quickly analyzed his answer. "So you've bitten vampires for . . . other reasons?"

"Only women." He looked away, frowning. "In the right situation it can be a pleasurable thing."

"How?"

"You'll have to trust me on that." He glanced at her and his eyes turned a brilliant green. "Unless you'd like a demonstration?"

"No." She scooted further away in the booth.

His jaw shifted as he reached for his drink. "I'm no monster, Abigail. I won't hurt you."

She winced inwardly. He thought she feared him as a monster.

How could she admit she feared her attraction to him?

By Kerrelyn Sparks

KERRELYN SPARKS

Sexiest VAMPIRE *Alive*

AVON

An Imprint of HarperCollinsPublishers

This is a work of fiction. Names, characters, places, and incidents are products of the author's imagination or are used fictitiously and are not to be construed as real. Any resemblance to actual events, locales, organizations, or persons, living or dead, is entirely coincidental.

AVON BOOKS
An Imprint of HarperCollins*Publishers*
10 East 53rd Street
New York, New York 10022-5299

First Avon Books mass market printing: October 2011

Avon Trademark Reg. U.S. Pat. Off. and in Other Countries, Marca Registrada, Hecho en U.S.A.
HarperCollins® is a registered trademark of HarperCollins Publishers.

Printed in the U.S.A.

10 9 8 7 6 5 4 3 2 1

In loving memory of
Janice,
always there with a warm hug,
great advice, and homemade cookies.
Thank you for believing in me and being proud.
It was an honor to be part of your life.

Acknowledgments

There would be no sexiest vampire alive without the sexiest husband alive. I am forever grateful to my husband, Don, for deftly demonstrating how a man can be serious, yet funny. Strong, yet charming. My thanks to my children, who are always encouraging, and my best friends/critique partners, who are extremely wise and know exactly when to give me a hug or a needed kick in the rear.

My thanks to everyone at HarperCollins/Avon Books: Pam from publicity, Adrienne from marketing, Tom from the art department, publisher Liate, executive editor Erika Tsang, and assistant editor Amanda. Thanks also to my agent, Michelle Grajkowski of Three Seas Literary Agency.

And finally, I cannot express how grateful I am to all you readers. Thanks to you, the Love at Stake series has been more successful than I ever dreamed.

Sexiest
VAMPIRE
Alive

Chapter One

*S*imone tore the man's shirt open and skimmed her hand down his smooth, hairless chest and rippled abs.

"I have a hunger that cannot be denied," she murmured in her husky French accent.

The man turned his chiseled jaw to expose his neck. "Take me. My body, my blood—I'm all yours."

She trailed a finger along his carotid artery, then suddenly shoved him away. "No! I can no longer bear it!"

With a dramatic swish of her pink silk negligee, she rose to her feet. The voluminous skirt swirled around her long legs, allowing a peek at her matching pink stilettos.

She lifted a pale hand to her brow. "What is a vampire to do? For so many years I have endured the same taste. How I long for something different!"

She moved forward, lowering her hand with a graceful flutter. "I need something new, something rich, robust, and sophisticat— Ack!" She tripped on her nightgown and fell flat on her face.

"Cut!" The director cursed under his breath, then leaned toward Gregori and whispered, "Are you sure we have to use her?"

Gregori hid his frustration, like he normally did, and gave Gordon an encouraging smile. "She'll be fine. She's the most famous model in the vampire world."

"Yeah, you've mentioned that about five times. But she can't act. Hell, she can't even walk."

Gregori's smile faltered slightly as he inwardly winced. He thought he'd scored a coup, convincing the famous Simone to star in his commercial introducing the latest creation in Vampire Fusion Cuisine, Blardonnay. But after three hours of shooting, there wasn't a single successful take.

The director and film crew at the Digital Vampire Network in Brooklyn had already polished off the crate of twenty-four bottles he'd brought as a gift. The mixture of synthetic blood and Chardonnay was no longer strong enough for the director. Gordon tipped back a bottle of Blissky, then gave Gregori a sour look.

"The sun will rise in about ninety minutes," he muttered. "I'm calling it quits before my tortured crew runs outside to fry themselves in a blaze of glory."

"It's not that bad," Gregori assured him. "With some careful editing, we'll have—" *Zip.* "You'll still get paid for your time."

Gordon snorted and took another swig of Blissky.

Gregori adjusted his tie while he considered his options. He was the one who would have to answer to his boss for spending a small fortune on a commercial that wasn't happening. It wouldn't help matters if he criticized Simone. She might look frail and delicate, but, enraged, she could inflict a massive amount of damage with her superior vampire strength.

There was the time she'd destroyed a dance club in

Manhattan when no one had recognized her. Gregori had used a huge amount of vampire mind control to wipe the memory of every terrified mortal who had witnessed her temper tantrum. Unfortunately he hadn't been around to clean up when a paparazzo in Paris had snapped her photo without her permission. She'd tossed the photographer clear across the Champs Élysées. *Le Figaro* had speculated that her odd display of strength meant she was high on PCP. She'd retaliated the next night by ripping a street lamp out of the sidewalk and crashing it through the newspaper office's plate-glass window. Somehow, she thought she'd proved them wrong.

He adjusted his cuff links as he resigned himself to the only logical course of action: playing the role of the kind and sympathetic friend, otherwise known as major suck-up. Sheesh, the stuff he had to do for his job.

He stepped onto the set, which consisted of thick ivory carpet and an ivory satin settee. The male model sat sprawled on the settee, not even attempting to help Simone, who remained tangled in her negligee, wallowing on the carpet like a nearly starved, beached whale.

"Simone, sweetheart, are you all right?" He lifted her carefully to her feet. She was so thin, it was like propping up a broomstick in a strong wind. "It's not like you to fall down." *Twelve times.*

"It is these ridiculous shoes you made me wear. They're too big." She raised her voice so everyone in the studio could hear. "You know I wear a size five."

She wore an eight. Gregori knew because she'd begged him to buy her a pair of Jimmy Choo sandals last Christmas. He'd done it, not out of any special affection for Simone, but for business reasons. As marketing director at Romatech Industries, he knew the value of staying chummy with the most influential personalities in the vampire world.

"Is your gown too long?" he suggested. "We could have it shortened a bit."

"I like it long. It makes me look taller. And thinner."

Good God, if she was any thinner, she'd be two-dimensional. "You look beautiful, Simone. But . . . I'm afraid your concentration is off just a tad. Perhaps if we—"

"It's *his* fault!" She pointed a perfectly manicured pink nail at the male model who was busy taking off the shirt she'd ripped. "He's too ugly to work with."

Gregori glanced at the model. "He looks fine to me."

"Why, thank you, handsome." The male model winked.

Oh shit. "Simone, we can't keep replacing the guy for you. This is the eighth one. The talent agency is running out of guys, and we're running out of time, so do you think you could possibly bring yourself to work with this one?"

She stuck out her bottom lip in a pout. "He's repulsive. I shudder when I have to touch him."

The male model wagged a finger at her. "It's not like I'm enjoying it either, girlfriend."

"It's called acting, Simone," Gregori whispered. "You have to pretend to desire him. He could be as ugly as a turnip, but you make us believe he's stunning."

"But I *am* stunning." The model flipped his long blond hair over his shoulders.

Gregori groaned inwardly. It was impossible to whisper around a bunch of Vamps. They could hear everything. He grasped Simone by her bony shoulders. "Let's be honest about this, Toots. It's not the shoes, or the gown, or the guy on the couch—"

"The name is Pennington," the male model interrupted. "Pennington Langley, the Third. But please don't call me Penny for short. I would hate to sound cheap." He gave Gregori a flirtatious smile.

Suppressing a shudder, Gregori smiled back. Sheesh, the crap he put up with for his job. "Simone. I've seen you glide down a jillion runways as graceful as a swan. You can do this."

She ducked her head as she pressed her hands against his chest. "All right, I'll be honest. I-I'm afraid."

"Afraid of what? Failure?" He winced when her steel-like nails dug into him.

"*I never fail*," she hissed.

"Right. Right, I knew that." He grabbed her hands to keep her pink claws from ripping through his best suit. "What are you afraid of, then?"

Her bottom lip trembled against her fangs. "The sun will rise soon. I'm afraid of dying."

"Sweetcakes, we die at every sunrise."

"I mean *real* death! *La mort finale!*" She clutched his lapels with her fists. "I heard Corky's show tonight. *Live with the Undead.* She said we're all in grave danger!"

"You'll be fine, Simone. You'll be staying at Roman's townhouse where we have guards to keep us safe."

"Then Corky is *right*?" Simone shrieked and gave

him a hard shake. "The mortal world knows about us now?"

He pried her bony fingers loose from his lapels. "Corky ought to know. She's the one who posted the damned video."

Three nights earlier, Corky Courrant had filmed the battle at Mount Rushmore that had climaxed with the death of her lover, the Malcontent leader, Casimir. While Gregori could understand why a woman might be a little miffed over the decapitation of her lover, he still thought Corky had severely overreacted. She'd posted the video on YouTube, claiming it was proof that vampires were real. That was an unforgivable, traitorous act in their world, and yet Corky was still employed at the Digital Vampire Network. Apparently her infamy was good for ratings.

Simone's eyes filled with tears. "She said the mortals will hunt us down and slaughter us in our sleep!"

"Oh my God!" Pennington sprang to his feet. "Is that true?"

The boom operator glowered at him. "Don't you watch the *Nightly News*? Stone Cauffyn said the secret is out, and it won't be long before the mortals decide to kill us off."

With a soft moan, Simone sank onto the carpet. Her tears, tinted with blood, left pink streaks down her gaunt cheeks. *"La mort finale."*

"It's the end for us all," the cameraman grumbled.

"We're doomed." The makeup artist sniffed and wiped tears from her face.

"The Vampire Apocalypse," Gordon muttered, then took another swig of Blissky.

Good God, no wonder the director and crew had jumped on that case of Blardonnay. "Get a grip, guys," Gregori told them. "Just because Corky posted a video that looks like vampires getting their heads cut off and turning to dust, that doesn't mean any mortals will believe it."

"Right," Gordon sneered. "Because mortals are always making home videos where they cut each other's heads off."

"If you look at the comments, a lot of people are calling it a hoax," Gregori said.

"It only takes one mortal with one stake to do me in," the boom operator mumbled.

"We're doomed!" The makeup artist collapsed on the floor, clutching an empty bottle of Blardonnay. "*Doomed!*"

"No, we're not! You guys got the official memo from Roman, right?" Gregori asked. Roman Draganesti was not only his boss and CEO of Romatech Industries, he was also Coven Master of East Coast Vampires. "He wants everyone to remain calm and go about your lives in a normal manner."

"Yeah, we know." Gordon upended his Blissky bottle, then scowled when he discovered it was empty. "That's why we all showed up for work today."

"We should be looking for some caves to hide in," the cameraman grumbled, then his eyes lit up. "I know! We could hide in mausoleums."

"Right." The boom operator scoffed. "Mortals would never think about looking for us in a graveyard."

"We're doomed—"

"Enough!" Gregori interrupted the makeup artist.

"Chillax, people. It's going to be all right. Roman's got a strategy meeting tonight with a bunch of Coven Masters."

"Do they have a plan?" Pennington asked.

"I'm sure they'll come up with something." Gregori didn't know much about the situation except that Roman and the head of MacKay Security and Investigation, Angus MacKay, had spent the last two nights discussing the matter with Sean Whelan—CIA operative, newly turned vampire, and Roman's father-in-law. "The best thing for us to do is to behave normally and not bring any attention to ourselves. Just go to work, go home, drink your blood from bottles, and no one will ever suspect you're a vampire."

"That's easy for you to say," Gordon grumbled. "You and your buddies have security guards to watch over you during the day. We do our death-sleep in apartments that mortals could break into."

"We're doomed!" the makeup girl cried.

Gregori loosened his tie as he considered. Corky's damned video was probably inciting panic all over the vampire world. And the more the Vamps panicked, the bigger the chance that one of them would do something really stupid that made the problem even worse. They needed to feel safe.

He retrieved his smart phone from his jacket pocket. "I'll tell you what. I'll ask Angus MacKay to send a day guard here. We'll turn the building into an emergency shelter. Then Vamps can do their death-sleep here, knowing they'll be safe and protected."

Gordon jumped to his feet and swayed a little. "Are you serious? You can do that?"

"Of course." Gregori smiled. "I'll make the arrangements, so hurry up and announce it on air."

"Great!" Gordon dashed out of the studio.

The makeup artist eased to her feet and gave Gregori a shaky smile. "Thank you."

"Not a problem." Gregori selected Angus's number on his Droid while the rest of the crew thanked him. "Let's get ready for another try at the commercial, okay?"

"Yes, sir!" the boom operator shouted with a grin.

Pennington put on a new shirt, while the makeup girl applied new powder and lipstick to Simone.

Gregori breathed a sigh of relief. Maybe they'd get the commercial done after all. Angus's phone sent him to voice mail, so he left a short message explaining the need to turn DVN into an emergency shelter for frightened Vamps.

"Excuse me."

Gregori glanced up from a quick look through his e-mail to see Pennington standing nearby. "Yes?"

"I'd like to thank you for keeping us all safe tonight."

"Glad to help."

Pennington shoved his long blond hair over his shoulders. "And I'd like to thank you for giving me the opportunity to star in a commercial."

"No problem." Gregori didn't want to remind the model that he was the talent agency's eighth choice, and he wouldn't be here at all if Simone hadn't sent the first seven guys packing.

Pennington sidled up closer. "What I mean is I'd like to thank you . . . personally."

Yikes. Gregori stepped back. "No thanks. Sorry."

"But you're gay, right? I mean, you dress so well, and you were so nice and sensitive to . . . *her*." Pennington wrinkled his nose at Simone.

"A straight guy can't be nice?" Gregori muttered.

Simone snorted while the makeup girl brushed her hair. "Why do you continue with this charade, *mon ami*? You refused to have sex with me. You must be gay."

His mouth dropped open. The crew started whispering, latching on to this tasty morsel of gossip. *Shit.* "Simone, have you been spreading rumors about me?"

"No, of course not." She waved a hand dramatically. "I know how much you enjoy your reputation as a young playboy. But really, *mon ami*, you should stop acting so cowardly and admit the truth. You'll feel much better for it."

Cowardly? He reached into his pocket for a stress ball. Dammit, he'd left them all at the office.

It was true that he'd rejected Simone without giving her much of a reason, but it hadn't seemed diplomatic at the time to be honest. He simply wasn't attracted to her. And he wasn't gung-ho over the prospect of being lover number five hundred and sixty-three. Simone actually kept count in her journal. Along with a rating from one to ten.

She'd shown him the journal several times. It was rare, she'd pointed out, for a man to score over a five. That was why she was burdened with the sad task of trying out hundreds in order to find a few who were worthy.

He'd let her down as gently as possible since he needed to stay friendly with the celebrities of the vampire world so he could be successful in his career. And right now, success meant getting the damned commercial recorded. That meant he couldn't afford to insult Simone or Pennington, who was still regarding him with a hopeful smile. Damn, the bull crap he put up with for his job.

"I—" His Droid vibrated. Thank God. "I've got to take this. Excuse me." He paced across the studio. "Hey, Angus. Excellent timing. So do you have a day guard you can send?"

"Aye," Angus replied. "I asked Robby and some of the lads to teleport over there and leave Rajiv."

"Great. Thanks, dude."

"We're just about done here with our plan of action. Talk to you soon." Angus hung up.

They had a plan. Excellent! Gregori smiled as he pocketed his phone.

Gordon rushed back into the studio. "We aired the announcement. Vamps are already teleporting into the lobby."

"How many can you take in?" Gregori asked.

"Sly thinks we can take in hundreds," Gordon referred to Sylvester, the station manager. "We have six large studios and an enormous basement."

"Great!" Gregori gave everyone a thumbs-up. "You'll all be safe with Rajiv watching out for you. He's a were-tiger who can shift whenever he wants."

"A were-tiger?" The makeup artist's eyes grew wide. "Oh my. He sounds so . . ."

"Sexy," Pennington whispered.

Gregori winced. At least the Vamps would be dead during the day, so Rajiv wouldn't have to fight off a bunch of advances. He slapped his hands together. "So now that everybody's happy, how about we get this commercial done?"

The crew shouted a victory cheer.

"Places!" Gordon shouted, and everyone scurried into position on or off set. "Let's do it, people! Mark it."

"Take number seventy-two." A crew member clapped the sticks together on the slate.

Simone lounged on the ivory satin settee and leaned toward Pennington. Her eyes burned with hot passion. "I have a hunger that cannot be denied."

Pennington flipped his hair back to expose his neck. "Take me. My body, my blood—I'm all yours."

She ripped open his shirt. One of the buttons popped off and hit her in the eye.

"Ack!" She jumped to her feet, catching the boom operator by surprise and ramming her head into the large microphone suspended over them.

"Aarrgh!" She collapsed on the floor.

Everyone stared at her unconscious body for a few silent seconds.

"Cut," Gordon muttered.

"Am I interrupting anything?" Robby MacKay strode into the studio.

"No," the entire crew moaned.

"Rajiv is in the lobby." Robby did a double take at Simone's unconscious body. "We left a few cases of Chocolood and Bleer in the lobby so no one will go hungry."

"Chocolood?" The makeup artist ran from the room.

"Free Bleer!" The male crew members dashed after her.

Robby motioned to Simone. "Is she all right?"

Gregori sighed. "She will be. I'll teleport her back to the townhouse."

Robby shook his head. "Leave her be. Angus and Roman want you at Romatech."

"I'll drop her off on the way—"

"Nay," Robby interrupted. "They want you there now."

Now? The sun would be up in less than an hour. What was so important that it couldn't wait another night? Gregori turned to Gordon. "If Simone comes to, tell her I was called away. We'll try again tomorrow."

Gordon grimaced. "Must we?"

"Yes, I'll—"

"I said *now*," Robby interrupted Gregori and gave him a stern look.

"Okay! Don't get your panties in a wad." He glanced at Robby's green and blue plaid kilt. "If you even wear underwear."

Robby frowned as he grabbed on to Gregori's arm. "Let's go."

Gregori stiffened with surprise. He was being escorted? What was the big hurry— His thoughts cut off as everything went black.

Chapter Two

$\mathcal{T}$ he big strategy meeting had to be over. Gregori spotted about a dozen Coven Masters leaving the Romatech conference room as Robby ushered him down the hall.

He pulled his arm from Robby's steel-like grip. "Look, dude, tell me what's going on."

Robby shrugged one shoulder. "Angus told me to bring you here now."

"Yeah, I got the *now* part." Gregori noted most of the Coven Masters were teleporting away. No doubt they wanted to leave New York before sunrise. He nodded at two who remained in the hall. "Hey, guys. What's up?"

Rafferty McCall shook his hand. "Great idea about making emergency shelters."

"Thanks," he answered the West Coast Coven Master. Was that why he'd been summoned? They might need his help coordinating shelters across the world.

"I should get back to Louisiana." Colbert GrandPied slapped Gregori on the shoulder. "*Bonne chance, mon ami.*"

"Aye," Rafferty agreed. "Good luck to you, lad."

"For what?" Gregori asked, but the two Coven Masters teleported away.

"Why do I need luck all of a sudden?" Gregori asked Robby, but the Scottish vampire merely opened the conference room door and motioned for him to enter.

Gregori tamped down on his frustration. If there was any luck to be had, he sure as hell wasn't getting any. The commercial was a disaster. Thanks to Simone, everyone at DVN would be spreading a rumor that he was gay. And then there was that little matter of the Vampire Apocalypse and their imminent deaths at the hands of wild-eyed mortals driven into a murderous frenzy by Corky's damned video. An irritating prickle on the back of his neck warned him that it was about to get even worse.

If there was one thing he hated, it was walking into a situation uninformed and unprepared. He was accustomed to succeeding at whatever project he was assigned to, and as far as he was concerned, the secret to success was information. He liked to have all the facts beforehand, everything thoroughly researched, documented, and organized into strategic plans of action. He never walked into a conference room empty-handed . . . like he was doing now. Hell, he didn't even know what this meeting was about.

Out of habit, he reached into his pocket for a stress ball, but no luck. He'd just have to bluff his way through, show them some positive attitude. *Stay cool. Act like you belong. It's the best way to fit in.*

He slipped his tie back into place, then marched purposefully into the conference room. The long table was empty except at the far end, where five Vamps stopped their whispering to look at him.

He smiled. "You wanted to see me?"

No smiles in return. The prickle on the back of his neck grew more insistent. He'd known these guys for years. Why were they studying him like he was some sort of specimen?

At the head of the table his boss, Roman Draganesti, nodded his head slightly. Sitting to Roman's left was Jean-Luc Echarpe, who retained his title of Coven Master of Western Europe even though he spent most of his time in Texas and only teleported to Paris once a month to preside over Coven Court. Next to him sat Zoltan Czakvar, CM for Eastern Europe, headquartered in Budapest. On Roman's right, Angus MacKay narrowed his eyes. He was not only head of MacKay Security and Investigation, but also CM for the British Isles.

Next to Angus, Sean Whelan sat with a fierce scowl on his face. Actually that wasn't so unusual. Gregori had never seen Sean Whelan when the guy wasn't scowling. First he'd been pissed that his daughter Shanna had married Roman. Then he'd been livid when his other daughter Caitlyn had married Carlos and become a were-panther. His head had nearly exploded when Shanna's husband had transformed her into a vampire. Tough news for a guy who was the leader of the CIA Stake-Out team, dedicated to killing vampires. And if that wasn't bad enough, Sean had gotten himself mortally wounded fighting vampires, so Roman had transformed him.

No one was sure how Sean would react to becoming

the creature he hated the most, but Shanna had begged her husband to save him. Sean had been a vampire less than a week now, but he appeared to be taking it in stride. Apparently his desire to survive was stronger than his desire to kill Vamps.

"Sit down, please." Roman motioned to the end of the table.

A mile away from them? Why did he feel like a lab rat in one of Roman's scientific experiments? Gregori took a seat and rested his forearms on the table. "So do you need my help coordinating emergency shelters?"

"Nay," Angus said.

"Each Coven Master is responsible for the safety of the Vamps in his region," Roman explained. "I appreciate your help with my area. I've been . . . distracted with other matters."

Gregori nodded and adjusted his cuff links. "Then you devised a plan of action?"

Roman gestured to his father-in-law. "Sean is using his government contacts to negotiate a deal."

"We're waiting on approval from the president," Sean said. "I've arranged for us to meet with the president and his advisors tonight after sunset."

"What kind of deal are you talking about?" Gregori asked.

"Basically, we're asking the government to declare the vampire video a hoax and state categorically that vampires do not exist," Sean explained.

"So the government would lie to the people," Gregori muttered. "That's new for a change."

Roman frowned disapprovingly at him. "Surely you can understand why we need this lie."

Sean leaned toward Angus and whispered, "He won't do."

"Aye, he will," Angus insisted quietly.

The prickle on Gregori's neck crept down his spine.

"Sean, the sun will rise soon," Roman said quietly. "You should see Shanna and the children while you still can."

Sean glared at his son-in-law, then slowly rose to his feet. "Don't think you can leave me out of the loop."

"We appreciate your help," Roman told him. "We'll let you know our final decision."

Sean snorted, then glanced at Gregori. "I'll talk to you tonight after sunset." He strode from the room.

Gregori watched the door shut, then turned back to face Roman. "I won't be here. I'm shooting a commercial for Blardonnay."

"They'll have to do it without you," Roman said.

Gregori sat back. "But they need—"

"Like Sean said, we need approval from the president," Roman added.

Gregori shrugged. "What has that—"

"Is it true that all your meals have been bottled?" Jean-Luc interrupted him.

What? What did his eating habits have to do with this?

"You're very young for a Vamp," Jean-Luc explained. "By the time you were transformed, we already had synthetic blood. So are we correct in assuming you've taken all your meals from bottles?"

What the hell? They were on the verge of a Vampire Apocalypse and these guys wanted to tease him again for being a bottle-fed baby?

"Lad," Angus grumbled impatiently. "We need to know if ye've ever bitten anyone."

He moved his hands into his lap so they wouldn't see him clenching his fists. "My fangs work just fine."

Zoltan leaned forward. "Then you have bitten someone?"

This was getting too damned personal. "I have never bitten for food. And I've never bitten a mortal."

"Good. I thought so." Roman nodded approvingly, then glanced at the other CMs. "Gregori has always taken the Romatech mission statement quite seriously. Make the world safe for mortals and Vamps alike."

"Ye have never given a mortal reason to fear you?" Angus asked.

Gregori's jaw shifted. Did they think he was some kind of wimp? "I'm sure I have, but they don't remember it. I always wipe memories and clean up after myself."

Roman nodded again. "For a young Vamp, Gregori has shown an impressive talent for mind control."

Again with how young he was. Gregori gritted his teeth. Next they would congratulate him for being potty trained.

"He also has an excellent track record for getting a job done," Roman continued.

Gregori arched a brow. "Am I applying for a new job?"

"Have you ever fought in battle?" Zoltan pressed. "Ever killed anyone?"

Gregori glared at him. "Why? Are you looking for an assassin? I left my résumé at home with my AK–47."

Angus chuckled. "Ye're no' a killer, lad."

Don't push me. Gregori shoved back his chair and stood. First Simone had called him a coward, and now these guys were insinuating it. "Enough with the bullshit. You guys know I never fought in battle. I wanted to. I trained for it, but Roman promised my mom he'd never put me at risk. I went along with it for her sake, but that doesn't mean I need to grow a pair. If there's a fight in our future, you can count on me."

"We're no' questioning yer bravery, lad," Angus said. "In fact, we're relying on it."

"For what? Tell me what you want."

"You have different skills than we do," Jean-Luc said. "Because of your youth you know how to maneuver through the modern world of business and technology."

Roman smiled. "And you've proven yourself adept at handling people and persuading them to do what you want."

"Without threatening them with a sword," Angus added. "Ye have a modern approach that we're lacking."

Gregori frowned. No doubt they thought they were complimenting him, but somehow he felt like he was being called manipulative. Using a sword might be old-fashioned, but it was blatantly honest. "I'm not that bad with a sword, you know. I've been practicing with Ian at the school during my time off."

"We don't need a swordsman for this job," Zoltan said.

Angus drummed his fingers on the table. "The problem is we doona want Sean Whelan to act as our sole representative to the president."

"We don't trust him," Zoltan muttered.

"So we need our own special envoy," Jean-Luc added. "Someone we can trust to represent the best interests of Vamps all over the world. A Vamp who is modern, works hard at a steady job, and has never bitten a mortal. A Vamp who appears completely safe and harmless."

Safe and harmless. Somehow those words felt like the worst of insults. Gregori yanked at his tie to loosen it. "You're choosing me 'cause you think I'm an Undead Pillsbury Doughboy?" He shook his head. "No. Hell, no."

Roman gave him an irritated look. "You're a marketing expert, Gregori. You understand the importance of how we are perceived. If we're seen as a bunch of dangerous, bloodthirsty monsters, it could mean the end for us. You can honestly present the image we want because it is what you are: a modern-day, well-educated, hardworking, harmless Vamp."

Harmless. Shit. He was tempted to sink his teeth into a mortal just to prove them wrong. But he kept his frustration in check. "Look, it's late, so let's continue this conversation tonight. If you give me a few hours, I'm sure I can come up with a better plan."

"Nay!" Angus thumped a fist on the table. "We doona need another plan. The decision was made. The vote was unanimous."

"All the Coven Masters agreed." Roman stood, his expression stern and stubborn. "Gregori, we're counting on you. You are the plan."

Chapter Three

$\mathcal{T}$hey were counting on him. Every freaking Coven Master in the Vamp world. Gregori headed for his office at Romatech, still reeling from the news.

He didn't let anyone see how tense he was. He even grinned at Laszlo when he passed him in the hall, and gave him a high five. *Stay cool. Act like you belong. It's the best way to fit in.* That was the mantra Gregori had adopted eighteen years ago, after the shock of waking up to find himself Undead.

And now he was the *plan*? He didn't know if he should be flattered or pissed. Flattered, maybe, if thousands of Vamps were trusting him to keep them safe.

He snorted as he wrenched his office door open. *Safe?* What a joke! For the last eighteen years, he'd been the one the old warrior guys threatened to kill for the fun of it.

He shut the door, then hit the light switch so hard, it cracked the plastic cover plate in two.

"Shit." He strode across the office and skirted his desk to peer outside the window. Lampposts illuminated the parking lot, but as always, his gaze wandered to the same dark spot, the place where he'd died as a mortal.

There were no cars to obstruct his view. Most Vamps simply teleported from place to place. Sometimes Gregori drove to work to make sure he remembered how, but as the years slipped by, those mortal skills seemed increasingly unimportant and unnecessary.

Memories swirled through his mind—the dark night, the terror and pain of the attack, the hot burn of blood and icy fear of death, the muted screams from his mother as he'd faded away. The memories haunted him for only a few seconds before he knocked them away. Over the years, he'd learn to react quickly.

He'd been transformed in 1993, six years after Roman invented synthetic blood, so he was something of a rarity in the vampire world. It gave the old guys one of their favorite labels for teasing him. The bottle-fed baby.

A few nights after being transformed, he had realized that if he was going to succeed in his new life, he needed to embrace it. Leave the old world behind. *Stay cool. Act like you belong.*

So he'd worked hard at fitting into the vampire world. He'd practiced mind control, levitation, and teleportation until he was just as skilled as the old guys. He'd worked hard at Romatech, and in 1998 he'd become vice president of marketing.

In the mortal world, he would have been considered a great success, but in this world, surrounded by crusty old warriors, he could never escape the stigma of his youth. He hated being the new kid, the bottle-fed baby, the one they referred to as the *fledgling*. That made him feel like a helpless little bird with its mouth wide open, begging the older and wiser birds to bring him a freaking worm.

It frustrated him no end, but he put up with the crap. Why? Because he loved being eternally young.

Who wouldn't love it? For eighteen years he'd enjoyed the body and energy of a twenty-nine-year-old. He could work hard, play hard, and party all night. Totally forget that if he were still mortal, he'd be a forty-seven-year-old dullard, saddled with a wife and a couple of kids.

Only his mother seemed aware of his true age. She reminded him of it daily when she lamented her lack of grandchildren.

With a sigh, Gregori turned away from the window. What an ironic twist of fate. The same Vamps who had teased him for being young now needed him for his youth.

Flattered or pissed? Flattered, yes. Being special envoy to the president was a big job, and he'd assured the guys in the conference room that he would succeed. But damn! If they were going to hinge their plan of action on him, they should have invited him to the meeting.

Pissed. Definitely. He grabbed a stress ball off his desk and gave it a squeeze. How dare they plan his life without consulting him? The old geezers were centuries old and still thought being a Coven Master was akin to being a king. If they wanted his help, they should have asked. They should have shown a little respect. But no, they believed they had the right to decide things for him.

The *fledgling*. The new kid who was safe and harmless. Who couldn't hurt a fly.

Pop! The stress ball exploded in his hand.

"Shit." He tossed it in the trash where it landed on top of three more exploded stress balls.

He glanced at his watch. Thirty-six minutes till sunrise and so much to do. First, he needed some sustenance, so he retrieved a bottle of synthetic blood from his mini-fridge and popped it into the microwave. While it warmed up, he undid the top buttons of his shirt, then took off his tie and tossed it onto the couch. It landed in VANNA's lap.

"Hang that up for me, will you?" he muttered, knowing she would just stare into space with her glass eyes.

VANNA was a Vampire Artificial Nutritional Needs Appliance, his brainchild from about six years ago. He and Laszlo had taken a female, humanoid sex toy and filled her with synthetic blood so a Vamp could pretend he was getting his food the old-fashioned way. Unfortunately, VANNA had not proven to be a very good chew toy. Her rubbery skin was hard to puncture and had literally ripped out one of Roman's fangs.

Even so, Gregori still kept VANNA around for parties. She never got insulted if the guys tried to undress her or nibble on her. Nor was she offended by their crude jokes or belching.

He had dragged her out of his supply closet earlier in the evening and put a red bikini on her and big red bow around her neck. She was going to be a surprise gift to Connor for his five-hundredth birthday.

"Maybe you can cheer up that old grouch." Gregori saluted her with his warmed-up bottle of blood, then drank while he considered what to do about the commercial. What he needed was someone who could oversee the production in his stead, someone he could trust who was familiar with Simone and DVN.

"Aha!" He set his bottle on the desk and called Maggie O'Brian. She lived on a ranch in Texas now, but a few years back, she and her husband had been stars on DVN's popular soap opera *As the Vampire Turns*.

"Maggie, darling! How are you?"

She snorted. "I'm knee-deep in bat guano. How are you, Gregori?"

I'm in deep shit, too. "I'm great! Thanks for asking."

"Is it true what they're saying on DVN?" Maggie asked. "That the secret is out, and mortals will want to kill us?"

"Highly exaggerated, Sweetcakes. It's all going to be fine, trust me."

"Oh. Then Roman has a plan?"

Gregori gritted his teeth. "Yes. By the way, Maggie, how would you like to earn some extra money? I need someone to finish production on a Vampire Fusion Cuisine commercial at DVN, and of course, I thought of you. Gordon is the director. You've worked with him before, right?"

"Yeah. You . . . want me to do it?"

"Sure. You'd be brilliant! And you'd get to see Simone again. She's the star."

There was a pause. "This bat guano is starting to look pretty good."

"Maggie, I need you! And the vampire world needs more Fusion Cuisine. Imagine all those Vamps with sad and miserable taste buds. They're counting on you."

She laughed. "Right. Well, with Simone I may need hazard pay."

"You got it, Toots. And I'll send a case of Blardonnay to your home. Just come to DVN tonight at midnight, ready to crack the whip."

"Okay. That works out well, actually, since I'm teaching a drama class at the school tonight at nine." She referred to the Dragon Nest Academy where her daughter attended.

"Excellent. I'll let Gordon know to expect you. Thanks, Maggie!" Gregori hung up. "Yes!" He punched the air, then called Gordon but was sent to voice mail. Hardly surprising given how much Blissky the director had drunk. He was probably passed out under a table somewhere.

After leaving a message, Gregori tossed his suit coat on the couch, then removed his cuff links and rolled up his sleeves. He now had twenty-eight minutes to gather information and formulate his plans before falling into his death-sleep.

He sat at his desk and wrote, *Strategies for Dealing with the President* at the top of a yellow legal pad. Two lines down, he wrote, *Plan A*, and described it. This was basically what Roman, Angus, and Sean wanted him to do. Convince the president and his advisors that all Vamps were safe and utterly harmless. Then he would beg the president to protect them from those mean-spirited vampire haters who wanted to kill them.

He frowned. This plan did a good job at keeping their secrets, but how could he negotiate from such a weak position? And why would the president believe they were safe and harmless after seeing the video where Connor decapitated Casimir?

He dropped down two lines and wrote, *Plan B*. Instead of playing the victim, he'd present himself as a helpful ally. He'd reveal how well MacKay S&I had worked with Sean Whelan's Stake-Out team. In fact, two MacKay S&I employees were former CIA agents, and another two were formerly employed by the FBI. He could also reveal that the British government already knew about Vamps and had a healthy working relationship with them. He'd tell the story about how Angus MacKay had received a medal for rescuing some British Air Force guys during World War II.

This plan made more sense to Gregori, but he knew it had a few drawbacks. It could ultimately lead the government into using the Vamps, making them do their dirty work. And the president would probably want to know how Angus had managed to accomplish his secret mission behind enemy lines.

That brought Gregori to Plan C. Reveal some of the powers that Vamps possess. Explain the danger that the Malcontents presented to the mortal world. And then convince the president that only the Vamps were capable of destroying the Malcontents.

This was the boldest plan, but also the most dangerous. Some powers, like mind control and memory wipes, could appear too threatening. If the government suspected how powerful the Vamps truly were, they might condone the murderous acts of vampire slayers. Basically he had to persuade the president that the Vamps were friendly and committed to keeping mortals safe and protected.

It would help if he knew more about the man he would be dealing with. President Laurence Tucker.

He Googled the president's bio on his laptop. Shameful, he supposed, for an American to know so little about current affairs, but why bother to keep up with presidents who could change every four years? He'd left that world behind.

Or so he had thought. Now he was being dragged back into it. He grabbed another stress ball.

He scanned quickly through a summary of President Tucker's early years. A stint in the U.S. Navy, where he acquired the nickname Torpedo. Graduated from Harvard Law School. Made a name for himself as a tough D.A., combating organized crime. Served as state attorney general for four years before running for Congress. After four years in the House, he ran for the Senate. The media had claimed the Torpedo was blasting his way through Washington straight to the White House. They had been right.

Gregori yawned and dropped the stress ball. So what if Tucker was starting his second term? Eight years was nothing compared to the hundred-year stint of a Coven Master. And a president's power was measly compared to what a Vamp could do.

He studied a photo taken of Tucker and his wife, Belinda, when he'd first campaigned for the Senate fourteen years ago. His hair had been brown back then, not gray like it was now. His wife, blond and perky, waved and smiled at the camera.

Gregori glanced over at VANNA. "I've found the perfect job for you."

He scrolled down further to look at more photos. There was Senator Tucker with his wife and children: a pretty blond girl who looked like her mother and a son with brown hair like his dad. The perfect all-American family, all with perfect smiles. Even the golden retriever in front of the kids was smiling.

Gregori read the caption underneath. The dog was named Grover. The boy, Lincoln. The girl, Madison. Sheesh! Had Tucker purposely named his children and pets in a way to further his political career? The dog was even wearing a stars-and-stripes bandana around his neck.

I may puke, Gregori thought, then narrowed his eyes on another name. Abigail. Where was she? He studied the small photo and spotted another kid half hidden behind Belinda and obscured by Lincoln's waving hand.

A tug of sleepiness dragged at him, and he glanced at the time. Nine minutes till sunrise. Damn, he needed to hurry up. He scanned a few more articles and photos. Apparently teenagers Madison and Lincoln had traveled with Tucker when he'd first campaigned for president. There were a bunch of photos of him sandwiched between his grinning daughter and son.

Belinda and Abigail were nowhere in sight.

Lincoln was now a senior at Harvard, while twenty-year-old Madison was a sophomore at a prestigious art school in Washington, D.C. She'd become quite a celebrity in the last few years, constantly followed by paparazzi when she went on extensive shopping trips in

New York City or when she accompanied her father to black-tie events, playing hostess in dazzling designer gowns. He had to admit she was a beauty, and in spite of her young age, quite at ease in high society. Then again, she'd grown up in the life.

But where was the mother? And the other daughter?

"Gregori!" His own mother, Radinka Holstein, cracked open his office door and peeked inside. "It's awfully late to still be working."

"Hey, Mom." He exited all links and powered down his laptop. "What's up?"

"Just wanted to let you know that I'll be out of town. Roman has asked Shanna and the kids and me to stay at the school for a while. We'll be leaving tonight right after sunset."

"That's a good idea. You'll be safe there." No one in the mortal world and very few in the vampire world knew where the Dragon Nest Academy was located. He folded the page with his strategy plans, then stuffed it into his pants pocket as he stood up. "I have to go out of town, too. What do you think of the president?"

Radinka tilted her head in confusion. "Why are you asking about him all of a sudden?"

Gregori closed the blinds on his window. "I have a meeting with him later tonight."

"Oh." Radinka's eyes widened. "That's quite an honor!"

He shrugged. "Maybe. Maybe not if he's an ass."

Radinka scoffed. "That's no way to talk about the president. I really admire his wife. She's been battling lupus for years, you know. And now I hear she has diabetes, too. Poor thing can't get a break."

"Oh." Maybe that was why she'd disappeared from the publicity photos. Gregori cast a guilty glance toward VANNA. He shouldn't have indulged in insulting thoughts toward the first lady. "What about the daughter?"

"Madison?" Radinka waved a hand in dismissal. "She's in all the magazines with her silly little dog named Dolly."

"No, I mean the other daughter."

"There's another daughter?"

"Yes." *Abigail.* "She's not in any of the pictures."

"Maybe she's shy," Radinka suggested.

Or ugly, Gregori thought with a snort. Another wave of sleepiness pulled at him. He strode toward his mom and pulled her into his office for a hug. "Take care. I'll see you in a few days."

She hugged him back, then gasped. "Gregori, what is *she* doing in here?" She glared at VANNA. "Didn't I tell you to get rid of that disgusting thing?"

"I am getting rid of it. I'm giving it to Connor for his five-hundredth birthday."

Radinka slapped at Gregori's shoulder. "You can't give that to him! Haven't you heard? Connor got married!"

Gregori stepped back, stunned. "What?"

"Connor got married. He called Angus tonight to request a month off for his honeymoon." Radinka grinned. "Isn't it wonderful?"

"*What?*" Gregori shook his head. "Who on earth would marry Connor? He's a grouch. And he's totally against us Vamps marrying mortals."

"He didn't marry a mortal. He married an angel."

Gregori's jaw dropped. Marielle had given up heaven to marry Connor? "Snap! You've got to be kidding me."

"No, I'm not. They're married." Radinka clasped her hands together over her heart. "Isn't it beautiful?"

Gregori swayed. The sun must be nearing the horizon. Or maybe he was reeling from shock. Connor was married? To the beautiful Marielle? Hell must have frozen over. He glanced at the beaming look of delight on his mother's face. Oh yeah, it was coming. *Wait for it. Five, four, three—*

"I wonder if they'll be able to have children," she whispered.

Gregori groaned. She was picking up speed.

"You know, Robby and Olivia are expecting." She gave Gregori a pointed look. "That means Angus and Emma will be grandparents soon."

"I'd love to discuss it in great detail for about three hours, but gosh darn, Mom, I'm about to fall over dead."

She scoffed. "You've used that excuse before. Don't think I'll forget about this."

"I'm sure you won't."

"All the Vamp men are having children except you."

"I would need a wife first. Or a uterus. Either case is highly unlikely."

Her eyes narrowed. "You need to stop playing around."

"Good night, Mom." He kissed her cheek, then stumbled toward the closet. "Oh, before I forget—will you send a case of Blardonnay to Maggie's ranch in Texas? And lock the door when you leave, okay?"

"Okay. Good night, dear."

Gregori shut himself inside the large walk-in closet. Not as comfy as a bed, but he didn't have time to get to one of the bedrooms in the basement. Besides, once he was dead, he really didn't notice how uncomfortable he was. He stretched out on the carpet as the tug of death-sleep crept over him.

Connor was married? What was the vampire world coming to? The apocalypse, apparently, if he didn't do his job well. No pressure there. After eighteen years of detaching himself from the mortal world, he was being forced back into it. Straight into the center of power.

The makeup artist's words came back to haunt him. *We're doomed. Doomed!*

Vamps around the world were depending on him. He had to succeed no matter what. One last thought came to his mind before he succumbed to total darkness.

He needed to order another case of stress balls.

Chapter Four

$\mathcal{Y}$ou look like shit."

"Thanks, Whelan. It's a pleasure working with you." Gregori motioned for Sean Whelan to enter his office.

The sun had set five minutes earlier. After waking from his death-sleep, Gregori had guzzled down a warmed-up bottle of synthetic blood, then he'd dashed down the hall to use the men's restroom. He'd been on his way back to his office when Sean had accosted him in the hallway.

He followed Sean into his office. "I guess you slept in one of the basement bedrooms?"

"Yes." Sean glanced around, then stiffened. "What the hell is that?" He pointed at the couch.

"She's a Vampire Artificial Nutritional Needs Appliance," Gregori explained as he shut the door. "Otherwise known as VANNA. Phineas has VANNA Black somewhere. This one is VANNA White."

Sean wrinkled his nose. "It's disgusting."

"Now don't be rude. You'll hurt her feelings." Gregori adjusted the red bow around VANNA's neck. "I was thinking she'd make a nice gift for the president."

Sean's mouth dropped open, and his complexion turned a mottled red. "You will do no such thing! You'd better—"

"Relax, dude. I was joking." Gregori picked VANNA up and tossed her back into his closet. When he turned around, he found Sean scowling at him. "What?"

"You look like you slept in those clothes."

"I did. I worked till dawn researching the president."

Sean snorted. "Don't bother. I'll tell you everything you need to know."

"Oh really?" Gregori wasn't about to admit that he'd formulated his own set of plans for dealing with the president.

"Yes." Sean crossed his arms over his chest. "This is how it will play out. We'll teleport to the safe house precisely at nine P.M., then I'll brief you for the meeting. The White House will send a car for us at nine-thirty. Our meeting with the president is at ten o'clock sharp."

Gregori nodded. He'd questioned the need for a safe house at the meeting last night. Teleporting back and forth would be so much easier. Angus had explained why they needed to arrive at the White House in a car like normal people. They wanted to severely limit the number of mortals who knew about vampires. Only a few at the top should know.

Although Angus agreed they should arrive by car, he was opposed to Sean and his Stake-Out team being in charge of the safe house. The future of Vamps depended on the success of this mission, so Angus had a plan to make sure they remained safe.

Sean smirked, apparently pleased that Gregori was

keeping his mouth shut and not questioning his authority. "For right now, you need to make yourself presentable."

"Really? That would have never occurred to me."

Sean scowled. "You can cut the sarcasm, especially when we're with the president. In fact, just keep your mouth shut and let me handle everything."

"The Coven Masters voted for me to represent Vamps. I intend to do my job, Whelan."

Sean gave him a skeptical look. "From what I hear, you spend all your time schmoozing with vampire celebrities—"

"And it was great training for this gig. I know how to get what I want."

Sean narrowed his eyes. "Your hair's too long."

Gregori grinned. Was that the worst he could come up with? Yeah, his hair was a little long for a businessman. The ends brushed his shoulders, but it was a good five inches shorter than the ponytails on the warrior Vamps.

He collected his tie, coat, and cuff links. "I'll see you here at nine."

"No. I want you here at a quarter till. We teleport *precisely* at nine."

"Chillax, Whelan. It only takes a second to teleport."

"A quarter till. I'm in charge of this—"

Before Sean could finish, Gregori teleported to his condo on the Upper West Side. Fifteen minutes later, he'd showered, shaved, and packed a suitcase. For the meeting, he decided to wear a gray Armani suit, crisp white shirt, and his favorite red power tie.

He paused in the middle of buttoning his shirt.

Roman had been right when he said it all boiled down to presenting the right image. He was supposed to be the safe, harmless Vamp who picked flowers instead of victims. Instead of biting young women, he helped little old ladies across the street.

With a groan, he yanked his shirt over his head, then tossed it onto his bed.

"Safe and harmless," he muttered as he selected a pale blue shirt. It would be a lot more fun to wear a tuxedo and vampire cape. And have a Hungarian accent like Zoltan. Instead, Gregori fastened his cuff links and put on a gray tie with thin blue stripes.

He removed his page of strategy plans from the pants pocket of his dirty clothes and studied the list, committing it to memory. He also had Angus's security plans to follow.

At thirteen minutes till nine, he teleported with his suitcase to the side entrance at Romatech, since arriving inside the building would set off an alarm. He swiped his ID badge and entered. Halfway down the hall, he passed by the security office.

The door opened and half a dozen MacKay employees spilled out into the hallway.

"Ye understand the plan, lad?" Angus asked.

"Yes."

"Yo, undercover brother." Phineas gave him a knuckle pound. "I'll see you soon."

"Sean's a little upset," Emma warned him. "He claims you're running late."

Gregori's mouth twitched. "By two minutes. Just to annoy him."

"Aye, doona let the bastard get to you." Robby

patted him on the back. "We'll be waiting for yer call."

After a round of well wishes, Gregori excused himself and wheeled his suitcase down to his office. His heart swelled when he realized how much trust his fellow Vamps were placing in him. In spite of all the teasing, they really did respect him. He grinned to himself.

"It's about time!" Sean yelled as he entered the room.

His smile faded. "Chillax, Whelan." He grabbed his phone charger off the desk and stuffed it into an outside pocket on his suitcase. He noticed Sean was still glowering at him, so he slipped a few stress balls into the suitcase.

"How much longer are you going to take?" Sean growled. "It's ten minutes till."

"I'm ready." Gregori picked up his Droid. "What's the number for the safe house?"

"I'll make the call." Sean whipped out his cell phone. "I'm the one in charge. You're just going along to show how safe and harmless you are."

Gregori gritted his teeth as he pocketed his Droid.

Sean punched a number on his phone. "Garrett, we're ready. Keep talking till we get there." He sidled up close to Gregori. "Grab on to me."

"You don't know how to—"

"Shh." Sean covered his phone with his hand. "I've been a . . . you-know-what for only a few nights, and we've been busy with one meeting after another. I haven't had time to learn any of your damned tricks."

Gregori nodded. And it looked like Sean had neglected to tell his fellow team members about his transformation. "Give me the phone." He held out his hand.

Sean hesitated.

"I have to hear the guy's voice to know where to go." Gregori accepted the phone, then motioned toward Sean's suitcase by the door. "Don't you need to take that?"

"Oh, right." Sean hurried to the door.

With a grin, Gregori grabbed his suitcase and teleported. He arrived in a living room that was sparsely furnished with what looked like rejects from a thrift store.

The other person in the room stopped talking in mid-sentence. His eyes grew wide. "What? Where's Sean?"

Gregori parked his suitcase next to the sagging couch of burnt-orange velvet, then set Sean's cell phone on the scarred coffee table. He extended a hand toward the other guy. Garrett Manning was a member of Sean's Stake-Out team, and he'd participated undercover in a reality show that Gregori had hosted a few years back at the Digital Vampire Network.

"We've met before, remember? I'm Gregori Holstein."

"Uh, yeah. I'm Garrett." He backed away, refusing to shake hands, his expression growing more confused. "Weren't you supposed to bring Sean with you?"

"Damn." Gregori slapped his leg. "I knew I was forgetting something."

Garrett winced. "Sean's going to be really pissed."

"What else is new?" Gregori pulled out his Droid and called Angus, who immediately put him on the speakerphone. "I'm at the safe house. Looks like Garrett is alone here. Is that true, Garrett? Are you alone?"

"Well . . . yeah, but—" Garrett gasped as four men materialized in the room. "What the—"

"This is Robby and Phil." Gregori gestured toward the two Vamps and the shifters they'd brought with them. "I believe you've met Phineas before. And this is Howard. They'll be in charge of security from now on."

Garrett flinched. "But that's my job! This is a CIA operation. You can't just take over like that."

"Dude." Phineas gave him a pointed look. "Are you going to argue with a werewolf and a were-bear?"

Garrett gulped as he eyed Phil and Howard. Gregori bit his lip to keep from laughing. The shifters had both affected their steely-eyed, vicious looks.

Phineas rested an arm on Garrett's shoulder. "Let me give you some advice, bro. Keep the kitchen well stocked. You do not want to share your house with a hungry bear."

"I—I didn't realize shifters were real," Garrett whispered.

"Yeah, well, we're gonna trust you to keep quiet about that, bro." Phineas patted him on the back. "Or we'll have to wipe your memory clean for a year or so."

Garrett turned pale. "I can keep a secret."

"Good lad." Robby smiled at him. "I'm going back now to report to Angus. Good luck to ye all." He disappeared.

"Got any donuts?" Howard lumbered toward the kitchen.

Garrett jumped out of his way. "There's a box on the counter. Eat all you want."

Gregori motioned toward the fridge. "Did you stock up on blood?"

"Yeah." Garrett gave him a wary look. "Are you going to get Sean now?"

"Soon." Gregori glanced at the large bay window. "Is there a safe place for Phineas and me to sleep?"

"Yeah, the basement. Sean told me to board up the windows and put two beds down there." Garrett frowned at Phineas. "Did he know there would be two of you?"

"Dude, there's gonna be *three* Vamps," Phineas said. "Gregori, me, and Sean."

Garrett's mouth dropped open. "What?"

Gregori attempted to keep a straight face. "Hate to break it to you, dude, but your boss is a Vamp."

"No." Garrett shook his head. "You're just messing with me. Sean hates vampires."

"Then he'd better get a therapist to deal with his self-loathing." Gregori glanced at his watch. "Time to go." He teleported back to the side entrance at Romatech, swiped his card, and strode inside.

"You bastard!" Sean shouted as he charged down the hall, dragging his suitcase behind him. "I'm reporting you to your superiors." He stopped in front of the MacKay security office and lifted a fist to pound on the door.

It opened and Angus filled the doorway.

Sean froze with his fist an inch from Angus's chest.

Angus arched a brow. "Is there a problem?"

"Yes!" Sean gestured wildly toward Gregori. "That asshole left without me! He's impossible to work with. You should fire him!"

"Now why would I do that?" Angus's eyes twinkled

with humor. "I believe he followed my orders perfectly."

"What the— I'm in charge here!" Sean jabbed a finger in Gregori's direction. "That idiot was supposed to take me!"

"Chillax, Whelan," Gregori said. "It wouldn't have been safe to take you and all our luggage at the same time."

"And he had other matters to take care of first," Angus added. "My men are now providing security for the safe house."

Sean flinched. "But they don't know where—" He turned to Gregori. "You bastard, what have you done?"

"I provided us the best security possible." He glanced at his watch. "Would you look at that? It's *precisely* nine o'clock, the exact time you wanted to go."

"Don't act like a smart-ass with me!" Sean growled. "I'm the one in charge of this operation."

"Then teleport yourself. I'll see you there." Gregori no longer needed a beacon. The location of the safe house was imbedded in his psychic memory.

"Wait!" Sean stepped closer and lowered his voice. "You have to take me. The president knows me. And all the other men at the meeting. They trust me. You need me there."

Angus folded his arms over his chest. "Do the president and his cronies know ye're a Vamp?"

"Of course not! It just barely happened." Sean shifted his weight. "I don't want them to know. It would destroy their trust in me."

Gregori nodded. He'd never seen Sean look so uptight and miserable. "Okay, I'll play along with that. But it's too late for Garrett. We already spilled the beans."

"*What?* Dammit, Holstein. It should be my decision when to tell people." Sean scowled as Gregori grabbed his arm. "You'd better remember from now on that I'm in charge. I'm getting fed up with your—"

Gregori teleported to the safe house, taking Sean with him.

"—sorry ass!" Sean completed his sentence.

"Are you talking to me?" Phineas asked.

"What?" Sean looked around. "Dammit! How many MacKay employees are here?"

"Three," Garrett muttered. "Phineas and those two shifters in the kitchen, eating all our food." He gave Sean an annoyed look. "You should have told me about shifters."

Sean shrugged. "Need-to-know basis."

Garrett scowled. "Is it true what they said? Are you a vampire now?"

Sean sighed and his shoulders drooped. "It's a long, painful story. It would probably take hours—"

"He nearly died in battle, so Roman transformed him to save his life," Gregori explained, then smirked at Sean. "End of story."

Garrett eyed his boss. "But he looks the same."

"And he acts the same," Phineas muttered.

Sean snorted. "I am the same."

Frowning, Garrett ran a hand through his hair. "How can you stay the head of the Stake-Out team? Isn't that a conflict of interest?"

"You expect me to stake myself?" Sean growled.

"I've got a nice, big one you can borrow," Gregori suggested.

Sean scoffed. "I think my new situation will actually help me in my fight against the bad vampires."

"But you said all vampires are bad," Garrett insisted.

Sean waved a hand in dismissal. "I was a bit premature in my observation. I know a lot more about it now."

Gregori and Phineas snorted.

Sean glared at them, then at Garrett. "No one in the government is to know about my new status. Understood?"

Garrett gave him a dubious look. "Aren't they going to notice that you're dead during the day?"

"That may be normal for a government worker," Gregori muttered.

Phineas snickered.

Sean waved that aside. "We've always done our work at night. That won't change." He took a seat on the couch. "We need to start the briefing."

Gregori sat and listened to Sean explain once again how he was supposed to keep his mouth shut during the meeting and prove just how safe, harmless, and boring he truly was.

At nine-thirty, the limo from the White House arrived.

As Gregori strode toward the door, he chanted softly, "I'm too sexy for my cape, too sexy for my fangs—"

"What the hell are you talking about?" Sean scowled at him.

"Just a little positive thinking, dude. To get psyched up. You should try it sometime."

Sean snorted, then paused at the door. "I've heard about you. You're . . . well, to be blunt, a womanizer."

Gregori gritted his teeth. His dear mother must have told Sean that. "What of it?"

"I know how you Vamps are around women," Sean muttered. "And for some weird reason, women tend to find vampires really attractive."

"Hoping to get lucky, Whelan?"

He shot Gregori an annoyed look as they stepped outside. "I'm warning you. You had better act safe, harmless, and boring."

"I'll attempt to smother my naturally charming personality."

"Just stay away from the president's daughter." Sean hurried down the steps to the waiting car.

"You mean if I ravish her it might put a little hitch in our negotiations?"

"Cut the sarcasm and stay away from her." Sean opened the car door, then climbed into the limo, followed by Gregori.

He gazed out the window as the limo turned onto a busy avenue. No doubt Sean was referring to pretty Madison who regularly graced magazine covers. But what about the older daughter, Abigail? How come he hadn't been able to locate one good photo of her? Why was she hiding from the world?

He smiled to himself. The evening wouldn't be entirely safe, harmless, and boring. He had a mystery to solve.

Chapter Five

*T*onight I will make you mine. Every inch of your flesh will beg for my touch. Your very soul will scream for me to possess you."

Abigail hesitated as the man's deep, husky voice filtered through the closed door. *Wow.* Mom had found a hot one for tonight.

She glanced at the Secret Service agent who stood next to the door. The poor guy could probably hear the racy dialogue going on inside, but his face remained expressionless and stoic.

She slipped quietly into the room. Not wanting to interrupt the audio book in progress, she simply waved at her mom and Nurse Debra.

Belinda squinted behind her eyeglasses, then smiled. "Hi, Abby."

"Hey, Mom." Was her mother's vision growing worse?

"Perfect timing!" Belinda motioned to the CD player on the table next to her recliner. "Maxim's about to get lucky."

Maxim ripped his shirt off and flung it aside, the narrator's voice continued.

Debra sighed. "I'm warning you. If your blood pressure goes up, I'm turning that silly thing off."

"Shh." Belinda hushed her. "You enjoy it, too, even if you won't admit it."

"Humph." Debra adjusted her reading glasses and went back to writing her report.

Abigail smiled. Debra had been her mom's private nurse for ten years now, and the two of them enjoyed fussing at each other.

The narrator's voice grew softer. *With graceful ease, he picked her up and tossed her onto his bed.*

"Maxim is very sexy," Belinda whispered.

"Well, that is a requirement for the hero." Abigail scanned the monitor to check her mother's vital signs.

She always tried to visit her mom when she was undergoing kidney dialysis, but with her long hours at the lab, it wasn't always possible. Thank God for audio books. Especially the romances. They kept her mom entertained for hours. No doubt sexy Maxim was also tall, dark, and handsome. And of course fabulously rich.

She sighed. Guys like that existed only in fiction. But she had to admit she'd learned a lot about the fine art of lovemaking thanks to her mom's books. Some mothers sat their daughters down for a heart-to-heart talk about sex. Belinda May Tucker simply invited them to listen to her audio books. Unfortunately that only left Abigail feeling uneasy since her forays into the world of romance had not produced the soul-searing, multi-orgasmic epiphanies that her mother's beautiful heroines experienced. Regularly. Without fail.

Maxim lay down beside her, marveling over the perfection of her lovely face and long blond tresses.

Abigail wrinkled her nose. "Why are the heroines always blond?"

Debra huffed. "Because only a blonde would be stupid enough to—"

"Excuse me?" Belinda gave her nurse an indignant look.

Abigail exchanged a grin with Debra, then patted her mom on the shoulder. "We can't all be blond like you."

Her smile faded when she noted strands of silver in her mother's hair. When had that happened? Even Debra's short and tidy Afro had acquired hints of gray among the black.

She stuffed her hands into the pockets of her lab coat so her clenched fists wouldn't show. Time was flying by, and she'd hardly made any progress at all. Her chest tightened with the same fear that had haunted her for a dozen years. *Failure is not an option. Failure means your mother dies.*

"Take a seat." Belinda motioned to the chair beside her. "The good part's coming up."

Abigail perched on the edge of the chair and gripped her jeans-clad knees. She needed to relax and enjoy the time she had with her mother. And not feel guilty that she wasn't at the lab.

"Are you ready for me, my love?" he whispered.

"Oh yes, Maxim! Take me. I need to feel your manly rod of steel deep inside me."

Abigail snorted. "I think he has a penile prosthesis."

Debra laughed.

Belinda scowled at them both.

Maxim caressed her face, then sliced through her night-gown with his claw.

"What?" Abigail sat back. "His *claw*?"

Belinda nodded. "I told you he was sexy."

Debra rolled her eyes. "Only a blonde would be stupid enough—"

"He's got a *claw*?" Abigail jumped to her feet and picked up the case for the audio book. "*Wild and Wicked Nights with a Werewolf*? You mean Maxim has hairy palms and never cuts his nails?"

Belinda sighed. "You might as well turn it off. You've really destroyed the mood now."

"Who could ever be in the mood for a *claw*?" Abigail punched the off button and dropped the CD case on the table. "What happened to the Greek billionaire tycoon and his secretary?"

Belinda shrugged. "I wanted to branch out. Try something new. I never get out of the house, you know. I can at least let my imagination roam free."

Abigail swallowed hard. "You're right. I'm sorry." Even though the house in question was the White House, it was still a prison for her mom.

"Hi, guys!" a cheerful voice greeted them from the doorway. A dog yipped.

"Madison?" Belinda squinted, then smiled. "Well, don't you look lovely! Is that a new dress?"

"Yes!" Madison waltzed into the clinic, carrying a pink rhinestone-encrusted dog bag.

She twirled, and her pink, sparkly cocktail dress swirled around her long, lean, perfectly tanned legs. "Isn't it gorgeous? It's a Versace. Oh, sorry, Dolly darling!" She patted the head of her toy poodle. "Little schnookums gets motion sickness, don't you, poor baby?"

"If that rat's going to puke, take it out of here," Debra grumbled.

Madison gave the nurse an annoyed look, then aimed her high-wattage smile at her mom and sister. "Guess what? I have the most exciting news ever!"

"There's a sale at Bloomingdale's?" Abigail muttered.

Madison gasped. "Is there? Oh." She waved a dismissive hand with perfect pink nails. "I can do that tomorrow. What's happening tonight is actually more important."

Belinda exchanged an amused look with Abigail. "How shocking."

"It is. Quite shocking." Madison set her dog bag on the carpet, then pressed a hand to her chest. "There's no easy way to say this, so I'll just blurt it out. Debra, be sure to monitor my mother's blood pressure. This may be . . . *too* shocking."

Debra gave her a wry look over the top of her reading glasses. "I've got it covered."

"Very well. Here goes." Madison took a deep breath. "Vampires are coming to the White House."

Abigail bit her lip to keep from laughing out loud.

Her mom smiled. "Honey, vampires aren't real."

Madison flinched. "How can you say that?" She motioned toward the audio book on the table. "You were so happy when I bought the werewolf book for you. If you believe in werewolves, then you should believe in vampires, too. If you don't, then it's like . . . racist, or something."

"Girl, are you on medication?" Nurse Debra asked.

"No, of course not," Madison answered impatiently.

"Maybe you should be," Debra muttered.

Abigail covered her mouth to hide her grin.

"I'm totally serious," Madison insisted. Her dog yipped in agreement.

Belinda shook her head. "Vampires and werewolves aren't real, sweetie. It's called fiction."

"That's what everybody used to think." Madison brushed her long blond hair over her shoulder. "But vampires *are* real. It's all over the Internet, so it has to be true. Besides, I have proof."

Abigail assumed a serious expression. "If you're referring to that video on YouTube, I've seen it, too, and it doesn't actually prove anything. How did you reach the conclusion that vampires are coming to our house?"

Madison heaved a frustrated sigh. "Okay. I'll explain it to you." She ticked off a list with her fingers. "Number one, I heard Dad is holding a top secret meeting tonight at ten o'clock. And you know vampires can only meet at night."

"That's not actual proof." Or even a logical train of thought, although Abigail refrained from telling her younger sister that.

"Number two," Madison continued. "I heard that all the top defense guys will be here, like the CIA and Homeland Security directors. So you know they're meeting someone really important . . . like vampires."

Abigail shrugged. "That's still not proof."

"Okay, then number—" Madison glanced down at her hand to see which finger she was on. "Three. I checked in the kitchen, and they just received a special delivery." She lowered her voice to a dramatic hush. "It was *blood*!"

Abigail groaned inwardly. Didn't Madison realize it was necessary to keep a supply on hand in case their mother needed a transfusion?

"It's probably for me," Belinda muttered.

"Does your blood come in bottles?" Madison asked. "And arrive in the kitchen?"

Abigail shot Debra a questioning look, and the nurse shook her head.

"Did you see these bottles of blood?" she asked Madison. "Where did they come from? Were they the same blood type as our mother's?"

"I don't know." Madison gave them all an indignant look. "It doesn't matter. It's obvious those bottles are for the vampires who are coming tonight. If you don't believe me, then come with me and I'll prove it to you."

Abigail sighed. Of all the silly things . . .

"Go on," Belinda nudged at her. "I want to hear all about it."

Abigail noted the twinkle in her mother's eyes. She was enjoying Madison's latest drama. "Very well. I shall investigate the matter and report back to you."

Belinda clapped her hands together. "Excellent."

"Come on!" Madison grabbed her dog bag, and Dolly yipped. "The vampires will be arriving any minute now."

Abigail waved bye to Nurse Debra and her mom, then joined her sister in the East Sitting Hall. A second Secret Service agent was standing nearby—Josh, the poor guy who was assigned to Madison. She smiled at him, and he nodded ever so slightly, his face expressionless. She'd managed to make him crack a smile once by telling him if anyone ever tried to kidnap Madison, they'd give her back in ten minutes.

Madison looked her over, frowning. "Jeans and a T-shirt? And why do you always wear that ugly coat? It has no style whatsoever."

"It's a lab coat. I came straight from work."

Madison sighed. "I wish there was time for you to change. First impressions are important, you know. But no matter, we need to hurry." She strode down the hall, her high heels silent on the thick carpet.

Abigail walked beside her, and Josh followed discreetly at a distance. "So you wore that dress for the vampires?" she asked.

"Of course." Madison marched across the Center Hall and into the Yellow Oval Room. "I want to look my best. Everyone knows vampires are extremely attractive."

"I thought they were kind of pale and . . . dead."

"Undead," Madison corrected her. "And yes, they're a bit pale, but in a sparkly sort of way. I thought they would like this sparkly dress. And Dolly's rhinestone bag. It's important to make them feel comfortable, you know."

Abigail shrugged. "You're the expert." Her sister had always loved sparkly things, so much so that the Secret Service used Sparkle for her code name.

Madison slanted an annoyed look in her direction. "I know you don't believe me, but you'll see I'm right." She opened a French door that led onto the Truman balcony of the South Portico. "This way."

"But what about the meeting?" Abigail stepped outside into the cool night air. "Shouldn't we go to the West Wing?"

"Yes, but we'll see them here first." Madison set the dog bag down, then strode to the edge of the upper balcony that overlooked the south entrance of the White House.

Josh stationed himself by the door and murmured their location into the communication device on his wrist.

Abigail rested her hands on the wrought-iron railing and peered down at the circular drive two floors below. "There's no one here."

Madison huffed. "Do you expect them to pull up in a car? They're vampires! They'll fly in. I expect they'll want to land right here on the balcony." She scanned the night sky. "Do you see them? They'll probably be in bat form."

Abigail crossed her arms and leaned against a thick white column. She could hear horns blaring and the hum of traffic in the distance, but here, they were in a small green oasis of quiet. The grounds were well lit and colorful with spring blossoms. She really ought to enjoy the gardens before the heat of summer invaded. Take time to smell the roses. But she could always feel the clock ticking, warning her she was in a race against time to save her mother.

She sighed. "You do realize it's physically impossible for a full-grown man to shrink his mass down to the size of a bat?"

Madison gasped and pointed. "Is that one?"

"Looks like a crow."

"Oh." Madison pressed a finger to her mouth as she considered. "The meeting's going to start soon. I wonder what's taking them so long."

"Well, it's a long flight from Transylvania."

Madison scoffed. "Don't be silly. They're already here in America. They're all around us."

"I guess I've missed them somehow."

"Well, duh! Of course you missed them. We never know when we're actually seeing them. They're good at blending in. Oh!" Madison's eyes widened. "I know what the problem is! They can't enter our house until we invite them."

"Really?"

"Yes! It's a vampire thing. Trust me. I'm a bit of an expert. I've read all the latest books." Madison stretched her arms out and raised her voice. "Oh, creatures of the night! I call upon the Undead! You are welcome in our humble abode!"

Humble? Abigail stifled a laugh. "Maybe it's working." She pointed to a limousine that was turning into the driveway.

"Don't be silly, Abby. They'll fly in as bats." Madison scanned the horizon.

"What happens when they change into human form? Will they go into the Oval Office completely naked?"

Madison giggled. "That would be so cool! But no, they'll be very well dressed. Tuxedoes, probably. They have expensive tastes."

Abigail watched as the limo came to a halt on the driveway. A group of Secret Service agents swarmed the car with their high-tech gadgets, making sure it hadn't been tampered with. The head Black Suit opened the door, and a man climbed out.

Her breath caught. There was something about him that immediately seized her attention. That alone was strange since she'd never been the type to ogle men. Maybe it was the way he straightened as he got out of the car. He was graceful, but manly, as if he had great strength and power that he kept quietly in control.

She could only see his back, but . . . *wow*. He was tall and lean, and his expensive suit fit his broad shoulders to perfection. His dark brown hair was a bit long, the ends reaching past his collar, but it looked soft and thick and so very tempting to touch. If only she could see his face.

A second man emerged from the limo. Shorter, stockier, older, with a reddish-blond buzz cut. He acted like he was in charge, talking urgently to the Secret Service agents. The mystery man seemed content to stand silently by. The shorter guy introduced him to the head Black Suit, and he turned to shake hands.

He was stunning. Abigail leaned against the railing for a better view. All she could see was the right side of his face, but what a profile. Good Lord, a man could melt butter with a profile like that. A sharp, straight nose, high cheekbone, and a jawline that curved into a strong chin. *Wow*. He should be on the cover of one of her mother's books.

Who was he? He seemed too young to be a politician. Maybe the older guy was the politician, and this guy was his aide? But tonight's meeting was being attended by experts in defense, so he might be from the CIA or the Pentagon.

She edged closer into the shadow created by the column so she could spy on him unnoticed. He was listening to the head Black Suit now. His skin was a bit pale in comparison to the other men. Hmm, pale skin, extremely attractive, well dressed, expensive tastes. She might be able to convince her sister that a vampire had indeed arrived at the White House.

"I don't understand," Madison mumbled, still scanning the horizon. "Why haven't the vampires come?"

Something happened with the mystery man. It was a minute, subtle change, but clear as day to Abigail. His shoulders suddenly seemed broader, and his head tilted ever so slightly. Had he somehow heard Madison? Impossible! They were two floors up.

He turned and peered up at Madison. He *had* heard her! And his face. His entire face was visible now.

"Wow," Abigail whispered.

His gaze immediately shifted to the side.

Straight at her! Good Lord! Abigail gasped and scrunched deeper into the shadow. How could he hear a whisper? And how could he possibly see her in the dark?

She waited. Any second now, his gaze would shift back to Madison. Men always looked at Madison. She was standing beneath a porch light, her blond hair gleaming, her pink dress glittering. She was the princess of the White House.

Abigail struggled to catch her breath. He was still looking at her. Oh God, she was feeling light-headed, like she might faint. *Don't be silly. You never faint. You're a scientist.* This was nothing more than a chemical reaction. It had never happened to her before, but she understood the process. Her brain was simply releasing dopamine. *By the bucketful.*

She edged around the back of the column. She was good at disappearing. After all, she was the forgotten daughter, and that was the way she liked it.

She waited while seconds ticked by. He would have given up on her by now. He'd be focused on Madison. She peered around the column.

She gasped. He was still looking at her! She pressed a hand against her chest. Good Lord, her heart was going crazy.

And then he smiled. A slow, devastating one that curled to the left in a lopsided fashion before transforming into a full-fledged smile. With dimples.

She slumped against the column. Dopamine overload. Skyrocketing tachycardia. *Okay, now you can faint.*

Chapter Six

Come on!" Abigail rushed toward the staircase.

"What's the big hurry?" Madison struggled to keep up with her. She passed her dog bag to Josh. "I can't run in these heels. I'm afraid I'll fall and hurt Dolly."

Josh's jaw shifted slightly, his only sign of annoyance, but Abigail noticed it.

"I'll take her." She grabbed the dog bag and ran down the stairs, quick and nimble in her athletic shoes.

"Not so fast!" Madison yelled. "You'll scare Dolly!"

Abigail glanced at the bag. Dolly was poking her head out and grinning like she did whenever she was in a car. "She's fine!"

"What about you?" Madison's voice filtered down the staircase, along with the clunking sound of her heels. "Why are you acting so weird?"

Good question. Abigail paused when she reached the ground floor. It wasn't like her to fixate on a man. "I . . . want to know who he is."

"Who?" Madison clambered down the last of the stairs with Josh beside her, making sure she didn't fall.

"The guy who got out of the limo." Abigail started down the Center Hall and called back over her shoulder. "There was something different about him. Don't you think?"

"I didn't get a good look at him. I was too busy looking for— Oh my God." The sound of Madison's footsteps stopped abruptly. "You think he's a *vampire*?"

Abigail blinked. Did she? No, of course not. Vampires weren't real. She glanced down at the bag in her hand, and Dolly tilted her head, regarding her curiously. "That would be crazy, wouldn't it?" she whispered.

Dolly yipped in agreement.

"The voice of reason." Abigail continued toward the West Colonnade. She'd seen the hysteria all over the Internet. She'd even watched the video that claimed to show a vampire being beheaded. It had looked like a movie clip to her, starring a kilted Scotsman as the hero, killing his foe with his mighty claymore. The guy he'd supposedly decapitated had turned to dust, but that was easy enough to fake with special effects.

As soon as she entered the West Colonnade, the toy poodle began to bark. Abigail stopped. She'd never seen Dolly this agitated. The dog was scratching at the sides of the leather tote bag, her yipping growing more frantic.

Madison ran to catch up with them. "Abby! What did you do to my baby?"

"Nothing." Abigail winced when Dolly tried to leap out. She quickly set the bag on the floor.

Dolly jumped out and scampered into the West Wing. Abigail chased after her, then halted at the doorway that led into the waiting room outside the Oval Office. Madison and Josh stopped beside her. Two Secret Service agents were stationed across the room,

just outside the door to her father's office. Her heart
stuttered when she spotted the mystery man halfway
across the room, seated beneath a painting.

Dolly advanced toward him, growling and baring
her sharp little teeth. He stood, his attention focused
entirely on the dog. Abigail opened her mouth to tell
Dolly to stop, but the dog suddenly collapsed onto the
carpet, limp and silent.

"Dolly!" Madison ran to her dog and fell to her knees.
She lifted her dog's head. "Dolly, speak to me! Oh
my God, what's wrong with her?"

"She's fine," the mystery man said, glancing back
at the pair of Secret Service men, who remained quiet
and expressionless. "I think she's . . . sleeping."

"Sleeping?" Madison repeated, her eyes wide.

Josh leaned over to inspect the dog. "She's okay.
She's still breathing."

"Oh." Madison pressed a hand to her chest. "Thank
God." She peered down at her pet with a perplexed
look. "Poor baby. She must have worn herself out."

Abigail watched silently from the doorway, her gaze
darting back and forth between the limp dog and the
mystery man. A strange thought seeped into her mind,
that somehow he had shut the dog up and caused her
to fall asleep. She opened her mouth to question him,
but then his gaze shifted to her.

And she forgot how to talk.

She'd almost fainted before from seeing him at a distance. Now that he was close, she could hardly think.
Hardly breathe. Her heart pounded, and her mouth
grew dry. She licked her lips, and his gaze flickered to
her mouth, then back to her eyes.

His eyes were green, she noted. A grayish-green that reminded her of green moors shrouded with mist. Beautiful, but mysterious. And potentially dangerous.

He inclined his head, never taking his eyes off her. "How do you do? I'm Gregori Holstein."

Gregori? He pronounced his name in an Eastern European fashion, but his accent seemed American. Abigail bit her bottom lip, not certain how to proceed with him. Could he possibly possess some sort of strange psychic power?

"I'm Madison." Her sister scrambled to her feet, cradling Dolly to her chest and apparently unaware that Mr. Holstein had not been talking to her. "Josh, would you be a dear and fetch the dog bag?"

Josh glanced at the other two guards, then strode from the room to do Madison's bidding.

Abigail eased into the room. It was decorated in typical White House fashion: uncomfortable chairs grouped around antique tables, expensive draperies, paintings and ornate mirrors on the walls. She looked about nervously, pretending not to notice that the mystery man was still staring at her. But she was aware. Skin-tingling aware.

Madison eyed him curiously. "Did you say your last name is Holstein?"

"Yes." His gaze flicked to her, then back to Abigail.

Madison sidled close to her sister and whispered, "He can't be one of them. No self-respecting vampire would ever be named after a cow."

He grinned.

Good Lord, his smile. Abigail's pulse jumped into warp speed, but then she blinked and narrowed her eyes. His canine teeth looked very pointed. And his hearing was extremely good. "You—you saw us on the balcony?"

He nodded, his eyes twinkling with humor. "The next time you try to hide in the shadows, you should take off the white lab coat."

Oh, of course. Her cheeks grew warm. That was how he'd managed to see her. Although she could have sworn he'd been looking at her face.

"Are you a doctor?" he asked.

She shook her head.

"You are too," Madison whispered, then raised her voice. "She has a Ph.D. in biochemistry."

His eyebrows lifted slightly.

Abigail couldn't tell if he was surprised or impressed, but he was certainly watching her closely. That alone was enough to make her pulse jump to warp speed six. "You seem to have excellent vision and hearing."

The corner of his mouth curled up just enough to show a dimple. "How kind of you to notice."

"Excuse us a moment, please." Abigail pulled her sister outside the door and glanced back at him. He turned politely away to study a painting, presenting her once more with a devastating view of his profile. *Good Lord. No man should be that handsome.*

"Do you realize he fits every item on your checklist?" she whispered to Madison. "Expensive taste, pale skin, *extremely* attractive?" She spotted his grin once again. *Blast him!* "His sense of hearing is downright scary."

Madison sighed. "I can see where you're going, but that guy's not a vampire. He doesn't sparkle. And he didn't fly here as a bat."

He turned toward them, chuckling, and Abigail ignored his dimples to zero in on his canines. His extra-sharp and pointed canines.

He squelched his smile.

Interesting. She strode back into the room. "There's a rumor going about that the Undead will be visiting the White House. What do you think, Mr. Holstein? Do you believe vampires could be living secretly among us?"

His eyes narrowed, and she felt an invisible crackle of tension as if the air between them had suddenly turned electric.

Warp speed seven. She lifted her chin. "Are you living a secret life, Mr. Holstein?"

His eyes gleamed a brighter green as he stepped toward her. "What about your secret life, Abigail?"

She blinked.

"You are Abigail Tucker, aren't you?" He stepped closer. "Why do you hide from the cameras?"

"I don't want attent—" She did a double take at the mirror on the wall. She was reflected, but he wasn't! With a gasp, she glanced back at him, but he'd moved out of the way. Very quickly.

Had she imagined it? It had all happened so fast. She looked at the mirror, briefly noting her own pale and shocked expression. Madison was also reflected. And her Secret Service man, Josh, who had just returned with the dog bag. They were too busy lowering Dolly into the bag to notice anything amiss.

She cast a nervous glance at Mr. Holstein. He was frowning, his mouth thin with annoyance. He adjusted his tie with an angry jerk.

"You could use the mirror to fix your tie," she suggested quietly.

He clenched his fists tight, then relaxed them.

He was nervous, she realized. He didn't want to be . . . discovered.

She gasped. His gaze cut immediately to her, the green of his eyes growing more intense.

Warp speed eight. Her heart thundered in her ears. Could it be true? No. She was a scientist, and all her years of study were clamoring in her head screaming *no!* She could not accept this.

"I don't believe it," she whispered.

He remained silent as he fiddled with his cuff links.

She moved in front of him. "You can relax, Mr. Holstein. I'm not going to accuse you of something that's not scientifically possible."

He arched a brow at her. "And what is scientifically possible, Miss Tucker?"

"Facts. What I can observe or measure."

"And what about the intangible? Do you believe in feelings? Anger, fear, love?"

"Of course. Love is actually scientific." She stuffed her clenched fists in the pockets of her lab coat. "It generally begins with physical attraction which triggers a chemical reaction that releases dopamine into the bloodstream—"

"Is that why your heart is racing?"

Her heart lurched. *Warp speed nine.* "I don't know what you're talking about. My pulse is perfectly normal."

His mouth curled into a slow smile. "Tell me, Abigail. Why does a beautiful woman like you hide in the shadows?"

She froze. If he was trying to throw her off her guard, he was certainly succeeding.

He moved toward her. "Do you go by Abby? Or Gail?"

"I—" Good Lord, she could hardly remember her own name with him so close. She lifted her chin. "Do you go by Greg? Or does Gori suit you better?"

His mouth twitched. "Do I seem gory to you?" He leaned in close enough she could feel his breath against her cheek. "Is that why your heart is pounding? Do you think I'm frightening?"

Could he actually hear her heartbeat? She swallowed hard. "I'm not afraid."

He moved back, his smile fading. "Maybe you should be."

Her skin prickled with goose bumps. "Who are you? What do you want?"

His eyes narrowed, glittering with green intensity. "I'm not so different from you. I want to be left alone to live in the shadows."

A shiver skittered down her spine. *Warp speed ten.* Had he just admitted to being one of the Undead?

No! She refused to believe it.

The door to the Oval Office opened, and a voice called out. "Mr. Holstein, the president will see you now."

Gregori inclined his head. "Abigail." He turned and strode into the Oval Office.

She watched him go, her heart still thumping, her head still echoing with the soft way he'd said her name.

"Abby?" Madison sidled up close. "What was going on? Was he trying to pick you up?"

"No." She eyed the closed door.

"Are you sure?" Madison whispered. "It looked kind of intense to me."

Abigail drew in a deep, steadying breath. "How's Dolly?"

"Still asleep. It's the strangest thing."

"Yes, it is." Abigail couldn't shake the feeling that somehow, Mr. Holstein had caused Dolly's sleep. With her scientific training, she naturally discounted the existence of vampires, but even she had to admit the circumstantial evidence was piling up. No reflection in the mirror, possible psychic power, heightened senses, pale skin, pointed canine teeth, and something unusual about his eyes. Then there was his aura of power and mystery. "I never thought I'd say this, but you might be right."

"Really?" Madison grinned, then looked confused. "About what?"

"Dad's secret meeting with the Undead." Abigail glanced toward the Oval Office. "Mr. Holstein . . ."

"You really think he's a vampire?"

"I'm not totally convinced vampires are real. I'll have to study this further." *Study him further*.

Madison grinned and grabbed hold of Abigail's arm. "Can I help? I love vampires!"

Abigail winced. "Don't say that! I don't care if Mr. Holstein is the most handsome and charming man on earth. If he's a vampire, then loving him would be the height of folly."

Madison rolled her eyes. "Chill, Abby." She brushed her hair back over her shoulders. "I didn't think he was all that handsome and charming."

"Are you crazy?" Abigail bit her lip. *Damn*. Gregori Holstein had better be human.

Chapter Seven

*

*S*hit. Gregori clenched his fists, then forced his hands to relax. He'd completely screwed up. He was supposed to convince the guys in power that he, along with every other modern-day Vamp, was safe and harmless. But he'd just asked Abigail Tucker if she thought he was frightening.

She'd given him several opportunities to deny he was a vampire. He should have said he didn't believe in such nonsense. After all, it was also his mission to make sure only a small group of mortals knew that vampires actually existed. And that small group did not include Abigail.

Dammit, he should have played it safe. He should have acted aloof. As if he couldn't hear her heart racing every time she came near him. As if his heart wasn't racing, too.

He should have looked her in the face and lied.

Why hadn't he? It wasn't like he was a stickler for honesty and honor like the old Vamps. He could have lied to Madison without giving it a second thought. This was business, and he had a job to do. Thousands of Vamps were depending on him.

So why did he screw up? What was it about *her*?

As usual, he didn't let his frustration show. He entered the Oval Office with a smile, playing the charming diplomat while Sean Whelan made the introductions: Secretary of Defense George Ralston; National Security Advisor Frank Garcia; chairman of the Joint Chiefs of Staff General Bond; CIA director Nick Caprese; head of Homeland Security Alan Schiller; and the president, Laurence Tucker.

Their smiles were as false as his own, Gregori thought. There was no disguising the wary glint of suspicion in their eyes. Nor the implied warning that came with the steely grip of their handshakes. They were sizing him up as a potential threat to the American people.

The president took a seat at the end of a coffee table in the chair closest to his desk. Sean Whelan motioned for Gregori to take the chair at the other end of the coffee table, then he and the remaining men squeezed onto the two long sofas that flanked the table.

President Tucker gestured to an ice bucket perched on a metal stand next to him. "We provided you with some refreshment. Help yourself."

Gregori glanced at the bottle of synthetic blood resting in ice. "Thank you, but I'm not really hungry."

Sean cleared his throat and rolled his eyes toward the bottle.

They wanted to see him drink blood? Gregori grabbed the bottle and unscrewed the top. "A little would be nice. Thank you." He took a sip and carefully refrained from grimacing at the taste of cold blood.

The mortal men stared at him like he was a circus freak.

"I was informed three nights ago of the existence of vampires," President Tucker began. "Mr. Caprese tells me the CIA has been aware of your kind for over six years."

The CIA director nodded. "It was our agent, Mr. Whelan, who first brought your species to our attention when he was stationed in St. Petersburg. Since your kind exists all over the inhabited world, we've always felt the Agency is best equipped for keeping track of you. Mr. Whelan's Stake-Out team has given us a lot of valuable information."

"I see." Gregori wondered just how surprised Caprese would be if he knew Sean Whelan was now Undead.

"Of course we've always shared any national developments with Homeland Security to make sure our citizens are protected," Caprese continued. "We've also been monitoring the Digital Vampire Network. Your *Nightly News* program keeps us well-informed." He gave Gregori a smug look. "You've made our job easy."

Gregori took another sip of blood and remained quiet.

President Tucker leaned forward, studying him. "Mr. Whelan tells us the vampire community has selected you as their representative. Is that true? Do you admit to being a vampire, Mr. Holstein?"

Gregori glanced at the Secret Service man at the door. There were two more outside. Had they been told to attack if he confessed? Was Abigail still outside, hoping to confirm her suspicions?

A chill tickled the back of his neck. He'd never confessed to a mortal before, and the words were surprisingly hard to force out. He knew the second he did, his life would never be the same.

He was tempted to say no, it was all a hoax, but there were too many people who believed the stupid video. It wouldn't take long before the Buffy wannabes started hunting. And if they videotaped themselves in the act of staking a vampire with the poor Vamp turning to dust, it would fuel the fire. More vampire hunters. More death.

The Vampire Apocalypse.

The Vamps needed the government to declare the video a hoax. *Here goes Plan A.*

He shifted in his chair. "Yes, I'm a vampire, but I can assure you that I'm not dangerous. My fellow Vamps and I are morally opposed to causing mortals any harm."

He glanced toward the Secret Service man, but the guy didn't budge. No one moved. They sat still, staring at him.

Even the president seemed speechless. He might be called the Torpedo, but as far as Gregori could tell, that honor belonged to his daughter. Abigail Tucker had completely blown him out of the water.

Since the night before, he'd come up with a few reasons why a president's daughter would hide from the spotlight. It could be the president who wanted her hidden. If she had a history of crime or drug abuse, he wouldn't want the media to know. If she was suffering from a mental disorder, he might keep her locked up in the proverbial attic. Or maybe she was simply an embarrassment. A few tacos short of a combination plate. Or too ugly. Or too shy.

Shy? What a laugh. She'd marched right up to him and let him have it. *Who are you? What do you want?*

Mentally challenged? Ha! She was a scientist. A Ph.D. And she looked only about twenty-five. The girl was obviously brilliant.

And beautiful. Not in the skinny, carefully crafted superstar look that her sister Madison had mastered. Abigail was a little shorter, a little more curvy, and a hell of a lot more exciting. She was different. And real.

At first he'd thought she had pretty hazel eyes and curly brown hair. But when she drew closer and more into the light, he'd become fascinated with the subtle changes in her appearance. Flecks of gold and green glimmered in eyes that were big and beautiful without makeup. Her pink mouth was sweetly sculpted, her lovely face so expressive.

Across the room, her curls had seemed sweetly innocent, but close up, they looked wild and soft to touch. He'd noted a glint of dark auburn in her chin-length hair and a pale smattering of freckles over her sharp little nose.

There was a fire in her just waiting to be lit.

And like a fool, he'd completely screwed up. He'd been so focused on her, he'd forgotten about the stupid mirror.

Sean Whelan cleared his throat and nudged Gregori with his foot, forcing him back to the present.

The men in power were grumbling among themselves. Gregori didn't need super hearing to realize they were busy determining his future and the future of vampires around the world. As if they had the right to decide who was worth saving. He took another sip of cold blood to cool the frustration simmering inside him.

"So what if they drink from bottles now?" the national security advisor asked. "They must have fed off humans for centuries. I don't see how we could ever trust them."

"Exactly," the director of Homeland Security agreed. "I don't believe for a second that they're harmless, not when I know some people in South Dakota and Nebraska were murdered by vampires."

"It's true they could present a serious threat," CIA director Caprese said. "But if we ally ourselves with them, we could direct that threat at our enemies."

Gregori sipped more blood. Plan A was already falling apart. No big surprise there. But Plan B might succeed.

"This all sounds ridiculous to me." General Bond glared at Gregori, then at the CIA director. "How come you didn't tell me about this sooner? You wait till tonight to show me a weird-assed video, and you expect me to believe it? It's bullshit!"

"I understand how you feel," President Tucker told the general in a conciliatory tone. "I was skeptical, too, when I first saw the video."

"Excuse me, General," Sean Whelan cut in. "As head of the CIA Stake-Out team, I can confirm the existence of vampires. I've been studying them for six years."

"So you say," the general muttered. "But where's

the proof? Have you killed any of these so-called vampires?"

"I can't bring you a head to mount on your wall," Sean said. "They turn to dust when they die."

"Really?" General Bond gave Gregori a speculative look as if he were contemplating testing Sean's claim.

Gregori stuffed the bottle back into the ice bucket. "If you don't believe me, fine. Maybe a lot of people will refuse to believe it. We can spread the word ourselves that it's all a hoax, so I won't waste any more of your time." He stood.

"Wait." The president raised a hand. "We still have much to discuss. Please have a seat, Mr. Holstein."

Gregori hesitated.

"Already two of the major networks have examined the video and declared it authentic," President Tucker continued. "We estimate over forty percent of the public now believes, and that number is growing daily. To be blunt, Mr. Holstein, you need our help. We are prepared to discuss a mutually beneficial alliance with your kind."

Gregori sat down. *Here goes Plan B.* "We will gladly consider an alliance. We already have one with the British government."

A bunch of jaws dropped. Gregori ignored Sean's fierce scowl and proceeded to tell the other men about MacKay Security and Investigation and how Angus MacKay had come to the rescue during World War II.

"I'll have to verify that information," Caprese said.

"Of course." Gregori leaned forward, focused on the president. "Before we agree to an alliance, I need to know that you're willing to declare the video a fraud and denounce the existence of vampires."

"We will certainly consider it," the president said.

"Easy to do," the general muttered, "since it's all a bunch of bullshit. No one here has given me any proof."

CIA director Caprese sighed. "I told you we've been monitoring the Digital Vampire Network—"

"Which could be produced by a bunch of loons who are either crazy or acting," General Bond interrupted. "Just because someone claims to be a vampire on television, doesn't mean it's true."

Gregori tamped down on his frustration. How could he succeed with Plan B when the general wouldn't even agree that vampires existed?

"Show him your fangs," Sean Whelan whispered.

Gregori shot him an annoyed look. *Show him yours*. With an inward groan, he opened his mouth.

The secretary of defense sat back. "Those do look awfully sharp."

"And pointed," the national security advisor added.

Homeland Security director Schiller shook his head. "Those teeth aren't long enough to pierce a hot dog, much less someone's neck."

"The fangs elongate before they bite something," Sean explained, then turned to Gregori. "Go ahead, show them."

He gritted his teeth. Sean was such a newbie, he didn't know a vampire needed some motivation to get his fangs to shoot out. Hunger. A beautiful woman. Hot sex. There was none of that here. Just a group of stodgy old men who expected him to perform tricks like a well-trained dog.

"What's taking you so long?" The general smirked. "Are your fangs rusty?"

"We don't use them much anymore." Gregori motioned toward the ice bucket. "We drink our meals from bottles."

General Bond crossed his arms with a dubious look.

"He speaks the truth," Sean added. "The modern-day Vamp no longer feeds off humans. They're completely safe and harmless."

Instead of looking relieved, the men eyed him with a mixture of suspicion and disdain. Gregori fisted his hands again, wishing he had a stress ball he could explode. Sean was still trying to make Plan A work, but he'd suspected from the beginning that the safe-and-harmless routine was doomed to failure. Worse than failure, for it made Vamps look like incompetent wimps. Maybe some nice sharp fangs would garner him some respect. He closed his eyes to envision a beautiful woman. Simone. Inga. All the beautiful Vamp women he'd dated over the years.

Nothing. Not even a tingle in his gums.

The image of Abigail sneaked into his thoughts. Her eyes, her lips, her mop of curls and curvaceous body. Good God, how he'd like to get his hands on her. He'd show her just how high her dopamine levels could go.

With a hiss, his fangs sprang out. And his vision turned red, a sure sign that his eyes were glowing.

The men all flinched, staring at him with alarmed expressions. Hell, he was shocked, too. Red glowing eyes meant one thing. He was hopelessly hot for Abigail.

"Excellent," President Tucker whispered.

Gregori closed his eyes, willing the redness to fade away. The president wouldn't be so thrilled if he knew it was his daughter who had inspired the demonstration.

"All right," the general grumbled. "You convinced me."

"Good." President Tucker rubbed his hands together. "Let's get down to business. We are prepared to declare the recent vampire mania a complete hoax."

Gregori forced his fangs to retract. "Thank you. We simply wish to live in peace and keep our existence a secret. Not only are we morally opposed to causing mortals injury, but intellectually, we understand that harming people would only serve to reveal our existence and ultimately bring about our own destruction."

The president nodded. "You sound very sensible. I believe we can work well together."

Gregori stood. "Then I will convey the good news of our agreement to my people."

"Not so fast." Schiller from Homeland Security raised a hand to stop him. "We will need a list of every vampire in the country. Their names and addresses."

Gregori had suspected they would make such a request. "There is no list." Actually the Coven Masters did have lists, but there was no way he would admit to that. Vamps were essentially sitting ducks during the daytime, completely unable to defend themselves. He couldn't trust the government to leave them alone.

Schiller snorted. "Of course there's a list. If vampires

are drinking from bottles, like you claim they are, then there's a list for distribution."

Gregori sat once again. "Most vampires don't get home delivery. It would look odd to have blood delivered to your house, and vampires are experts at blending in and going unnoticed. We simply want to go about our jobs and our lives in secret."

"Do you really expect us to believe you're harmless?" the secretary of defense asked with a dubious look.

"For the majority of Vamps, that is true. Synthetic blood was invented in 1987, and since then, most Vamps have switched over entirely to bottles."

"*Most* Vamps?" General Bond asked. "So some vampires are still going around attacking innocent people?"

Gregori shifted in his chair. It looked like he'd have to go to Plan C. "Yes, just like there are some bad mortals, there are some bad vampires. We call them Malcontents."

"They're a small faction that takes pleasure in feeding off humans and killing them," Sean Whelan explained. "The good Vamps have been fighting them in order to protect us. Just a few nights ago, the Vamps defeated a small army of Malcontents. Their leader, Casimir, was killed in battle. That's what you saw on the video."

"The video showed a decapitation," Schiller said. "That doesn't sound harmless to me. Why should we trust you?"

"You can trust us because we've been risking our lives for centuries to protect you." Gregori leaned forward, his elbows on his knees. "You say you want an alliance with us? The alliance is already there. You just didn't know about it."

"What sort of things can you do for us?" the national security advisor asked. "What kind of powers do you have?"

There it was, the question Gregori had feared would come up. "Our sight and hearing is a little better than normal, but that's about it."

"What? You don't have special powers?" President Tucker shot an alarmed look at the CIA director. "You said they have supernatural powers."

Caprese regarded Gregori with narrowed eyes. "We believe they do."

Gregori shrugged. "We don't fly or turn into bats."

The general eyed him with a disgusted look. "If you can't do anything for us, why should we help you?"

Gregori adjusted his cuff links. He'd tell Roman and Angus that he had no choice but to demonstrate some powers. Otherwise these guys thought Vamps were worthless. "We have a few abilities you might find useful."

The president smiled. "Now that sounds more like it."

The general snorted. "We don't need these Vamps. They can't do anything our armed forces can't do."

Gregori leaned forward. "Mortals are not equipped to fight the Malcontents. We are. And we're willing to fight them to protect you."

The general shrugged. "We can solve that problem by getting rid of all of you. It's not like we'd be killing you. You're already dead."

"We're American citizens," Gregori said. "We go to work, pay our taxes, and follow the laws—"

"You're damned unnatural is what you are," the general insisted. "The world will be much better off without you."

Gregori clenched and relaxed his fists, wishing once again that he had a stress ball. There was no reasoning with the general. He'd have to go with Plan C. Show off some of his powers.

He removed the ice bucket from the stand and set it on the coffee table. Rising to his feet, he grabbed the thick wrought-iron stand and bent it easily into a circle.

"Excellent," the president whispered, his eyes gleaming with excitement.

"Let me see that." The secretary of defense took the metal loop and tried to straighten it. His face turned red with exertion.

"Superior strength," Caprese said. "Impressive."

The general shrugged. "Big deal. I have servicemen who are that strong."

Gregori zoomed around the men in a flash of vampire speed. The men reacted with gasps and startled expressions.

"Amazing!" the president said.

Gregori came to a halt behind General Bond and tapped him on the shoulder. "If you were a Malcontent, I would have snapped your neck."

The general leaped to his feet. "He threatened to kill me! Arrest him!"

"No, I didn't—"

"Arrest him now!" the general ordered.

The Secret Service man lunged toward him, but Gregori teleported to the other side of President Tucker.

"Mr. President, I wasn't—"

"*What?*" President Tucker jumped back. "How did you get there?"

"The president is in danger!" the general boomed.

"In here, now!" the Secret Service man yelled into his wrist communicator, then leaped onto the president.

The door crashed open, and two more Secret Service men dashed straight for Gregori. He levitated to the ceiling.

Abigail and Madison Tucker rushed inside with their Secret Service guard. The other two guards were jumping, trying to grab his legs, while the first one was pulling their father out of the way. The men were arguing with one another. Whelan was cursing at him. And the general was pointing at him and shouting.

Madison grinned and clapped her hands together. "This is so awesome!"

Abigail's stunned gaze lifted to him on the ceiling.

"I can explain," Gregori began, though he doubted she could hear his voice over all the noise.

She crumpled onto the carpet in a dead faint.

Chapter Eight

Abigail blinked her eyes as the world slowly came back into focus. For a fuzzy moment, she wondered why she was lying on the floor. And why was there so much shouting? Her father and Madison were kneeling beside her and watching her closely.

"She's fine, Dad," Madison yelled over the noise. "She just fainted."

Fainted? She never fainted.

Dad touched her cheek and smiled. "That's my girl."

When he stood, Abigail's gaze lifted and she gasped. Good Lord, now she remembered what had caused her to faint. Gregori Holstein was floating on the ceiling! And three Secret Service agents were bouncing on the sofas trying to grab hold of him. "What—?"

Madison squeezed her arm. "You were right, Abby! He's a vampire!"

"What?" She blinked, and he was still there, watching her with a worried look. Good Lord, this was real. This was horrible! "*No!*" She scooted back on the floor.

A grimace of pain flashed across his face.

Her breath caught. Had she hurt his feelings?

He turned away from her and slowly floated down to the floor.

"Arrest him!" the CIA director shouted, and two Secret Service agents seized his arms.

Abigail scrambled to her feet. "Don't hurt him!"

His gaze snapped back to her.

Her heart lurched. Out of all the noise in the room, he'd heard her voice. She pressed a hand against her pounding heart, terrified he was a monster and equally terrified he would be hurt.

"Everyone, quiet!" Dad shouted, and the room grew silent. "Now let's sit down and discuss this calmly." He motioned to the Secret Service men. "You can let him go."

"Laurence, no!" Mr. Caprese gritted his teeth. "Mr. President, he threatened to kill the general."

Abigail gasped.

"Oh my God," Madison whispered.

Mr. Holstein cursed under his breath. The Secret Service men continued to hold him.

"He must be arrested and detained," Caprese continued.

"I seriously doubt we *can* detain him," the president replied. "Am I right, Mr. Holstein?"

"Yes, sir. I could vanish from here or any holding cell, and you would never find me." His gaze shifted to Abigail. "You would never see me again."

That should be a good thing, she thought, considering he was a vampire and he'd threatened to kill one of her father's advisors. So why did the notion of never seeing him again give her a strange sensation of loss?

She looked away, her heart racing. It was baffling.

Part of her feared him. He was some sort of unnatural creature. But another part of her found him oddly attractive. It had to be scientific curiosity. He presented an intriguing subject for study. *Right. And his handsome face has nothing to do with it.* She winced, directing a spurt of anger at herself for finding a dangerous creature like him attractive.

She turned back to him, her fists clenched. "Is it true? Did you threaten to kill the general?"

His eyes flashed with anger. "Do you believe I'm capable of killing in cold blood?"

"I have no idea what you are capable of."

He stared at her a moment, then inclined his head. "You are correct. Trust has to be earned."

Her mouth dropped open. That was not the response she had expected. "Why—why did you threaten him?"

"I said I'd kill him if he were a Malcontent, but he isn't one, so there was no threat. I was merely giving a demonstration. Like this." He vanished, leaving the Secret Service men grasping at air. He reappeared, standing behind her father's desk.

Abigail gasped. He could actually teleport!

"Awesome," Madison whispered.

Mr. Holstein spread his hands. "I have no intention of harming anyone."

Could that be true? Abigail wondered. Could there be such a thing as a *harmless* vampire? It sounded like an oxymoron.

"You can believe Mr. Holstein," the stocky man who had arrived with him said. "Even though the Vamps have a number of impressive powers, they are basically safe and harmless."

"Stow it, Whelan," Mr. Caprese muttered. "That's not what you told me when you started the Stake-Out team. You said the Undead were dangerous, and this one has just proven it."

Mr. Holstein folded his arms over his chest. "If I was truly dangerous, none of you would be alive to talk about it. But as Mr. Whelan has discovered over the last few years, we are harmless. We're morally opposed to causing any injury to humans."

"Of course." The general sneered at him. "You wouldn't want to diminish your food source."

Mr. Holstein glared at him. "We're not inhuman monsters. We all started our lives as humans. We had human parents and a human childhood. Many of the older Vamps have descendants. Younger Vamps like me still have family. How could I view a human as food when my own mother is still alive?"

He was a young vampire? Abigail wondered what had caused him to become Undead. What exactly did it mean to be Undead? Gregori Holstein was moving about, thinking, talking. Didn't these things require an active circulatory system? Her mind raced with one question after another. So many unknowns, but one thing was for certain. Mr. Holstein was fascinating.

She winced inwardly. She couldn't allow herself to be distracted by this man, no matter how mysterious and handsome he was. She had to hold firm to her mission. All her years of study and hard work had been aimed at one goal: discovering a cure for her mother. She had no time for studying this . . . vampire, no matter how fascinating he was.

"Mr. Holstein makes an excellent point," her dad said.

"He's still basically human. I think we can trust him."

The Homeland Security director, Mr. Schiller, snorted. "Are you kidding? He has powers we can't hope to compete with."

"But we don't use them to harm mortals," Mr. Holstein insisted.

"What other powers do you have?" the national security advisor asked.

Mr. Holstein shrugged and skirted the desk. "You've witnessed most of them. Levitation, teleportation, super speed and strength."

"And heightened senses," Abigail murmured softly.

He looked at her, and that shot her heart rate into warp drive. The corner of his mouth lifted.

Blast him. He could hear it.

"Any other powers?" her dad asked.

His smile widened. "I'm an excellent dancer."

Dad chuckled, but her breath caught in her chest. He was deflecting. She knew it. He had more powers. Powers he didn't want them to know about. For one thing, she was ninety-nine percent certain that he had caused Madison's dog to fall asleep. If he could do that to an animal, he could probably do it to humans. What other tricks could he play on the human mind?

A chill skittered down her arms, giving her goose bumps. Mr. Holstein could be far more dangerous than her father realized. She needed to warn him, but she didn't want to make accusations she couldn't prove.

"Dad?" She sidled up close to him. "Can I have a word with you in private?"

He turned to her, his eyes sparkling with excitement. "You're thinking the same thing I am, aren't you?" He squeezed her shoulder. "That research trip you wanted to take? I think it's possible now."

She gasped. Good Lord, that hadn't occurred to her. She'd proposed that trip two weeks ago.

"I hated having to turn you down," her dad whispered. "But this changes everything. And the fact that it happened now, just when we need it, it makes me believe this was *meant* to be."

Her heart squeezed in her chest. She couldn't blame her father for believing that fate had somehow stepped in to help him keep his beloved wife alive. But could fate take the form of vampires?

She glanced at Mr. Holstein. He was watching them curiously, and no doubt he could hear every word. "Dad, we need to talk about this. Alone."

"It'll be fine. Trust me." He patted her shoulder, then turned to his advisors. "My decision is made. We will proceed with the alliance. These Vamps possess special abilities that will come in handy." He glanced back at Abigail and winked.

She gulped. Dad might be jumping into this alliance out of desperation to save Mom. Such an alliance shouldn't be based on emotional reasons, but she couldn't help but share his surge of hope. Mr. Holstein's ability to teleport meant he could get her into China without the Chinese government even knowing about it. She might find the plants that had the most potential of saving her mother.

But what if Mr. Holstein had dangerous psychic powers? How could she possibly trust him? On the other hand, how could she pass up an opportunity to help her mother?

"Alan." Her dad turned to the director of Homeland Security. "I'm putting you in charge of making that video disappear and proving to the public that vampires are nothing more than fantasy. Get started immediately."

Alan Schiller nodded with a resigned look. "Yes, Mr. President." He strode from the room.

"Thank you," Mr. Holstein told her father. "We'll be happy to assist you with any problems that might arise." He glanced at Abigail and lifted his eyebrows with a questioning look.

She turned away, her cheeks growing warm. Would Dad actually do it? Would he ask a vampire to take her on her research trip?

"I have something personal I'd like to discuss with Mr. Holstein," her father said. "General, George, Frank, thank you for coming."

General Bond shot Mr. Holstein a disgusted look, then marched from the office, followed by the secretary of defense and the national security advisor.

"Mr. President?" Josh asked. "I'll escort your daughters back to the residence floor now."

"You can take Madison, but I'd like Abigail to stay."

She swallowed hard. Yes, Dad was going to do it.

"But that's not fair!" Madison latched on to Abigail's arm. "If Abby gets to stay, then so do I."

Dad lowered his voice. "Sweetie, we have business to discuss with Mr. Holstein."

"I can do that! I'm a vampire expert!"

Dad's mouth twitched. "I doubt you could know more than the vampire himself."

"Oh." She tucked her chin down. "I suppose that's true."

"If the young ladies wish to remain, I would be honored to have their company." Mr. Holstein gave them a dazzling smile.

Abigail's pulse jumped. Did he know the power of that smile? It was every bit as striking as his phenomenal hearing. The man who had accompanied him, Mr. Whelan, nudged him with an elbow and gave him a warning look that he seemed to find amusing.

"Oh, thank you, Mr. Holstein!" Madison grinned and extended a hand. "I'm so excited to meet you. I have long been an admirer of your . . . species."

He shook her hand. "Please, call me Gregori."

She giggled. "I love your name! It's so vampirish. Don't you think so, Abby?"

"I suppose." She avoided eye contact with him, but still saw his hand reach out to her.

"Abby?" he asked softly.

She swallowed hard. Why did his voice have to be so deep and sexy? "Gori." She clasped his hand, intending to give it one quick shake and release, but he held tight until she lifted her gaze to meet his.

A small frisson of energy shot through her, giving her a shock. Where had that come from? His eyes? His hand? Or both? She pulled her hand from his grip, jerking back hard enough that she lost her balance and fell onto her rump on the couch.

"Yes, let's all have a seat." Her dad sat in his chair at the head of the coffee table, apparently unaware that anything odd had happened.

The CIA director and Mr. Whelan sat on the other couch. Josh and the three Secret Service agents remained standing.

Had she imagined that little jolt? No, her right palm still tingled with residual electricity. Abigail clenched her hands together. Maybe it was just her. She ventured a glance at Gregori.

He was regarding her with a puzzled look.

"Gregori." Her dad cleared his throat. "Do you mind if I call you Gregori?"

"No, that would be fine." He sat in the chair at the end of the coffee table.

Madison set her dog bag on the coffee table next to the ice bucket, then sat next to Abigail. "I'm so sorry, Gregori, that I didn't recognize you right away. I was expecting you to fly in as a bat."

He nodded with a hint of a smile. "We try to be inconspicuous."

Abigail snorted. As if Gregori Holstein could ever be inconspicuous.

He glanced at her, and his eyes darkened to an intense green.

Her heart went back into warp drive. Dammit, he could probably hear that.

Abigail's dad leaned forward, his forearms resting on his knees, as he studied Gregori. "Now that we're helping you with your problem, I'm sure you realize that we expect something in return."

Gregori shifted in his chair as he unbuttoned his suit coat. "What do you have in mind?"

Mr. Caprese cleared his throat. "Your ability to teleport makes you an excellent candidate for covert operations."

Gregori nodded. "We can do covert. We've been covert for centuries." He leaned forward, his expression earnest. "But you must understand that our commitment to not harm mortals remains firm. We will not torture or assassinate for you."

Mr. Caprese huffed. "What makes you think we do that sort of thing?"

Gregori arched a brow, then pulled a bottle from the ice bucket.

Madison nudged Abigail and whispered, "Look! He's going to drink blood!"

"He can hear you," Abigail muttered.

He glanced at her, lifted the bottle in salute, then took a sip.

Yeech. She suppressed a shudder.

His eyes twinkled with humor as he licked his lips.

She looked away, her cheeks warm. The rascal was purposely trying to unnerve her. And succeeding.

"We won't ask you to do something you find morally offensive," her dad said.

The CIA director raised a hand in objection. "They were caught decapitating someone on video. I don't buy the morally superior act."

"That was a battle against the Malcontents." Gregori took another sip of blood. "Our warriors kill in self-defense like any good soldiers."

"So if you were attacked while on a mission," Mr. Caprese said, "we could expect you to kill in order to defend yourselves?"

Gregori frowned. "If necessary, yes. But it is rarely necessary when we can simply teleport away."

Mr. Caprese smirked. "Is that your usual reaction to danger? Run away and hide? I suppose that's how you've managed to exist in secret for so many centuries."

Abigail sucked in a breath. Gregori looked pissed. His eyes had narrowed and turned a more brilliant, luminescent green.

His voice was deadly soft. "Vamps have been risking their lives in battle against the Malcontents for centuries in order to protect mortals. You will not question their bravery."

"Of course not," her dad agreed.

Abigail watched Gregori, fascinated by the changes in his eyes. He seemed to be calming down now, and his eyes were returning to their normal shade of grayish-green. Still, while he'd been upset, the intensity in the room had felt electric and exciting.

He definitely didn't like being considered cowardly. She wondered what other hot buttons he had. What would happen if he completely lost control? Was there a bloodsucking monster inside him just waiting to burst free?

"Who are the Malcontents?" she asked.

"They are the true enemy," Mr. Whelan explained. "Evil vampires who believe they have the right to feed off mortals and kill them. Mortals would be defenseless against them in battle. But the Vamps have the same powers as the Malcontents, so they're our best bet at defeating them. We need the Vamps on our side."

"Then on behalf of our country, I would like to thank you for protecting us," the president said.

Gregori inclined his head. "You're welcome."

Strange, Abigail thought. Mr. Whelan made the

Vamps sound like heroes. Protectors of the Universe with their black vampire capes and super powers. Come to think of it, she wouldn't mind seeing Gregori in a spandex costume.

"I'd like to hear more about teleportation," her dad continued. "How far can you travel?"

She sat up, anxious to hear his answer.

"I can go anywhere in the world," Gregori replied. "But it has to be nighttime wherever I'm going."

Abigail's dad exchanged a look with her, then turned back to Gregori. "Can you take someone with you when you teleport?"

Gregori nodded. "One person. Some of the older Vamps can manage two, but we usually stick with just one to be safe."

Abigail's heart raced even faster.

Gregori leaned forward. "What sort of project do you have in mind?"

"Nothing violent." Her dad waved a dismissive hand. "It would be more of a . . . humanitarian mission."

"Mr. President," the CIA director whispered. "We need to discuss this first."

He nodded. "We will. I just wanted to gather some facts beforehand." He turned to Abigail and lowered his voice. "What do you think? Would you be comfortable traveling and working with him and his kind?"

Her heart pounded in her ears. "It's hard to say." She cast a nervous glance toward Gregori. "I hardly know him."

"Then you need to get better acquainted." Her dad turned back to Gregori. "Would you mind spending some time with my daughter? Tomorrow night? Perhaps you could introduce her to your world and some of your associates."

His eyes widened. "If you wish. Yes, sir."

Abigail gulped. Did her father just set her up on a date with a vampire?

"I want to come!" Madison bounced on the couch with excitement. "Please, Daddy. I want to see the vampire world!"

"Yes." Abigail grabbed her sister's arm. "I'd like Madison to come, too." *Anything to keep me from being alone with Gregori Holstein.*

"Oh, thank you, Abby!" Madison hugged her. "It's going to be so much fun!" She turned to Gregori. "Where will you take us?"

"I—" He adjusted his tie and glanced at Mr. Whelan, who had just cursed under his breath. "Somewhere . . . public. I don't know any vampire places in D.C. There's a new vampire nightclub in Manhattan that's very popular right now."

"A vampire nightclub!" Madison clasped her hands together over her chest. "That sounds so exciting!"

Their dad frowned. "What goes on at this club? Is it a safe place for my daughters?"

"Completely safe. All the Vamps there will be drinking from bottles," Gregori explained. "They just go there to talk and dance."

"Then I guess it would be all right." Dad motioned to two of the Secret Service men. "Josh and Charles will provide transportation. They'll need to be with you at all times, and they'll report directly to me every five minutes. The girls will arrive in Manhattan tomorrow. We'll let you know where they're staying."

"Dad." Abigail touched his sleeve. "I have to go to work tomorrow."

"They can give you a few days off." He squeezed her hand. "This is important. We have to know if you can get along with this vampire and his friends." He glanced at Gregori. "And I need to know if I can trust you with my daughter."

Gregori nodded. "I will guard her with my life."

"Me too!" Madison clapped her hands merrily.

Their dad stood and gave Gregori a stern look. "I will hold you to that promise. My daughters are to stay safe and protected. If anything happens to them, if they come home just feeling *unhappy*, then our deal is off, and you and your vampire friends are on your own."

"I understand." Gregori stood and turned stiffly toward Abigail and Madison. "I will see you tomorrow evening at nine in New York."

Madison jumped to her feet. "Thank you!"

He nodded at her, then gave Abigail a questioning look.

Her cheeks blazed with heat. A date with a vampire? Her whole world had suddenly turned topsy-turvy.

Her dad gestured to one of the Secret Service men. "Charles will drive you back now."

"Thank you, but no. It's not necessary." Gregori took hold of Mr. Whelan's arm and glanced at the dog bag on the coffee table.

Dolly opened her eyes and sat up.

Abigail stiffened and stared at Gregori. "You—"

"We can talk tomorrow," he interrupted.

Before she could respond, he vanished, taking Mr. Whelan with him.

Chapter Nine

$\mathcal{G}$regori landed close to the side entrance to Roma-tech. He swore silently as he dug his ID card out of his wallet. Of all the stupid things—nowhere in his strategy plans had he counted on being a damned babysitter. He swiped his ID card while Sean Whelan pivoted in a circle.

"What the hell are we doing here?" Sean demanded.

Gregori opened the door. "After you."

"We need to go to the safe house. Take me there now."

"No." Gregori strode down the hall. How the hell had this mess happened? As far as he could tell, the fate of Vamps around the world now depended on how well he could babysit the president's daughters.

"You can't tell me no." Sean followed him. "I'm in charge of this operation."

Down the hall, the door to the MacKay security office opened, and Angus and Emma MacKay stepped out.

"Did ye finish yer meeting with the president?" Angus asked.

Before Gregori could answer, Sean lunged in front

of him, jabbing a thumb toward him. "This idiot's not doing as he's told. He was supposed to take us to the safe house."

Gregori glared at Sean. "Who's the idiot? You had the Secret Service pick us up there. I don't consider it safe."

"Of course it's safe," Sean insisted. "The president just made an alliance with us."

"Och, that's good news," Angus said.

Emma smiled. "Well done, guys."

Gregori shrugged. "I wouldn't bank on it yet." He still had to take the daughters out dancing. And keep them *happy*, or he and his friends were screwed.

"That's why we should stay in D.C.," Sean said. "We need to be close by for further negotiations."

Gregori shook his head. "We'll just teleport."

Sean gritted his teeth. "I can't teleport."

"Learn how."

"I can't!" Sean ran a hand over his buzz cut hair. "Don't you see the bind I'm in? I have to keep acting like I'm human. If they find out the truth about me, they'll fire me and I'll lose their trust."

"He has a point," Emma said. "Sean can help us more if he retains his current position."

"All the more reason for him to stay away from the safe house." Gregori turned to Sean. "What if your CIA buddies came to see you during the day and found you in your death-sleep?"

He gulped. "I—I would be in the basement. Garrett wouldn't let them down there. He would protect me."

"Garret works for the CIA," Gregori gritted out. "He'll do whatever Caprese tells him to do."

"And he knows the truth about you, aye?" Angus asked. "Did ye no' train him to hate vampires as much as ye do?"

With a grimace, Sean paced away a few steps. "It's not fair! I'm the same person I was before. I've worked for the CIA for over thirty years! Why would they think I've suddenly become a monster?"

Gregori scoffed in chorus with Angus and Emma.

Sean gave them a sheepish look. "Okay. I get it. I was a little . . . judgmental toward you guys."

"Ye were an arse, Whelan," Angus muttered.

"Fine." He scowled. "Rub it in. But how the hell am I supposed to keep my job when I'm . . . Undead?"

"It's better than being dead," Gregori told him wryly.

"If ye end up getting fired, ye can always work for me," Angus suggested.

Sean grimaced as he raked a hand over his hair. "I'll have to think about it. I'm still trying to . . . adjust."

"Have you told your wife yet?" Emma asked.

"No. She thinks I've been overseas for the last two weeks. I . . . don't know how to break the news to her."

Emma patted him on the shoulder. "Once she gets over her shock, it will all be for the best. She can see Shanna and Caitlyn again. And once she sees how adorable her grandchildren are, she'll recover soon enough."

Sean's face softened. "Those kids are really special."

Gregori exchanged a look with Angus. Those kids were a lot more *special* than Sean knew. "Back to the matter of the safe house—it's not really safe. Not when that asshole General Bond is claiming the world would be better off without us."

Sean snorted. "Well, you didn't help matters by threatening to snap his neck."

Angus stiffened. "*What?*"

Gregori winced. "It's a long story. Before we get into it, I think we should get our guys back here."

Angus nodded. "Agreed. I never did like that safe house."

Sean huffed. "I went to a lot of trouble to set that up for us. And that's where the CIA will contact us for further negotiations."

"Then Garrett can remain there and relay any messages to you," Angus said. "Like it or not, Whelan, ye're in our world now, so ye have to start doing things our way."

Five minutes later, Angus, Robby, and Phineas had teleported the shifters and everyone's luggage back to Romatech. Phil was transported back to the Dragon Nest Academy to help guard the school since most of the women and all the children were there. The remaining MacKay Security and Investigation employees filed into the conference room along with Sean Whelan and Coven Masters Roman and Zoltan.

Gregori sat at the table in the same seat he'd occupied the night before. As he gazed around the table, seeing some of his best friends—Phineas, Robby, Olivia, Howard, Angus, Emma, Zoltan, and Roman—the pressure to succeed bore down on him. Had he done well tonight or totally screwed up?

"So the president has agreed to help us?" Roman asked.

Before Gregori could answer, Sean jumped in. "Yes, he has. He ordered the director of Homeland Security to scrub the video, and the whole vampire story will be declared a hoax."

Cheerful comments reverberated around the table.

"Excellent work." Roman smiled at Gregori.

Olivia tilted her head, studying him. "You don't look very pleased, Gregori."

He shrugged. "It was like a poker game with a lot of maneuvering and bluffing going on. Even though the president agreed to get in the game with us, he has yet to show his hand. I'm not sure what he's expecting from us in return."

"But it was an excellent start," Sean insisted. "President Tucker was eager to form an alliance with us, and he seemed quite willing to trust us."

"Because he wants something," Gregori muttered.

"At least we have his support," Roman said. "What about the other men?"

Gregori took a deep breath. "The Homeland Security guy was ordered to get rid of the video, but he doesn't really trust us because I refused to give him a list of all the Vamps in the country."

Angus winced. "Nay, we canna do that."

"The CIA director wants to be our ally so he can use us as a weapon against their enemies," Gregori continued. "The secretary of defense and national security advisor are suspicious and not readily inclined to trust us. General Bond of the Joint Chiefs of Staff would prefer to wipe all the vampires off the planet. That's why I didn't think we should remain at the safe house in D.C."

A moment of silence settled in the room.

Roman sighed. "I guess it will take them a while to learn to trust us."

Gregori nodded. "I tried the safe-and-harmless routine, but they were interpreting that as weak and worthless, and they only want us around if we're useful. I had to prove we were worth saving, or they might agree with the general that it was better to just eliminate us."

"So how much did you tell them?" Zoltan asked.

"Tell them?" Sean scoffed. "He *showed* them. He bent an iron rod, zipped around at vampire speed, teleported, and threatened to break the general's neck."

Everyone gasped.

Gregori shot Sean an annoyed look. "It was a demonstration of strength so they would respect us." He adjusted his tie. "I believe it was an effective strategy."

"Apparently so, since you weren't arrested," Emma said. "And the president agreed to help us."

Gregori shrugged one shoulder. "He has an agenda. A humanitarian mission, he called it, that involves teleporting somewhere."

"We can do that." Angus leaned forward. "Did he say where?"

"No." Gregori fiddled with his cuff links. "But I believe it involves taking his daughter."

Angus sat back with a surprised expression.

"You mean Madison Tucker?" Olivia asked.

Gregori shook his head. "The oldest daughter. Abigail." He was met with blank looks. "She's not well-known." But she was fascinating.

A small part of him was excited about seeing her again. He wanted to know what she was up to, why she was hiding, what made her tick. And how good she would feel in his arms. He winced. *She's the presi-*

dent's daughter, you fool. A bigger part of him knew she represented sheer disaster. If the CIA knew what kind of thoughts he was having, they'd have a hit man assigned to him in a second.

"You don't like her?" Emma asked.

He stiffened. "What?"

"You were scowling," Emma said.

"Oh." He shifted in his chair. "I'm . . . not happy with the . . . uh, situation."

"Yeah, it's a bad situation," Sean agreed. "The president asked Gregori to introduce his daughters to the vampire world. He wants to see if Abigail can get along with us."

Olivia's eyes widened. "The president wants you to take his daughters out? You mean like a date?"

Gregori gritted his teeth. "It's not a date. It's a . . . diplomatic mission."

Sean nodded. "Exactly. It's serious business. The girls will arrive in Manhattan tomorrow with a Secret Service detail."

Phineas snickered. "Can you handle two women, bro? Or do you need a little help with your date?"

Gregori jerked at his tie. "It's not a date. It's a damned babysitting job. The president made it clear. If the girls are harmed in any way, or just *unhappy* about how the evening goes, then the whole alliance will be canceled."

Roman stiffened. "That seems harsh."

Robby's mouth twitched. "Luckily, Gregori is an expert at keeping lassies happy."

Phineas gave him a thumbs-up. "You da man!"

"Are you guys crazy?" Sean growled. "If he lays a

finger on them, we could all be screwed. I wanted to stop the president, but how could I tell him he was sending his daughters off with the most notorious womanizer in the vampire world?"

"Gee, thanks, Sean." Gregori glared at him. "Like I was planning to ravish them both." *Only one.* He slapped himself mentally. *Don't even think it!*

"Where are you taking them?" Emma asked.

"Everlasting Night. It's a vampire nightclub in SoHo that's very popular right now. I'll buy them a few drinks, let them dance a little and gawk at the Undead, then drop them off at their hotel. They'll have two Secret Service guys with them the whole time. It should be easy enough." Gregori shrugged. "It's just a stupid babysitting job."

Angus nodded. "Still, we canna afford to have something happen to the lassies while they're in yer care. Phineas, I want you to go with them."

"All right." Phineas grinned.

Sean groaned. "What are you thinking? The future of Vamps around the world depends on this, and you're subjecting those poor innocent girls to a playboy and the self-proclaimed Love Doctor?"

Phineas huffed. "Dude, I can be a perfect gentleman."

"On what planet?" Sean growled.

Angus chuckled. "I believe we can trust Gregori and Phineas to make sure the lassies are happy with their evening."

Emma smiled. "I agree. They can be very charming."

"You hear that, bro?" Phineas grinned at Gregori. "We're like Prince Charming."

"More like toads," Sean grumbled. "You'd better behave yourselves with the princesses."

Olivia leaned close to her husband and whispered, "Maybe one of them will be smart enough to recognize a prince in disguise."

"Like you did?" Robby squeezed her hand.

One of them was smart, all right, Gregori thought. Sharp and observant. She'd known he was different from the start. But she'd looked horrified when she'd learned the truth. When they shook hands, she pulled away from him so hard, she fell onto the couch.

He sighed. It was better that way. Better if she found him repulsive.

The meeting came to a close with Angus and Roman stressing the importance of his keeping the president's daughters safe and happy. He strode to his office, needing to get away from everyone. But once he got there, he found no peace. He grabbed a stress ball off his desk and squeezed it as he paced back and forth.

Memories of Abigail Tucker kept sneaking into his thoughts. He had a feeling she suspected him of messing with the little dog. She didn't trust him. And she didn't want to be alone with him. He'd noticed how fast she'd coerced her sister into going on their night out.

What kind of mission did Abigail have in mind that it had to be done in secret? What was she up to? He tossed the stress ball on his desk and turned on his laptop so he could find out more information about her.

He paused halfway into typing her name. What was he doing? Feeding an obsession with her? He needed to stop thinking about her.

He closed the laptop, pulled out his Droid, and called Maggie.

"Hi, Sweetcakes." He leaned back in his chair. "How's the commercial going?"

Maggie groaned. "It's not. Every time Simone moves, something bad happens."

"It's not my fault!" Simone's voice shrieked in the distance.

Maggie sighed. "Gordon and I have stopped for the evening. We decided to rewrite the commercial in a way that keeps Simone as stationary as possible. Can you be here tomorrow night when we shoot it?"

He grabbed the stress ball. "I wish I could, Toots, but something's come up."

"Everyone here is still upset about the Vampire Apocalypse," Maggie said. "The makeup girl keeps saying we're doomed. Can you tell me if Roman has started on the plan yet?"

He squeezed the stress ball. "It'll be all right, Maggie. I met with the president tonight."

"*The* president? Of the United States?"

"Yep. That's why I couldn't do the commercial."

"Sweet Mary and Joseph! What happened?"

"I'd rather not say just yet, but we're hoping the government will help us out. I'll try to stop by DVN tomorrow night after I'm done babysitting."

"Babysitting?" Maggie asked.

He gave the stress ball another squeeze. "I'm taking the president's daughters to a vampire nightclub."

Maggie laughed. "Once they see how well you can dance, they'll definitely want to help us." There was a pause, then he heard her mutter, "No, Simone, you can't go with them. You have to be here for the commercial."

Gregori winced. Simone had overheard his plans. "Talk to you later, Maggie. Thanks for helping out." He hung up, tossed the stress ball to his other hand, then called his mother. "Hey, Mom. How's everything at the school?"

"Oh, we're fine. Is it true?" his mother asked in a rushed, excited voice. "I heard you have a date!"

The stress ball exploded in his hand. "Shit."

"Excuse me? What was that noise?"

"It's nothing." He tossed the ball in the trash. "It's not a date, Mom. It's a diplomatic mission. And how the hell did you hear about it?"

"You seem a bit agitated, dear. Are you nervous about your date?"

"It's not a date!" He grabbed another stress ball. "I'm as calm as can be. I just have the fate of every Vamp in the world on my shoulders."

"Oh, well, some days are harder than others. So who is the young lady you're dating?"

"I'm not dating! I'm taking the president's daughters on a friendly little outing to prove how trustworthy I am."

His mother made a tsking noise. "I'm not sure if that Madison Tucker is the right girl for you."

"I'm not interested in her. And how did you hear about this?"

"Well, Emma called. And then Olivia called. So are you interested in the other daughter? Shall I come back to Romatech so I can meet her?"

"No. Stay away."

She huffed. "That's not very nice. I just want to meet your new girlfriend."

"I'm not dating!"

"There's no reason to raise your voice."

Gregori took a deep breath and carefully squeezed the stress ball. "I gotta go now, Mom. Important stuff to do. Talk to you later."

"Very well. Have a wonderful time on your date."

He hung up and threw the stress ball across the office. "Important stuff to do." He pulled a bottle of Blissky out his bottom desk drawer and wrenched off the top.

He took a drink and wiped his mouth. "It's not a date."

But you wish it was.

He took another long drink to drown out the foolish voice inside him.

Chapter Ten

*M*adison's pretty blue eyes widened. "Wow! I haven't seen you look this good in years!"

"Gee, thanks," Abigail muttered as she eyed herself in the mirror. What would Gregori Holstein think of her now? She tugged at the neckline of the black cocktail dress her sister had picked out for her on a whirlwind shopping trip that afternoon. "I still think this is too revealing."

"Will you get off that?" Madison tilted her head, frowning. "But it does need something. Just a minute." She rummaged through her Louis Vuitton suitcase and pulled out a velvet jewelry case. "I should have something here."

Abigail sat on the edge of the bed and winced at how much of her pale legs were showing. She hadn't worn a dress in years. She hadn't taken a day off work in years, either. Mom was always telling her she needed a life, but her mom deserved to live, too.

When she'd explained to her mom that Madison had actually been right and not only were vampires real, but they would be going out with one tonight, her mom had taken the news quite well. In fact, Abigail couldn't recall the last time she'd seen her mother this excited. She'd looked five years younger when she'd seen them off this morning.

So Abigail had decided not to feel guilty for missing work. Or for costing Dad a small fortune. Madison was used to traveling to New York on a private jet, but Abigail had never indulged in the glamorous lifestyle. What was the point? She'd realized years ago in college that having a six-hundred-dollar tote bag wasn't going to help her pass a chemistry exam. And now she worked in a lab where everyone wore white coats. Her colleagues got excited over formulas and life-forms, not the latest trend in the fashion world.

After landing in New York, Josh and Charles had whisked them immediately into a black Suburban limousine and taken them to the Waldorf Astoria, code name Roadhouse. She and Madison were sharing one bedroom of their elegant suite, so the guys could use the other. The agents planned to sleep in shifts so one of them would always be on guard duty.

Abigail sighed. The combined cost of the hotel suite and her dress was more than she earned in a month. She had to admit, though, it had been exciting, running around Manhattan with the paparazzi chasing them and the Secret Service guys guarding them like they were something special.

"This will be perfect!" Madison held up a glittering rhinestone necklace. Her grin faded. "What are you doing sitting? You'll wrinkle your dress."

Abigail returned to the spot in front of the mirror, wobbling on the borrowed high heels. "I'm going to fall over in these things. I'd rather wear the flats I brought."

"Don't be silly. You need the heels. You're a little short, you know." Madison looped the necklace around Abigail's neck and latched it in the back.

Abigail winced. A long string of sparkling rhinestones ended in the valley between her breasts. It was like a flashing billboard that advertised, *Look what I've got!*

This was crazy. A vampire nightclub? Sexy cocktail dresses? This was nothing like the mission she'd proposed to her dad. That trip would require hiking through rough mountainous terrain. But she supposed this was a safer way to get acquainted with Gregori and his world.

Madison checked her makeup in the mirror, then glanced at Abigail. "You need some lipstick. Here, this color will suit you."

Abigail frowned at herself in the mirror. She'd put on lipstick ten minutes ago, but it was gone. She must have chewed it off. She'd probably poisoned herself just to impress a vampire. An incredibly handsome vampire.

With a groan, she pulled the top off the lipstick tube. She needed to calm down. Relax. He was just a guy. A gorgeous, mysterious guy who happened to be Undead.

She applied the copper-red shade. Great. This would probably remind him of blood. *Stop fixating on him!* Why would he care what her lips looked like? He'd be a lot more interested in her carotid artery. Or in playing mind games with her and putting her to sleep like he had Madison's dog. And that would really be a shame, because if he ever played games with her, she'd want to be fully awake.

She winced. What on earth was she thinking?

The phone rang and she jumped, smearing the lipstick across her cheek. "Oh no!"

"Don't worry about the phone." Madison checked her mascara. "The guys will pick it up." She looked at Abby and flinched. "Oh my God! What have you done?"

"I slipped."

"Sheesh! I leave you alone for ten seconds and you turn into the Joker!" Madison dug into her cosmetic case. "I'll find a makeup remover pad. Hang on."

A knock sounded at the door. "That was Gregori," Josh announced. "He's down in the lobby."

Abigail's heart lurched.

"We're almost ready," Madison called out as she wiped the lipstick off Abigail's cheek. "Are you nervous about tonight?"

"How'd you ever guess?" Abigail muttered. "Aren't you nervous?"

"No. Not too much. Dad sent the two biggest Secret Service guys to watch over us." She lowered her voice. "Have you seen Josh without his jacket on? Oh my God—"

"Madison, our guards may be strong, but they don't have supernatural powers like the vampires. In fact, I strongly suspect Gregori didn't reveal all his powers. He may have some strange psychic abilities."

Madison shrugged. "Probably so. It's one of those vampire things. Kind of sexy when you think about it." She tossed the dirty makeup remover pad in the trash can.

"Sexy? It's downright dangerous."

"Abby, chill. You heard Dad. If we're unhappy about anything tonight, he'll call the alliance off. Gregori won't dare do anything to upset us. The way I see it, that puts us in the position of power."

Abigail bit her lip. She wouldn't call their position powerful, not when Gregori was the one with the powers.

"It's all about attitude," Madison continued. "I've played hostess at a lot of events, and I've met people from strange countries and cultures. You just smile and act like everything's okay. You can do this."

"Okay." A twinge of guilt pricked at Abigail that she'd never given her sister the respect she deserved. For the past few years, Abigail had congratulated herself for being the one most dedicated to helping Mom. She worked long hours trying to come up with a cure for lupus, while she considered her sister the frivolous party girl.

But now she realized that in her own way, Madison was helping their mother, too. Serving as hostess at state dinners and parties couldn't be easy, and as nervous as she was tonight, Abigail knew it was a job she couldn't manage half as well as her sister.

"Thank you, Madison. I don't know what I'd do without you."

Madison's eyes widened. "Well, I suppose I have my uses." A blush spread over her pretty cheeks. "You like him, don't you?"

"Who?"

Madison gave her a pointed look. "Do you want some alone time with him tonight?"

"Good Lord, no. I'd rather you keep him busy."

Madison smiled as she picked up her small rhinestone-encrusted clutch. "So you do know who."

Abigail grabbed the black pashmina shawl and black beaded clutch she was borrowing from her sister. "He's a vampire." *And he's waiting downstairs in the lobby.*

On the elevator ride down, Abigail looped the end of her shawl over one shoulder so it covered her from the neck past the bodice of her dress. Beside her, Madison smirked. She was striking in a blue sparkly dress that matched her eyes. In front of them, Josh and Charles stood facing the elevator doors. They wore their usual black suits, and each sported an earpiece and wrist communicator so they could converse with each other.

The elevator doors opened. Josh held the doors and blocked their departure until Charles determined it was safe for them to emerge.

Abigail tensed when she spotted Gregori across the lobby. *Wow.* Still more handsome than should be legally allowed. Women could have car accidents if they spotted him on the sidewalk. Or they could choke on their food if he wandered past a café. He was clearly a menace to society.

She slapped herself mentally. Of course he was a menace. He was a vampire!

He was talking to another man. Both were well dressed in expensive suits, although the new guy was more casual. No tie, and the top buttons of his dress shirt were undone. Was he a vampire, too?

"Oh look." Madison flipped her hair over a shoulder. "Gregori brought a friend. It'll be like a double date."

"It's not a date," Abigail mumbled.

She and her sister accompanied the security guys across the lobby. Gregori's gaze drifted over the guys and Madison, then settled on her. His face remained blank, but there was a growing intensity in his eyes that sent a shiver down her spine. She wobbled on her high heels, and Charles grabbed her elbow. Gregori's gaze shifted to Charles's hand, and his mouth thinned.

Madison switched into hostess mode, beaming a smile at Gregori and extending a hand. "Gregori! How delightful to see you again."

"Madison." He shook her hand, then nodded at Abigail. "How do you do?"

She nodded back. "Good evening." So he didn't intend to shake her hand or even say her name? Abigail squeezed her hands around her clutch, feeling the little beads bite into her fingertips. So what if he wanted to act stiff and formal? It was better this way.

Meanwhile her sister aimed her dazzling smile at the new guy. "I don't believe we've met. I'm Madison Tucker."

"I'm Phineas McKinney." He shook her hand. "Also known as Dr. Phang."

Her eyes widened. "Really? I guess that means you're"—she lowered her voice dramatically—"one of them."

He winked. "You bet your sweet blood type I am."

She giggled and leaned close to Abigail. "Isn't he cute? He's just like Denzel, but younger."

"He can hear you," Abigail muttered.

Josh and Charles quickly introduced themselves, then Charles hurried off to retrieve the limo from its special parking place. While they waited, Josh called their father and gave him a brief update.

"This is my sister, Abigail," Madison introduced her to Phineas. "She's a doctor, too. What is your area of expertise, Dr. Phang?"

"I'm the Love Doctor. Everyone turns to me with their romantic queries, and now our world is full of happily married couples."

Madison gasped, then whispered, "You mean your . . . kind like to get married to each other?"

"Actually, most of the guys have hooked up with luscious-looking mortal babes." He smiled. "Like you."

Madison gasped again, then gave Abigail a wide-eyed, excited look. "Did you hear that?"

"Don't even think about it," Abigail whispered, casting a nervous look at Josh. "Dad would kill us."

"No, he would kill us," Gregori said softly.

Abigail met his eyes for an electric second before he looked away. Good Lord, was that why he was acting so distant? But if he was concerned about getting involved with her, then it had to mean . . . *He's attracted to me.*

A part of her was shocked to admit it. But another part, deep inside her, had sensed it from the beginning. The way he had looked at her, smiled at her, watched her so intently.

It's impossible, she reminded herself. And thankfully, he knew it was.

Still, it might make traveling with him a bit awkward. She slanted a look at his expensive suit. Could he rough it in the wilderness? His super strength and other abilities would certainly come in handy, but what about his liabilities? What happened to him during the day? What happened if he ran out of bottled blood?

"Charles is pulling up now," Josh announced. "Let's go."

They stepped out onto the sidewalk on Park Avenue. The night air was chilly, so they hurried to the waiting car.

A flash of light blinded Abigail, and she lifted a hand to shade her eyes.

"Madison! Give us a smile!" A paparazzo eased closer, lifting his camera for a second photo.

"Quickly." Josh opened the door to the Suburban limousine and ushered Madison inside.

The paparazzo halted suddenly, and his face went blank. He raised his camera overhead and hurtled it to the sidewalk. It smashed into pieces, but his face remained expressionless.

Good Lord! Why would he destroy his own camera? A crazy thought screamed through Abigail's mind. *He was forced to.*

She spun toward Gregori, but stumbled in her high heels. He caught her, grasping her arms.

She planted her hands on his chest to keep from falling against him. "Did you do that?"

"Do what?" He leaned closer and whispered, "Are you all right?"

The feel of his breath against her cheek made her heart pound wildly. Dammit, he could probably hear it. Her gaze lowered to her right hand. Was that a heartbeat?

She splayed her hand more firmly against him. Yes! She could feel it. She pressed an ear against his chest.

Tha-thump. Tha-thump. He had a heartbeat! It was a bit fast. Like hers.

He cleared his throat. "We're being watched."

She jumped back and discovered him looking at her with glittering green eyes. Phineas was grinning at her. Josh was frowning. "It's okay. I was checking his heart. In the interest of scientific research."

"You want to check mine, too?" Phineas asked. "You gotta do a thorough job on your research, you know."

"That's enough. Let's go." Josh motioned for Phineas to get in the limo. After the young Vamp climbed in, Josh leaned into the vehicle to tell him where to sit.

Abigail glanced back at the paparazzo. He was still standing there, his face blank. A chill crept down her spine, and she turned back to Gregori. "You have psychic powers, don't you? And you're not really dead."

He looked around the busy sidewalk. "Let's not discuss it here, okay?"

He wasn't denying it. She had to be right.

She took a wobbly step toward the limo, then realized her hands were empty. "My purse!" She spotted it on the sidewalk, then leaned over to get it.

"I've got it." Gregori picked it up, then froze, his head turned toward her.

She gasped. Her shawl had slipped off her shoulders, and her breasts were practically falling out! She jerked to a standing position and pressed a hand to her chest. Oh God, she'd given him an eyeful.

And why was he straightening so slowly? Was he checking out her legs? He continued to straighten, his gaze inching up her dress to her neckline. Her face grew hot. Good Lord, she knew she shouldn't have worn this dress.

She cleared her throat. "My purse?"

His gaze shifted to her face, then to his hand as if surprised to find the purse there. "Here."

She took it. "Thank you." With hot cheeks, she hurried to the car and sat on the long side seat next to Madison.

Josh and Gregori climbed in. As they drove away, she heard the paparazzo bellow in outrage.

He must have been released from Gregori's mind control. She glanced warily at him. How often did he play with people's heads? Her gaze wandered to the shiny chrome-plated ceiling of the limo. She could see her own pale face reflected, but not his.

With a shiver, she wrapped her shawl tightly around her shoulders.

"Hey, Snake." Gregori greeted the huge bouncer outside the plain black door at the end of a dark alley.

The bouncer grunted and narrowed his beady eyes. Gregori assumed he was called Snake since he had a snake tattoo that curled up his neck onto his bald head, but he'd never asked. Snake was not a talkative guy.

The bouncer sniffed and curled a lip. "Mortals."

Gregori nodded. "They're my guests for the evening."

Snake grunted. "You know the rules." He opened the door and let them in.

"What rules?" Josh asked as he entered with Gregori.

"It's nothing," Gregori lied. It wasn't unusual for a Vamp to bring a mortal boyfriend or girlfriend to the club, but when their relationship ended, the Vamp was supposed to erase the mortal's memory.

"What rules?" Josh asked again as he scanned the room.

Gregori sighed. He'd have to make something up. "We're not supposed to let mortals drink blood. It tends to make them sick."

Josh nodded, apparently accepting the story. As the girls filed in, he remained close to them. Charles moved toward the center of the empty dance floor, then he pivoted, scanning the room.

It was a rectangular room, simply designed with a wooden dance floor in the middle, flanked on each side by small round tables and wooden chairs. On the right wall, the DJ stood behind his counter. A long bar ran the length of the left wall, and only one bartender was on duty this early in the evening. About two dozen Vamps were at the round tables, quietly chatting and sipping blood from wineglasses. On the far end of the room a few couples were cuddled up in half-moon-shaped booths upholstered in tufted red velvet.

Slow music was playing, but no one was dancing. The crowd was smaller than usual, and more subdued. Vamps probably didn't feel like partying, not with the Vampire Apocalypse hanging over their heads.

"This is it?" Madison frowned as she looked around. "It looks so normal. Even the people look normal."

What was she expecting? A naked Roman orgy? "It's only nine-thirty," Gregori explained. "Things don't really heat up till about three when most Vamps get off work and the West Coast crowd starts teleporting in." He didn't want to admit how worried Vamps were.

Madison sighed. "The music's turned down a little low."

Gregori nodded. "We have sensitive hearing. If the music's too lòud, it could be painful for us."

"I like it this way." Abigail glanced at her sister. "We'll be able to hear each other talk."

She was avoiding looking at him. *Great.* He was supposed to keep the girls *happy* but Madison was disappointed and Abigail was freaked. He could hardly blame her. First he'd scared her by using vampire mind control on the paparazzo. Then he'd embarrassed her by ogling her sweet body. And finally he'd frightened her on the ride over. He didn't reflect in the limo's chrome-plated ceiling, but he could see in it, and he'd watched her shudder and recoil in horror.

"I'll talk to the DJ," Gregori offered. "Phineas, why don't you escort the ladies to a booth?"

"Sure. Ladies?" Phineas led them across the dance floor to a red velvet booth, with the Secret Service men following close behind.

"Hi, Gregori!" Two Vamp women waved at him from a table close to the DJ.

He waved back. They looked familiar. He'd probably danced with them before. The blond one was Prudence? Prunella? He'd called her Pru. "Hi, ladies. You're looking lovely tonight," he said on his way to the DJ.

They giggled.

"Hey, Gregori!" The DJ shook his hand.

"How about some real music?" Gregori asked, slipping a fifty-dollar bill on the counter. "And some lights. The whole show."

"You got it, dude." The DJ punched some buttons.

The house lights grew dim, the sparkly disco ball started spinning, and red and blue laser lights darted across the room. Fast-paced, thumping techno music filled the room.

The two Vamp girls jumped to their feet, clapping their hands. They lunged toward Gregori and latched onto his arms.

"I say, Gregori!" Pru said in a British accent. "Be a good sport and dance with us."

"Sí," the other said with a Spanish accent. "You are so hhhhot!" She said her *h* sound as if she was coughing up phlegm.

"I'm sorry, but I'm with that party over there." He motioned with his head to the booth Phineas had chosen, and noticed that Abigail was watching him. *Sheesh*. Ten minutes ago she didn't want to look at him, but now she was eyeing him like a hawk.

"But that's hardly fair," Pru objected. "Those two girls have three men with them, and we don't have any."

"And we want you 'cause you are so hhhhot!"

"Sorry." He untangled himself from their grip. "Another time, all right?"

Pru stuck out her bottom lip. "That's what you said the last time."

He had? He strode across the dance floor to the bar.

"Hi, Gregori!" Two Vamp women seated at the bar grinned at him.

"Hi, ladies." He smiled back, then turned to the bartender. While he ordered drinks, the two women sidled up close to him.

"Want to drink with us again?" one of them asked. "We had so much fun last time."

When was that? He couldn't remember. Eighteen years had flown by since he'd become a vampire. What if his mother was right? What if he was taking eternity for granted and wasting his time? He'd been playing around for years. With so many women. He couldn't even remember these girls' names.

He'd always told himself he was doing the Vamp women a favor, keeping them entertained. But didn't they deserve a real friend who could remember their names?

This sort of thing had never worried him before, so why this sudden change of heart? He glanced at the booth and found Abigail still watching him. *Shit*. That was the problem. She was studying him like a new-found species. And he wasn't sure he liked what she was discovering about him.

"Sorry, another time." He grabbed the two martinis and headed toward the booth.

He set the drinks in front of the ladies. "They have just a few mortal drinks here. These are apple martinis."

"Wonderful!" Madison took a sip and smiled. "It's delicious! And I love the lights and music. Thank you."

"Would you like to dance?" Phineas asked.

"Oh yes!" Madison jumped up and strode onto the dance floor with Phineas.

Pru and her friend joined them, and then a dozen more Vamps moved onto the floor. Madison laughed and twirled around, clearly delighted to find herself surrounded by flashing lights and dancing vampires.

Gregori sighed with relief. At least one of the girls was happy now.

He turned back to Abigail, who was fiddling with the

stem of her martini glass. "Would you care to dance?"

She shook her head. "No thank you."

"Is your drink all right? I can get you something nonalcoholic, if you prefer."

She glanced at him with a shy smile. "A Diet Coke would be nice. Thank you."

"Coming right up." He strode back to the bar, but more Vamps had arrived and he had to wait in line.

He glanced back at Abigail, sitting alone in the booth. She should be all right. If a male Vamp tried to make a pass at her, one of the Secret Service guys, standing nearby, would stop him.

She'd wrapped her shawl around her shoulders again to hide her breasts. Her perfect, luscious breasts.

He clenched his fists. *Don't think about her breasts.* Or her legs. Or her pretty eyes. He couldn't afford to have his eyes turn red. It might scare the hell out of her.

"Gregori!" One of the girls at the bar latched on to his arm. "You came back for us!"

"I'm just getting drinks." He pulled his arm free, then glanced over at Abigail. What the hell? Pru and her friend were sliding into the booth next to Abigail.

Phineas was busy dancing with Madison so he hadn't noticed. Secret Service man Josh was talking on his cell phone, probably reporting to the president. Charles was watching carefully, but he didn't advance.

Why should he? Gregori thought. What harm could come from Abigail talking to a few female Vamps? Wasn't that the purpose of tonight's outing? To give Abigail a taste of the vampire world?

Unfortunately, he suspected that taste would be sour.

Chapter Eleven

*H*ello, there. I'm Prunella Culpepper, but everyone calls me Pru."

Abigail turned to find two women behind her in the neighboring booth. One was fair and blond, the other a beautiful brunette. Both were smiling, their sharp canine teeth gleaming. *Vampires.* And if she wasn't mistaken, these were the same two women who had drooled all over Gregori at the DJ's station.

"I am Constanza Maria Hhhortencia," the brunette said, stressing the *h* in a way that made Abigail move back to keep from being spit on.

"Who are—" Constanza's brown eyes widened. "Santa Maria, you are hhhuman."

Pru leaned over the booth and sniffed. "By George, you're right! You can always smell 'em."

What the heck? Abigail glanced over at Gregori. He was in line at the bar, but he was watching her with a worried look. Charles was standing about ten feet away, watching her, too.

Constanza huffed and tossed her long black hair over her shoulder. "I can't believe Gregori would stoop so low."

"Precisely," Pru agreed. "He's never dated a mortal before. What could he possibly see in this chit?"

"Maybe she tastes good."

Pru sniffed again, then shook her head. "Type O. Dreadfully common, don't you know."

Abigail cleared her throat. "Excuse me?"

Pru winced. "Sorry, luv, but it simply makes no sense at all. Why would Gregori date a mortal when he has so many Vamp women eager to date him?"

"Hhhundreds of them," Constanza clarified. "They say hhe is excellent in the sack."

Abigail sat back. Gregori was a . . . *playboy*?

"I would sleep with hhim in a second," Constanza added.

"Any sensible woman would," Pru murmured. "Alas, I am still waiting my turn."

Constanza gasped. "I thought you already did it! I saw you kissing hhim on the dance floor two weeks ago."

Pru smiled with a dreamy look. "By George, that man can kiss. I haven't been kissed like that since 1762."

Abigail blinked. "You've been a vampire that long?"

Pru shook her head. "I was mortal then, don't you know. I was working in a tavern in Dover when a dashing young highwayman pulled me onto his lap and gave me a kiss that curled my toes. Then he asked me if I'd be his mistress."

Constanza grinned. "And you said yes?"

"Of course. Any sensible woman would."

"And then what happened?" Constanza asked.

"I became his assistant," Pru continued. "I dressed

in knee breeches and hid my hair under a tricorne. We robbed coaches at night and had a jolly ole time of it."

Abigail scooted closer, thoroughly intrigued. It was like talking to a live historical figure. "Did you say, 'Stand and deliver?'"

Pru nodded. "Of course. Everything was just dandy until we stopped a coach that belonged to a vampire. He jumped my poor highwayman and fed off him till he was dead as a doornail."

Abigail gulped. Her gaze shifted to Gregori. Did he ever attack people like that? Surely not. He'd claimed last night that he and his friends were morally opposed to injuring mortals. And they were fighting the bad vampires in order to protect mortals.

"So what happened to you?" Constanza asked.

Pru smiled. "The vampire was a rich and handsome viscount. When he discovered I was a beautiful young woman, he offered me the eternal life of the Undead if I would agree to be his mistress. I said yes, of course. Any sensible woman would."

"Of course," Constanza agreed.

Abigail winced, wondering if Pru had left her dead former lover on the side of the road.

"He taught me proper English, don't you know." Pru's eyes narrowed. "We were happy for years until he tossed me aside to marry Lady Pamela."

"That bitch," Constanza hissed.

Pru shrugged. "All water under the bridge. The point is I've known quite a few good kissers over the years, but none of them compare to Gregori. By George, that man can kiss."

Abigail's gaze drifted back to him at the bar. Oh

brother. Now there were two more girls hanging on him.

She shook herself mentally. She needed to get over her attraction to him. He was a vampire and a playboy. And he had strange psychic powers. Three major points she could never reconcile herself to. The sad truth was he was impossible. Completely, irreparably impossible.

A heaviness settled in her chest, and she closed her eyes briefly. It shouldn't hurt this bad. She'd only met him last night.

But she'd never met anyone like him before. Physically, he made her heart race, her knees weak, and her dopamine levels skyrocket. Intellectually, he fascinated her. With her mind and body both drawn to him, how could she resist?

"So why didn't you sleep with hhim?" Constanza asked.

"I wanted to. I invited him to my flat, but . . ." Pru hesitated, her eyes gleaming. "You'll never guess what he told me."

Constanza leaned toward her. "What?"

Abigail eased closer to make sure she heard.

"He said the sun would rise in thirty minutes, and it wasn't enough time. Someone as beautiful as me deserved an entire night where I could be worshipped and pleasured to my heart's content." Pru pressed a hand to her chest. "It was the most romantic thing I've ever been told."

Abigail's heart squeezed. *Wow.* He sounded like one of the heroes from her mother's books. If he ever talked to her like that, she'd probably melt at his feet.

"Ooh, he is so hhhot." Constanza turned to Abigail. "You are so lucky, hhuman. You should sleep with hhim tonight."

"Any sensible woman would," Pru added. "And it's still early, so you can let him pleasure you all night long."

She swallowed hard. *All night long.* "I-I'm not really dating him."

Pru sat up with a hopeful smile. "Then you won't mind if I take him?"

Abigail glanced at him. He was headed toward them, a glass in each hand and his eyes focused intently on her. Her heart started to pound. *You must resist.* He was completely, irreparably impossible.

But she could pretend, couldn't she? Just for one night, she could pretend that a handsome, sexy man like Gregori was choosing her over everyone else.

"No," she whispered. "He's with me."

Pru huffed. "You want him for yourself?"

Abigail gave her a wry look. "Any sensible woman would."

Pru's eyes narrowed with anger. "How do you intend to keep him? You're just a mortal."

"Sí," Constanza agreed. "You can't even do levitation sex."

"Excuse me?" Abigail asked.

"You know." Constanza pointed up in the air. "On the ceiling."

Abigail's mouth dropped open as she recalled seeing Gregori floating on the ceiling of the Oval Office. Levitation sex? Was such a thing possible?

Pru shook her head and tsked. "You've never done it

on the ceiling, have you? Do you really think someone as inexperienced as you can keep Gregori satisfied?"

The man in question set the drinks on the table with a clunk and frowned at the two vampire women. "If you will excuse us, I'd like to be alone with my date."

The ladies scooted out of their booth and rushed over to lean against him.

"I'm still waiting for you, Gregori," Pru whispered.

"Me too." Constanza ran her fingers down his arm.

My date, Abigail thought. He'd called her *my date.* Of course he could be saying it just to get rid of the vampire women, but her heart ignored that notion and thumped wildly.

The women sneered at Abigail, then flipped their hair over their shoulders and strode back to the dance floor.

Gregori slid her drink in front of her, then sat, not across from her, but right next to her. She eased to the side just a fraction. Hopefully he wouldn't notice.

"Are you afraid of me?" he whispered.

He'd noticed.

She shook her head, then gulped some of her Diet Coke. *Afraid* wasn't the right word. Unnerved. Freaked. But strangely attracted. Curious. *Sex on the ceiling?* And she was a bit . . . miffed, to be honest. She didn't like the mental picture of him kissing Pru on the dance floor. Prunella Culpepper, who could leave a lover dead on the side of the road and take off with his murderer. Gregori deserved better than that.

"You look upset." He peered closely at her. "Did those women say something to disturb you?"

"No, no, I'm fine." Her gaze lowered to his mouth,

and Pru's words taunted her. *By George, that man can kiss.* She scooted down the booth a little.

"Your father wanted us to get better acquainted. Can you tell me what sort of project he has in mind?"

"I'd rather not say just yet." She drank some more soda. How on earth could she travel with this man? He was too . . . alluring. Too dangerous. Too damned sexy.

He moved a little closer. "Do you have any questions you'd like to ask me?"

"Yes. Ah . . ." *Do you really worship and pleasure a woman all night long? On the ceiling?* She mentally shook herself. There were more important issues she needed to address. "What happens to you during the day?"

"I sleep."

"That's . . . all?"

The corner of his mouth curled up. "I don't snore."

She looked away from the power of his dimple. "What kind of psychic abilities do you have?"

He sat back, then moved his glass closer. "Are you going to report whatever I say to the CIA?"

"I don't mean to cause you any trouble, Mr. Holstein, but I need to know if it's safe for me to be with you."

"I would never hurt you." He paused, then added wryly, "Miss Tucker."

Was he mocking her for trying to keep some distance between them? "If you'll answer my questions honestly, then I won't repeat whatever you tell me."

He nodded. "Deal."

"Did you make that man break his camera?"

"It seemed the best recourse at the time. I didn't want my photo in a paper." He glanced at her. "And I figured you didn't want the publicity, either."

That was true. But she wasn't going to thank him. "So you admit that you can mess with our minds."

His mouth thinned. "We have the right to protect ourselves. How do you think we managed to keep our existence secret?"

She snorted. "You've never been secret. There have been horror stories about your kind for centuries."

"That just means we didn't *mess* with your minds enough. We allowed too many memories to stay intact."

She winced. "You can erase a mortal's memory?"

He shifted on the padded booth, turning to face her. "Vampires survived for centuries on human blood. The usual procedure was to feed, then wipe the memory. It kept the vampire safe, and it protected the mortal from any bad memories."

"How thoughtful of you," she said wryly.

He arched a brow. "You don't think vampires have the right to survive or protect themselves?"

"You don't have the right to screw with our minds."

His mouth curled up. "How about your bodies?"

She scoffed and inched down the booth. "Did you make Madison's dog fall asleep?"

"Self-defense, Miss Tucker. It was about to gnaw on my leg."

"Can you do the same to a human?"

"I could." He inched closer. "If you're planning to gnaw on my leg."

Her face warmed with a blush. "I don't gnaw on people. That's your specialty."

His mouth twitched. "I don't gnaw on people, either, Miss Tucker. I'm a young Vamp. I take my meals from bottles."

"You've never bitten anyone?"

"I've never bitten a mortal. And I've never bitten for food, so you can relax. You're completely safe."

Instead of feeling reassured, she quickly analyzed his answer. "So you've bitten vampires for . . . other reasons?"

He looked surprised, then adjusted his tie. "You're a smart one, aren't you?"

"Then I'm right? You've bitten vampires?"

"Only women." He looked away, frowning. "In the right situation it can be a pleasurable thing."

A frisson of heat sizzled through her. "How?"

"You'll have to trust me on that." He glanced at her, and his eyes turned a more brilliant green. "Unless you'd like a demonstration?"

"No." She scooted farther away in the booth.

His jaw shifted as he reached for his drink. "I'm not a monster, Miss Tucker. I won't hurt you."

She winced inwardly. If only she *could* think of him as a monster. It might help her squash this strange attraction she felt for him. Could he actually make a bite feel pleasurable?

She watched him drink the red liquid topped with pinkish foam. When he licked the foam off his lips, her heartbeat sped up. *By George, that man can kiss.* She slapped herself mentally. *Don't think about that!* "What—what are you drinking?"

"It's called Bleer. Half synthetic blood, half beer. It's one of the more popular drinks in Vampire Fusion Cuisine."

Her mouth dropped open. *Vampire Fusion Cuisine?* She looked at the foamy drink, then back at Gregori. "Are you kidding me?" She reached for the glass.

"Abigail." He grabbed the glass, his hand covering hers. "Don't drink it. It could make you ill."

"I just want to smell it." She glanced up.

He was leaning toward her, his face close to hers. "Okay."

She inhaled deeply, then closed her eyes to concentrate on her other senses. The yeasty smell of beer and metallic scent of blood. And the warmth of his hand on hers.

She opened her eyes and found him studying her face. Her heartbeat screamed into overdrive. She set the glass down and pulled her hand away. "So you need blood to stay alive? You are alive, aren't you?"

He nodded. "At the moment, yes. My heart is beating just like yours." His mouth curled up, making his dimples show. "But not quite as fast."

Her face grew warm. So he could actually hear her heartbeat. She motioned toward Josh, who was standing two booths down and talking quietly on his cell phone. "Can you hear him?"

Gregori tilted his head as he focused on Josh. "Sparkle's still on the dance floor." He turned to her with a questioning look.

"We all have code names. Madison is Sparkle."

He smiled. "It suits her." He leaned close to Abigail, his eyes twinkling. "So what's your code name?"

She shrugged. "Not important."

"That's a lousy code name."

"That's not my—"

He chuckled. "Let me guess. Your sister is Sparkle, so you're . . . Brilliant."

"No." Her cheeks grew hotter.

"But you are brilliant."

Unfortunately, her face probably was a brilliant red.

"Well, if you refuse to talk, I have other ways of finding out." He glanced at Josh, who had put away his cell phone and was now murmuring to Charles on his wrist communicator. "Sailor? Who's that?"

"My dad."

Gregori's eyebrows lifted. "He didn't want to be an Admiral?"

"All of our names start with *s*. And Dad likes being Sailor. He's a Navy man, and he thinks it makes him sound humble."

Gregori gave her a dubious look.

"I know. He doesn't always appear very humble. But it's hard to look modest when you're trying to show a lot of confidence and competence as a leader." She ran a finger around the rim of her glass. "He's different when he's with us. Especially when he's with my mom. He loves her so much. When you're watching someone you love slowly die, and there's nothing you can do to stop it, it's very humbling."

Her hand stilled. What on earth was she doing? Opening up to a vampire? She glanced at Gregori. His eyes had a faraway look to them, a look of remembrance and pain.

She sipped some of her Diet Coke. He remained silent, and she wondered what sad place he had drifted off to.

She reached out to touch him, but changed her mind and lowered her hand to the table. "I'm sorry if I made you sad. I didn't mean to—"

"It's all right." He smiled, but the sadness lingered in his eyes. "I'm really sorry about your mother."

She blinked when tears threatened. It had been a long time since she'd talked to anyone about her mom. She usually kept her fears and anxieties bottled up. And when she was with her mom, she always tried to be cheerful. "Her code name is Serenity."

"That's an excellent name for her."

"Yes." Abigail clenched her fists, determined to keep her emotions in check.

Gregori rested his hand on top of hers. "It'll be all right."

She froze. His hand felt perfectly warm and human. And his touch was light and . . . tender. Her gaze darted to Josh, who was standing two booths to the right, and then Charles, two booths to the left. "I—"

"Sorry." Gregori lifted his hand. "I didn't mean to make you uncomfortable."

Uncomfortable? She was tempted to hold hands with him under the table. There was a kindness to him that she hadn't expected. It made him even harder to resist.

"You're a sneaky one." He eyed her with an obviously fake suspicion. "You never did tell me your code name." He eased closer. "Is that it? Sneaky?"

She shook her head, smiling. This was more of his kindness. He was teasing her out of her moment of sadness. And making her like him even more.

"I know! It's Secret, because you live a secret life."

She shook her head again. "It's not anything very exciting."

"Hmm." He studied her closely. "Sweet? Sugar? Spicy?"

She grinned.

"Sex Kitten?"

She laughed. "Are you crazy?"

"It sounds right to me."

She shook her head, ignoring the heat of her blush. "They based it on my . . . brain."

"Ah." He gave her a wide-eyed innocent look. "Simpleton?"

"What?" She swatted his shoulder. "How dare you?"

He laughed. "I'd rather have you attacking me than scooting away. We've moved halfway around the booth."

She pressed a hand against her hot face. "I'm sorry."

"It's all right." He leaned closer. "So your code name is . . . Scientist? Super Brain? Smarty Pants?"

She laughed. "I'm Scholar."

"Scholar?"

"I warned you. It's not very exciting."

"Oh, but it is." He tugged at one of her curls, then let it go. "I can't imagine anything more exciting than a . . . scholarly pursuit."

She gulped. Was he making a pass at her? A part of her leaped with joy that such a handsome, charming, mysterious man could desire her. But another part warned her he was impossible. Completely, irreparably impossible. She couldn't allow herself to fall for a vampire.

Besides, Pru and Constanza were probably right. Why would he be interested in a mortal when so many Undead women wanted him? She had to seem boring compared to vampire women who could have sex on the ceiling.

A terrible thought weaseled into her mind. What if he was just pretending to like her for political reasons? He might be charming her to ingratiate himself and his kind with her father. A playboy would be an expert at charming women.

She groaned inwardly. It was foolish, wishful thinking to believe Gregori was attracted to her. The guys who usually gravitated toward her were the geeky type—lanky build, nerdy glasses, and totally immersed in science. She'd dated a few like that in college and grad school. The relationships had been . . . comfortable.

But they were not the men she dreamed about. After years of listening to her mother's audio books, she'd found herself wanting more than *comfortable*. She wanted heat and passion. Desperate desire. She wanted to long for a man who would long for her. She wanted a man who believed she should be worshipped and pleasured to her heart's content. All night long.

She'd feared such men existed only in fiction.

Now she feared they were all too real.

She couldn't let herself fall for a vampire. Or a playboy. A vampire expected sex on the ceiling. A playboy would find her sister attractive. Not her.

She sighed. "I know about you."

His green eyes widened. "What do you know?"

"You're a playboy."

Chapter Twelve

Shit. Gregori sat back and adjusted his cuff links. There was no mistaking the censure in Abigail's voice, which meant there were now two points against him: vampire and playboy. No wonder she kept scooting down the booth. She expected him to either bite her or ravish her.

He'd figured Pru and her friend were up to no good. They had their own agenda, obviously, and that included scaring Abigail away from him. He'd heard them talking as he'd approached the table.

He took a sip of Bleer and set the glass down. "Just for the record, I've never had sex on the ceiling."

Abigail stiffened and her cheeks turned pink. "It's none of my business." She ventured a glance his way. "Is that true?"

"Yes. Did those ladies claim that I slept with them?"

"No." She shook her head, and her blush deepened. "But they want to. Along with hundreds of others."

"*Hundreds?*" He tried not to laugh. "I'm not much of a playboy, am I, if I've neglected to sleep with hundreds of willing victims?"

She tilted her head, considering. "That would depend on how large a pool of volunteers you started off with."

He lifted his eyebrows. Did she think he was operating in the thousands? "Well, thank God I'm with a scholar. I'm sure you can devise a formula for determining the correct number."

She frowned at him. "It's none of my business."

"No, it's not." He gulped down the last of his Bleer.

She drank some of her soda.

So he hadn't been a saint. She had no right to judge him. He clunked his empty glass onto the table. "After about five thousand or so, I stopped counting."

She gasped. "*Five thousand?*"

He glowered at her. "I was kidding."

"It's not amusing."

"I'm not laughing." He leaned toward her. "Why are you so prickly all of a sudden? Are you jealous?"

She snorted. "Jealous of what?"

"Five thousand make-believe lovers."

She lifted her chin. "If you must know why I'm upset, it's because I have serious doubts you can be trusted. I don't want to be left abandoned in the middle of China while you take off chasing women."

"China? Is that where we're going?"

"*We* aren't going anywhere. I'll have to report to my father that you're not suitable."

Shit. He loosened his tie. The personal insult was bad enough, but he had too many Vamps depending on him to make sure the alliance with the president went through.

He twisted to face Abigail, resting one arm across the back of the booth and the other along the table.

"You judge me guilty without a trial? Where's your evidence? How many women here have I slept with?"

She shrugged.

"The answer is none," he continued before she could answer. "If you don't believe me, call them over and ask them yourself."

"You would have slept with Prunella Culpepper if you had more time."

"How do you know that?"

"You told her the sun was setting in thirty minutes, and you needed the entire night to worship and pleasure someone as beautiful as her."

He snorted. "That was a rejection line. I turned her down."

"Because you only had thirty minutes."

"I'd take thirty minutes with *you*!" He froze. What the hell was he saying? She looked equally shocked, her pretty eyes wide and her soft lips parted. It had been so long since he'd kissed a mortal. Her lips would be warmer than a Vamp's. Sweeter.

"Well, don't you two look cozy?" an amused voice asked.

Gregori shifted to face front and gave Phineas an annoyed look. Abigail attempted to scoot farther away from him, but since his arm was stretched along the back of the booth, he grabbed on to her shoulder and blocked her movement. She nudged him in the side with her elbow.

"I'm having a great time!" Madison grinned as she sat down. "Dr. Phang is a wonderful dancer."

"You're pretty hot yourself." Phineas winked at her. "You make the other chicks look half dead."

Madison laughed, then beamed a smile at her sister and Gregori. "I'm glad you two are getting along. Dad will be so relieved."

"Be sure and tell him that," Gregori said with a smile that only wavered slightly when Abigail nudged him harder in the ribs.

"I'm going to get something to drink," Phineas said. "Anybody want something from the bar?"

"I'm fine, thank you," Abigail murmured.

"Me too." Madison took a long drink from her martini.

"I'll take another Bleer," Gregori said.

Phineas nodded and strode toward the bar.

Madison set her martini glass down and gave him a confused look. "Did you say beer?"

"Bleer. Half blood, half beer," Gregori explained. "It's part of Vampire Fusion Cuisine. We call it VFC for short."

"VFC?" Madison's eyes lit up. "Oh my gosh, that's like KFC, but for vampires." She giggled. "You guys are so funny."

Gregori smiled. "We aim to please."

Abigail turned toward him an inquisitive look. "Is there a lab that comes up with this stuff?"

He nodded. "Romatech Industries."

Her eyes widened. "The lab that invented synthetic blood?"

"Yes. That's where I work."

She blinked. "You have a job?"

He gritted his teeth and lowered his voice. "You think I spend my entire life partying?"

"So are all the Vamps here drinking Bleer?" Madison asked as she peered around the room.

"They could be drinking a number of things," Gregori explained. "Straight synthetic blood in their favorite blood type or something like Chocolood, chocolate-flavored synthetic blood."

Madison grinned. "Oooh. If I was a vampire, that's what I would drink."

Gregori smiled. "It's very popular among the ladies. And for those who overindulge, we can help them shed a few pounds with Blood Lite."

Madison laughed. "You guys are so cute." She gulped down the rest of her martini.

"Dietetic blood?" Abigail asked.

He nodded. "It has an extremely low blood sugar and cholesterol count. And then there's Bubbly Blood: half blood, half champagne, for those special vampire occasions."

Madison laughed. Even Abigail looked amused.

"And there's a new one, a favorite among the Scottish vampires—Blissky. Half blood, half—"

"Whisky?" Madison guessed.

Gregori winked at her. "You got it, Sweetcakes."

Madison giggled, then leaned toward her sister. "A vampire called me Sweetcakes."

Abigail grimaced. "I can hit him, if you like."

"Why?" Madison asked as she reached for her sister's neglected martini.

"It's embarrassing," Abigail muttered.

Madison took a sip. "It is?"

"I wasn't embarrassed," Gregori said. When Abigail

shot him an irritated look, he smiled and squeezed her shoulder.

Madison drank some more and licked her lips. "Tell me some more funny vampire drinks."

"We're introducing a new one in a few weeks. Blardonnay: half blood, half—"

"Chardonnay!" Madison lifted her arms like she'd score a touchdown, then burst into giggles.

Gregori grinned. "You got it, Toots."

Abigail shuddered. "*Toots*?"

Her sister giggled some more, then hiccupped.

Abigail winced. "Maybe you should stop drinking."

Madison waved a dismissive hand. "I always get loopy at nightclubs. It doesn't matter. Josh won't let anything bad happen to me." She lifted her martini glass and saluted the Secret Service man who was watching her carefully from a short distance. "Love you, Josh!"

An angry look flashed over the guard's face before it returned to its usual deadpan expression.

Gregori felt a surge of sympathy for the two Secret Service men. They were babysitters just like he was.

"What do you do at Romatech?" Abigail regarded him with a hopeful look. "Are you a chemist?"

Damn, he hated to disappoint her. Again. "No. I'm vice president of marketing."

"Oh." She fiddled with her glass.

"Here's your Bleer." Phineas slid one across the table to him, then sat on the booth opposite Madison. "Cheers." He clinked his glass against Madison's martini glass.

"Bottoms up!" Madison downed the rest of her drink.

Abigail turned toward him again. "If Romatech manufactures Vampire Fusion Cuisine, then it's operated by vampires?"

Gregori nodded. "My boss is a vampire. And a brilliant scientist."

Her eyes widened. "Roman Draganesti?"

"You've heard of him?"

"Every scientist in the world has heard— Oh my gosh, he's a vampire?"

Gregori nodded. "And a really nice guy. Lovely wife, two beautiful children."

Her mouth dropped open. "He . . . fathered children?"

"Like I said, he's a brilliant scientist. He figured out a way."

"How fascinating." Her eyes gleamed with excitement. "Is it possible to meet him? I would love a tour of the labs."

At last, something he could do that would impress her. "I'd be happy to arrange it for you. How about tomorrow night?"

She nodded, smiling. "Yes. Thank you."

Excellent. Gregori took a long drink. The more he thought about it, the better he liked the idea of taking Abigail to Romatech. This nightclub might have won Madison over to the Vamp cause, but Abigail needed to see smart, hardworking Vamps like Laszlo. She needed to meet Roman, whose invention of synthetic blood saved thousands of mortal lives every year.

His Droid vibrated in his pocket and he pulled it out to check the text message. Maggie and Gordon had finished filming two new versions of the Blardonnay commercial and wanted him to see them.

He took a sip of Bleer. "Would you guys mind if I left for about ten minutes? I need to teleport to DVN—"

"What's that?" Madison asked.

"The Digital Vampire Network. It's a television studio. Vamps have their own shows to watch. Soap operas and such."

"Oh my God," Madison breathed. "That is so awesome."

Gregori adjusted his tie. Maybe this would impress Abigail. "I produce all the commercials for Romatech. I'm having a new one made to advertise Blardonnay."

Abigail's eyes widened, but she remained silent.

"It stars Simone, the famous model," Gregori continued.

"I know who she is!" Madison bounced on her seat. "Oh my God, do you think I could meet her? That would be so cool!"

Gregori inclined his head. "I can arrange it."

Phineas grinned and gave him a thumbs-up. "Gregori's da man! He knows all the hot vampire chicks."

Abigail scoffed. "I bet."

He gave her an annoyed look and whispered, "Still jealous, *Toots*?"

Her eyes narrowed. "Don't call me Toots."

"You prefer Sweetcakes?"

"If we were alone, I'd slap you."

He leaned close and whispered in her ear, "If we were alone, I'd give you a good reason to slap me."

Phineas choked on his Bleer.

"Are you all right, Dr. Phang?" Madison asked.

He nodded and slanted an amused look at Gregori.

So he had heard. Gregori scooted down the booth. "If you guys will excuse me, I'll be on my way."

"But I want to go!" Madison jumped to her feet and clasped her hands together as if she were begging. "Please! I want to see the television studio!"

Gregori stilled. "I-I'm teleporting there. I'll be back soon."

"But I want to go," Madison whined. "Please!"

"Is it far away?" Abigail asked quietly, her cheeks still flushed from his last verbal poke at her.

"Brooklyn," Phineas said. When Gregori shot him an angry look, he shrugged. "We gotta keep them happy, bro."

"Yes!" Madison squealed. "It would make me so happy!"

Gregori sighed. Phineas was right. They had to keep the girls happy, no matter what. "Very well. We're all going to DVN."

"It's complicated," Gregori whispered to Maggie and Gordon thirty minutes later at DVN. "But if you want to help us avoid the Vampire Apocalypse, you'll let these girls do whatever they want. We have to keep them happy."

"All right," Maggie agreed. "I recognize the blonde. She's the president's daughter."

"They're both the president's daughters." Gregori glanced at them across the recording studio. "Madison is the one gushing all over Simone. Abigail's the other one."

Abigail and Josh were looking curiously about. Charles had driven them to the Digital Vampire Network using Gregori's directions. Upon arrival, he had decided the entire location needed to be checked, so he was running about while Josh remained with the girls.

"I didn't know there was a second daughter," Maggie whispered.

"She's a bit of a mystery," Gregori said as he watched Abigail. He still didn't know why she kept herself so carefully hidden from the public eye, but he suspected it had something to do with her mother. Or maybe her job as a biochemist. The mission she planned to do in China was certainly being kept secret. What on earth could she want in China?

He could understand their desire for secrecy. If she traveled there as the president's daughter, it would become a media event, and her every move would be scrutinized by journalists and the Chinese government. Obviously she wanted to see something that the Chinese were reluctant to show her. Or she planned to take something without their knowledge.

Maggie tugged at his sleeve, drawing his attention. "Gregori, Gordon said your name three times. You didn't hear."

"Oh, sorry. Lot on my mind lately."

Her eyes twinkled as she glanced at Abigail. "I can see that."

"Do you want to watch the commercials?" Gordon asked.

"Yes, of course." Gregori walked over to the monitor with Maggie and Gordon.

"You must see me acting!" Simone motioned for her new entourage to follow her to the monitor. "I was brilliant!"

"Oh, I'm sure you were." Madison rushed after her.

Abigail and Josh followed after them.

"Both commercials have potential," Gordon explained as he punched some buttons. "But we may need someone with a stronger presence than Pennington to pull them off."

"Mais oui." Simone waved a dismissive hand. "That Pennington is too weak." Her gaze settled on Josh. "Oh, *mon Dieu*, don't you look nice and strong." She sidled up close to him, and he stepped back.

"Simone." Gregori shook his head and gave her a warning look.

She huffed. *"Pourquoi pas?* You want him for yourself?"

He cursed silently and clenched a fist, wishing he had a stress ball.

The commercials started. Pennington did his lines, then Simone came onscreen.

"That's me!" Simone pointed at herself.

Gregori watched amazed as Simone completed both commercials without falling over or injuring herself.

Maggie turned to Gregori when the commercials were done. "Well, what do you think?"

"I like them! You did a great job, Maggie." He gave her a high five. "Thank you."

"I did well, too!" Simone cried.

He smiled at her. "Yes, you did. I was very impressed." He looked around the studio. "Is Pennington still here?"

"We told him he was done for the night," Maggie said. "We've been debating whether we should try another guy."

"I think you're right," Gregori admitted. "He didn't quite pull it off."

"I know who could do it!" Madison grabbed Phineas's arm. "Dr. Phang! He would be excellent."

Everyone turned to look at Phineas.

He shrugged.

"And I want to do it, too!" Madison clasped her hands together. "Please! I've always wanted to be in front of a camera."

What a surprise, Gregori thought. He caught Gordon's attention and nodded his head.

"Why, yes, of course." Gordon smiled at Madison. "We would be delighted to have you in a commercial."

"Wheeee!" Madison bounced for joy. "I'll do the first one with Dr. Phang, and Abby can do the second one with Gregori!"

Abigail gasped. "What?"

"Oh, come on, Abby." Madison leaned against her sister and gave her a soulful look. "It'll be fun. When's the last time you ever had any fun?"

"Good question," Gregori muttered. Abigail scowled at him, but he simply lifted an eyebrow. "I'll do it if you'll do it with me."

She snorted. "You've probably done it in front of a camera before."

He chuckled. "No, sweetheart. You're my first."

"Yes!" Madison punched the air with her fists. "Then it's all settled."

"Madison," Abigail whispered. "We can't make commercials. We're not allowed to endorse anything."

"It's not for real." Madison waved a hand impatiently. "It's just for fun. And it'll make me happy."

"Then you do it." Abigail frowned. "I don't know if I can."

"Of course you can." Madison patted her on the shoulder. "You only have one line. 'Take me.' It's easy."

"Take me," Abigail repeated, then cast a nervous glance at Gregori.

He smiled slowly, enjoying the blush that crept up her cheeks.

After twenty minutes of makeup and practicing their lines, Phineas and Madison were ready to tape Blardonnay commercial number one.

"Roll 'em," Gordon said.

Standing alone in a bathroom set, wearing a towel fastened around his hips, Phineas began in a deep voice, "Hello, ladies. Come closer. Look at my eyes."

The camera zoomed in.

"You're hypnotized now, aren't you? Look at my chest. That's right. Do as I say. You're under my command."

The camera moved back as Phineas walked into a bedroom set.

"This is my bedroom. Wouldn't you like to join me? Look at the man next to you. Now look at me. Yes, you want to be with me."

The camera moved right to catch Madison running toward him. Meanwhile, Phineas was handed a bottle of Blardonnay.

"Oh yes, Dr. Phang!" Madison exclaimed as she reached his side. "I want to be with you."

"Of course you do." Phineas lifted the wine bottle. "And if you want me, you'll want my Blardonnay."

"Oh yes, Dr. Phang!" Madison leaned against him and placed a hand on his bare chest. "Can I pop your cork?"

"Anytime, baby. I have a corkscrew under my towel." He winked at the camera. "If you love me, you'll love my Blardonnay."

The camera zeroed in on the bottle of Blardonnay, then Gordon said, "Cut."

"Yes!" Madison squealed, then threw her arms around Phineas. "You were fantastic!"

He laughed. "So were you!"

Maggie strode toward them, grinning. "You guys were great!"

Gordon looked at Gregori. "What do you think?"

Gregori chuckled. "It was good."

"It was *damned* good!" Gordon yelled.

Everyone clapped and cheered except Simone, who shrieked, "But what about me?"

"All right!" Gordon shouted. "Let's do commercial number two."

The crew rolled the bedroom/bathroom sets out of the way, then brought in a brick wall and lamppost. Crinkled newspapers were scattered on the floor to make the scene look like an inner city alleyway. The lights were dimmed, so the only light appeared to come from the lamppost.

Gregori's suit had been okayed for the shoot. Abigail's dress, too, but without the shawl. He watched her as she approached the set. The makeup girl had made her eyes look sultry and sexy, her lips bloodred. Her dress clung to her curves, the black color making her pale skin look luminous. Her necklace sparkled, leaving a glittering trail of rhinestones down to the valley between her beautiful breasts.

He swallowed hard. They'd succeeding in making her look glamorous, but she still possessed a wide-eyed innocence, a fresh-faced, wholesome sweetness that was vulnerable and endearing and, surprisingly enough, sexy as hell.

"Are you ready?" Maggie asked.

Abigail nodded.

"You know your lines, Gregori?" Maggie asked. "First you say, 'Mortal, I have you now.' Then after she says, 'Take me,' you say, 'No, I'm tired of the same meal every night. I want something different. I want Blardonnay.'"

He nodded. "Got it."

Gordon settled into the director's chair. "Let's do it. Roll 'em."

Chapter Thirteen

*A*bigail was tempted to pinch herself to make sure this was all real. Vampire Fusion Cuisine. The Digital Vampire Network. And now she was about to do a vampire commercial?

At least Mom would get a kick out of this story. It was crazier than any of her audio books.

The vampire named Maggie smiled at her and motioned for her to begin. Abigail took a deep breath, then ran into the alley, not too fast since she was still wearing high heels.

A blur zoomed in front of her, blocking her, and she stopped with a jerk. Gregori? No need for her to act startled. She *was* startled. He'd moved incredibly fast.

He advanced toward her with the fierce look of a predator. She stumbled back, bumping into the brick wall.

"Mortal, I have you now." He planted his hands on the wall, pinning her in, then leaned forward to study her face.

A hunter examining his prey. No doubt he could hear the wild drumming of her heart. He was so close she could see the strong line of his jaw and the shadow of whisker stubble. Her gaze settled on his mouth, his wide, expressive lips; and Pru's words flitted through her mind. *By George, that man can kiss.*

When her gaze drifted upward, she found his eyelids lowered, fringed with thick, dark eyelashes. Her heart squeezed in her chest. Such a beautiful man. Why did he have to be a vampire? She might be able to reconcile herself to him being a playboy. After all, a rake could possibly be reformed. But a vampire? As far as she knew, he could never be brought back to life.

She realized with a small jolt that while she was thinking, his downcast eyes were focused on her breasts. The rascal. Her heartbeat quickened. He looked up, and her breath caught. His eyes had lost their grayish-green tint and turned a brighter emerald color.

Good Lord, had she caused that change in him? Her emotions ricocheted from one end of the spectrum to the other—a strong surge of awe that she wielded such womanly power and a trembling desire that made her weak in the knees.

His right hand touched her neck, gently caressing her skin until he located the throbbing pulse of her carotid artery. He leaned forward and his breath tickled her ear.

She shivered. With his fingers, he traced the line of her artery. On the other side of her neck, the tip of his nose nuzzled her.

She held her breath, wanting, longing to feel his lips against her skin. *Kiss me, please. Just once.*

What was she thinking? She was standing on a set, being watched by about twenty people. She couldn't let this continue. Why didn't he say his lines?

Oh, she hadn't said hers.

She inhaled a shaky breath and whispered, "Take me."

He groaned, then drew her earlobe into his mouth. At last, his mouth on her skin. Her eyes closed as sensations washed over her. His lips nibbled a path down her neck. His fingers reached her shoulder, then trailed her necklace over her collarbone and down to her breasts.

"Your line, Gregori," Maggie whispered.

Abigail's eyes popped opened. *Good Lord!* She'd forgotten for a second where she was. She placed her hands on his shoulders to push him back, but then his lips brushed across her cheek. Oh God, was he planning to kiss her mouth?

His fingers curled around the strand of rhinestones, and his knuckles nestled in the valley of her breasts.

"Gregori!" Maggie hissed.

"Cut!" Gordon shouted.

With a jerk, Gregori released her necklace. His gaze lifted to her face.

Red glowing eyes! "Aagh!" She pushed at his shoulders. "You're going to bite me!"

Gregori stepped back. "I wasn't—"

Bam! Josh body-slammed him onto the floor.

"Abby!" Madison ran toward her. "Are you all right?"

She pressed a hand against her thundering heart. "His eyes turned red! Glowing and red!"

"Really?" Madison glanced at Gregori, still pinned underneath Josh.

"I wasn't going to bite you." Gregori frowned at Abigail, his eyes returning to their usual grayish-green.

"His eyes were *red*?" Simone asked. "Impossible!"

"I saw it," Abigail whispered. She'd been a fool to let herself be attracted to a vampire, to think that he might want her for anything other than a snack.

"Abby, I can explain," Gregori told her, then glared at Josh. "Get off me! I could teleport away. Or throw you across the room."

Josh didn't budge. "I can't allow you to hurt her."

"I'm not going to hurt her!" Gregori shouted.

"It's true!" Maggie said as she stepped onto the set. "When a vampire's eyes turn red, it doesn't mean hunger. He wasn't going to bite her."

"That's right." Phineas gave Abigail an encouraging smile. "Chillax, dudette. He didn't want to *bite* you."

She wondered if she'd overreacted. "He didn't?"

"Naw." Phineas smirked. "He just wanted to jump your bones."

Her mouth fell open.

"Phineas," Gregori growled. "Let me handle this."

"I think you've scared her enough," Maggie told him, then turned to Abigail. "I'm sorry you were needlessly frightened. I would have warned you if I had known Gregori would . . . react like that."

Abigail nodded, still stunned. She didn't know what to say, but a whirlwind of thoughts kept circling in her mind. *He wants you.* A vampire wanted her. A playboy was attracted to her. It wasn't political. It wasn't an act. He actually wanted her.

Gregori pushed at Josh. "Will you get off me now?"

Josh slowly straightened. "I'm watching you. Keep a distance from her."

He scrambled to his feet. "I am *not* going to hurt her."

"No, definitely not," Maggie agreed. "The fact that his eyes turned red proves that he has . . . developed tender feelings toward her."

Phineas snorted. "That's putting it mildly."

Gregori shot him a warning look.

He shrugged. "Don't give me the evil eye. You were the one about to star in an X-rated porno flick."

Abigail gasped. He wanted her that badly?

"Oh my God," Madison breathed.

Gregori glared at Phineas. "Don't you know when to shut up?"

Phineas grinned. "We could call it *Undressed by the Undead*. Or *Debbie Does the Undead*."

"Enough!" Gregori yelled.

"C'est impossible!" Simone marched onto the set. "Gregori cannot desire a woman. He is gay!"

Abigail blinked. *What?*

Gregori spun toward the French model. "I am not gay!"

"Of course you are! You refused to sleep with me. You must be gay."

He clenched his fists, then released them. "Simone, the truth is . . . I didn't want you."

She gasped. "How can you say that? It is an honor to share my bed!"

"I'm sure all your lovers felt extremely honored. I just didn't want to be number five hundred and sixty-three."

She huffed. "I see how you are. You were afraid! You thought I would give you a bad ranking in my journal."

"I don't like to be judged," Gregori told her, then glanced at Abigail. "By anyone."

She winced. She'd judged him unfairly, assuming he was a playboy just because Pru and Constanza had made him sound that way. He obviously didn't sleep with every woman who wanted him. He'd refused Prunella and the model Simone. He didn't want them.

But he wants you. She swallowed hard. At last, a man who desired her as much as she desired him. The attraction was mutual.

But impossible.

Simone stalked up to Gregori. "I am the most beautiful woman on earth, but you prefer that"—she glanced at Abigail with a sneer—"that mortal to me?"

"Yes."

"You bastard!" Simone slapped him so hard he stumbled to the side. "I will never star in a commercial for you again!" She teleported away.

"Good riddance!" the director shouted. "Now we can finally do a decent commercial."

The crew cheered and applauded.

Abigail watched Gregori as he rubbed his jaw. "Are you all right?" It looked like Simone had walloped him with super vampire strength. He glanced at her, and her heart stuttered. He hadn't hesitated to confess his attraction to her.

He stepped toward her. "Abby, can we talk somewhere in private?"

"No!" Josh pulled her back. "He's not getting near you again."

"But I have to—" Abigail started.

"No," Josh interrupted her. "We're leaving."

"But Josh—" Madison whined.

"I said *no*! We're leaving now."

Madison gasped. "Why, Josh. It's not like you to be so . . . forceful." She bit her lip as she looked him over.

He spoke into the communicator at his wrist. "Charles, meet us out front. We're leaving now." He grabbed Abigail with one hand and Madison with the other and steered them toward the door.

Abigail glanced over her shoulder at Gregori, who was watching her with a frown. "I'll see you tomorrow night at Romatech?"

Josh halted, an incredulous look on his face. "How can you even consider seeing him again? You're not safe with him."

She pulled her arm from Josh's grasp. "It's my decision, not yours."

His eyes narrowed. "It's your father's decision, and when he finds out what happened here—"

"Nothing happened!" The beginning of panic seized hold of her. If Josh told her father to cancel the alliance, then her trip would never happen. "You'll report *nothing*."

"My first priority is your safety." He pointed toward Gregori. "You are not safe with that man."

"He'll behave himself." Abigail raised her voice. "You will behave, won't you, Gregori, in order to keep the alliance between my father and your people?"

"Yes." His hands clenched, then relaxed. "I will do whatever it takes to keep my people safe and to help Abigail successfully complete her mission. You have my word."

"There, you see?" Abigail lifted her chin. "So you will not report this . . . this *accident* to my father. You will not destroy his last chance to save his wife, or my last chance to cure my mother."

"She's my mother, too," Madison insisted. "If you tell Daddy what happened here, I'll tell him you're lying. Abby will back me up."

"Have you both lost your minds?" Josh spun around to glare at Gregori. "Have you done something to them?"

"No."

Josh scoffed. "Like you would tell the truth."

"He would never do that," Abigail insisted. "The Vamps need this alliance as much as we do." She lowered her voice. "Come on, Josh, you know there's no way I can sneak into China on my own. We need their help."

He shook his head. "I don't like it. I don't trust them."

"Look at it this way," she continued. "It's to our advantage that he likes me personally. He'll be better motivated to keep me safe on the mission."

"That is true." Gregori stepped toward them. "I would never let any harm come to her. I would protect her with my life."

Abigail's heart squeezed in her chest, but she didn't dare look at Gregori. She couldn't let Josh see her face soften with desire.

Josh gave Gregori a long, hard look, then turned back to her. "Very well. We will continue with this alliance for now. For your mother's sake. But you are never to be alone with him, do you understand?"

She nodded. "Agreed." She risked a quick glance at Gregori, expecting him to look relieved that she'd saved the alliance and saved his neck. Dad would not have reacted well to Josh's report of a red-eyed vampire lusting for his daughter.

But Gregori was scowling at her. Why was he angry?

"What time shall I come to Romatech tomorrow night?" she asked.

His hands fisted. "Ten o'clock."

She nodded. "I'll be there."

"Madison?" Maggie asked. "There's a casting call tomorrow night for one of the soap operas. You could audition, if you like. Phineas, too."

Madison gasped, then clasped her hands together. "Really?"

Josh shook his head. "You shouldn't do it."

"Are you kidding?" Madison squealed. "This is my chance to be a star!" She bounced up and down. "Thank you, thank you, Maggie! I'm so thrilled! Isn't this exciting, Dr. Phang?"

Phineas grinned and punched the air with his fist. "Oh yeah! The Love Doctor strikes again!"

Josh groaned. "This is a disaster."

"No," Abigail corrected him. "It's the beginning of a whole new future. For all of us."

Her gaze met Gregori's. He was still scowling at her, still watching her with a fierce, hungry look. She had no doubt he intended to keep the alliance with her father. And he intended to honor his vow to help her with the mission and keep her safe.

But his promise to behave himself?

She didn't believe that for one second.

Chapter Fourteen

$\mathcal{T}$ he following night Gregori paced across his office at Romatech, stress ball in hand. He'd told Angus and Roman that everything was progressing well. Luckily Phineas had backed him up, claiming the date with the president's daughters had been a great success.

Bullshit. He gave the ball another squeeze. He'd come damned close to completely blowing his mission. Thousands of Vamps depended on him to forge an alliance with the U.S. government and prevent the Vampire Apocalypse. And what did he do? Molest the president's daughter in front of an audience. In front of a Secret Service man!

"Stupid, stupid," he muttered to himself. At least Gordon had erased the video so Corky Courrant couldn't get her evil hands on it and post it on YouTube.

But he couldn't erase his actions. The whole alliance could have fallen apart if Abigail hadn't stepped in. She'd saved his ass. Not because of any affection she felt for him. She'd saved him out of desperation to save her mother.

Just as he had suspected, the secret trip to China

was connected to her mother. No doubt her Ph.D. in biochemistry was also connected to her mother. Everything Abigail did was due to her determination to save her mother.

Such love. Such dedication. She was incredible. Brilliant, beautiful, and capable of so much love.

But not for him. Her description of his lovemaking kept repeating in his mind.

An accident.

The stress ball exploded in his hand.

"Shit." He threw it away and grabbed another one.

An accident. Had she felt nothing at all? Had she stood there, bored and mentally compiling a grocery list, while he spiraled completely out of control?

He'd never felt an attraction like this before. Romance was supposed to be fun. He loved the thrill of the chase, the giving and taking of pleasure. Simple, easy fun. But there was nothing simple or easy about Abigail.

She was impossible, but it didn't deter him. She was forbidden, but that only made her more tempting. A desperate desire had dug its claws into his heart and was threatening to consume him entirely. *Shit*. What was she doing to him? He'd actually forgotten he was in the studio.

He could have sworn she'd felt something. Her heart had definitely raced. But then, her heart rate always sped up whenever he came near. It could mean that she was afraid. Or worse. Repulsed.

Vamp women didn't care if he was a Vamp. But it could be a deal breaker for a lovely mortal like Abigail.

She'd fallen on the couch in the Oval Office, trying to escape his handshake. She'd fainted when she saw him on the ceiling. And she'd scooted halfway around the booth at the nightclub to get away from him.

Could it be that she didn't even like him? So many Vamp women had chased him over the years, maybe he'd lost the ability to know when he was being rejected.

What a joke. The *womanizer* falls for the one woman who doesn't want him.

He threw the ball against the wall, and it burst in a cloud of white powder. He was crazy to fall for Abigail. The president wasn't going to allow his daughter to get romantically involved with a vampire.

Josh clearly didn't approve of him. When Gregori had teleported home an hour ago to put on a fresh suit, he'd discovered that his condo had been searched. Probably Josh and Charles, looking for something negative to report to the president so the alliance could be broken. Or maybe they had hoped to find him asleep and vulnerable to attack.

Thank God he'd slept at Romatech. He wasn't sure how far Josh and Charles would go to keep Abigail safe from the evil clutches of a vampire.

And he still wasn't sure how she felt. That alone was enough to drive him completely bonkers.

The desk phone rang, and he picked it up. "Yes?"

"She's here," Emma told him. "The limo with Abigail Tucker just went through the front gate."

He picked up another stress ball. "I'll meet her at the front entrance. Can you tell Roman she's here?"

"I'm afraid not," Emma replied. "He had to leave for a moment."

"*What?*" Gregori squeezed the stress ball. "He agreed to meet her. He knows how important this is."

"Don't worry," Emma reassured him. "Roman will be back soon. There's a bit of a family drama going on right now. He and Angus had to teleport to the school to bring Shanna and Caitlyn back."

"Why? What's wrong?" Gregori felt a twinge of worry for the women. Shanna had only recently been transformed and was still adjusting. Caitlyn had undergone the painful transformation into a were-panther and was now expecting twins. "Are they all right?"

"They're fine, but their mother isn't," Emma explained. "She called Caitlyn, and apparently, she was screaming and terribly distraught—"

"Darlene is never distraught!" Sean Whelan shouted in the background. "She's always perfectly calm!"

"Well, she isn't calm now," Emma told him. "Gregori, Roman's coming back soon. Caitlyn and Shanna are meeting their mother here at Romatech."

"All right." Gregori hung up, wondering what was wrong with Sean Whelan's wife. Maybe she'd finally figured out what a jerk he was.

He stuffed the stress ball in his pocket, and strode to the main foyer.

The night shift at Romatech was small compared to the large number of mortals who worked during the day, but he had warned them that the president's daughter would be touring the facility. The marble floors had been polished, the offices and laboratories tidied up. He'd arranged for the cafeteria to be kept open late, and a gourmet chef had been brought in to cook a few of his specialties.

Phineas had requested the night off, so he could return to DVN with Madison. He'd called earlier to report Josh was watching him like a hawk. Gregori supposed Charles would be coming with Abigail.

He punched the code on the security pad by the front door to unlock it, then stepped outside to wait. A light rain had left the black-topped parking lot wet and gleaming under the lampposts. As usual, his gaze drifted to the spot where his life as a mortal had ended eighteen years ago. Casimir had attacked him and left him dying on the dark asphalt.

Then there was the other spot where he'd been caught in the blast of a car bomb set by the Malcontents. There'd been a church service that night in the Romatech chapel, led by Father Andrew. The chapel was a sad and empty place now, just a vase of flowers on the altar in memory of the mortal priest who had become a father to them all.

Gregori sighed. Everyone was glad Casimir was finally dead, but the cost had been too high.

His gaze wandered back to the first spot where he'd been transformed. Twice he'd cheated death in this parking lot. *You're not immortal, you fool*. He could die as easily as Father Andrew. He should stop playing at life and make his life mean something. But what gave life meaning?

Father Andrew would have said *love*.

Headlights flashed in the distance, pulsating like a strobe light as a limo passed through the wooded grounds.

Abigail.

She was coming. His heart squeezed with a knot of longing.

The limo came to a stop under the porte cochere. While Charles climbed out of the driver's seat, Gregori opened the back door.

"Step back, please." Charles gave him a stern look, then rushed over to assist Abigail.

Gregori moved back. Apparently Charles had been warned that the lusty vampire wanted to jump on Abigail like a rabid dog.

Unfortunately, the minute he saw her emerge from the limo, he did want to get his paws on her. He had to swallow hard to keep from drooling. And it wasn't like she was dressed in a sexy outfit. She was wearing jeans, a navy and green plaid blouse, and a green raincoat.

She was beautiful.

The mist in the air had made her hair curlier, her cheeks rosier, and her skin look even more dewy soft. Her eyes sparkled with excitement as she looked around.

He inclined his head. "Welcome to Romatech, Scholar."

She smiled. "The place is huge! And the grounds are beautiful. I'm already impressed."

"Great." Gregori swiped his ID to unlock the front door, then followed them inside the foyer.

"I've noticed several cameras," Charles said as he watched Gregori punch in the code to reactivate the locks. "Is there a security problem here?"

Gregori considered how to respond, then decided

honesty would be best. "We've been bombed a few times."

Abigail gasped. "Why? Synthetic blood saves thousands of lives. Who could object to that?"

"The Malcontents," Gregori explained. "They hate synthetic blood. They figure if they can get rid of Romatech, they can force Vamps to go back to biting."

Charles frowned. "If Miss Tucker is in danger, then we should leave."

"She'll be safe," Gregori reassured him. "We have an excellent security force. Would you like to see their office?"

"Yes." Charles nodded.

Gregori led them down the hall on the left. He reached in his pocket to squeeze the stress ball. The damned Secret Service man was hovering close to Abigail. At this rate, he'd never get some time alone with her to know how she truly felt.

"Our security is provided by MacKay Security and Investigation," he explained. "The CEO is Angus MacKay. If you have a secret mission in mind, he can provide you with the best operatives in the Vamp world."

Charles looked doubtful. "Do they have any field experience?"

Gregori snorted. "Some of them have centuries of experience. A few of the newbies used to work for the FBI and CIA. There's one guy who teleports into Langley without you guys knowing."

Charles's eyes narrowed. "I doubt that."

"Do you want to see the medal the Brits gave Angus? During World War II, he teleported behind German lines and rescued some Royal Air Force guys. Got them all out alive in one night."

"Then the British government knows about vampires?" Abigail asked.

Gregori nodded. "I told your father about it the other night. We'd like to have the same sort of relationship with the American government."

"That sounds good to me," Abigail said. "I'm going to recommend to my father that we go ahead with the mission."

"Miss Tucker—" Charles started.

"I can't afford to lose any more time," she interrupted. "If the British trust these Vamps, then I will, too."

Charles glanced at Gregori with a look bordering on disgust. "Josh told me about him. He's not to be trusted."

Gregori gritted his teeth. "I would never harm Miss Tucker. I'm sure she knows that." He wasn't sure at all, but he hoped she would verify it.

She didn't. She looked away, her cheeks turning pink.

Damn. Did she not even like him?

As they approached the MacKay office, the door opened. No doubt the people inside had been watching them on the monitors.

Emma stepped outside. "Good evening. I'm Emma MacKay, vice president of MacKay S and I." She smiled. "I worked for the CIA for a short time."

"She's a vampire?" Abigail whispered.

"Yes, I am." Emma's smile widened, and she pointed to her ears. "Super hearing. Please, come inside."

Gregori stepped into the office, followed by Emma

and Charles, who motioned for Abigail to remain in the hall.

"Remember me?" Sean Whelan shook hands with the Secret Service man. "I'm head of the CIA Stake-Out team."

Charles quickly scanned the room, then gestured for Abigail to enter.

"Wow," she whispered as she approached the wall of monitors.

"Impressive." Charles eyed the stash of weapons in the caged-off area at the back.

"Miss Tucker?" Sean shook her hand. "Delighted to see you again. If there's anything I can do to assist you, please let me know."

"Thank you." She gave him a curious look. "So you're a friend of the Vamps?"

"Yes." He nodded. "Of course I didn't start off that way. As head of the Stake-Out team, my original goal was to terminate all vampires. But over time, I learned that the good Vamps were on our side, helping to protect us from the Malcontents."

Charles's eyes narrowed with suspicion. "Why are you here?"

"I drop by every now and then to keep an eye on things." Sean wandered over to the table and poured a cup of coffee. "Would you like a cup?"

Charles shook his head.

Gregori bit his lip to keep from laughing at how Sean was pretending to still be mortal.

"My husband, Angus, will be back soon," Emma said. "In the meantime, I'd be happy to answer any of your security questions."

Abigail gasped and pointed at a monitor. "Four people just appeared out of thin air."

Emma glanced at the monitor. "Yes, that's my husband, Angus, and Roman Draganesti, CEO of Romatech. They're teleporting Roman's wife and sister-in-law here."

Charles studied the monitor. "They arrived outside?"

"Yes, they're coming in the side entrance now," Emma explained. "Teleporting straight into the facility sets off an alarm. That way we can tell if any Malcontents have entered."

"Excuse me." Sean hurried out into the hallway.

"Dad!" Shanna called out to him. "What are you doing here?"

Sean winced and closed the office door.

"Dad?" Charles stepped closer to examine the monitor. "Those women are Sean Whelan's daughters?"

Emma exchanged a look with Gregori.

He shrugged. They could hardly hide the truth. "Sean's daughter Shanna is married to Roman Draganesti."

Charles scoffed. "No wonder he's friends with them."

"Actually," Emma muttered, "it took Sean several years to accept Roman as a son-in-law."

Charles nodded, then shot Gregori an annoyed look. "No man would want his daughter involved with a vampire."

Gregori scowled back. "Some women might think Vamps make excellent husbands. They don't have to cook for us. We never snore. And while we're passed out all day, they have free access to our credit cards."

Emma chuckled.

Abigail continued to study the monitors, ignoring him, but her mouth twitched.

"What do you mean by *passed out*?" Charles asked. "You're unconscious during the day?"

Gregori exchanged another look with Emma. "Something like that."

"There's a car pulling into the parking lot." Abigail motioned to another monitor.

Emma winced, then gave them a bright smile. "Perhaps you should continue with your tour now." She opened the door and stepped outside. "Come along."

Gregori reached for Abigail, but Charles grabbed her arm first and ushered her into the hall.

Emma whispered to Shanna and Caitlyn, "Your mother has arrived."

"I'll let her in." Caitlyn hurried down the hall to the foyer.

"Mr. Draganesti?" Abigail approached Roman.

He turned toward her.

"Roman, this is Abigail Tucker." Gregori quickly made an introduction. "If you could talk to her later—"

"Of course." Roman shook her hand, smiling. "I'd be happy to."

"This way." Gregori motioned for Abigail and Charles to follow him. Hopefully they could get out of the way before all hell broke loose.

"Dad, go inside the office," Shanna said behind them. "Mom doesn't want to see you right now."

"But I have a right—" Sean objected.

"She figured it out, Dad!" Shanna interrupted him. "She knows what you did to her."

"Impossible," Sean replied. "I've always had complete control of her mind."

Abigail stopped to listen.

"Come on." Gregori reached for her arm.

"Back off," Charles growled.

"He was controlling his wife's mind?" Abigail whispered. "Is he a vampire?"

Gregori winced. "Sean has always had a lot of psychic power. That's why he's head of the Stake-Out team. He can resist any sort of mind control. Now, let's move on." He led them farther down the hall.

"You're no longer in control of your wife." Roman's angry voice echoed down the hall. "The control was probably broken when you went into a vampire coma."

Charles halted.

"Dammit!" Sean shouted. "This is all your fault, Roman!"

"How can you say that?" Shanna fussed at him. "He saved your life!"

"You call this *life*?" Sean roared. "He turned me into a—" He glanced down the hallway and spotted Gregori with Abigail and the Secret Service man. "Shit!" He ran into the security office and slammed the door.

"He's a vampire?" Charles asked softly.

Gregori sighed. "He was mortally wounded in battle about a week ago. Shanna begged her husband to transform him. It was the only way to save his life at the time."

"You can save someone's life by transforming him?" Abigail asked.

Gregori squeezed the stress ball in his pocket. He shouldn't have let Abigail and that damned Charles come here. They were learning too much. He could practically see the wheels turning in her mind. Was she considering having her own mother transformed?

"Sean is here?" a woman shrieked in the foyer. "He told me he was out of the country. That filthy liar! Where is he?"

"Mom, calm down!" Caitlyn told her.

Shanna ran toward the foyer. "Mom!"

Abigail followed, so Gregori and Charles went after her. They stopped at the entrance to the foyer.

"Shanna?" A middle-aged woman stared at Shanna, then burst into tears. "My baby! It's been so long!"

"Mom!" Shanna hugged her, then Caitlyn joined in the embrace.

Darlene Whelan touched Shanna's face. "Look at you. You're so beautiful. I missed you so much."

Shanna's eyes glimmered with tears. "You're back now, Mom. We have you back."

They continued to hug each other and weep. Gregori glanced over at Abigail and found her watching with tears in her eyes. Hopefully no one would notice that Shanna's tears were tinted pink.

Darlene wiped her face, then clenched her fists. "I know what he did to me. That control-freak bastard! I can hardly remember the last fifteen years. He stole them from me!"

"I know you're angry, Mom," Caitlyn said. "I was angry, too, when I found out what he did to you."

Darlene gritted her teeth. "Anger doesn't begin to describe how I feel. If I ever see him, I'm going to kill him!"

"Mom—" Shanna began.

"I have my bags in the car," Darlene announced. "I'm leaving him. I was hoping I could stay with one of—" Her mouth dropped open. "Caitlyn, you're pregnant?"

She patted her swollen belly. "Yes, with twins."

"I have two children myself," Shanna added.

"Oh my." Darlene went pale. "I didn't realize you two were married." She frowned. "You are married, aren't you?"

"Yes." Shanna grinned. "I know the perfect place for you to stay. You can see your grandchildren every day."

"Oh. Oh my." Tears ran down Darlene's face. "That would be wonderful."

"Come." Shanna wrapped an arm around her mother's shoulders. "Let me introduce you to my husband."

Gregori, Abigail, and Charles moved to the side to let the three women pass. Roman, Angus, and Emma were still waiting in the hallway in front of the security office.

"Does the mother know about Roman?" Abigail whispered to Gregori.

He shook his head.

"Oh brother," she murmured. "She's in for more drama tonight."

"Yep," Gregori agreed. Not only would Darlene Whelan find out her daughter was married to a vampire, but her daughter had recently become one as well. And her other daughter, Caitlyn, was now a were-panther and expecting kittens.

The security office door opened and Sean jumped out. "Darlene! Don't leave me!"

"You bastard!" Darlene charged down the hall. Her daughters grabbed her to slow her down.

"Darlene, I only did it because I love you!" Sean shouted.

"The devil take it." Angus shoved Sean back into the office. "Doona come out until ye know how to treat a woman."

"But she's going to leave me!" Sean bellowed.

"And ye deserve it." Angus shut the door in his face.

"Never a dull moment around here," Gregori muttered. "Come on, I'll show you around." He led Abigail across the foyer and through some double doors into another hallway.

She walked beside him with Charles trailing behind. "Sean Whelan was using mind control on his wife?"

Gregori nodded. "He sent Shanna away as a teenager when he discovered he couldn't control her."

Abigail shuddered. "No wonder his wife is so angry. If someone messed with my mind, I'd want to kill him, too."

He glanced back at Charles, then lowered his voice. "For the record, I think what Sean did was unconscionable. It's not how you treat someone you love."

She didn't answer, but he noticed her hands were clenched. "Here." He handed her the stress ball. "These seem to help."

She accepted the ball and gave it a squeeze. "What do you have to be stressed about? Can't you live forever?"

"We're not immortal. We can die. And we see people die."

She nodded and dropped the ball into her raincoat pocket. "I think that would be the worst part of being a vampire—watching your mortal friends and family die."

She grew quiet until they arrived at Laszlo's laboratory. Laszlo invited them in with a shy smile.

"Amazing." She looked around, her eyes wide. "Tell me what you're working on."

"Of course." Laszlo launched into a long monologue that made no sense to Gregori at all, but Abigail was nodding and agreeing.

Laszlo was clearly delighted to have someone who understood what he was doing. Charles stood by the door, silent and watching. Gregori ended up standing nearby, silent and watching, too, because he couldn't understand what the hell they were talking about. Whatever it was, it certainly had Laszlo excited for he was twirling the buttons on his new lab coat. Abigail seemed excited, too. She was talking fast, her hands were gesturing, her eyes gleaming.

Gregori sighed. He was doomed. She was way too smart for him. Way too alive for him. Way too forbidden for him.

She mentioned some plants she wanted to find in the Yunnan province of China, and one of Laszlo's buttons popped off and bounced onto his black-topped table.

"Yes! Roman used a plant from that province when he invented the Stay-Awake drug." Laszlo fiddled with another button. "The drug works, but it has the unfortunate side effect of aging the Vamp one year for every day he ingests it."

"Amazing," Abigail said for about the tenth time.

"Roman still has the plant in his lab," Laszlo continued. "Perhaps you would like to examine it?"

"I would love that!"

"I've been working on the Stay-Awake formula to try to minimize the side effects, but it's hard to find a Vamp who's willing to test it. They don't like taking a chance that they could age a year."

Abigail gasped. "You test your formulas on your fellow vampires?"

Laszlo chuckled. "We don't have any vampire mice. Besides, if a formula ends up making a vampire ill, it won't last for very long. His body will automatically heal during his death-sleep—"

"Laszlo!" Gregori stepped behind Abigail and made a cutting motion across his neck.

"Death-sleep?" Abigail asked. "He'll automatically heal?"

Laszlo's eyes widened as he realized he'd said too much. "Oh, I—I meant—" He nervously plucked at a button.

"What he means is vampires have superior strength," Gregori said. "We tend to heal more quickly than mortals. Of course we can still die. And if we lose a body part, we can't regenerate. We have a Vamp friend who lost a hand in battle."

"True." Laszlo nodded. "Our healing abilities are quite limited. Shall I go find that plant for you?"

"Ah, yes, thank you." Abigail watched as Laszlo scurried from the room.

"Let me show you my office." Gregori grabbed her elbow and steered her out the door.

Charles frowned at them and followed.

"What did he mean by death-sleep?" she asked.

Gregori winced inwardly. Vamps would be in deep shit if the government knew how helpless and vulnerable they were during the day. How easy they were to kill. "It's just a term we use to describe our sleep during the day. It's a . . . very deep sleep."

"So if you teleported me into China, you would have to sleep during the day?"

"Yes, but remember we can move super fast at night and teleport hundreds of miles. We can do more in one night than a mortal could do in a week. Besides, if you want to remain covert, you're better off doing things at night."

"I suppose that's true." She walked beside him, chewing her bottom lip. "What did he mean by automatically heal?"

Shit. He should have never invited Abigail here. She was too smart, too quick at figuring out their most guarded secrets. "I told you, we tend to heal more quickly."

She stopped abruptly. "Would you let me examine you?"

He gave her a slow, seductive smile, hoping it would distract her. "Do I get to strip?"

She blushed, but waved a dismissive hand. "I'm sure your anatomy is basically the same as a mortal man. What I need is a few tissue samples and some vials of your blood."

His smile faded. "Scholar, I'll take you anywhere you want in the world. I'll protect you with my life."

"I appreciate that, but right now, all I want is some blood."

"I . . . can't. I'm sorry."

Her eyes narrowed. "If there's some sort of special healing properties in your blood, I need to know. It might help my mother."

He clenched his hands. This was what he had feared the most, what every vampire in the world feared, that mortals would not only learn that vampires existed, but that their blood could heal. "We can't let you examine our blood."

She gasped. "I'm right, aren't I? Your blood has healing properties." She touched his arm. "Please, this is for my mother."

He shook his head. "Every Vamp in the world is trusting me to keep them safe. If mortals thought our blood could heal disease, they would hunt us down and drain us all dry. It would be mass murder."

Her eyes filled with tears. "You would let my mother die?" She gripped his arm. "Just give me a little. I won't tell anyone where I got it from. I can keep a secret."

"Secrets have a way of getting out. Look how well the vampire secret was kept."

She moved closer. "Gregori, please."

He winced. She wasn't going to let this go. "I'm sorry."

She released his arm and stepped back. "I can force you. Give me a blood sample, or I'll tell my father to break the alliance."

A chill ran down his back. Without the alliance, Vamps could be in serious danger. But if he gave her a blood sample, they would be doomed. "Abby, don't do this. Don't push me."

A tear rolled down her cheek. "You're not giving me any choice."

Shit. There was only one way out of this mess. He hated to do it, but what choice did he have? Thousands of Vamps were counting on him.

Her words came back to torment him. *If someone messed with my mind, I'd want to kill him, too.*

He squeezed his fists. He had no choice.

He shot a surge of mind control at Charles, and the agent slumped against the wall. *You will forget everything you heard since we left the foyer.*

He grabbed Abigail by the shoulders. "Forgive me."

She blinked. "For what?"

He hesitated. Why not? This might be his only chance. He kissed her.

She stiffened in surprise, then slowly relaxed as he poured his apology into the kiss. Her lips molded against his so soft and sweet. *Forgive me, Abby.*

He broke the kiss and invaded her mind.

You will forget everything that has happened since we left the foyer.

Chapter Fifteen

*A*bigail stumbled as a wave of dizziness swept over her.

Gregori caught her by the upper arms. "Are you all right?"

"I—" She rubbed her brow. "I think so." Why on earth was she feeling faint? She never fainted. Correction, she'd fainted two nights ago when she saw Gregori floating on the ceiling. From the moment she'd met him, her life had gone haywire.

"When's the last time you ate?" he asked, still holding her steady.

"I—" She searched her fuzzy mind. "I'm not sure." Where was she? Oh, right, Romatech. She'd just witnessed a family drama and discovered that Sean Whelan was a vampire.

And something more . . . but she couldn't quite put a finger on it. It was like trying to remember a person's name when it was on the tip of your tongue. Somehow she knew it was important, but it flitted away and was gone.

She gazed up at Gregori, who was watching her

carefully. His brow was furrowed with worry. His eyes . . . strange, he looked upset. And his mouth, there was something familiar about his mouth.

Her lips tingled, and she licked them.

He sucked in a breath of air, and his grip on her arms tightened.

"Miss Tucker, are you all right?" Charles asked.

She glanced at the Secret Service man, who was rubbing the back of his neck and frowning. "Yes, I—"

"Let's go to the cafeteria," Gregori interrupted. "I had a gourmet chef brought in. He'll be terribly disappointed if you guys don't stop by to eat."

"Oh, that was very kind of you." Abigail let him escort her down the hall. She resisted an urge to touch her mouth. Why did she feel like she'd been kissed?

Charles followed close behind.

The hallway was lined with windows on both sides, and the gardens outside were well lit. To the left, she spotted a basketball court.

"It's a lovely facility," she murmured. "I'd love to see one of the labs."

"Of course," Gregori said quietly.

"Do you actually produce synthetic blood here?"

"Yes." He nodded. "We package synthetic blood intended for mortal use in plastic bags. We do that 24/7. At night, when the Vamp employees come in, they bottle synthetic blood and Fusion Cuisine for the Vamp population."

"Do the mortals who work here know about Vamps?" Her gaze wandered once again to his mouth.

A pained expression crossed his face. "Most of them

have no idea." He opened some double doors and ushered her into the cafeteria.

It was a typical-looking employee cafeteria—rectangular-shaped tables and plastic chairs, but she liked the view of the basketball court and garden. "There's no one here."

"Most of the night shift are Vamps, so they don't eat here," Gregori explained. "Make yourselves comfortable. I'll bring you some food." He strode away to the kitchen.

She sat where she had a view of the garden. In the distance she could see a gazebo with some sort of flowering vine growing over it. Very pretty and romantic-looking. If she had enough courage, she'd ask for a tour. Just her and Gregori. And maybe he would kiss her.

She shook her head. Why was she so obsessed with kissing all of a sudden? It was ridiculous when she had so many important things to worry about. Like her mother. The trip to China. But she'd fallen asleep last night remembering the feel of his hands and mouth on her skin. He'd come so close to kissing her when they'd shot the commercial. And she had wanted it.

She touched her mouth. A kiss from a vampire. What folly.

Charles leaned over to whisper in her ear. "You had a moment of dizziness?"

She lowered her hand. "Yes."

"So did I. Something's not right." He straightened, frowning as he surveyed the room.

It was definitely strange. It wasn't like her to feel dizzy and weak. She'd had dinner with Madison at seven. She glanced at her watch. Ten forty-seven? She'd been at Romatech for forty-seven minutes?

"Hello!" a woman's voice said behind her.

Abigail twisted in her chair to see a woman entering the cafeteria. Late sixties perhaps? Abigail estimated her age by the gray streaks in her dark hair and the thin lines on her face, but she was still a handsome woman. A very happy one, too, since she was smiling broadly. She was wearing expensive black pumps and a stylish suit that reminded Abigail of the way her mother used to dress on the campaign trail.

"How do you do?" She strode straight toward Abigail. "I'm delighted to meet you."

Charles held up a hand to stop her. "Identification, please."

The woman halted. "I didn't bring my handbag." She planted her hands on her hips with a huff. "Really, young man, do I look like some kind of terrorist to you?" Her eyes glimmered with humor as she looked him over. "On second thought, I might insist that you search me thoroughly."

Charles gulped. "That won't be necessary."

Abigail smiled as she rose to her feet. Whoever this woman was, she liked her.

"Mom!" Gregori strode toward them, carrying a tray. "What are you doing here?"

"Is that any way to greet me?" She gave him a stern look. "I came to meet your date, of course."

"She's not a date," Gregori gritted out between clenched teeth as he set the tray on the table.

Abigail's smile widened. The emotions crossing

Gregori's face were priceless. Shock, horror, then mortification.

"What is this?" His mother inspected the two dishes on the tray.

"Lobster and asparagus risotto," he mumbled, setting the dishes on the table. "One for each of my guests. I don't recall inviting you."

"Well, it smells lovely!" his mother exclaimed. "I'll take one. Thank you."

"Mom," he muttered. "This is a business meeting."

"I'd be delighted for you to stay," Abigail said. It was just too much fun watching Gregori squirm.

"Aren't you the sweetest thing?" She extended a hand. "I'm Radinka Holstein. Please call me Radinka."

"I'm Abigail Tucker."

"Don't shake her—" Gregori groaned when Abigail shook his mother's hand.

Radinka clasped her hand in both of hers and held tightly. Then she let go with a wide grin. "Yes, at last! She's the—"

"*No!*" Gregori shouted, then winced. "Sorry." He leaned close to his mother. "Wishful thinking, that's all."

She huffed. "I'm never wrong about these things."

Gregori's hands clenched, then released. "Take a seat, Mother. Have some risotto." He grabbed a set of eating utensils wrapped in a napkin and banged them onto the table. Then he set a plate of risotto in front of her.

Abigail sat across from his mom, and Gregori handed her a napkin and the other risotto.

"Fair warning," he whispered. "She'll bring up children in less than five seconds." He straightened. "So how did you know I was here tonight, Mother?"

She unrolled her napkin. "Roman, Angus, and Emma just teleported to the school, and they brought Shanna and her sister and mother with them. The mother wanted to meet her grandchildren." She smiled at Abigail. "Did you know vampires are able to father children?"

Gregori groaned.

Abigail's mouth twitched. She recalled Gregori mentioning this at the nightclub, but she was curious to hear more. "How very interesting."

"So what brings you here, Mom?" Gregori asked.

"It's very simple." She shook out her napkin and placed it in her lap. "Emma told me you were here with your date, so I asked her to teleport me here, so I could meet her."

"She's not a date," Gregori muttered. "She's the president's daughter."

"I know that." She looked at Abigail, her eyes gleaming. "She's everything I ever hoped for. And as pretty as can be. Don't you think she's pretty, Gregori?"

"Mom—"

"Now don't be shy. You should tell her how you feel."

Abigail covered her mouth to hide her grin. The big tough vampire couldn't control his mother. She glanced at him to find him glowering at her.

"She's beautiful," he whispered.

Her heart stuttered. Memories from last night swirled in her head. He'd admitted that he wanted her. His eyes had glowed red with desire.

Her gaze settled once again on his wide sensual lips. Good Lord, she was obsessed with the man's mouth. All she could think about was kissing him.

"Now leave us alone a minute." Radinka motioned toward Charles. "Don't you need to bring the gentleman some food? And we need something to drink."

Gregori grunted and stalked toward the kitchen.

"How is your mother, dear?" Radinka asked. "I have always admired her. She seems to have a great deal of inner strength."

Abigail swallowed hard. "Yes, she does. Thank you." She fiddled with her napkin. Somehow she had a feeling that Gregori didn't understand how desperately she wanted to help her mother. "I'm trying to find a cure for her."

"That's very admirable of you." Radinka tried the risotto. "Excellent. Is my son treating you well?"

"Yes." Abigail felt a blush sweeping across her face as she recalled Gregori's lips and fingers caressing her neck.

She watched him as he approached them with a tray. He set glasses of ice water in front of each of them, then gave Charles a plate of risotto.

He turned toward them, frowning. "This is just the first course. The chef has Chilean sea bass coming up next. And he selected a wine for you."

"Wonderful! Thank you." Radinka smiled at him, then at Abigail. "Isn't he sweet?"

Abigail grinned. Radinka's matchmaking efforts were far from subtle.

"May I ask why you've been so careful to stay out of the public eye?" Radinka asked.

Her smile faded.

Gregori lifted his eyebrows, obviously waiting for her answer.

"I was never comfortable with all the attention," she mumbled.

He crossed his arms over his chest. "And?"

"And when I went to college, I wanted to be left alone so I could concentrate on my studies. My papers were all published using my mother's maiden name, May."

"Abigail May?" Gregori asked.

She nodded. "I did my doctorate on a formula I developed that would put a person into stasis. I intended to use it for accident victims to keep them stable until they made it to surgery. Or if my mother took a sudden turn for the worse, we could use it to keep her stable."

"How interesting," Radinka said.

Abigail sighed. "The military wanted to develop it as a weapon, a way to put the enemy combatant into stasis. I went along with it because I thought it was better than killing the enemy. So I let them work with the formula, and they gave me free use of their labs and resources for my own research. It's a secret military installation, so I can't afford to have any media following me."

"You've dedicated much of your life to helping your mother," Radinka concluded.

"Yes." Abigail glanced at Gregori. "I'll do whatever it takes."

He adjusted his tie. "I'll see if Roman is available to meet you now." He dashed toward the double doors and left them swinging in his wake.

He'd certainly been in a hurry to leave. Abigail picked up her fork and poked at her risotto.

Radinka huffed. "He forgot to bring us the wine."

Abigail shrugged. "I'm not sure he understands how important my mother is to me."

"He may not want to admit it, but he does." Radinka sighed. "You see, my husband died from bone cancer. Gregori had just started his master's degree at Yale when we got the news. He quit school, came home, and spent all the time he could with his father. He knew what was coming, but he was still devastated when Heinrich died. We both were."

"I'm so sorry," Abigail said. So this was the sad place Gregori had gone to when she'd told him about her mother's illness. He did understand what she was going through.

Radinka's eyes glimmered with tears. "It was a difficult time. So much sadness. And so much debt. Gregori lived at home and worked two jobs to help pay it off. I took a job here as office manager for Roman Draganesti. As soon as the debt was paid off, Gregori finished his master's at NYU. He's such a good man. So loyal and hardworking. I hope you don't hold it against him that he's a vampire."

Abigail didn't know what to say. "Well, I—"

Radinka reached across the table to squeeze her hand. "Please don't think ill of him. It was all my fault."

"Your fault? How?"

Radinka sat back and sniffed. "After a few months of working the night shift here, I started to catch on. Roman is a brilliant scientist, but a bit absentminded when he gets involved with a project. He would leave half-empty bottles of blood in his office. And since I was raised in the old country, Czechoslovakia, I was aware of all the old vampire tales. I soon figured it out."

"Did you tell him?" Abigail asked.

Radinka nodded. "And I swore to keep the secret. I needed the job. And Roman needed me. It worked out well until Gregori got it into his head that it wasn't safe for me to work and commute at night. He wanted me to work during the day, but of course, that was impossible. We argued about it."

She sighed. "I lost my temper and told Gregori I worked for vampires. You can imagine his reaction."

Abigail took a sip of water. "What did he do?"

"At first, he was afraid I'd lost my mind. Then when he started to suspect it was true, he was worried for my safety. He drove here to confront Roman. And that's when it happened." A tear ran down Radinka's face. "My poor son. He was only trying to protect me."

Abigail leaned forward. "What happened?"

"He was attacked in the parking lot. We found out later it was Casimir, the leader of the Malcontents. He overpowered Gregori and ripped open his neck. Drank his full and left him to die."

Abigail swallowed hard. Poor Gregori.

"We didn't have all the security cameras back then. A guard finally found him when he was making his rounds." Radinka wiped a tear from her face. "I'd already lost my husband. I couldn't bear to lose my son, too. I begged Roman to transform him. And he did."

Abigail took a deep breath and let it out slowly. She couldn't blame Radinka. She'd be desperate, too, to save a loved one. "It must have come as a great shock to Gregori."

"Yes, I believe it did." Radinka dabbed at her eyes with her napkin. "But he tried not to show it. He's tried so hard to fit in. Roman offered him a job here, and he's worked awfully hard. He's vice president of marketing now, you know."

Abigail smiled. Radinka was clearly proud of him. "How old was he when was transformed?"

"Twenty-nine." Radinka ate some risotto. "But that was back in 1993. It's high time he stopped playing around with those silly Vamp women. He needs to settle down with a nice mortal girl. I won't live forever, you know, and I want some time with my grandchildren."

"I'm sure you do." Abigail tasted the risotto. It really was excellent. She glanced over at Charles, who had cleaned his plate. "There's more food in the kitchen," she called to him. "And some wine. Could you bring it out?"

He frowned, looking Radinka over, then hurried off to the kitchen.

Radinka snorted. "Does he really think I'm going to hurt you? My own future daughter-in-law?"

Abigail's mouth dropped open. "I—I think you may have misunderstood my relationship with your son. We're not dating."

Radinka shrugged. "All in good time." She pointed a fork at Abigail. "But I'm not getting any younger, so don't wait too long."

"But I—"

"At least two grandchildren," Radinka continued.

Abigail stuffed her clenched fists into her raincoat pockets, then felt something bump against her knuckles. She peered into her pocket and found a ball. Where on earth did this come from? She pulled it out to look at it.

Radinka chuckled. "Did Gregori give you one of his stress balls?"

Abigail gave it a squeeze. Did he? When?

Chapter Sixteen

*G*regori found Roman in his office, enjoying a Bleer with Angus. "I—" He dragged a hand through his hair.

"Out with it, lad. I'm no' getting any younger." Angus lounged back in his chair and took a long sip from his bottle.

Roman set his bottle on his desk. "Would you like me to talk to Miss Tucker now?"

"In a little while." Gregori yanked the knot of his tie loose. "I-I've done something awful."

The two men stared at him for a while.

"How awful?" Roman asked finally.

Angus sat up. "Did ye bed the lass?"

"No!" Gregori huffed with indignation. "What would give you that idea?"

The two men stared at him again.

He shifted his weight. "I realize I have a bit of a reputation, but I don't—"

"We're no' blind, lad," Angus muttered. "We can tell ye're attracted to her."

"You can?" When they continued to stare at him, he swallowed hard. "All right, it's true."

"You slept with her?" Roman asked.

"No! I find her attractive." He grimaced. "I erased her memory. About fifteen minutes' worth. The Secret Service guy, too."

Roman and Angus exchanged a worried look.

"Do they suspect?" Angus asked.

"I don't think so." Gregori groaned inwardly as he ran a hand through his hair. "If she ever finds out, she's going to be so pissed."

"With good reason." Roman frowned at him.

"I know it's bad, but I didn't see any other way out. We were in Laszlo's lab, and he accidentally let it slip that we heal automatically in our death-sleep."

Roman winced, and Angus muttered a curse.

"I tried to cover it up, but she's really smart, you know. And the next thing I knew she was asking for tissue and blood samples, and I explained why I couldn't, but she wouldn't back down. She even threatened to have her dad break the agreement with us if I didn't give her some blood."

Roman shook his head. "We can't let them know that our blood heals."

"The government would definitely say we doona exist," Angus growled. "And then they would secretly come after us and drain us all dry."

"They would become an enemy instead of an ally," Roman concluded.

Angus gulped down a swallow of Bleer. "I know ye doona like it, lad, but ye did the right thing."

Gregori sighed. He still felt guilty.

"Do you know any more about the mission she wants to go on?" Roman asked.

"She mentioned to Laszlo that she was looking for some plants in the Yunnan province of China."

Roman's eyes widened. "That's where I got the—"

"Yes, I know, for the Stay-Awake drug," Gregori interrupted. "Laszlo told her about it. Of course, she doesn't remember that now."

Roman nodded. "I'm not surprised she wants to go there. It's extremely biodiverse. Over two thousand plants are endemic to the area."

"And I can understand why her father wants the trip to remain secret," Angus said as he rose to his feet. "I'll put together some plans. Stop by the security office later tonight." He strode from the office, the bottle of Bleer in his hand.

"Where is she now?" Roman asked.

"In the cafeteria, eating a gourmet meal," Gregori replied. "I'll take her to my office in about ten minutes. You can meet her there."

"All right." Roman sipped some Bleer. "You're doing very well, Gregori."

He balled his fists. "If she ever finds out—"

"We'll make sure she doesn't."

"I feel like an ass, especially when I keep trying to convince her I'm trustworthy."

"You are trustworthy. You have thousands of Vamps trusting you to keep them safe."

Gregori sighed. "I guess the needs of the many outweigh the needs of one." Even if he was falling for the one.

He strode back to the cafeteria. Roman and Angus had both confirmed he'd done the right thing, but he still felt guilty. She didn't remember going to a lab, but he suspected that on some subconscious level, she remembered the kiss. She kept looking at his mouth.

Did that mean she wanted to kiss him? Could he be that lucky? He'd admitted last night that he was attracted to her, but he still didn't know how she felt about him.

He did know how she felt about mind control. Her words came back to taunt him. *If someone messed with my mind, I'd want to kill him, too.*

He jammed a hand into his pocket to squeeze his stress ball, but it was empty. Oh, right. He'd given it to her.

He stopped with a jerk. .

Shit. He adjusted his tie. If the ball caused any trouble, he'd bluff his way through.

Back in the cafeteria, the chef had taken a seat at the table with the ladies, and they were all eating and drinking wine while Charles sat at another table, eating and watching.

The chef gave him an annoyed look. "You did not tell me I would be cooking for ze president's daughter," he said with a French accent. "I would have made many more dishes."

Abigail smiled and touched her stomach. "I'm so full. I couldn't have eaten any more. And it was all fabulous. Thank you."

"Yes," Radinka agreed. "It was superb. Thank you."

The chef inclined his head. "You are most welcome. And if you ever need a guest chef at the White House, you will remember me, *non?*" When Abigail nodded, he slapped his hands together and grinned. "*Merveilleux!*"

"We need to go to my office now," Gregori told Abigail. "Roman will meet you there."

"You go on without me." Radinka stood and gave Abigail a hug. "I'll see you later, my dear." She sat back down and poured more wine into her glass. "It's not often I get a night off."

As they walked toward Gregori's office, Charles followed about ten feet behind. Gregori glanced back at him, wondering how he could get rid of their shadow. Mind control would be the easiest solution, but he didn't want Abigail to see that.

She leaned close and whispered, "I'm afraid your mom thinks we're dating."

"Is that all?" He gave her a wry look. "I'm surprised she didn't pick out names for all five of our children."

"Five? She only mentioned two." Abigail blushed.

Gregori chuckled. "Don't let her get to you. She's been trying to marry me off for years."

"You . . . were never tempted?"

He shook his head. "I wanted to be free. No worries, no responsibility."

"No debt?"

He shot a look at her. "She told you about that?"

She nodded. "And about your father. I'm very sorry."

A sharp pang of remembrance jabbed at him, but he mentally shoved away the old pain. "I don't have to deal with that anymore. Vamps can live for centuries."

"Is that why you date Vamp women? Because they're more . . . permanent?"

He scoffed. "There's nothing permanent about Vamp females. They're a bunch of butterflies, flitting here and there. They have so much time, it ceases to have any value to them."

"So you don't want anything permanent?"

No. He'd wanted to avoid falling in love. It hurt too much to lose someone you loved. So much safer to simply give and take pleasure. He glanced at Abigail. "Why all the questions?"

Her cheeks bloomed a brighter pink. "I'm just trying to get to know you better. So I can trust you."

Trust me? The vampire playboy who had messed with her mind? "I have a reputation as a womanizer." He scowled at her. "And I earned it. I spent my first few years as a vampire making Undead women happy."

She frowned and was silent for a while. "You were coming out of a long period of grief and financial difficulty. I can see why you wanted to have some fun. Your mother said you tried very hard to fit in."

He shrugged.

"Oh my gosh. You're vice president of marketing." She halted and stared at him. "You were marketing yourself."

He flinched. Of all the ridiculous things to say. He opened his mouth to disagree, but paused.

It was true. He'd tried to always be charming and successful, the life of the party. Gregori, the gregarious. But after a few years, he'd grown tired of the game. He'd wondered why the sex wasn't as pleasurable as it should be.

Because his heart wasn't in it. He was pretending to be something he wasn't.

He swallowed hard. "I woke up one night Undead. I couldn't go back. I could never be mortal again." Years later, Roman figured out how to transform a person back, but it had been too late for him. "I just wanted to fit in."

She nodded. "So you tried to please everyone."

He grimaced and looked away. *Shit.* All those years he'd thought he was being cool, he'd been an insecure idiot. He was like a school kid trying to get into the inner clique.

It was time to grow up. Figure out who he really was and what he really wanted.

He glanced at Abigail, and a wave of possessiveness flooded over him. He wanted her. He wanted her beauty. Her brains. Her bravery. Her insightfulness. Her kindness.

Her love.

He wanted to pull her into his arms and kiss her. But he couldn't, not with Charles standing ten feet away, glaring at him.

"My office is this way." He hurried down the hall.

"I found it!" Laszlo called out from down the hallway. "I have the plant you wanted." He rushed toward them.

Abigail stopped with a confused look on her face.

Gregori stepped forward. "Laszlo." He gave him a pointed look. "I don't believe you have met Miss Tucker." He turned to face her, smiling. "Abigail, this is Laszlo Veszto, one of our chemists here at Romatech."

"Delighted to meet you." She shook his hand. "I would love to see your lab if that's possible."

"Ah, yes, of course." Laszlo fiddled with a button on his lab coat.

Gregori patted him on the back. "I was just telling Laszlo last night that you were interested in going to China. So we thought you might like this plant."

"Yes." Laszlo handed her a plastic container. "It's a rare plant from the Yunnan province."

She gasped. "That's exactly where I want to go." She took the container. "Thank you, Laszlo."

"Glad to help." He plucked at a button. "I think I'll be going now." He scurried back down the hallway to his lab.

"Is he all right?" Abigail asked.

"Sure." Gregori opened the door to his office. "He's just a little shy."

Charles rushed forward to enter the office first. He pivoted, looking about, then motioned for Abigail to enter.

"It's very ni—" She halted when Charles jumped back from the closet he had just opened.

"Please step out of the room," he said quietly as he pulled a cell phone from his pocket. "I'm calling the police."

"What?" Gregori asked.

Charles gave him a disgusted look. "There's a female body in your closet."

Gregori scoffed. "You mean VANNA? She's not alive."

Abigail gasped.

"I mean she was never alive!" Gregori strode toward the closet.

Charles grabbed his arm. "You can't go in there. It's a crime scene."

"Don't be ridiculous." He flipped on the lights in the closet. "You see? It's a doll."

"A doll?" Abigail moved closer. "In a red bikini?"

Charles held up a hand to stop her. "Stand back. I'll investigate the matter." He eased inside the closet.

"Oh come on," Gregori growled. "It's just a stupid doll."

Charles leaned over to inspect VANNA. "It looks like a sex toy." He shot another disgusted look at Gregori. "The ribbon around its neck could be used to simulate strangulation."

Abigail stiffened. A horrified look flitted over her face, then she ran from the room.

"Abby!" Gregori followed her. "It's not what you think."

She turned to face him. "What should I think? That you've been strangling a life-sized sex toy in your closet?"

"No! VANNA is a Vampire Artificial Nutritional Needs Appliance. Laszlo and I invented her. He put in some tubes to simulate veins and a battery-operated pump to make synthetic blood flow through her. But it didn't work. Her skin is too rubbery for biting."

"You bit her?"

"No! Not me. It was Roman."

"Talking about me?" Roman sauntered down the hall toward them.

Gregori winced. Now he'd made his boss sound like a perv. "They found VANNA in the closet."

Roman chuckled. "Don't let VANNA upset you, Miss Tucker. She was a failed experiment from a few years ago."

"Oh." She gave Gregori a wry look. "And yet, she's still in your closet."

"I was going to give her to Connor for his five-hundredth birthday. As a gag gift. That's why there's a bow around her neck. But Connor just got married, and . . . I don't think his new wife will appreciate it."

Roman laughed. "No, definitely not."

Charles stepped into the hall, carrying VANNA. "It's harmless. Sorry for causing you alarm, Miss Tucker."

Gregori grabbed the doll and bent her over his arm. "See the opening we cut in her back to insert a circulatory system?" He peeled back the rubber skin to show her.

"Interesting," she murmured.

"We thought VANNA might be useful for Vamps who were still addicted to biting," Roman explained. "I know it must seem a bit odd, but our ultimate goal is to protect mortals and keep them from being attacked."

"I see." She nodded. "She's a substitute victim."

"Exactly." Gregori straightened the doll. When Abigail frowned, he realized his hand was planted on VANNA's breast. He quickly lowered it to her waist.

"Would you like to see how we manufacture synthetic blood?" Roman asked Abigail. "I'd be happy to take you on a tour and answer any questions."

"That would be wonderful." She smiled. "Thank you."

Roman patted Gregori on the back. "You look like you could use a break."

"I'm okay." Just one near disaster after another. Laszlo reappearing, then VANNA. And the way Abigail had seen right through him, opening his eyes. He'd marketed himself to make everyone in the Vamp world like him. The truth was there was no way to please everyone. He should just be himself and only worry about the people he truly cared about.

Like Abigail.

"Maybe you can use this?" She pulled a stress ball from her pocket. "I'm not sure how I got it, but your mother said it belongs to you."

He swallowed hard. "I slipped it into your pocket when you weren't looking. You can keep it. I have a bunch more."

"Okay." She stuffed it back into her pocket, apparently accepting his explanation.

"You can leave the plant in my office if you like," Gregori offered, and she handed the plastic container to him.

"We'll see you in about twenty minutes," Roman told him as he walked off with Abigail, Charles trailing behind.

Gregori went back into his office, set the plant on his desk, then tossed VANNA in the closet and shut the door. Unable to relax, he grabbed a stress ball and paced. When that didn't work, he retrieved a bottle of synthetic blood from his mini-fridge and gulped down half of it.

He strode to the security office to hear what plans Angus had come up with. Emma was gone, having teleported his mother back to the school. He sat across the desk from Angus, and the two were deep in discussion when the phone rang.

"Aye, he's here," Angus spoke on the phone. "I'll send him yer way." He hung up. "Roman finished the tour. He and the lass are looking for you."

Gregori dashed toward his office and ran into Roman, Abigail, and Charles in the hallway.

Roman turned toward her. "It was a pleasure meeting you, Miss Tucker. If there's anything I can do for you, just let me know. And if you ever need a lab, you're welcome to use one of ours."

"That's very kind of you. Thank you." She smiled. "I'm going to recommend to my father that he befriend you and your people."

"Excellent." Roman shook her hand. "And we will do everything in our power to make your trip to China successful."

"I was with Angus just now, making plans for the trip," Gregori said.

"I'll leave you to discuss it. I need to see how my wife and children are doing. Good evening." Roman inclined his head, then teleported away.

"Wow," Abigail breathed. She turned to Gregori. "That's how I'll get into China?"

"Yes. But before you go, we'll have everything planned out. It would help if we knew exactly what you're looking for."

"Three rare plants that are endemic to the Yunnan province. They're used in some ancient Chinese remedies, and from my research, I believe they might be helpful in boosting my mother's immune system. I tried to get hold of some samples legally, but the government wouldn't allow it. I have the information on the plants at work, including the mostly likely areas for locating them."

"Good." Gregori nodded. "That would help a lot. For now, we're busy selecting the right team, those who have experience in covert missions and know the native language."

She frowned. "But you're going, aren't you?"

"I would like to, but I don't have any experience—"

"You have to go." She grabbed his arm. "I don't know the others."

"You'll get to know them."

"Not like you. I—I need you there. I trust you."

Trust. He didn't deserve her trust, not after wiping her memory.

Her grip tightened on his arm. "Please. I'll feel safer with you."

"I'll tell Angus you want me to go." Did this mean she really liked him? He glanced over at Charles, who was glaring at him. "Before we take off across the world, we need to test how well you can handle teleportation."

Her eyes widened. "What happens if I can't handle it?"

"You . . . might get nauseated." He pointed out the window. "See the gazebo? I'll teleport you there, so we can see if you can stomach it."

She touched her tummy and winced. "On a full stomach. Great."

"I don't like it." Charles stepped toward them. "I have to be able to monitor her at all times."

"You'll be able to see her through the window," Gregori assured him.

"Charles," Abigail said, "we have to know if I can do this."

"All right." Charles frowned at Gregori. "I'll be watching."

He extended a hand to Abigail. "I have to hold on to you."

"Okay." She placed her hand in his.

"Like this." He pulled her into his arms, and she

stiffened with surprise. He heard her heart rate speed up.

Charles's eyes narrowed.

"And I need you to hold on to me," Gregori continued. "You don't want to get lost on the way."

"No, that would be bad." She wrapped her arms around his neck.

He gazed into her pretty hazel eyes. "Ready?"

She nodded and squeezed her eyes shut.

Everything went black for a second, then they landed by the gazebo. The grass was damp from a recent rain. The air was thick with humidity and the scent of climbing roses.

"You can open your eyes now," he whispered.

She did, and her eyes widened as she looked around. "Oh my gosh, we actually did it. I hardly felt a thing."

He waved at the window in the distance where Charles was watching. "Let him know you're okay."

"Right." She waved at the Secret Service agent. "I'm not nauseated at all. Isn't that great?"

"I . . . sorta lied about that. Mortals usually teleport just fine."

Her mouth dropped open. "Why would you lie?"

"Because I wanted to get away from all the cameras." He grabbed her hand and pulled her into the gazebo. "And away from Charles."

"He'll just come after us."

"He'll have trouble finding an unlocked door so he can get out here."

She winced. "This is going to make him angry."

"It'll be worth it." Gregori released her and stepped back. "Finally. We're alone."

Chapter Seventeen

*A*bigail's mind raced, along with her heart, as she mentally ticked off any reasons Gregori might have to be alone with her. Unfortunately, no matter how she figured it, she kept reaching the same conclusion: he was planning to seduce her.

It was dark inside the gazebo, so she couldn't see his expression to gauge how serious he was. His posture seemed tense.

She took a deep breath of the heady rose-scented air. "If you're concerned about the alliance, I can assure you that my father will honor—"

"I'm sure he will. That's not why I brought you here."

She swallowed hard. Seduction remained on top of the list. "If you're concerned about the doll we found, then you needn't be. Roman explained it all to me. He said you only bring her out of the closet for bachelor parties."

He nodded. "I never dated her. She's hard to talk to."

Abigail smiled weakly. "Well, you can always talk to me."

"That's exactly what I want to do."

She blinked. "It is?" What happened to seduction? Well, this was a relief. Or was it? She winced inwardly with a sudden realization.

She was disappointed.

Good Lord, she must be losing her mind.

He shifted his weight. "I want to talk about us."

Us? "I . . . hope we'll be traveling together to China in a few days—"

"How do you feel about me?"

She hesitated. What on earth could she say? That he was the most handsome, attractive, and charming man she'd ever met? That he was the sort of man she'd dreamed of? That she wanted him to long for her as much as she longed for him? That his act of stealing her away made her dizzy with excitement? He'd taken charge with boldness, and it made her knees tremble.

But how could she admit any of that? He was a vampire. As much as she yearned for heat and passion, she was still, underneath it all, a sensible, practical person. She couldn't fall in love with a vampire.

He yanked at his tie. "Are you . . . repulsed that I'm Undead?"

She winced. "No. You were attacked. You didn't ask for this. You did the best you could under the circumstances."

He stepped toward her, and she stepped back.

"Are you afraid of me?"

"Should I be?"

"I would never hurt you." He took another step toward her. "I'm going to kiss you."

Seduction. She'd been right all along. She stuffed her

hands in her coat pockets. When she bumped into his stress ball, she clenched a fist around it. "Don't you think you should ask permission first?"

He shook his head. "If I ask, you might refuse."

Bold and aggressive. He sliced right through her defenses and seized hold of that secret primitive part of her that ached to be loved by such a strong, determined man. An Alpha hero like the guys in her mother's books. A man like Gregori who would take an entire night to worship and pleasure her to her heart's content.

But she couldn't give in. A relationship with him was impossible. Completely, irreparably impossible.

She lifted her chin. "You would kiss me against my will?"

He touched her chin with his finger. "I would have to change your will."

"I doubt you—" She stopped when he dragged the tip of his finger down her throat. Goose bumps skittered down her arms, and she shivered.

"Scholar," he whispered.

"Gori," she whispered back.

The corner of his mouth curled up, causing his cheek to dimple. "The brain and the beast?"

Unfortunately her brain wasn't working well. There had to be a dozen reasons why she needed to stop him, but she couldn't think of a single one.

His hand slipped around to cup the back of her neck. His gaze met hers, and his eyes had turned a brighter, more emerald green. "Do you know how much I want you?"

She shook her head.

"You're so brilliant." He kissed her brow. "So brave." He kissed her temple. "And beautiful." His lips skimmed over her cheek.

"No." She planted her hands against his chest to stop him as his mouth hovered less than an inch from her own. Good Lord, she wanted him so much.

But she had to resist. "It's impossible."

His hand tightened around her neck. He leaned his head forward till his brow rested on hers. After a moment of silence, he whispered, "You can say it's difficult. Hard. Challenging. Don't say it's impossible."

She pushed at his chest. "But it is. You know it is."

He released her and stepped back, frowning. "Why? Why is it impossible?"

She fisted her hand around the stress ball in her pocket. "We don't have a lot in common. I'm a . . . scientist, and you're not. I'm—"

"You're alive, and I'm not," he interrupted.

She winced. "My father could never accept you."

"What about you?"

"I . . . I don't know." She squeezed the ball. "I don't know you that well, really. We only met a few nights ago."

"Abby, you do know me. You see things about me that no one else does. Even myself. I haven't been able to look at myself in a mirror for eighteen years, but you . . . you are my mirror. When I see your tears for your mother, I feel the ones I shed for my father. And when you suffer, I understand that, too." His eyes glimmered with tears. "We lost someone we loved a few nights ago in battle."

"I'm so sorry," she whispered.

"And we do have a lot in common," he continued. "We're both hardworking and goal-oriented. We've both lived in the shadows, hiding from the public. We both get stressed out." He reached in his pocket and removed a ball. "It shows up in our hands."

She scoffed. "That doesn't bode well for a stress-free relationship."

He smiled. "I like your sense of humor." He stepped toward her. "I like everything about you."

Her chest tightened. She liked everything about him, too. Except the vampire part. That was a tough one to swallow. "It's still impossible. Completely, irreparably—"

"Don't say it!" He stared at her for a moment, then turned abruptly to walk to the other side of the gazebo.

She was so tempted to run to him, put her arms around him, and comfort him. *Don't do it. You must resist.*

He placed his hands on the railing and looked out at the stars. Moonlight fell on his face, and she eased to the side so she could see his handsome profile bathed in silvery light.

"I used to go camping in the mountains with my father, and we loved to get up early to watch the sunrise. Now, I can never see the sun. It's impossible."

"Would the sun harm you?" she asked.

"It would kill me." He tilted his head, still watching the stars. "When Dad's cancer spread to his liver, they told me there was no hope. It was impossible."

Her heart ached for him, but when she opened her mouth to say she was sorry, he continued talking.

"When I lay dying in the parking lot, and my mother

begged Roman to give me a transfusion, he said it was too late. It was impossible."

Tears stung her eyes. She couldn't bear the thought of him dying. And he'd lost so much—the sun, his father, his mortality.

He touched a rose that was growing on the vine close by. "When I woke up Undead, I asked if I could ever be mortal again, and they said it was impossible."

A tear rolled down her cheek.

He plucked the rose. "It is possible now. Roman figured out a way, but I don't have any samples of my mortal blood. My mother burned the bloody clothes I was wearing when I was attacked." He pinched a thorn off the rose stem and tossed it outside into the flowerbed. "So for me, it's impossible. You can see why I dislike that word."

He turned and held the rose out to her. "Why can't you be possible?"

Her heart cracked. How could she hurt him when she was falling in love with him?

She drew in a shaky breath and wiped her cheek. She took a step toward him. Then another one.

His eyes widened.

She realized she was giving him hope, the first hope he'd had in years. She ran to him.

The rose tumbled to the ground as he caught her in his arms. "Abby." He held her tight, lifting her feet off the plank floor and swinging her around. The minute her feet touched ground, he was scattering kisses over her face.

A seed of joy burst in her heart and swept over her. "Gori." She clutched at his shoulders. He was so strong, so solid, and so wonderfully focused on her.

His nose nuzzled against hers, and his breath puffed gently against her lips. "Abby."

She lifted her gaze to meet his and stiffened. His eyes were glowing and red.

"I have no control over it," he whispered. "You will always know when I long for you."

Her hands delved into his soft hair and she cradled his head. "I thought you were planning to kiss me?"

A corner of his mouth curled up. "I don't need to ask permission?"

"I changed my mind."

"I always knew you were brilliant." He touched his lips to hers gently, then pulled back a fraction, waiting.

She closed her eyes, savoring the tension that hummed in the air between them, a dam about to break. And it did.

It shattered into a million pieces. He planted his mouth on hers, devouring her with passion.

She rode along on the flood, clinging to him as he held her tight. His lips were sweet and relentless. He tasted her, nibbled and coaxed till he took full possession, invading her with his tongue.

Heat and desire washed over her. A tiny voice in the back of her mind warned her she was in over her head, but she didn't care. She'd never been kissed like this. She could drown in his desire and beg for more. His passion pounded against her, one wave after another, lifting her higher and higher.

She groaned with disappointment when he suddenly broke off the kiss. "Gregori—"

"They're coming."

"You can—" Of course, she realized. He could hear.

"Charles and Angus," he whispered, his eyes gleaming red in the darkness. "They came out the side entrance. Charles must have gone to the security office to make Angus unlock a door." He tightened his grip on her. "Trust me."

Everything went black for a second, then she stumbled onto the ground.

"Are you all right?" He steadied her.

Hell, no. Her knees were wobbly, her heart was pounding, and her lips were still tingling. *By George, that man can kiss.*

She'd done it. She'd kissed him. She reached up to touch his cheek.

He turned his head to kiss her palm. "They're coming."

She looked around, but only saw trees. "Where are we?"

"At the back of the garden. You asked for a tour, and being a gentleman, I naturally obliged."

"Really?"

"That's our story, and we're sticking to it." He took her hand and led her down a path she could barely see in the moonlight.

In the distance, she saw Charles running toward the gazebo. Angus MacKay followed behind, his kilt swishing about his knees. She withdrew her hand from Gregori's. Their moment alone was over.

"Miss Tucker!" Charles disappeared inside the gazebo, then emerged seconds later. "She's not here!"

"Charles!" She waved at him and quickened her pace until she reached a well-lit area. "I'm fine!"

Relief swept over his face, quickly replaced by anger. "Don't ever do that again!"

"I was perfectly safe," she assured him. "I just wanted to see the garden." She glanced at Gregori, and thankfully his eyes were no longer red and glowing.

Charles shot a suspicious look at Gregori, then turned back to her. "I should take you back to the hotel now."

She nodded. "In a moment. Mr. MacKay, I understand you've been making plans for my trip. I want Gregori to come with me."

"Och, is that so?" Angus's eyes twinkled with humor. "I'm sure that can be arranged. If Gregori is willing."

"I am," he said quietly.

Abigail touched his arm. "Can you come to the White House tomorrow night and explain your plans to my father? I'd like to get his okay, so we can proceed as soon as possible."

Gregori nodded. "I can do that. Why don't you and Charles head toward the limo? I'll fetch your plant from my office and bring it to you."

"All right. Thank you."

His mouth curled up. "I hope you enjoyed the tour."

Her face warmed. She watched as he dashed toward the building at an incredible speed.

"He moves awfully fast," Charles muttered.

"Yes." Her blush grew hotter. It had taken him only a few nights to make her melt in his arms.

Angus led her and Charles back to the side entrance at a much slower pace. By the time they reached the foyer, Gregori had returned with the plastic container containing the plant she wanted to examine.

Angus entered the code to unlock the front door. "Rest assured, lass, that we will do everything in our power to keep you safe on yer trip."

"Thank you." She stepped outside.

While Charles circled the limo to the driver's seat, Gregori opened the back door for her. "I'll see you tomorrow."

"Yes." She tried not to blush as she climbed into the car.

He leaned over and whispered, "Take a look inside the box." He winked, then shut the door.

As Charles drove away, she peeked inside the plastic container. Inside there was a dried root wrapped in plastic. And a note.

She opened it and found a number scrawled at the top.

My dear Scholar,

Here's my cell phone number. If you're alone any time at night and wish to see me, call and I will come.

And remember—with love, anything is possible.

She sighed. If only that were true.

She was falling in love with him. But it was still impossible.

Chapter Eighteen

$\mathcal{T}$he next evening, Abigail headed upstairs to the family floor so she could check on her mother. She and her sister had flown back to D.C. that morning, and she'd spent the rest of the day at the lab, gathering information for the meeting tonight with her father. And Gregori.

By George, that man can kiss. Prunella Culpepper had been right about that. She'd hardly slept a wink last night. Memories of kissing Gregori had filled her mind, and she'd relived the scene over and over, treasuring each detail she could recall and eventually imagining what could have happened if they hadn't been interrupted.

She tightened her grip on the handle of her leather portfolio. She'd have to act cool at the meeting with her father. Not stare at Gregori with red-hot cheeks. Her files were inside the portfolio, along with Gregori's note, safely stashed away in a zippered pocket. Could she work up the nerve to call him? She would need to be alone to do it. She couldn't let a Secret Service agent overhear her flirting with a vampire.

She hadn't found a moment alone since sunset.
She'd worked late at the lab with some other scientists.
An agent had picked her up and delivered her to the
White House. Even now, as she made her way to the
clinic, there were Black Suits stationed here and there,
always watching. Always on alert for danger. And no
doubt they considered Gregori a danger.

She knew she should keep a distance from him. It
was the smart thing to do, and all her life, she'd always
done the smart thing. But it was already too late. She'd
stepped off a cliff and didn't know how to stop the fall.
Wasn't sure she even wanted to stop.

Falling for Gregori was a crazy, irresponsible act. Totally out of character for her. And totally exciting. How
strange that it took an Undead man to make her feel
so alive.

She nodded at the female agent who stood by the
clinic door. Inside, she could hear laughter—her mother's and Madison's.

She slipped inside. "Hello."

"Abigail!" Her mother waved her over. "We were just
watching Madison's commercial. Come and see it."

"She already saw it live." Madison reached for the
remote control. "But if you'd like to see it again?"

"Sure. I'd love to." Abigail hugged her mom and
quickly looked her over. She looked tired with dark
circles under her eyes. "Is Debra gone for the evening?"

"She's on her dinner break," Belinda said. She
leaned close and whispered, "We're not supposed to
talk about vampires when she's here. Top secret, you
know."

Abigail nodded, noting the twinkle in her mother's

eyes. All the recent excitement seemed to be invigorating her mother. Her sister, too. Madison had chattered nonstop all the way home about her new friends at the Digital Vampire Network. Maggie had given her a DVD of the pretend commercial she'd done with Phineas.

"It's starting!" Madison hushed them.

Abigail sat and watched her sister and Phineas. "It's really good." Thank God Maggie hadn't included the commercial she'd done with Gregori.

Belinda clapped her hands. "I love it. I'm so proud of you, Madison."

"And guess what?" Madison jumped to her feet, grinning. "Last night I auditioned for a mortal role on one of their soap operas. They usually have vampires play those roles because mortals don't know about DVN, but Gordon—he's the director—he said it doesn't work very well 'cause everyone can tell they have fangs. So there's a good chance that I could get on one of their shows and be a real actress!"

"Wow." Abigail glanced over at their mom, who looked more alarmed than happy. "That's really exciting, Maddie."

"I know!" Madison clasped her hands together with a dreamy look. "I could be a real star."

"I thought you said the commercial was pretend, just for fun," Belinda said. "I didn't realize you were serious about acting."

"I didn't realize I'd be so good!" Madison exclaimed.

"But what about art school?" Belinda asked.

Madison waved a dismissive hand. "I'm only going there 'cause I didn't know what to do with myself. I'm not all that good at art, you know. But Maggie said I show real potential for acting. And Gordon said I look fabulous in front of the camera."

"Yes, dear, you do," Belinda conceded, "but this is a *vampire* network."

Madison blinked. "So?"

Abigail winced inwardly with a sinking feeling.

"I'm delighted you were able to discover a new talent," Belinda continued. "But you need to develop it among your own kind. DVN is not the sort of environment you should be visiting every night."

Madison looked stunned. "Why not?"

"All this excitement lately over vampires—it's been great fun, but . . ." Belinda sighed. "It's a nice world to visit, but you don't want to live there."

Madison frowned. "You have something against vampires?"

"I'm sure some of them are very nice, but—let's be honest about this, Maddie. They're dead. I don't want you to get involved with any of them."

"But I wouldn't," Madison insisted. "I'm not attracted to any of them." Her gaze shifted to Abigail.

Please don't say anything, Abigail beseeched her with her eyes.

Madison's frown deepened. "I don't understand, Mom. It's not like you to be so . . . prejudiced."

"I don't mean to be rude. I just don't want you to form a relationship with any of them. Think about it. They can live for centuries, right? They would either tire of you after a few years, or they would insist on making you a vampire. How can I possibly condone that?"

Madison bit her lip and glanced at Abigail. "Some might think it's romantic."

Belinda scoffed. "Only in fiction. In reality, he would be killing you."

Abigail swallowed hard. Her mom was bringing up valid points. Even she had warned Madison several nights ago that falling for a vampire was sheer folly.

It was like that old saying her grandmother used to joke about. If you're going to fall in love, it might as well be with a rich man. And if she was going to fall in love, why couldn't she find a *live* man?

Her shoulders slumped. She needed to admit the truth. A relationship with Gregori was truly impossible. But how could she possibly find anyone as wonderful as him? He was everything she'd ever dreamed of. Except for the vampire part.

Madison stuck out her bottom lip. "I thought you would be happy for me. I really want the job at DVN."

Belinda sighed. "It would worry me too much for you to be around vampires."

Madison huffed. "But Abby's going to be around them when she goes to China!"

Abigail jerked up in her seat and shook her head.

"*What?*" Belinda gave her a shocked look. "You're doing what?"

Madison winced. "Sorry, Abby. I thought she knew."

Abigail shot her an annoyed look, then turned to her mother. "It's a research trip, that's all. Just a few days."

Belinda's eyes narrowed. "Is your research connected to me?"

"It'll be fine, Mom. The Vamps will only be there to

protect me. They're super strong and fast. They have special abilities like superheroes."

"Yeah!" Madison nodded. "It'll be like traveling with Superman and the Justice League!"

Belinda frowned. "I don't think you should go."

"Mom—" Abigail started to say she was doing it for her, but that would only make her mother more opposed to the trip. "I need to do this."

Belinda's eyes shimmered with tears. "Sweetie, my health is *my* problem. You can't take responsibility for everything."

Abigail blinked to keep her eyes from misting up. "How can I live with myself if I don't try everything I can do?"

A knock sounded at the door, and the Secret Service agent cracked it open. "The meeting has started in the Oval Office. The president requests Miss Abigail's attendance."

"I'll be right there." She stood and picked up her portfolio. "It'll be fine, Mom."

Her mother sighed wearily. "I hope so."

She waved at Madison as she crossed the room. "See you later."

"Good luck." Madison eased up close to her and lowered her voice. "With *everything*."

Was she referring to Gregori? "Thank you." *Thank you for not mentioning him to Mom.*

With a smile, Madison patted her on the shoulder. "You've always worked so hard. You deserve to be happy."

So Madison approved? Abigail nodded and left the room.

Sure, she wanted to be happy, but could happiness be found with a vampire? She'd certainly felt happy in Gregori's arms last night, but what if that sensation proved to be fleeting? Could her happiness endure if it made her parents unhappy? What if her mother was right and Gregori's attraction to her faded away as she grew older? What if he expected her to become a vampire, too?

She shuddered. Kissing Gregori was one thing, but getting involved to the point that he'd want her to become a vampire, too—that was really frightening.

She should stop this now before she fell totally, irreversibly in love. Stop falling in love? A chill prickled the back of her neck.

It might already be too late.

Gregori stood when Abigail entered the Oval Office. His chest tightened, and he fought an urge to pull her into his arms. She was wearing a lab coat as if she'd just come from work, and she had a leather portfolio gripped in one hand.

"Good evening." He kept his face blank.

She glanced at him and nodded. "Gregori." She smiled slightly at her father and the CIA director, Nick Caprese. "I hope I didn't miss anything important."

"We're just getting started." Her father motioned to the couches, then sat in the chair at the head of the coffee table.

Gregori sat to the president's right and set his folder on the coffee table. Abigail took a seat on the couch across from him, next to Caprese. She must be trying to keep a distance from him. Hopefully that only signified she was trying to keep their relationship a secret. He didn't want to consider that she might be having second thoughts.

She laid her portfolio on the couch beside her, then shifted her gaze straight to her father.

"Gregori teleported straight to this office from New York," the president told her. "Very impressive. And he tells me you practiced teleporting with him last night and did extremely well."

She nodded. "Yes."

She was purposely trying not to look at him, Gregori thought. "I was just telling the president and Mr. Caprese about MacKay Security and Investigation."

"And I verified with the British prime minister that they have a good working relationship with Angus MacKay and his employees," Caprese said.

"Excellent." The president turned to Gregori. "So you were about to tell us about a plan you developed with Mr. MacKay?"

"Yes." Gregori opened his folder. "Angus and I selected the members for the team last night. We're calling it the A-Team. A for Abigail."

Her father smiled. "I like it."

Gregori glanced at Abigail. She was focused on his folder, her cheeks slightly flushed.

He picked up the paper on top. "This is a brief bio and photo for the team captain, J.L. Wang. He speaks fluent Mandarin and can blend in among the locals. He's been a vampire for two years. Before that, he was a FBI special agent stationed in Kansas City. For the past year, he's been head of security for the West Coast Coven, headquartered in San Francisco."

"Sounds good." The president scanned J.L.'s profile, then passed it on to Caprese, who glanced at it, then set it on the coffee table.

Abigail slid the paper closer to her so she could see it.

Gregori picked up the next profile. "The second vampire on the team is Russell Ryan Hankelburg. He was a major in the Marine Corps during the Vietnam War. He's an expert in weaponry and survival techniques."

The president looked over his profile. "He was declared MIA in 1971. What happened to him?"

"He was discovered by some MacKay employees a year ago in a cave in northern Thailand," Gregori said. "We believe he was in a coma for thirty-nine years. Angus managed to revive him by transforming him. The minute he heard about this mission, he volunteered. He's eager to serve his country once again."

"Admirable." The president handed the profile to Caprese.

"So not only did he wake up Undead, but he lost thirty-nine years of his life?" Abigail asked. "That must have been traumatic."

Gregori shrugged. "He's a Marine. From what I hear, he adjusted quickly to all his new vampire capabilities."

Caprese scanned his profile, then set it on the table. "These two men appear to be excellent choices. I'll have to vet them, of course."

"Of course. As vampires, we won't be able to do much during the day." Gregori refrained from saying they were actually dead. It was a vulnerability they didn't want the government to know about. "We don't want to leave Abigail unprotected while we sleep, so we're bringing a few day guards."

He lifted the next profile. "This is Howard Barr. He was a defensive lineman for the Chicago Bears."

President Tucker took the paper and frowned. "I can see why you might need some humans, but why not take Josh and Charles?" He motioned to Charles, who stood by the door.

"Or some operatives from the Agency," Caprese offered. "They have experience in this sort of mission."

"Yes, but they're not going to have abilities like our day guards."

Caprese snorted. "I say we go with a few of my men. It'll show that you Vamps are willing to work with us."

Gregori winced. "I'm afraid we have to insist on our own guys."

"Why?" Caprese sat back. "What's so special about them? Do they crap golden eggs?"

"Something like that," Gregori muttered. He and Angus had debated this for an hour. The shifters expected the Vamps to keep their secret. But if Abigail traveled with them, she'd have to know. And if she knew, then her father should know. If he found out after the trip was over, he'd be understandably angry that they had withheld the information.

Gregori leaned forward, resting his forearms on his knees. "The information I'm about to tell you is top secret even in the vampire world. I'd like your word that it never leaves this room."

The president and CIA director exchanged looks, then nodded.

"There is another group of . . . people, supernatural like vampires, but different. They wish to remain secret for obvious reasons. I need your word that you will never attempt to hunt them down or harm them. They have trusted us to keep their secret, and it would be dishonorable for us to betray them in any way."

"You have my word," President Tucker said, then gave Caprese a pointed look. "If you can't keep a secret, leave the room now."

Caprese arched a brow. "I was quiet about vampires for six years. I can keep my mouth shut."

"All right, then." Gregori glanced at Abigail, whose face had turned pale. "Howard is a shifter." When he was met with blank looks, he explained further. "A shape shifter. He changes form at will."

She gasped. "You mean like a werewolf?"

"The majority of shifters are werewolves," Gregori admitted.

Caprese scoffed. "I don't believe it."

Abigail shook her head. "I don't see how it's physically possible."

Gregori gave her a pointed look. "There are a lot of things that can be possible." *Like a relationship with me.* Her cheeks blushed, so he assumed she'd understood his point. "If you need proof, I could bring Howard here and let him shift. He might rip the sofas in two, but—"

"Wait." The president lifted a hand. "If he turns into a beast, will my daughter be safe?"

"Yes." Gregori nodded. "He has complete control. And even in human form, he has super strength and speed and heightened senses. He can protect Abigail better than any human."

"He's a werewolf?" she asked him.

"Actually, he's a were-bear. A Kodiak bear. Nobody's going to mess with Howard."

She stared at him with a stunned expression.

"The second day guard is Rajiv." Gregori picked up the last profile.

"Do you know Maxim?" Abigail interrupted.

Gregori blinked. "Who?"

"Maxim. He's a werewolf."

The president stiffened. "Abby! You know a werewolf?"

"No! He's the hero in Mom's book . . . but I guess he's not real." Her face flushed. "Sorry. I hardly know what's real anymore."

Gregori refrained from smiling.

The president's face softened as he regarded his daughter. "I understand how you feel, sweetie. We've had a lot thrown at us these last few nights." He took a deep breath and exhaled. "Werewolves and were-bears—who would ever believe this?"

"You can add were-tigers to the list." Gregori passed him the last profile.

Abigail gasped. *"Tigers?"*

Gregori chuckled. "Wolves, tigers, and bears, oh my!"

When the others continued to stare at him with stunned expressions, he cleared his throat and assumed a serious expression. "Rajiv has been working for MacKay S and I for a year. His tribe is from Thailand, but they originated in the Yunnan province. Came down the Mekong River, and then settled in northern Thailand. Apparently the were-tigers like to have a set territory for each tribe, and they ran out of room in Yunnan. The good news is Rajiv has relatives there, and he knows one of their local dialects."

"And he shifts into a tiger?" President Tucker passed the profile to Caprese.

"Yes. He can shift at will." Gregori closed his now-empty folder. "I'll be going, too. And Abigail. So you have the six members the A-Team."

"Why only two day guards?" Caprese asked.

"We'll be teleporting around," Gregori explained. "Three vampires means we can safely transport only three—Abigail plus the two shifters."

Caprese gathered the profiles together in a stack. "I'll let you know if I approve of these . . . men."

Gregori gave him a wry look. "Try to do it within a few hours. The *men* are already in San Francisco. As soon as the sun sets in Hawaii, they'll teleport there. Then they'll move on to the MacKay office in Tokyo. In twelve hours they could be in the Yunnan province setting things up."

Abigail sat up with an alarmed look. "They're leaving without me?"

"You and I will follow as soon as everything is ready," Gregori said. "The other four will establish bases around the province. Since the terrain is fairly mountainous, they'll be looking for caves or abandoned buildings away from populated areas. They'll set up beacons in these bases that only Vamps and shifters can hear. We use the beacons to know exactly where to teleport. And each base will be stocked with supplies: food, water, synthetic blood, sleeping bags, and so forth. I'm afraid we'll be roughing it."

She nodded. "I was expecting that."

Gregori shifted to face the president. "The plan is this—careful and thorough preparation, everything set up, and then when it's time to take Abigail in, we do a quick strike. Get her in and out as fast as possible. Two or three nights at the most. No one will ever know she was there."

The president smiled. "I like it."

"Laurence," Caprese said, "I hope you realize the ramifications if your daughter is discovered. The Chinese could hold her prisoner, claiming she's a spy."

"I'm counting on the Vamps being able to teleport her out at the first sign of trouble," the president replied.

"What if the Chinese realize she's stolen some of their plants for research?" Caprese asked. "She could be in serious trouble, and your career would be over."

"If I can save my wife, I don't give a damn what people think of me," President Tucker said. "I'm on my second term, so my career's over anyway."

"If I discover something useful with one of the plants," Abigail said, "I'll find a way to synthesize it so we won't have to go back. We should only have to go once."

"Exactly," her father agreed. "What's important right now is managing Abby's trip without putting her in any danger." He turned to Gregori. "I'm counting on you guys for that. Don't let me down."

Gregori nodded. Personally, he didn't know how he could live with himself if something happened to Abigail. And if something bad did happen and the president blamed the Vamps, then they could all be in serious trouble.

He adjusted his tie. "If Abigail can give us some information on the plants, we'll do our best to locate them ahead of time. Then we'll take her in, grab them, and leave."

She removed a short stack of papers from her portfolio. "I have the information here."

"Great." Gregori smiled at her, then turned back to her father. "Our first priority is your daughter's safety. That's why we're trying to minimize the time she'll be in China. But it would be seriously remiss of me if I didn't suggest letting our men take care of the entire mission. With enough information, we should be able to find the plants she wants."

She gasped. "You would go without me?"

Gregori winced inwardly at the shocked and injured look on her face. "I'm sorry, but it's something we should consider."

She pressed a hand to her mouth, then to her chest. "I can't believe this. You know how important this is to me."

Her father gave her a sympathetic look. "He has a valid point, Abby. The best way to protect you is to keep you safe here."

Her eyes glistened with tears. "There's more to life than always being *safe*." She glanced at the Secret Service man. "Everywhere I go, everything I do, I'm watched so I'll be safe. We've had bodyguards since you first entered Congress. It's been going on for fifteen years!"

"It's all right," the president said gently. "I'm sure they can locate the plants without you."

"No!" She shook her head, and tears tumbled down her cheeks. "Don't tell me I can't do this! I'm always being told what I can't do. You can't wear that. It doesn't look classy enough. You can't have those friends. They're not prestigious enough. Don't frown like that. You can't look unhappy in public. Don't say anything in front of the media. They might print it. I had to go into hiding to get a life!"

Gregori sat back, stunned. He squeezed his hands into fists to keep from reaching out to her. He glanced at her father. President Tucker looked equally stunned.

"Abby," her father whispered. "I—I didn't know . . ."

"Oh God." She wiped her cheeks. "I'm sorry. I didn't mean to . . ." She stuffed her papers back into the portfolio, her hands shaking. "I'm going on the trip. I won't share my information until you agree." She rushed toward the door and stopped in front of Charles. "I want to leave."

The Secret Service man glanced at the president, who nodded, then he opened the door and Abigail ran out.

President Tucker slumped in his chair, rubbing his forehead. "I didn't realize my career was so hard on her. She never complained. Not once."

Gregori shifted on the couch. The CIA director was just sitting there with a blank face. Charles was expressionless as usual. "Sir, I've only known your daughter a few days, but I can tell she loves her family very much. She would do anything for you."

The president nodded with tears in his eyes. "She's so brave. So smart." He leaned forward suddenly and grasped Gregori's shoulder. "Give me your word you won't let anything happen to her."

He gazed into the president's eyes. They were hazel like Abigail's. "You have my word. I'll defend her with my life."

The president watched him closely, then nodded. "Good." He sat back and took a deep breath. "You were right to suggest she stay here. It occurred to me, too. But you can see how strongly she feels."

Gregori nodded. "Yes, sir."

"She's very passionate about this mission. She hopes it will save her mother. I have the same hope, or I would never put her at such risk."

Gregori rose to his feet. "Then it's settled. We'll take her." And God help them if anything happened to her.

Chapter Nineteen

*A*bigail slammed the safe door shut and twirled the combination lock. She'd tossed all her plant information inside. It was her personal safe at the lab, and only she knew the combination. Of course, the info was also on her computer, but no one could access it without a password. If Dad sent Gregori and his buddies to China without her, they wouldn't know what to look for.

She groaned. This act of rebellion could condemn the mission to failure. And condemn her mother.

Tears burned her eyes. The trip had been her idea, dammit. How could they decide she shouldn't be allowed to go?

She'd been afraid this would happen. Her whole life had revolved around two lists—what was allowed, and what wasn't allowed, and the second list had always been ten times longer than the first.

She paced across the lab, still angry. Still hurt. Still mortified. She'd completely lost it. Years of frustration and resentment had erupted all at once.

She'd been too upset to remain at the White House. Her poor father had looked so shocked. And hurt. He'd worked so hard over the years, and she was proud of him. It wasn't his fault she'd never adjusted to public life. Madison and Lincoln thrived on it. Even Mom had loved it before she became ill.

She couldn't face her mother, either. She sure didn't want to hear another lecture about keeping away from vampires. One more item to add to the not-allowed list. Good Lord, her parents would have a fit if they knew she'd kissed Gregori. They'd want to kill him.

They'd have to wait their turn. She was ready to clobber him herself. How could he kiss her one night, then betray her the next? She'd thought he was on her side.

Her mother didn't want her to go to China. Her father had originally rejected her request. He was only going along with it now because he thought the Vamps could sneak her in undetected and keep her safe. It was bad enough to have both parents opposed to the idea, but then Gregori had to join in?

She strode to her desk to boot up her computer, then changed her mind. She was too upset to work. The stress ball from Gregori sat on her desk, mocking her. How dare he betray her! She grabbed the ball and gave it a squeeze.

"*Et tu, Brute?*" She tossed it back onto her desk and strode to the black-topped table where she'd started examining the plant he had given her. No, she couldn't concentrate right now.

She paced across the laboratory. It was small, but it was all hers. She stopped by the window and looked out. The parking lot was mostly empty, but the soldiers were still at the entrance gate. She spotted another soldier walking along the perimeter of the chain-link fence topped with barbed wire. The grounds were well lit and dotted with security cameras. And there were more military personnel in the lobby. The installation was so well guarded, she didn't need a Secret Service agent here. They dropped her off and returned to the White House.

With a sigh, she closed the blinds. She didn't want to see the soldiers, see the proof that she merely moved from one prison to another. The room was dim now, the only light coming from the lamp on her desk. She wandered over to the long, black lab table. The epoxy resin surface was cool to the touch and bare right now except for her microscope and the plant at the end of the table. She'd cleared away all her work in anticipation of her trip to China.

How could Gregori recommend she not go? Didn't he understand how important this trip was to her? She ought to give him a piece of her mind. Vent, then maybe she could relax.

She paced over to her desk, then dug his note out of her portfolio.

"Feel my wrath," she muttered as she punched in the number.

He picked up the call right after the first ring.

"I am so angry with—"

"Where are you?" he interrupted.

She huffed. How dare he not even let her finish a sentence! "I'm at work because I'm too upset to sleep. But I'm too upset to work, so I—"

"Are you alone?"

"Of course I'm alone. I can't chew you out in front of

an audience. I'm so angry that you could kiss me one night and betray me the next! You know how important this trip is to me!"

"Yes, I do."

She glanced at her cell phone. It didn't seem to be working right. "Did I mention how angry I am? Feel my wrath, Gori!"

"I'll feel yours if you feel mine."

She gasped. "Pig!" She disconnected, then heard a chuckling sound behind her. She whirled around and gasped again. The phone tumbled from her hand.

Gregori lunged forward in a blur of movement and snatched the phone before it hit the ground.

She stumbled back. His speed had been amazing, but she was not in the mood to compliment him. "Did I give you permission to come here?"

"I don't ask for permission, remember?" He set her phone on her desk, then looked around. "So this is where you work?"

"What are you doing here? I don't want to see you. I'm still mad at you!"

A knock sounded at her door, and her heart lurched up her throat. How on earth could she explain Gregori's presence here when he'd bypassed all the checkpoints? She dashed to the door to make sure it was locked. "Yes?"

"Miss Tucker?" A guard called from the hallway. "Are you all right? I thought I heard yelling inside."

"I'm fine! I was just talking on the phone."

There was a pause.

She glanced over her shoulder, hoping that Gregori had teleported away. But no, he was still there.

"If you need anything, just call us on the intercom," the soldier said.

"All right. Thank you!" She listened to his footsteps fade away, then she peeked through the closed slats on the blinds that covered the window portion of her door. "Okay, the coast is clear."

"I guess you're not too angry," Gregori said softly. "You didn't turn me in."

She spun around to face him. "You know good and well I can't explain how you got here. And I'm not finished being angry with you."

"I know you're upset. It nearly killed me to see you crying. And it hurts to think about how much you've been suffering over the—"

"Please!" She held up her hands. "I don't want to talk about it. I'm mortified that I . . ." She pressed her hands against her hot cheeks. "I said terrible things."

"You spoke the truth."

She shook her head. "It was a pity party. My parents have always been good to me. I've never lacked for anything—"

"Except freedom."

She winced. "Well, we have to learn to live with the hand we're dealt."

His mouth thinned. "True."

So she lived without freedom and he lived without mortality. "You hurt me. I'm still in shock that you would betray me."

"I did not."

"Yes, you did! My mother doesn't want me to go to China. My dad is this close"—she lifted a hand with her forefinger and thumb pressed together—"to forbidding me to go. He's only allowing it because he trusts you to keep me safe. And what do you do? Tell him I'm safer at home!"

"You *are* safer at home."

She scoffed. "Why don't you want me to go? You don't want me to have any adventure in my life? Afraid I'll have some fun?"

He arched a brow. "I'd love to have some fun with you."

"Not funny. I'm still angry with you."

"I hear makeup sex is really hot."

"Good Lord, is that all you think about?" She waved a hand. "Don't even bother to answer that. But do me a favor and try to get past your overabundance of testosterone to understand that I'm trying to save my mother's life."

His eyes narrowed. "Try to get past your PMS to understand why I said what I did."

"How dare you bring up PMS!"

"My testosterone made me do it. Now why would a caveman like me suggest you remain safely at home?"

"Good question."

"And I've got a good answer." He stepped toward her. "I don't want you in a dangerous situation because I care about you."

She blinked. Then swallowed hard.

"I can't bear the thought of anything bad happening to you." He yanked the knot of his tie loose. "I think about you all the time. And not just about sex." He grimaced. "It's downright . . . strange."

Her heart squeezed in her chest. Was the poor womanizer in over his head? "You . . . care about me?"

"I care a hell of a lot." He gave her an exasperated look. "Couldn't you tell while I was kissing you?"

Heat rushed to her cheeks. "Well, it was certainly . . . passionate. But there is an obvious reason for that. You have a lot of experience, so it was simply indicative of a high level of expertise—" She stopped when he placed a finger on her lips.

"Scholar."

"Yes?" she whispered against the pad of his finger.

"Think about it." He leaned close. "The kiss was passionate because I'm falling in love with you."

Her heart lurched, and she stepped back. "That—that's highly unlikely. We've known each other only a few nights."

"I started falling the minute I saw you on that balcony."

She gulped. She'd started falling the minute she saw him emerge from that limo. "Well, I have to admit that instant attraction is rather . . . instant."

The corner of his mouth curled up, and his dimple showed. "You ran into my arms last night. You kissed me back. Rather passionately, I might add."

Her cheeks blazed with heat. "That was last night. Tonight I'm angry."

"You're beautiful when you're angry."

"Don't think I can be swayed with flattery. The only reason I'm not screaming at you is because the guards would hear. I'm sorely tempted to slap that smile right off your face, but luckily for you, I'm exercising a great deal of self-control."

"I see." He nodded, his cheeks dimpling. "Then

you'll be able to refrain from screaming when I bring you to climax?"

Her mouth dropped open. "*What?*"

He winced. "That was a little loud. I'm not sure you can keep from screaming—"

"I don't scream!" She scoffed. "I never scream."

"Then you've been with the wrong men."

Goose bumps skittered down her arms. "And you believe you are the right one?"

"I know it." He stepped toward her. "Your scream-less nights are over."

Her heart thumped. "My, aren't we sure of ourselves."

"Must be an overabundance of testosterone."

She snorted. "Well, I'm not a pushover, you know. It's not easy to get me into the sack."

"We could always try the ceiling."

She laughed. When he grinned, she realized what he'd been up to. "You're just teasing me, aren't you? So I won't be mad at you anymore."

"Maybe. Maybe not." He slipped a hand around her waist. "Are you still mad at me?"

"I'm . . . recovering."

"I've always wanted to do this." He grasped the top button on her coat and gave it a twirl. "Laszlo gets such a kick out of doing this."

"Really?" She tilted her head. "Well?"

He shrugged. "Not much fun. Got anything else I can play with?"

She snorted. "You never give up, do you?"

"Not until I make you scream." He dragged his hand

up to her neck, and she shivered. "Your skin is turning pink, your lips a dark, rich red."

She glanced at his eyes, and they were starting to glow. It was a heady feeling, knowing that she affected him so strongly. It made her heart race wildly. And her thighs squeeze together.

Desire swept over her, pulling her under like a drug. She'd never wanted someone this badly before. It wasn't like her to be so . . . mindless with passion.

Mindless? She shivered when he kissed her right below the ear. "Gregori?"

"Hmm?" He nuzzled her neck.

"You would never mess with my mind, right?"

He pulled back with a wary look. "What?"

"It's just that . . . I've never fallen for someone so fast before. It's not . . . normal for me."

"You think I'm *making* you like me?" He released her and stepped back. "I would have to force it on you? I'm not . . . likable on my own?"

She winced. "I didn't mean that. You're very likable. And charming. And more handsome than any man should be allowed to be."

His mouth twitched. "Okay. I'm buying that part. But you still think I'm making you fall for me?"

She frowned. If he was controlling her mind, then most probably she wouldn't have the ability to question it. "I'm sorry. I shouldn't have asked that."

He gave her a wry look. "If I was controlling you, we would be naked."

She laughed. "That's true. Forget I said it. I'm sure you would never mess with my mind."

A pained look flitted over his face.

She sighed. She'd really destroyed the mood now.

Her cell phone rang.

"Don't answer it," he grumbled.

"But it might be news about the trip."

"I want to be the one to tell you." He took her hand. "You're going. It scares the hell out of me. Scares your dad, too. But you're going."

Joy and relief burst inside her. "Oh, thank you!" She wrapped her arms around his neck.

He held her tight, and she ignored the ringing cell phone. It felt so right in Gregori's arms. She nestled her head against his chest and listened to the pounding of his heart. If it wasn't for the fangs and the red, glowing eyes, she'd never know he was a vampire. And she was actually starting to like the red, glowing eyes. It made her feel powerful and womanly that she could cause his eyes to change.

Powerful and womanly—those were new feelings for her. She liked it. His super powers were exciting, too. Sex on the ceiling?

"All you need to bring is a backpack with a few clothes and personal items," he said. "We'll take care of the rest."

She smiled to herself. For once, she'd been thinking about sex and he hadn't. "Oh! You need the information on the plants." She hurried over to the safe. "I pinpointed the two most likely areas for finding them."

"That's good." He joined her by the safe. "Then we only need two base camps."

Just as she handed him the information, the phone on her desk rang.

He frowned. "They won't leave you alone."

"If I don't answer it, the guards will come to check on me." She picked up the receiver. "Hello?"

"Abby?" Her father's voice sounded agitated. "What are you doing at work so late? Why aren't you answering your cell phone?"

"Well, I—"

"I've sent Charles to pick you up. Your . . . your mother has taken a turn for the worse. The doctor is with her now. We may have to take her to the hospital."

Abigail swayed, and Gregori caught her. "I-I'll be there soon."

Her father hung up, and an icy cold wave shuddered through her.

Gregori took the receiver from her hand and hung up. "I could teleport you home in a second."

She shook her head. "They would know you were here." She touched his chest. "Send the men into China tonight. We need to leave as soon as possible."

Chapter Twenty

*W*hen Gregori returned to Romatech, he learned from Sean Whelan that the CIA director and president had approved of their A-Team. The two Vamps, J.L. and Russell, had already teleported the two shifters to San Francisco. Angus called to tell them to proceed with the plan.

The guys would teleport to Hawaii, then on to Tokyo. From there, they would call Rajiv's grandfather in the Yunnan province and use his voice as a beacon so they could safely teleport into the province. The grandfather's tribe of were-tigers lived along the Mekong River, and they had agreed to help the team find bases that would be safe for the Vamps during the day.

Once the two bases were established, they would teleport supplies in from Tokyo, and Gregori would start the process of teleporting Abigail west. Angus and Robby intended to go with them as far as Tokyo. Along with Japanese operative Kyo, they would remain on standby in case something went wrong with the A-Team.

In the security office at Romatech, Gregori, Emma,

and Angus looked over Abigail's notes to determine the areas she wanted to check. The first was the eastern plateau region known for its many lakes and karsts, odd stone formations that resembled a forest of stalagmites. The second area was in the northwest, closer to Tibet. It was rugged and mountainous with rivers rushing through deep canyons.

Abigail was hoping to find an ancient plant along the Yangtze River. It would be a rough area for hiking, but they were more likely to find a cave there for their base.

Angus e-mailed the information to Kyo in Japan. "That's all we can do for now."

Gregori nodded. "If we're lucky, we can spend one night at each base, and only be in China two nights."

"We'll expect you to check in with us in Tokyo every two hours," Angus said. "If we don't hear from you, we'll come looking for you."

"Good." Gregori stood and stretched. "I'll go to my office then. Get some work done." And hope that Abigail would call. She'd promised to let him know how her mother was doing.

Emma smiled at him. "Your mother told me that Miss Tucker was the one."

He groaned. "My mother talks too much."

Emma exchanged an amused glance with her husband.

"Are ye saying she isna the one?" Angus asked.

"I'm saying it's not easy." Gregori headed toward the door to make an escape. "The president isn't going to accept a vampire son-in-law."

"Ah." Emma's eyes lit up. "So you're considering marriage?"

Gregori gulped. "I didn't say that. I—I was speaking theoretically."

Angus grunted. "Well, lad, if she's good enough to bed, then she should be good enough to wed. Theoretically speaking, of course."

Gregori reached into his coat pocket and squeezed a stress ball. "Abigail and I are modern people. We're not tied to old-fashioned ideas of—"

"Och, I see. Ye're a generous soul, so ye plan to share her with other men."

"What?" The ball exploded in his pocket. "Shit." Now his coat pocket was full of baking soda.

Emma and Angus chuckled.

"Yeah, very funny." He stalked to his office. Tossed the exploded stress ball into the trash can. There was no message on his phone. He had Abigail's number now, since she'd phoned him earlier, so he called. No answer, so he left a short voice message. *Call me.*

He worked for an hour. Still no phone call. He teleported to his condo, showered, then threw on some jeans and a T-shirt. No call, no message. He sprawled on the sofa to watch DVN and guzzled a warm bottle of blood.

His Droid buzzed. Finally a text message from Abigail: *My mom is stable now, still at home. It's late, so going to bed. Good night.*

He called her number, but she didn't pick up. He texted her: *Answer your phone.*

She texted back: *No.*

Then call me.

No. You'll teleport to my bedroom.

He smiled. She was on to him. *Chicken!*

Bawk!

He drummed his fingers on the Droid, trying to come up with a reply that would make her call. *I have a stress ball that needs to be squeezed.* He winced and deleted that.

He'd teleported to the Oval Office before, so he could get fairly close to her. He texted: *I'm teleporting to the West Wing. Will search the White House until I find you.*

The phone rang.

"Bingo." He answered it.

"You can't wander around the White House," she fussed at him. "You'll get yourself arrested—"

He focused on her voice and teleported.

"—and then we'll never make it to China. And—" She jumped when he appeared next to her bed. "You rascal, I knew you'd do that."

He grinned as he turned his phone off, then stuffed it into a front pocket of his jeans. She was sitting against a blue tufted headboard on a queen-sized bed, glaring at him.

"You should leave." She set her phone on the bed-side table.

"But I just got here." And she looked so sweet with her damp curls and freshly scrubbed face and old-fashioned pajamas. Good God, how he'd love to peel those off. Before his eyes could turn red, he shifted his gaze to look around her room. "Very nice."

"Thank you. You can go now." She dragged the blue comforter up to her chin.

"Smart move. Those pajamas with little coffee cups on them are way too sexy. I can hardly restrain myself."

She smiled and shook her head. "I don't own any sexy lingerie."

"That's amazing." He sat on the edge of her bed. "Neither do I."

She laughed.

"See how much we have in common?"

She kicked at him from under the covers. "It's late, Gregori. After three in the morning."

"But a good Vamp can go all night long."

She nudged him again. "I've been up for twenty-two hours. I want to sleep."

"No problem." He stood and turned off the lamp on her bedside table. "Good night, sweetheart." He could still see well in the dark, and he grinned at the way she squinted her eyes to follow his movements.

"You're not leaving?" she asked. "What are you doing?"

He arrived at the other side of her bed and pulled back the sheet. "You wanted to sleep." He climbed in.

She gasped. "Not with you!"

He fluffed up his pillow. "You might as well get used to it. You'll be sleeping with me on the trip."

"I will not."

"You want to sleep with the other guys?" He lay down beside her. "I'll have to beat them up then. Not really good for team spirit, but—"

"You can't sleep in my bed!"

"Relax. I won't bite."

She snorted. "Gregori, you're in the White House. You don't sneak into a girl's bed in the White House!"

He glanced at the door. "Is it locked?"

"Yes, but—"

"Is there a guard at the door?"

She shook her head. "Down the hall by the stairs."

"Then we should be fine." He turned onto his side to face her and smiled. "As long as you don't scream."

She scoffed. "I'm going to sleep."

"I won't stop you."

She gave him a wary look. "Then why are you here?"

Why *was* he here? He'd never climbed into a girl's bed before just to talk. "I missed you. I wanted to know how you were doing."

She scooted down into a lying position. "I'm tired. Worried about my mom."

"How is she?"

"Stable. But not good. They may take her to the hospital tomorrow if she doesn't improve."

"I'm sorry." He brushed a curl back from her brow.

She sighed. "I sat with my dad for a few hours by her bedside. He told me how sorry he was that I'd been unhappy."

"He loves you," Gregori whispered.

"I love him, too. I love all my family." She smiled sadly at Gregori. "There are times, though, that I feel like I don't belong. Like an outcast."

"I know the feeling. I'm an outcast, too."

Her eyes widened as she gazed at him. It took all his control not to pull her into his arms.

She rolled onto her back and stared at the ceiling. "We do have a lot in common."

Time stretched out while he tried to think of something incredibly deep and insightful to say. Something that would impress her. "There's something hard in my pants."

She moaned. "Why am I not surprised?"

"Really uncomfortable." He reached down to his jeans to get a hold on it.

"Oh God, don't let it out."

"Got it!" He pulled his hand out and showed her the Droid.

She laughed.

He dropped the phone on the bedside table next to him, then snuggled up close to her.

"What are you doing?"

"We're going to sleep, right?"

"I thought you slept during the day."

"I do." He wrapped his arms around her.

She rested her head against his chest. "You're just going to lie there? Sounds kind of boring."

"Not at all." He stroked her hair. "I get to hold you. Listen to you breathe. Think."

She yawned. "About what?" She closed her eyes.

"Keeping you warm." He tucked the comforter around her. "Keeping you safe." Her breaths deepened, and her body relaxed against him.

He kissed the top of her head. "Keeping you mine."

Half asleep, Abigail reached for Gregori. She couldn't remember ever sleeping so well. She'd loved the feel of his arms around her and the way he'd stroked her hair. She'd felt safe and loved, and now that she wasn't so tired, she was remembering other things. Like how broad and muscular his chest was. How gentle and sweet his hands were. How he made her laugh. Made her hot.

"Gregori," she mumbled and stretched her hand out to feel his hard abs.

Nothing.

She jerked awake and sat up. She was alone. And good Lord, it was almost noon!

Gregori must have teleported away hours ago. She glanced at his pillow. It was still indented where his head had rested. She touched it. How sad that she had to wait till sunset to see him again.

She picked up the pillow and nestled her cheek in the valley. His scent filled her nostrils, and she hugged the pillow against her chest. She was falling fast. She'd been falling for some time, but things were a little different now. Before, she had hoped to somehow stop the feelings before they grew any stronger.

Now she knew there was no stopping it. She wanted him. She wanted years of laughter with him. And all those scream-filled nights he had promised her.

But there were always consequences. Could she actually live with a vampire? How could her parents accept him? What kind of future could she have with him?

With a groan, she tossed the pillow aside. She was tired of always approaching life like a scientist. Why couldn't she just enjoy herself for once?

She dressed and went to see her mom in the clinic. The doctor and Nurse Debra were getting her ready to take to the hospital.

She pulled Debra to the side and whispered, "Is she worse?"

Debra shook her head. "The same, but Doc wants to run some tests."

Abigail sighed. "I'll pack her a bag."

That afternoon, an ambulance took her mother to the hospital. The media was swarming the streets around the White House. Abigail covered her face as she dashed from the South Portico to the waiting limo. Her sister and father joined her, and they followed the ambulance. Her brother, Lincoln, had already been notified, but Dad told him to stay at Harvard since he had final exams coming up. His mom was just having a few routine tests done.

After a few hours of pacing at the hospital and drinking coffee, which only made her more edgy, she was told the first test was done. No results yet, but they could see the first lady.

Abigail's heart stuttered when she saw her mother, looking so pale and worn in the hospital bed. Her father sat on the edge of the bed, holding her hand.

He loved her so much. Abigail could see it in his eyes.

"We'll leave you alone a minute." She dragged her sister into the hall.

Madison frowned at her. "Why'd you do that?"

"I didn't want to cry in front of Mom." Tears stung her eyes. "She and Dad still love each other."

"Well, duh."

Abigail sniffed. "It's so beautiful."

"Yeah." Madison gave her a curious look. "When did you turn into such a mushy romantic?"

Abigail sighed and thought about Gregori holding her in his arms while she slept.

"Oh my God," Madison whispered, her eyes growing wide. "You're in love!"

Abigail started to object, then reconsidered. "You're not going to tell, are you? Dad might refuse to let me go on the trip, and—"

"I won't say anything." Madison grinned. "Has he tried to bite you?"

"No, of course not."

"Oh." Madison looked disappointed. "I'd let a vampire bite me."

Abigail smiled. "I'm going to go the lab for a few hours. This sitting around being useless doesn't work for me."

"You're lucky," Madison said with a wry look. "It works for me."

An hour later, Abigail was in her lab, printing out photos of the three plants they would search for in Yunnan. The one that looked most promising was in the eastern part of the province. It went by a name roughly translated as the Demon Herb. Ominous-sounding, but it was rumored to have a powerful effect on a person's ability to heal.

As the sun set, her thoughts returned to Gregori. Where had he slept? Was he getting up now? Was he thinking about her?

She turned on the desk lamp, then closed the blinds on the window. Back at her desk, she opened the clear plastic container she'd bought downstairs in the commissary. She took a bite of the turkey sandwich. Tasted like every other sandwich she'd bought at the commissary. She opened her Diet Coke and took a drink.

"Good evening, sweetheart."

She choked and spewed soda onto her lab coat. "Good Lord." She grabbed a napkin to wipe her face and coat. "You should give me a warning when you're about to come."

"Are you referring to sex?" Gregori asked, his eyes twinkling. "I'll remember to do that."

With a smile, she shook her head. "I missed you when I woke up alone." She strode to the door to make sure it was locked.

"I woke up alone, too. It was very sad." He gave her a droopy puppy-dog look.

She was so tempted to kiss him. "It was a dreary day. My mom went to the hospital to have some tests done."

"I'm sorry to hear that."

She nodded. "I don't like feeling useless. I'll be glad when our trip gets under way."

"The guys reported in. They've already set up one base. I think we should start teleporting west tomorrow night."

"Oh." Her heart raced. It was actually happening. She was going to travel to China. With no Black Suits. *Freedom.* She pressed a hand against her chest. "It's been years since I went anywhere without a Secret Service agent following me." Her lab coat was sticky, so she took it off and draped it over the back of her chair.

Gregori yanked his T-shirt over his head and dropped it on the floor.

Her mouth dropped open. "What are you doing?" Her gaze drifted to his bare chest.

"I thought we were undressing."

"I just took off the coat because it was stained." Her

mouth grew dry. What a chest. Broad, muscular, well-defined abs. She grabbed her soda and drank some more.

"There's a stain on your T-shirt, too."

She glanced down at herself, and sure enough, she'd spewed cola on her shirt, too. She set her drink down. If she had the nerve, she'd take off her shirt, too. She looked up to find Gregori watching her intently. His eyes began to darken.

Goose bumps shimmered down her arms. A fluttering sensation started in her belly, then eased down to her womb, where it settled, growing hotter and more tense with desire.

"I want you," he whispered. He held out his hand.

Her heart pounding, she walked toward him, then placed her hand on his.

He gripped her hand and retreated toward the black-topped lab table. When he grasped her around the waist and lifted her, she grabbed on to his shoulders.

He sat her on the table, then planted his hands on the table on either side of her and watched her closely.

Her cheeks grew warm as she smoothed her hands over his shoulders and chest. There was a light sprinkling of curly brown hair above his nipples. Soft and springy. She continued down to the ridges of his abdominal muscles, and she heard him suck in a deep breath.

She glanced up to find his eyes red and glowing. The aching sensation in her womb intensified, and she squeezed her thighs together.

"I'm in love with you," he whispered.

Her heart stuttered, and tears misted her eyes. "Gregori." She cradled his face with her hands. God help her, she loved him, too. She was in love with a vampire.

He grasped her knees and opened her legs. A shudder swept over her, and moisture pooled between her thighs.

He eased between her legs, his hands skimming up her thighs to her hips. "I want you."

"I want you, too."

He yanked her T-shirt off and tossed it aside. Then he pulled her tight and kissed her. Passion broke loose, and she was swept into a whirlwind of sensation. His lips, his tongue, his hands. She tried to keep up, stroking his tongue with hers and raking her hands into his soft hair.

He was delicious, sweet, and desperately hungry for her. Her heart pounded, her skin felt feverishly hot, and she ached with desire. All this—just from kissing him? She might die if he did more.

She might die if he didn't. She groaned and nearly fainted at the raw, husky sound of his answering growl. Her body responded, causing her back to arch and more moisture to slicken her legs.

Before she knew it, her bra was off, and he was lifting her higher so he could kiss her breasts. She wrapped her legs around his waist and moaned as he suckled hard. With his palms on her rump, he pulled her groin tight against him. More moisture seeped from her. More desperation.

"Gregori, please."

He set her on the table. "Lie back."

She stretched out on the black slab as he fumbled with the button and zipper of her jeans. He pulled off her shoes, then whisked off her jeans and underwear.

Her heart thundered as he looked her over with his red glowing eyes.

"You look like a feast." He rested a hand on her tummy, then skimmed it up to cup her breast.

She reached for him. "Gregori."

He smiled and kissed her. "My beautiful Scholar." He trailed kisses down her neck to her breast.

She arched when he drew her nipple into his mouth. She raked her hands into his hair and gasped when he rested a hand on the curls between her legs.

"Oh God." She'd never felt such a desperate level of need before. All modesty fled, and she opened her legs.

He glanced up at her. "No screaming, remember?"

She shook her head. "I've never felt so . . ." She moaned when he parted the folds.

"You're dripping wet."

That made even more moisture seep out. "*Please.*" She planted her feet on the table and pressed against him.

He gently stroked her clitoris. She gasped, struggling to breathe.

He rubbed her faster and faster till she knew he'd gone beyond what was humanly possible. And he was taking her with him, higher and higher.

Her climax ripped through her with such astonishing force, she didn't realize she'd screamed till his hand clapped over her mouth. Dots danced before her eyes, and her body throbbed.

Slowly her heart returned to a steady thud.

"Sorry about that." He took his hand off her mouth and grinned. "You came faster than I expected."

"Huh?" She managed to say.

"You're a screamer." He gathered her up in his arms. "We need to go somewhere private."

"Huh?"

He chuckled. "Trust me."

Everything went black, then she found herself in a strange place. "Huh?"

"This is my condo. Upper West Side."

She looked around the dim apartment as he carried her into a bedroom. "This is your home?"

"Yes." He dropped her onto his bed.

She sat up and gazed around the room. King-sized bed. Moonlight filtering through a window. Gregori kicking off his shoes while he unzipped his jeans.

"This is the infamous bachelor pad?"

He paused and looked at her. "I've never brought a woman here before. You're the one I want, Abby."

Her heart squeezed, and she smiled. "That's good, considering I'm in love with you."

He stared at her a moment, then his eyes glowed red. He dropped his jeans and his underwear.

She scooted back to make room for him. He moved onto the bed, crawling toward her, his red eyes coming closer. Her heart pounded faster. He had to be the sexiest man alive. Or Undead. She no longer cared which. As long as he was hers.

He lifted one of her legs and nipped at her toes. Then he nibbled a trail up her leg to her thigh. "You smell good."

He kissed her swollen and aching folds. "You taste good."

She whimpered as his tongue gently teased her clitoris.

He glanced up and his smile flashed white in the dark. "You can scream all you want here." He dove between her legs, and soon, she did scream.

"Gregori," she panted, reaching for him.

He stretched out over her, then eased his penis just inside. She gasped at the size. And hardness.

Slowly he stretched her out and filled her up.

"Oh God." She wrapped her arms and legs around him.

He rested his brow against hers. "You're the one, Abby. You're mine."

He pulled slowly out, then pushed back in. Again and again. Faster and harder.

He kissed her hard. "You wanted a warning. I'm about to come."

She laughed. "I love you." Her heart expanded till she thought it would burst. So much joy. So much love. And a trace of fear.

For she now believed in the impossible.

Chapter Twenty-one

I'm still not happy about this trip of yours," Belinda said the next evening.

"I'll be fine, Mom," Abigail assured her. "I should be away for only a few days."

Madison perched on the end of the hospital bed in their mother's private room. "It sounds exciting to me. Like super spy stuff with superheroes. I wish I could go."

"We'll be camping inside caves," Abigail muttered.

"You won't have a bathroom?" Madison's eyes widened in horror. "Or a television? How on earth will you survive?"

"I'll be *fine*." Abigail rolled her eyes over to their mom.

Madison looked confused for a second, then nodded enthusiastically. "Oh! That's right. She'll be perfectly fine, Mom. I'll TiVo all the good shows for her. And the Chinese will never catch her."

Belinda groaned and pressed a hand to her mouth.

"Don't worry, sweetheart." Dad patted his wife's shoulder. "Abby will be with the most powerful guards on the planet. And Gregori promised to keep her safe."

"Where is this Gregori?" Belinda motioned to the window. "It went dark an hour ago."

"I'm sure he'll call soon," Abigail said, even though she was wondering the same thing.

After a few hours of lovemaking at his condo, he'd teleported her back to the lab so she could put her clothes back on. She'd checked out at work, letting a Secret Service agent drive her home so everything would appear normal. Then he'd teleported to her bedroom at the White House and they'd had more fun in the shower.

Before leaving, he'd warned her to be packed and ready to go the next evening. Her backpack was now sitting next to the dresser in her mother's hospital room, and she was saying her good-byes.

"Be sure to wear layers," Belinda warned her. "And don't drink the water. Even when you brush your teeth."

"Yes, Mom." Abigail's phone rang. "That must be him." She stepped over to the corner of the room and answered the phone.

"Ready to go?" Gregori asked.

"Yes. What took so long?"

"We went through all the reports from the guys. The messages come in during the day and pile up. Besides, there's no need to hurry. We can't start teleporting till the sun sets in California."

"Oh."

His voice softened. "Are you all right, Scholar?"

She turned to face the wall as heat invaded her cheeks. "Yes."

"Are you in your bedroom?"

"I'm at the hospital. My mom wants to meet you before we go. Is that all right?"

"Sure."

"You can teleport straight here. I'm in my mother's private room. My dad and Madison are here, too."

Gregori appeared beside her.

Belinda gasped.

Madison grinned. "So cool."

Her father stepped forward, his hand outstretched. "Good evening, Gregori."

"Sir." Gregori shook his hand, then inclined his head toward Belinda. "How do you do, Mrs. Tucker?"

Her eyes widened. "So you're really a vampire?"

"Yes, ma'am."

She looked him over. He was wearing khaki pants, a khaki shirt, and a brown bomber jacket. "You don't look very vampirish."

"He's doing the Indiana Jones look," Madison told her mother, then frowned at him. "You forgot the hat and the whip. You know, accessories really make an outfit."

Belinda held out her hand. "Would you come here, please?"

Gregori walked forward and took her hand in his.

She searched his face. "My husband believes you can be trusted, that you'll take good care of our Abby. Is that true?"

"Yes, ma'am."

Abigail's heart warmed at the sincerity in his voice. She eased closer so she could see his face.

"Abby tells me you're a young vampire, and you've never bitten a human for food," Belinda continued.

"Yes, ma'am, that's true."

Belinda smiled. "You seem well mannered for a vampire."

He smiled back. "My mother will be pleased to hear that."

"Your mother is still alive?"

"Yes, ma'am."

"I've met her," Abigail told her mother. "She's mortal. And a big fan of yours."

Belinda shook Gregori's hand, then released it. "Very well. Have a good trip. And please bring my Abby home safe and sound."

"I will." He looked at Abigail. "Ready to go?"

She nodded. After a round of tearful hugs and good-byes, she swung her backpack over her shoulder. "Let's go."

"First stop, Romatech." Gregori wrapped his arms around her, and everything went black.

They landed outside the side entrance, and Gregori swiped his card to open the door. He led her to the security office, where she was able to look at the reports from the guys in China. Both bases were set up, and they had teleported in supplies.

The office soon grew crowded with Vamps and mortals who wanted to wish them a good journey. Abigail was introduced to Angus and Robby MacKay, who would be teleporting with them as far as Tokyo. When it was time to leave, both MacKay men pulled their wives aside to tell them good-bye.

Abigail was touched by the obvious love on their faces.

She leaned close to Gregori and whispered, "Are their wives vampires, too?"

"Emma's a Vamp," he whispered back. "Olivia's mortal. And expecting their first child."

Abigail's mouth dropped open, and she glanced at Robby and Olivia, who held each other tightly. "Oh my gosh." She grabbed Gregori's arm and whispered, "We didn't use any protection last night. And we did it five times. I can hardly walk."

Gregori winced as chuckles reverberated around the room. "Abby, there's no point in whispering around vampires. They can hear everything."

"Oh." Heat rushed to her cheeks.

"Don't worry." Gregori pressed a kiss against her temple. "My sperm is dead. I can't have children until Roman does one of his magic tricks."

She narrowed her eyes. "How does that work?"

"He would take live human sperm, erase the DNA, and put in mine."

"Oh." She nodded. "Interesting." So she could actually have children with Gregori. If they decided to get married.

She glanced again at Robby and Olivia. They seemed very happy. In fact, the room was filled with couples. Roman and Shanna. Caitlyn and her husband, and others whose names she couldn't recall, but they all seemed happy.

"Time to go," Angus announced. He and Robby grabbed their bags and her and Gregori's backpacks, then teleported away.

Gregori pulled her into his arms. "Ready?"

She nodded as she wrapped her arms around his neck. "San Francisco, right?"

"Yes. The West Coast Coven house. I've been there before, so I know the way. Hang on."

Everything went black, then her feet landed softly on a thick Persian rug. She looked around. Angus and Robby were standing close to the fireplace, talking to a dark-haired man in a kilt. The room appeared to be a parlor, richly furnished with wingback chairs and medallion-back sofas, all upholstered in dark red velvet, the color of blood. Fitting, she supposed, for a house full of vampires.

"Miss Tucker?" The kilted man approached her with a smile. "I'm Rafferty McCall, West Coast Coven Master."

"How do you do?" She shook hands with him. "Thank you for helping me."

Since they had to wait for the sun to set in Hawaii, Abigail spent the next few hours sightseeing with Gregori. Rafferty provided them with a chauffeured Town Car, and they roamed about the city, laughing and stealing kisses in the moonlight. No Secret Service agents watching their every move. She hadn't felt this free in years.

Then they teleported to a small beach house in Hawaii that belonged to a were-dolphin named Finn Grayson. He was a marine biologist who worked at a nearby sea park.

"If the MacKay dudes want something done on the islands, they rely on me," he told Abigail. "Vamps don't hang out here, you know. Too much sun." He grinned at the vampire men. "Take a load off, bros.

I've got some Bleer in the fridge." He shuffled to the kitchen in his flip-flops.

Abigail couldn't help but smile at the differences. The MacKays were huge, pale, redheaded men who wore kilts and carried claymores on their backs. Finn looked like a blond surfer dude with his tanned skin and his baggy shorts and Hawaiian shirt.

She took a long walk along the beach with Gregori. Just the two of them, hand in hand. Back at the beach house, he encouraged her to take a nap. Once they moved on to Japan and China, there wouldn't be much time for rest.

She woke several hours later and ventured into the kitchen to look for food. "Hello?"

Where was everybody? After fifteen years of bodyguards, it felt strange to have no one hovering around her. She spotted Finn and Angus on the back porch. Angus waved for her to join them.

The minute she opened the sliding glass door, she heard a grating noise, the sound of metal clashing over and over.

"Sparring session," Angus explained as he pointed to the beach.

Her mouth dropped open. There on the beach, Robby and Gregori were engaged in a swordfight. With real swords. Huge swords.

Her heart leaped up her throat. "Are they trying to kill each other?"

"Nay, they're just practicing," Angus said. "I wanted to see how well the lad can fight."

She cringed when Robby's sword slashed down toward Gregori's head. He blocked it in time, the swords colliding with a loud crash. "This is crazy!"

"Ye want a man who can protect you, aye?" Angus asked as he calmly watched.

"I want a man who's *alive*."

Angus chuckled. "They'll no' kill each other."

Gregori shoved Robby back, then advanced toward him, lunging and parrying. The two men moved back and forth across the beach, swords flashing in the moonlight. After a while, she realized she could relax. They were carefully cutting short any thrusts that would seriously injure or kill.

As the gruesome dance continued, she became intrigued. The men were beautiful to watch. Neither was wearing a shirt, and sweat glistened off muscles that rippled across their chests and backs. Even as the men circled each other, she could always tell which one was Gregori. They were the same height, but Robby moved like a tank and stood his ground like a brick wall. Gregori was long, lean, and fluid. If he took a hard knock to the ground, he merely rolled with it and sprang back up. And he did it with style and grace.

She smiled. That was Gregori. He rolled with the punches life threw at him, and nothing ever kept him down.

"That's enough," Angus yelled. "We doona want to wear out the fledgling."

She heard Gregori's muttered curse and Robby's laugh. "You call him a fledgling?"

Angus chuckled. "Aye, just to irritate him, but the lad holds his own. Ye've found a good man there, lass."

Yes, she had. She watched him as he approached. Beneath his charm and expensive suits, he was a fighter, a warrior just like the kilted Scotsmen. His biceps bulged from the weight of the claymore, his dark, damp hair clung along his brow and neck, curling slightly at the ends. He smiled slowly at her, his dimples denting his cheeks.

Good Lord, she wanted him.

"Did you have a nice nap?" he asked.

She nodded, her gaze wandering over his bare, slick chest.

He handed his sword to Angus, never taking his eyes off her. "I'll see you in a few minutes. I need to shower."

She stood there a moment, then followed him inside the house. "Shouldn't you be inspected for injuries? What if Robby cut something off?"

"God forbid." With a grin, he pulled her into the bathroom that adjoined the guest bedroom.

After a leisurely inspection in the shower, she declared him whole and healthy. He wrapped her in a towel, dumped her on the bed, then jumped on top.

She laughed. "Aren't you tired?"

"Sweetheart." He peeled the towel open. "A good Vamp can go all night long."

And he did.

A few hours later, they teleported to Kyo's estate outside Tokyo. She called home to let her family know she'd arrived in Japan. Then she showered, changed clothes, and ate a big meal of miso soup, rice, and shrimp and vegetable tempura.

The phone rang, and it was J.L. Wang. Night had fallen in the Yunnan.

It was time for her adventure in China to begin.

Chapter Twenty-two

*T*hey arrived in the dark, but Gregori's vision quickly adjusted. Abigail skidded a little in the gravel, and he steadied her.

"They're here," J.L. told Angus on his cell phone. "We'll report in two hours." He hung up.

"Hey, J.L." Gregori gave him a knuckle pound.

"Hey, dude. Welcome, Miss Tucker. I'm J.L. Wang."

"Please call me Abby." She shook his hand. "It's so dark out here. I can hardly see."

"Yeah, we're in the boonies," J.L. said. "We have some lamps inside the cave, so you'll be able to see in there. Lousy phone reception though, so we usually come outside to make our reports."

Gregori pivoted as he looked around. Behind him, an odd cone-shaped hill rose abruptly from the flat ground. In front of him, moonlight glittered on an expanse of dark water. "We're next to a lake?"

"Actually, we're in the middle of a lake," J.L. explained. "This is an island. It's a good defensive position."

Gregori nodded. The Vamps could easily teleport

across the lake, but any humans trying to reach them would have to cross by boat. "Where's the cave?"

J.L. motioned to the cone-shaped hill. "Inside. Weird-looking thing, isn't it?"

Abigail touched the brown rock that rose steeply from the ground. "This area is known for its strange rock formations."

"You want to see something really strange, it's over there." J.L. pointed to the south edge of the lake.

Gregori narrowed his eyes. It was indeed strange. The moon gleamed off gray rocks that jutted out of the ground, a whole army of rocks, standing at attention.

Abigail sighed. "I can't see that far."

"It's a whole field of rocky spikes," Gregori told her.

"A stone forest, they call it." J.L. pointed east. "There's a bamboo forest that borders the lake over there. Beyond it and to the north, the land is mostly flat farmland, but dotted with more of the cone-shaped hills. The nearest village is about a mile that way. Rajiv and I have visited a few times, bought stuff at the market, and befriended the local healer."

He gestured to the west. "Over that way, it's more hilly. More jungle-like. Nearest village is about three miles. We haven't been there yet."

"I really appreciate all you've done to help me," Abigail said.

J.L. smiled. "No problem. Come on, let me introduce you to the guys. And our humble home."

He led them around a pile of boulders to a narrow entrance that was covered with a makeshift screen of bamboo. "We don't want any locals to notice our lamps at night," he said, pulling aside the screen.

Gregori ushered Abigail inside the small cave, lit by two kerosene lamps. J.L. entered and pulled the screen back in place.

Howard jumped to his feet and gave Gregori a big bear hug, then shook hands shyly with Abigail.

"Hello, Howard," she said, smiling. "I remember your photo from the briefing. Thank you for helping me."

Howard ducked his head and mumbled, "No problem."

Gregori motioned to the young man with a long black braided ponytail, who was scrambling to his feet. "This is Rajiv."

"Delighted to meet you. Please call me Abby."

The were-tiger pressed his hands together and bowed. "It is an honor." He straightened with a smile. "Tomorrow I cook hot pot. Just for you."

"Thank you." Abigail smiled back.

"Today I buy something in market just for you." He scurried to the wall and returned with something wrapped in old newspaper. With another bow, he held it to her.

"Why, thank you. That's so sweet." Abigail gingerly peeled back a corner of the paper and winced.

"Chicken feet!" Rajiv announced proudly. "Very good in hot pot. I make for you tomorrow."

"Oh. Thank you." Abigail glanced at Gregori and grinned. "I can hardly wait."

"We can't cook at night," Howard grumbled. "We would have to make a fire outside, and the locals might see it. But we still have food here, if you're hungry. Would you like a donut?" He motioned to an area close to the entrance.

Gregori chuckled at the stack of donut boxes next to Howard's sleeping bag. "Sheesh, bro. You can't go a few days without your bear claws?"

With a grunt, Howard sat on his sleeping bag. "A man's gotta eat."

"He sniffed out a donut shop in Tokyo and insisted we teleport those here." J.L. sighed with a resigned look. "Could be worse. You don't want be around a bear going through sugar withdrawal." He smiled at Abigail. "He might start growling."

"I know what make Howard happy," Rajiv said, grinning. "Nice lady panda bear!"

Howard snorted. "I eat pandas for breakfast."

Gregori chuckled, then noticed the alarmed look on Abigail's face. He leaned close. "He was kidding."

The last member of the team rose to his feet in the back of the cave. Gregori had met Russell Hankelburg once before, just briefly before everyone was teleporting to the final battle with Casimir. The former Marine wore green army fatigues and still kept his dark hair short.

"Hey, Russell, what's up?" He strode toward him and shook hands.

Russell gripped his hand hard, then nodded at Abigail. "Miss Tucker, it's an honor to serve."

"Thank you. Please call me Abby."

"Yes, ma'am." Russell returned to the back of the cave, where he sat cross-legged. He appeared to be in the middle of cleaning his gun.

"I know it's dark outside," J.L. said, "but the night is young, and our vision is excellent. If you'd like to get started?"

"All right." Abigail set down her backpack and removed some photos from the front pocket. "These are the two plants I'd like to collect in this area. The first one translates as Demon Herb and the second one as Tiger Paw." She handed them to J.L.

Howard snorted. "I could collect you a tiger paw right here."

Rajiv made a face at him. "Just try it, Pooh Bear." When Howard growled, he grinned at Abigail. "I learn English watching television. It's a Jersey thing."

J.L. chuckled as he studied the photos. "I'll teleport to the nearest village and ask the healer if he knows where to find these."

Rajiv bounced to his feet like Tigger. "I go with you."

"Okay. Can you get the gardening stuff?" J.L. checked his shoulder holster underneath his jacket. "I don't expect any trouble, but I like to be prepared."

"Do you want me to come with you?" Russell asked.

"I'd rather you stick with Abigail," J.L. said, then turned to her with an apologetic look. "I know you're here for the plants, but our first priority is keeping you safe."

She nodded. "I appreciate that."

J.L. pulled up a pants leg to check the knife strapped to his calf. "If we learn anything useful, we'll call. You'll hear us better if you go outside."

"Got it," Gregori said.

J.L. pointed to a box close to Howard. "Flashlights are in there. If we go hunting for a plant tonight, bring one for Abigail."

"Will do," Gregori agreed.

Rajiv slung a canvas bag over his shoulder and grabbed on to J.L. "Let's go."

J.L. vanished, taking Rajiv with him.

"These are for you." Howard handed them two rolled-up sleeping bags and a bulky black trash bag.

Gregori found an empty space and rolled out the two bags next to each other.

Abigail dug two pillows and blankets out of the trash bag and arranged them on top of the sleeping bags.

"Not much to do here, really." Howard sat down on his sleeping bag. "You want a donut, Abby?"

"Yes, thank you." She selected one from his box, then sat on her sleeping bag to eat it.

Gregori located the ice chest and removed a bottle of synthetic blood and a water bottle, which he handed to Abigail.

He sat and drank. Howard stuffed his face. Russell finished cleaning one gun and started on another.

When Gregori finished his bottle of blood, he rose to his feet. "I'll wait outside in case J.L. calls."

"I'll go with you." Abigail jumped up and followed him outside.

He moved the bamboo screen back into place, then took her hand. "Let's check out this island."

It took them about five minutes to circumnavigate the island and end up back at the cave entrance. Abigail shivered and zipped up her jacket.

"Cold?" He pulled her into his arms.

She snuggled her cheek against his chest. "Not now."

"Having fun?"

She looked up at him and smiled. "I am, actually. I

keep expecting to see a Secret Service agent around the corner, but they're not there."

He kissed her brow. He needed to warn her about his death-sleep, but wasn't sure how to break the news. *Oh, by the way, when the sun rises, I'll die?*

"I need to tell you something—" His phone rang. "We'll talk about it later." He pulled out his phone. "What's up?"

He listened to J.L., then reported to Abigail. "They're on their way to find one of the plants. The Tiger Paw. Do you want to join them?"

"Yes, of course."

"Hang on a sec," Gregori told J.L. He left his phone with Abigail, then stepped into the cave to let Howard and Russell know they were leaving.

"I'm coming with you." Russell holstered a pistol, slung a rifle over his shoulder, and strode outside.

"I'll stay here and hold down the fort." Howard leaned back, munching on a bear claw.

Gregori grabbed two LED flashlights and went back outside. While he jammed the flashlights into his pocket, Russell leaned close to the phone Abigail was holding so he could hear J.L.'s voice. He vanished.

Gregori grabbed on to Abigail. "Keep talking," he told J.L. on the phone, then he teleported.

They landed on a dirt path that weaved through a forest of bamboo. Gregori handed Abigail a flashlight and turned on the second one.

"I thought you had excellent night vision," she said as she clicked on her flashlight.

"I do. I'm just making more light for you." Gregori noticed that Russell had already started down the path. Typical Marine. He had to be on the front line.

J.L. motioned for them to follow. "The local healer said Tiger Paw grows on the other side of this forest. Close to a canola field."

"Healer very nice old man," Rajiv added. "He like little blue pills J.L. give him for gift."

Gregori chuckled.

"Wait a minute." Abigail stepped over a fallen bamboo log. "Are you giving the locals Viagra?"

J.L. shrugged. "They like it. It helps them be more . . . helpful."

She snorted. "You mean you're bribing them."

"Could be worse," J.L. muttered.

Rajiv nodded. "Village people like J.L. very much."

They reached the edge of the forest. Gregori's flashlight beam caught the bright yellow color of a canola field to the left.

"Oh, how pretty," Abigail breathed.

"This way." J.L. led them toward the canola field. "The healer said it grew in great clumps in this area."

They spread out to search for it, although Gregori stayed close to Abby. Their flashlight beams moved back and forth over the green vegetation.

She gasped. "There it is!" She grinned at Gregori, then flung her arms around him. "I found it!"

Rajiv, J.L., and Russell rushed toward her.

"Here." Rajiv dug into his canvas bag and handed her clippers and a plastic bag.

"There's a trowel in there, too, and some plastic pots." J.L. motioned to the canvas bag. "We weren't sure if you wanted clippings or the whole plant."

"Oh, the whole plant would be wonderful. Sometimes the root is the best part. And then I can get a soil sample, too." Abigail grinned. "You guys are the best!"

Gregori grabbed the trowel and located a cluster of small Tiger Paw plants. Soon they had three unearthed and planted in the plastic pots.

"Let me see if I can get through to Angus." J.L. called on his phone. "Hey, boss. We've got a pickup for you. Three plants."

Angus, Robby, and Kyo materialized close by.

"Are ye all right, lass?" Angus asked Abigail.

"Yes." She smiled. "We're making wonderful progress!"

"We'll have Mikhail teleport these to Moscow." Robby lifted one of the pots. "And then he can take them on to London. We'll have them safe at Romatech within twenty-four hours."

"That's fantastic." Her smile widened. "Thank you!"

Gregori wrapped an arm around her and squeezed her shoulder. "One down, and two to go."

Russell turned to J.L. "Did the healer tell you where the second plant is located?"

J.L. exchanged a worried look with Rajiv. "He said the Demon Herb is west of here. Close to the village that's three miles away on the other side of the lake."

"Let's go get it," Gregori said. "Then we'll be done here tonight, and we can move on to the next base."

Rajiv shook his head. "We should not look for it. It is very bad."

"What do you mean?" Gregori asked. "Is it s kind of narcotic?"

"I'm not sure," J.L. replied. "The healer just told us to stay away. Apparently it's called the Demon Herb because it's so powerful. People say it's cursed."

"Surely that's just an old superstition," Abigail said.

Rajiv shook his head again. "It is very bad."

"What makes it so bad?" Robby asked.

J.L. sighed. "Those who go looking for it are never seen again."

Chapter Twenty-three

*A*bby, is that you?" Madison asked on the phone. "Are you in China?"

"I was about thirty minutes ago. Is Mom okay?"

"She's asleep, so I answered her phone. I'm in her hospital room. Where are you?"

"I'm close to Tokyo," Abigail explained. "Kyo's place. I needed to use the bathroom, and Gregori said I could either try the bamboo forest or he'd teleport me to a real bathroom. Guess which one I chose?"

Madison laughed. "That teleporting sure does come in handy."

"Yes." Abigail suspected Gregori had a hidden motive for offering to take her back to Kyo's house. The guys were worried about the accursed Demon Herb. Instead of spending the rest of the night going after the plant, they were trying to keep her safely ensconced at Kyo's luxurious estate.

She leaned back in the Jacuzzi tub. "You wouldn't believe the size of this bathtub I'm in."

Madison giggled. "Are you alone?"

Abigail snorted. "Yes." She'd locked the door so she

could enjoy a long hot soak in the tub. "This place is beautiful. Full of art and antiques. And the garden outside is heavenly. Kyo must be awfully wealthy."

"Really?" Madison sounded impressed. "Can I meet him?"

Abigail laughed.

Gregori suddenly materialized inside the room. She gasped and nearly dropped the phone in the water.

"Something wrong?" Madison asked.

"I . . . dropped the soap." So much for locking a vampire out.

Gregori winked at her, then pulled his shirt over his head and dropped it on the floor.

She watched as his trousers hit the floor. Then his underwear. Good Lord, could any man be more gorgeous?

"Abby? Are you still there?"

"Yeah." Abigail sat up so she could observe Gregori in the glass shower stall. "Tell Mom and Dad I'm fine."

"Okay. What about the plants?"

What plants? Abigail watched as Gregori soaped up his body. Oh God, he was lathering up his groin.

"Abby? Hello? I think there's something wrong with our connection. Did you look for your plants?"

Oh, plants! "Yes! We're making excellent progress. We've already collected one and we know the location of the second."

"Wow! That's awesome!"

"Yes. Awesome," she murmured as Gregori rinsed off. He turned his back to her, and rivulets of white lather slid down his back, then over his muscular buttocks and down his legs. "I need to go now, Maddie.

Tell everyone I'm fine." She hung up and dropped her phone on a white bathrobe she'd left on a nearby bench.

Gregori stepped out of the shower and smiled at her, his dimples showing. "Did you enjoy the show?"

"Yes." Her gaze lowered to his groin. *Wow.* He was already semi-aroused.

He walked toward her. "That's an awfully big tub."

"Yes." She sighed. "Totally selfish of me to keep it all to myself."

"Naughty girl." He grinned as he climbed in.

She moved over to make room for him, but he pulled her close into his arms. His eyes darkened to a red glow as he skimmed his hands over her rump.

"There's something I need to tell you," he began. "I don't want you to get scared later."

"You want me to stay here, don't you?" She ran her fingers along his whiskered jaw.

"In the tub? Actually, I thought we might move to a bed."

She poked a finger in one of his dimples. "I meant you want to keep me here in Japan."

"Ah." He teased the crevice between her buttocks. "You have to admit it's much more pleasant here than a cave."

"The plants are over there."

"Yeah, but you're safer here." His eyes returned to their normal grayish-green. "Why not let us do the dangerous stuff?"

"How can it be dangerous? I have three Vamps, a tiger, and a bear to keep me safe."

He gave her a dubious look.

"I can be very persuasive." She smoothed her hand down his chest to his abs. "What can I do to convince you?"

He sucked in a breath when her hand circled his penis. "You're on the right track." His eyes turned red again.

"Well, it's a big track." She tugged gently. "Hard to miss."

He winced. "You're too smart for me, Scholar. I came in here to seduce you into staying, and you . . . you . . ." With a groan, he leaned his head back.

"Shame on you." She kissed his ear. "Using sex to persuade me."

He snorted. "And you're not?" He grabbed her, and everything went black.

He tumbled her onto a bed. "We'll see who can be more persuasive."

Abigail smiled as she reached for him. He tried for several hours to persuade her, but in the end, she teleported back to the cave with him.

She woke hours later, cuddled beside Gregori on their sleeping bags. It seemed dark in the back of the cave, but then she noticed a wooden screen had been stretched across the cave, dividing it in half and blocking any sunlight that filtered through the entrance.

Back in the dark recesses of the cave, J.L. and Russell were in their sleeping bags sound asleep. It had to be daylight outside. The numbers on her digital watch glowed two-fifteen P.M. Good Lord, she'd slept most of the day away. Her body no longer knew night from day.

"Good afternoon," she murmured to Gregori, wondering just how deeply a vampire could sleep. She kissed his cheek. Goodness, he was cold.

"How can you sleep like that?" He'd left his blanket in a pile at his feet. She covered him up, then added her blanket on top.

"Is that better?" She tucked it in around his chin.

He didn't seem to be breathing.

"Gregori?" She leaned over him, but felt no air escaping his mouth. "Hey." She patted his cheeks.

No response.

She yanked the blankets down and ripped open his shirt. No heartbeat.

"Gregori!" Panic seized her. She forced his mouth open, felt around inside, then breathed into him.

She planted her hands over his heart and pushed.

"What are you doing?" Howard slipped around the screen and started toward her.

"CPR! He's dying!"

"He's already dead."

"Don't say that!" She pinched his nose and breathed into his mouth again.

"Miss Tucker!" Howard knelt beside her. "There's no point in doing that."

"I'm not giving up on him!" She went back to pressing against his heart.

"Abby! The Vamps always die at sunrise. This is their death-sleep!"

She sat back on her heels. "Their what?"

"Death-sleep. Gregori didn't tell you they go into a death-sleep?"

Tears stung her eyes. "He—he's really dead?"

"Yeah, but don't worry. He'll wake again at sunset."

She swallowed hard. "He's really . . . dead?"

Howard nodded. "But it's just temporary, you know."

"How can death be temporary?"

Howard shrugged. "I don't know. It's a vampire thing."

She looked at Gregori, and a tear ran down her cheek. "Oh my God! He's really *dead*?"

"Well, Undead is more accurate, I guess, considering that he wakes up again." Howard gave her a curious look. "He didn't tell you?"

"No." Or did he? She thought back to when they'd returned to the cave. She'd been worn out from their lovemaking and gone straight to the sleeping bag. He'd stretched out beside her.

"I need to warn you," he had whispered. "I sleep like I'm dead."

"Me too," she'd mumbled before slipping into a deep sleep.

"Oh my gosh," she whispered. He'd meant it literally.

A rush of anger swept over her. "That's how you tell me?" She yanked the blankets back up to his chin, then slapped him on the chest. "You scared the hell out of me! I thought I'd lost you!"

Tears streamed down her face. "He can't hear me, can he?"

"No, ma'am." Howard rose to his feet.

She stood and wiped her cheeks. "I'll have to wait till sunset to vent my rage."

Howard nodded. "Good plan." He shifted his weight. "You want a donut?"

A burst of laughter escaped her. "Oh God, I'm going crazy."

Howard stepped back with a worried look.

"Not really crazy," she assured him, then took a deep breath. Good Lord, it was after two in the afternoon. She'd cuddled up to a dead body for hours. "I need to get out of here."

"This way." Howard led her around the screen. "We put the screen up as a safety precaution. If any sunlight hits the Vamps, they'll die for real."

She shook her head. *Death-sleep*. Gregori had always inferred that he spent the day sleeping in the usual fashion. Why did he lie to her?

He was really dead. The poor guy had actually *died* while she'd slept next to him. Had he suffered any pain? He must have. She shuddered. It was terrible to even think about.

Howard pulled the bamboo door away from the cave entrance so they could slip outside.

"Miss Abby!" Rajiv waved at her. He had a fire going and a big pot suspended over it. "I make you hot pot."

"Thank you." She walked over for a closer look. "It smells wonderful."

He looked at her and frowned. "Miss Abby cry?"

She took a deep breath and gazed up at the blue sky. "I'm all right now. Thank you."

"She didn't know Gregori would be dead," Howard grumbled.

"Oh." Rajiv grimaced. "That's bad."

Abby nodded and motioned toward the other end of the island. "I'll be over there for a little while."

Rajiv nodded.

She went behind the hill and found a place to relieve herself. She washed her hands in the lake, then straightened and gasped. Now that it was daylight, she could see the south side of the lake. Gray stone stalagmites jutted up from a flat field. She'd read about karsts in her research, but hadn't realized how unearthly they would look. She stared at them for a while, then headed back to the shifters.

Howard had rolled up his pants and was standing knee-deep in the lake. He leaned over, concentrating, then suddenly *swoosh!* He scooped a fish out and tossed it onto the beach.

Abigail smiled. He fished just like a bear.

Soon he had a dozen fish on the beach.

"Are we supposed to eat all of these?" she asked.

Rajiv grinned. "Howard is big bear. He eat eight."

The were-bear lumbered out of the lake, then pulled a knife from his belt and hacked the heads off the fish.

"Fish heads!" Rajiv grabbed two heads and rinsed them out in the lake. "Good for hot pot." He dropped them into the pot with the chicken feet.

Howard beheaded all the fish while Rajiv insisted he was throwing away the best part.

"I have noodles." Rajiv ran into the cave and came back with a bag of noodles he dumped into the pot. Howard retrieved a frying pan and some oil from the cave.

Late that afternoon, they feasted on Rajiv's noodle soup and Howard's fried fish.

Abigail sat on the beach, propped up against a boulder, gazing at the karsts on the south side of the lake. "I'd like to see those close up."

"We have a boat," Rajiv said.

"We do? I didn't see it."

Rajiv smiled. "We hide it good. You want to go across the lake?"

"No," Howard said sharply. "She can't leave the island."

She winced. It was happening again. She was being told what she wasn't allowed to do. The Vamps had wanted her to stay in Japan. She'd had a hard time convincing Gregori to bring her back here, and now she was just sitting here spinning her wheels.

She motioned to the sun, which was lowering in the west. "Don't we need to go to the village over there?"

Howard nodded. "It's three miles across the hills. The Vamps haven't been there before, so we'll have to hike."

"In the dark?" That might not bother the Vamps, but she preferred hiking in sunlight. "Why don't we hike over there now, then when the sun sets, we can call the Vamps and they'll teleport over?"

Howard frowned. "I'm sorry, but you're not leaving this island until the Vamps wake up."

She clenched her fists and released them. Was this what life would be like with Gregori? Always waiting for him to wake up?

She stood. "I'm taking a walk."

She paced around the island, feeling more and more trapped, more and more upset. Why did Gregori lie about his death-sleep? Was there anything else he was hiding from her?

She made a complete circle and sat on a boulder by the cave entrance. Rajiv washed his pot in the lake, then doused the fire. Howard retrieved his box of donuts from the cave and gave her one as a peace offering.

She ate and watched the sun lower on the horizon. The lake sparkled. The sunset painted the sky with shades of pink, orange, and gold. It was absolutely beautiful. It was something she could never share with Gregori.

Tears came to her eyes. That was what really had her upset. She was completely, totally in love with Gregori. She'd realized that when she thought she'd lost him.

But what kind of life could she have with someone who was literally *dead* all day long? Would she end up wishing away her days, putting her life on hold, while she waited for him to wake up?

Her parents would never approve. She sighed. More people telling her what she couldn't do.

The last rays of sunlight disappeared over the horizon, and the temperature dropped a few degrees. She zipped up her jacket.

"I'll go see if they're up." Howard went inside the cave.

She turned toward the entrance. She could barely see it in the moonlight, but she heard some mumbling voices inside. A loud voice shouted, Gregori's voice.

"What? Shit!"

She winced. Howard must have told him.

Gregori ran outside, a bottle of blood in his hand. He paused on the beach, facing her.

Rajiv stalked toward him. "You make Miss Abby cry," he growled, then strode inside the cave, leaving her alone with Gregori.

Chapter Twenty-four

*A*bigail remained sitting on the boulder. She didn't know whether to yell at Gregori for being dead or cry with joy that he was now alive.

He took a sip of blood and approached her. "I heard you were upset."

She scoffed. "That's putting it mildly. You didn't tell me you would be dead."

"I said I slept like I was dead."

"It wasn't *like* death. It was death. You should have warned me."

He took another sip. "I tried to tell you twice. Once here and again in the tub."

"Why didn't you tell me sooner?" She stood. "I asked you about it at the nightclub, and you said it was just a sleep. You lied to me!"

He winced. "Abby, we're totally vulnerable in our death-sleep. And I have thousands of Vamps depending on me to keep them safe. There was no way I could let the government know how easy we are to kill during the day."

"I'm not the government."

"You work for them."

She flinched. "You don't trust me."

He paused.

Anger flared inside her. "You don't trust me!"

Someone cleared his throat, and she glanced to the side. J.L. was standing on the beach with the other three guys.

"Sorry to interrupt, but we're moving out." J.L. motioned to the west. "When we spot the village, we'll give you a call, so you can teleport over."

Gregori nodded. "All right."

J.L. and Russell each grabbed hold of a shifter, then they teleported away.

She sat back down on the boulder. "How can you claim to love me if you don't trust me?"

Gregori stiffened. "It's not a claim, dammit. It's the truth. And maybe I didn't trust you very much at the nightclub. That was a few days ago before we . . . got closer. I do trust you now."

He stepped toward her. "I was lying there completely helpless. I would have never fallen into my death-sleep with you next to me if I didn't know I could trust you."

Tears misted her eyes. "I hate to think of you dying every day at sunrise."

"I don't enjoy it much, either." He drank more blood. "I'm sorry it upset you."

She blinked away the tears. "I was terrified. I thought I'd lost you."

He moved close to her. "Sweetheart, you can't lose me."

She swatted at his arm. "I even tried to revive you with CPR."

"You did mouth-to-mouth on me?" His white teeth flashed in the dark. "I'm sorry I missed it."

"It's not funny."

"I'm not laughing. I'm just deliriously happy that you care so much about me."

She sighed. "I don't see how it can work."

His smile vanished. "What do you mean? We're doing just fine."

"I couldn't do anything this afternoon. I had to wait for you to wake up." She motioned toward the karsts that she could no longer see in the dark. "I couldn't even go look at the rocks."

"I'll take you there."

"That's not the point. I wanted to go, but I wasn't allowed to. It's like I traded one set of prison guards for another."

"Only while we're here in China. Abby, it'll be different once we're home. I would never imprison you. I know how much you value your freedom."

"Because it's always been so scarce."

"You'll have more freedom with me than you would with a mortal guy. You can do anything during the day, and I can't stop you. Hell, you could even have an affair during the day, and I wouldn't know."

"I wouldn't do that!"

"Well, that's good news." He set his bottle on the boulder next to her and grasped her hands. "Abby, I'll give you all the freedom and love that I can. We can make this work. Trust me."

Tears crowded her eyes once more. "I love you, Gregori."

He pulled her to her feet and into his arms. "I love you, too."

She held on to him in the moonlight for a long time. He stroked her hair.

"Is there anything else I should know about you?" she asked. "You don't turn into a fruit bat or something?"

"Well, there is something."

She leaned back. "What?"

"I love disco."

She grimaced. "You're kidding."

"Is it a deal breaker?"

She smiled. "It's close." She nestled her head against his chest. She loved him, and he loved her. Somehow, it would all work out. She needed to trust in their love.

J.L. called to let them know they'd sighted the village. She grabbed a flashlight and a bottle of water, then Gregori teleported her there.

They landed on the crest of a hill overlooking a valley where the village was situated.

J.L. hung up his phone. "No flashlights, please. We don't want to announce our presence to the villagers."

"What villagers?" Russell muttered as he scanned the valley. "I see chickens. Cows. No people."

"Maybe they at church," Rajiv suggested. "Or party."

"We would see lights," Howard grumbled.

"Strange," J.L. murmured. "Where did all the people go?"

An uneasy feeling crept along Abigail's skin. She squinted but could barely see the village in the dark.

"Is there any smoke coming from chimneys? Any signs of life at all?"

Gregori shook his head. "Nothing."

"I go look," Rajiv offered.

"I'll go with you." J.L. started downhill with the were-tiger.

The closer they came to the village, the more anxious Abigail became. Something was seriously wrong.

J.L. and Rajiv reached the edge of the village and stopped. J.L. called out in Mandarin Chinese.

No answer.

Rajiv shouted in the Bai language.

No response.

Abigail's uneasy feeling spiked into alarm. She sprinted down the hill.

"Abby!" Gregori followed her.

She reached the valley and turned on her flashlight. Gregori stopped beside her. She moved the beam of light around. Chickens pecked in the grass. A few cows were gathered in a pen.

They joined J.L. and Rajiv at the edge of the village. The main street was empty. No sound came from any of the buildings. Tables lined the street, covered with fruit and vegetables. A market with no buyers or sellers.

J.L. gave her a worried look. "I'm not sure if it's safe for us to investigate."

She aimed her flashlight beam at one of the tables and gasped. The food was rotting.

"Oh my God," she whispered, stepping back. "Don't touch anything."

"You think people sick?" Rajiv pointed at the insects buzzing around the food. "The bugs okay."

The cows and chickens were all right, too. And she couldn't detect the odor of decaying bodies, so that was an encouraging sign. "The villagers could still be extremely ill. Or for some reason, they all ran away."

"And left everything behind?" Gregori asked softly.

She winced. J.L.'s warning about the Demon Herb flitted through her mind. *Those who go looking for it are never seen again.*

"I could look around," Rajiv offered. "I would be okay. I have seven more lives."

She stiffened. "What?"

He grinned. "Were-cats have nine lives. I still have eight more. I be okay."

Stunned, she watched him head for the first building. "He has nine lives?"

"Eight," J.L. corrected her. "He lost one, so he's what you call a level two cat shifter, which means he can shift whenever he likes."

"Oh. Okay." She forced her mind to wrap around that strange bit of information. Good Lord, less than a week ago she wouldn't have believed any of this. Yet here she was in China with vampires and shape shifters, and something seriously bad going down in this village.

"Don't touch anything," she reminded Rajiv.

He nodded and kicked the door in. He looked inside.

"What do you see?" J.L. shouted.

"People," he called back, then stepped inside.

She held her T-shirt over her mouth and nose, waiting for him to return. A feeling of doom settled over her.

Rajiv came out and waved at them. Then he went into the next building, checked it out, and ran back to them.

"They all asleep," he reported. "They even lay on floors, sleeping."

"Like a death-sleep?" Gregori asked.

Rajiv shook his head. "No. I poke them with my shoe, and they groan. They still alive. Just sleeping."

Abigail swallowed hard. She'd come here to discover a way to help her mother. What if she brought back a terrible disease? "Did they look ill? Were they pale or sweaty? Was there any sign of vomiting?"

Rajiv shook his head. "They look fine to me."

She took a deep breath. "I'll have to examine them."

"No," Gregori said sharply. "You'll do nothing to risk yourself."

"They need help," she insisted.

"We'll find a way to alert the authorities," J.L. said. "For now, our top priority is keeping you safe."

"Let's go." Gregori grabbed her and teleported back to the top of the hill.

J.L. and Rajiv materialized beside them.

"Well?" Russell asked.

"They all asleep," Rajiv said.

She shook her head. "It's not normal. I'm afraid it's some kind of disease. And we've all been exposed."

"Did you see anything else that was unusual?" J.L. asked Rajiv.

Rajiv shook his head. "They look fine. But they all have tattoo on arm." He pointed to the inside of his right wrist. "It was something in Chinese."

Russell stiffened. "What did it say?"

Rajiv shrugged. "I don't read Chinese."

Russell pulled back the jacket on his right wrist. "Did it look like this?"

Abigail shone her flashlight on it.

"Yes!" Rajiv said. "That's it."

J.L. sucked in a breath. "It means slave. It marks the people who belong to Master Han."

Russell yanked his sleeve down. "I don't belong to the bastard."

"How did you get the tattoo?" Howard asked.

"How the hell would I know?" Russell growled. "I woke up in a damned cave, Undead with a tattoo on my arm. But if these people are his slaves, then it means I'm close."

"That's why you were so quick to volunteer?" Gregori asked. "You're searching for Master Han?"

"Why shouldn't I?" Russell snapped. "The bastard destroyed my life!"

"I can understand why you want revenge," Gregori said, "but our first priority here is keeping Abigail safe."

"Who is this Master Han?" she asked.

"A *chiang-shih*," Rajiv answered.

"A vampire," J.L. clarified. "We've run into him before."

A loud gong sounded in the distance.

"What the hell is that?" Howard grumbled.

"It came from the south." Gregori pointed. "Past those fields."

The gong sounded again.

"Look!" Rajiv pointed at the village.

One light after another flared till the whole village was well lit.

Abigail gulped.

The villagers were awake.

Chapter Twenty-five

*G*regori reached over to turn off Abigail's flashlight. "We should get the hell out of here," he whispered, although like the others, he didn't move. He was too damned curious about what would happen next.

Villagers poured into the main street, carrying torches. They stood there silently, their faces without expression. Even the children were still and emotionless, and Gregori knew from spending time with Roman's kids that this was not normal.

"Could be some sort of mass mind control," J.L. murmured.

"By Master Han," Russell added.

A third gong sounded.

The villagers turned en masse and marched toward the south. The light of their torches illuminated blank faces and robotic movements.

"I see this on television," Rajiv whispered. "Zombies."

Howard snorted. "They're not going to eat us."

"You sure?" Rajiv asked. "They not eating food in village."

Abigail winced. "That's true."

"Let's see where they're going." J.L. moved south along the crest of the hill.

Gregori held on to Abigail to help her maneuver in the dark, although he had a secondary motive for keeping a grip on her arm. If the situation turned dangerous, he wanted to be able to teleport her away in an instant.

The villagers came to a field and divided, half walking to the east side of the field, half to the west. They set their torches into poles that lined the field on each side.

The field was vast, row after row of knee-high leafy green plants. The villagers—men, women, and children—spread out among the rows. The adults pulled knives from their belts and cut leaves off the plants. The children gathered up the leaves and dropped them into baskets that were located every ten yards.

"They're slave labor," Abigail whispered. "This is terrible."

"What's Master Han doing with those leaves?" Russell asked.

Gregori leaned close to Abigail. "Is it the Demon Herb?"

"I can't tell from here," Abigail answered. "Can we get closer?"

"I'll see." J.L. moved down the hill and stopped behind a pile of rocks. He took a rock the size of a cantaloupe and rolled it into the field.

No reaction. The villagers went about their work. Those close to the rock simply walked around it.

"They remind me of the Borg from *Star Trek*," Abigail whispered. "They're so intent on their work, they don't notice anything unless it interferes with their mission."

"I could cut you some leaves," Rajiv offered.

"Are you crazy?" Howard growled.

"They all cutting leaves," Rajiv said. "They will think I one of them."

"Give it a try," Gregori said, "but be careful."

Rajiv moved quietly down the hill and joined J.L. behind the pile of rocks. He leaned close to whisper in J.L.'s ear, and J.L. nodded.

The villagers never looked in their direction, just kept working.

Rajiv eased out from behind the rocks, then walked quickly toward the field. He turned into the first row, pulled his knife from his belt, and started cutting leaves.

None of the villagers looked at him.

He dumped a handful of leaves into the nearest basket, then went back to work. He cut off a branch of leaves and slipped it under his shirt.

"Shit," Gregori whispered.

"What?" Abigail asked.

He pointed at two men with rifles who were walking along the rows toward the north end of the field where Rajiv was working. They reached the end of the field and turned to watch the villagers.

Rajiv glanced over his shoulder at them, then looked at J.L. He bent over and started cutting more leaves.

"I should teleport you out of here," Gregori whispered.

"Don't you dare." Abigail pulled her arm from his grip.

Another gong sounded.

The villagers slipped their knives back into their

belts and turned south. They moved quietly down the rows. The men picked up the baskets and carried them.

Rajiv hesitated.

One of the guards shouted at him.

He turned south and moved slowly.

The guard shouted again.

He dropped his leaves in the basket, then picked it up and walked down the row like the other villagers.

J.L. glanced back at the rest of the team on the crest of the hill. He pointed at a thicket of trees to the south and mouthed the word *teleport*.

Gregori was tempted to whisk Abigail back to base camp, but he knew she'd be furious if he decided what she wasn't allowed to do, so he teleported her to the spot J.L. had pointed to. Russell materialized with Howard.

They were now at the south end of the field, and from here, Gregori could see the gong. The large brass circle was sitting on a red lacquered table. There were three guards there, and they were busy filling wooden cups with a dark liquid and setting them on the table.

The villagers approached and dumped the contents of their baskets into a large brass bin. Each one was handed a cup. They drank, then turned and went back to work.

"That must be what's sustaining them," Abigail whispered. "Instead of food."

Rajiv was last in line. His eyes widened at the sight of one of the guards, and he ducked his head. He dumped his basketful of leaves into the bin, then accepted the cup.

"Don't drink the Kool-Aid," Gregori muttered.

A guard yelled at Rajiv. He turned away, still holding the cup. The guard strode toward him and yanked him around.

The guard stiffened. "You!"

Rajiv glared at him. "Sawat! Why you here? I thought you still in San Francisco, looking for your balls."

J.L. winced. "We've run into Sawat before. I'll grab Rajiv and we'll all teleport back to base—"

Russell zoomed down the hill and pointed his rifle at Sawat. "Where is Master Han?"

Another guard grabbed Rajiv and pressed a knife to his neck. The cup tumbled to the ground.

"Dammit." J.L. teleported behind the guard and smashed the butt of his pistol against his head. As the guard crumpled to the ground, J.L. grabbed hold of Rajiv. "We teleport now!"

"*No!*" Russell cocked his rifle and yelled at Sawat, "Where is Master Han?"

Sawat shouted something in Chinese. A guard drummed on the gong till the air vibrated with the metallic sound. The villagers turned and drew their knives.

"Master Han, Master Han," they chanted as they advanced on Russell.

"Holy crap." Howard raced down the hill and grabbed Russell.

Gregori pulled Abigail close. She was trembling.

"*Teleport!*" J.L. shouted, then he vanished with Rajiv.

Gregori teleported back to the beach with Abigail. J.L. and Rajiv were there.

"In here." J.L. rushed inside the cave and lit one of the kerosene lamps.

Gregori led Abby into the cave and winced at how pale and frightened she looked.

"Where's Russell and Howard?" she asked, then spun toward the cave entrance when the two men strode inside.

J.L. stalked toward the ex-Marine. "What the hell do you think you're doing?"

Russell's eyes narrowed. "I'm going to find Master Han."

"And what?" J.L. yelled. "If you had learned his location, would you have taken off and left Howard behind? We don't work that way!"

"I can take care of myself," Howard growled.

"Hey!" Gregori interrupted. "Our first priority is keeping Abigail safe."

"Exactly." J.L. took a deep breath. "We keep her safe, find her plants, and get the hell out." He glared at Russell. "That is the full extent of our mission."

"I have her plant." Rajiv pulled out the branch from under his shirt and handed it to Abigail.

"This is it! The Demon Herb." She fumbled in her backpack for a plastic bag. "Thank you, Rajiv."

Gregori wondered why Master Han was collecting so much of the Demon Herb.

"Excellent work, Rajiv," J.L. said. "Let's move on to the next base. Everybody, pack your essentials. Don't worry about sleeping bags. The other base is already supplied. Howard, keep watch outside."

"Will do." Howard lumbered outside and jammed the bamboo door back over the entrance.

"I'm going to stay here," Russell said quietly.

"No." J.L. stuffed his clothes into his backpack. "We

need all three Vamps in order to teleport the others."

"Master Han is close," Russell insisted. "We have to take him out."

"We're not risking Abigail's life so you can avenge yourself," Gregori said.

"What about the whole village he's enslaved?" Russell asked.

"We'll come back later," J.L. said.

"I want him *now*!" Russell shouted. "That bastard stole thirty-nine years of my life! By the time I made it home, my parents were dead, my brother was dead, and my wife had declared *me* dead and remarried."

Abigail winced. "I'm so sorry."

He dragged a hand through his short hair. "My daughter, she was just a baby when I left for Vietnam. She died two years ago at the age of forty from breast cancer. I never got to see her. So yes, I want revenge. When I get my hands on Master Han, I'm going to rip his heart out and stuff it down his throat!"

"Hey," Howard called through the bamboo door. "You guys need to see this."

They filed outside.

Fires from torches lit the south side of the lake.

"Is it the villagers?" Abigail asked.

"I don't think so." Gregori watched as the newcomers planted the torches into the ground. "They're all young men. And they got here too fast."

"How did they know where to find us?" she asked.

"Good question," Howard grumbled.

More and more torches were planted along the beach till the south side of the lake was well illuminated. Firelight gleamed off the gray karsts, making them gleam like silver daggers pointed at the sky. The men were dressed in white uniforms with red sashes around their waists and across their brows.

"I think they're soldiers from Master Han," Russell said.

Abigail sidled up close to Gregori, and he wrapped an arm around her shoulders. "They didn't bring any boats, so we're safe for the moment."

"We're not staying." J.L. moved toward the cave entrance, then froze. "What the—"

Abigail gasped.

A group of soldiers leaped high in the air and landed, each one perched on top of a karst. More soldiers advanced toward the lake, leaping from one karst to another. Their leaps were high enough that some did somersaults in the air before landing on top of the stone stalagmites. Some of the karsts were pointed on top, and the soldiers balanced on them with ease.

She pressed a hand to her chest. "That doesn't seem humanly possible."

"*Chiang-shih*," Rajiv whispered.

"Vampires," J.L. translated.

They were all vampires? Gregori swallowed hard. There had to be a hundred of them.

"That explains how they found us," Russell muttered. "They're able to hear our beacon."

"I don't hear anything," Abigail said.

"Only vampires can hear this frequency." Russell yanked the electronic gadget from its hiding place near the cave entrance and stomped his boot on it.

More of the *chiang-shih* hopped from stone to stone, then they leaped even higher, flying through the air to perch on top of the bamboo trees on the east side of the lake. The bamboo stalks swayed back and forth like pendulums, arcs ever widening until they dipped down to the water and deposited the soldiers on the surface of the lake.

They didn't sink.

"Oh shit." Gregori steered Abigail toward the cave. "Get your backpack. We're going."

"They walk on water?" Rajiv asked.

"I think they're levitating," J.L. said. "Come on. Let's go."

Inside the cave, Gregori slipped on his backpack while Abigail put on hers. He'd never been to the other base, so he would have to rely on the beacon. He wrapped his arms around her, closed his eyes, and concentrated.

"Do you hear it?" J.L. asked. "It's two fast beeps, then a long one."

"Got it." He gave Abigail a squeeze. "We'll be all right, sweetheart."

She nodded and linked her fingers behind his neck.

Everything went black.

Chapter Twenty-six

*A*bigail didn't let go of Gregori even though they had arrived. The place was pitch-black and cold, and her nerves were frazzled. How could everything go so wrong so fast? For goodness' sake, she was only looking for a few plants. But instead, she'd found a whole village of mind-controlled slaves and a whole army of acrobatic kung fu vampires.

She shuddered, and Gregori's arms tightened around her. It was so dark, she couldn't even make out his facial features.

"We're okay," he whispered.

In the distance, she could hear the low roar of rushing water. "Where are we?"

"A cave in northwest Yunnan," J.L. answered her. A match flickered and he lit a kerosene lamp. "Everyone here?"

"Yes." Russell yanked the electronic beacon off a rock ledge, dropped it on the cave floor, and crushed it under the heel of his boot.

J.L. gave him a wry look. "You could have just turned it off."

Russell scowled at him. "I felt like smashing something."

J.L. retrieved a different phone from his backpack. "We have to use the satellite phone out here." He headed for the entrance of the cave. "I'll call Angus and tell him what happened."

Howard lit the second kerosene lamp. "I hope my donuts are all right." He opened a metal trunk and withdrew a pastry box.

Abigail released her death grip on Gregori and lowered her backpack to the floor so she could get out her sweater. "It's chilly here." She took off her jacket, put the sweater on, then the jacket back on.

"We're close to Tibet." Russell removed a sweatshirt from his backpack. "And we're at a much higher altitude."

"A couple of thousand feet up a damned mountain," Howard grumbled, then bit into a bear claw.

"At least we found a cave that faces south." Russell pulled on his sweatshirt. "We're sheltered from the colder winds."

"And direct sunlight," Gregori added as he retrieved a sweater from his backpack.

"What about all those vampires?" Abigail asked.

"We're over two hundred miles away from them." Russell smirked. "And our beacon is experiencing technical difficulties."

"I keep wondering why they came after us," she said. "Is it because we found that village? And all those plants? Why is Master Han collecting so much Demon Herb?"

"Because he's up to something nasty," Russell growled. "The sooner I kill him, the better off we'll all be."

"Just remember our mission right now is to keep Abigail safe," Gregori told him as he pulled on his sweater.

"Damn, it's cold out there." J.L. rushed back inside and pocketed his phone. "Angus wants us to call every two hours. And he wants us to teleport to Japan no later than tomorrow night, whether we find the third plant or not."

"Then we'd better get to work," Gregori said.

J.L. turned to Abigail. "What can you tell us about it?"

She took a photo from the outside pocket of her backpack. "The name translates as Flower of the Golden Sands. It's a flowering bush that grows on the south side of mountains near the Yangtze River. People here call it the River of Golden Sands."

"*Jinsha Jiang*," J.L. murmured as he studied the photo, then passed it to Rajiv.

"We look for it now?" Rajiv asked.

"Yes." J.L. pulled a sweater from his backpack. "The terrain is rough outside. And the wind really rips through the canyons. We're on a gorge above the Yangtze River."

Rajiv smiled. "It's the Leaping Tiger Gorge." He passed the photo on to Russell.

"That's the Yangtze River I hear?" Abigail asked.

"Yes." J.L. put on his sweater. "We need you to stay here, Abby. It's too dark outside."

She stiffened. "I'll be fine. I'll use a flashlight."

J.L. shook his head. "The wind is so strong, it could knock you off your feet. One slip, and you could fall a few thousand feet into the gorge."

She swallowed hard. "Okay. I'll look for it during the day then."

"Hopefully we'll find it before sunrise, so we can get the hell out of here," J.L. said. "Howard, will you stay here with Abby?"

"Sure." He offered her the pastry box. "Want a donut?"

She sighed. "No."

Gregori pulled her toward the back of the cave. "I know how you hate not being allowed to do things, but your time will come. Once we get home, you'll be doing all the work with the plants."

She nodded and gave him a weary smile. "You're right. It would be crazy for me to scramble around a mountain in the dark."

"Okay." He kissed her brow. "Wish us luck, so we can go home."

"Good luck." She hugged him tight.

The Vamps and Rajiv bundled up, retrieved some flashlights from a metal box, then headed out.

She ventured outside a few steps and watched the flashlight beams swing back and forth as the men searched the south side of the mountain. The edge of the cliff was barely visible to her, but she could hear the loud roar of the river far below.

A strong, cold wind slapped at her, threatening to knock her down, so she went back inside the cave. She helped Howard unroll sleeping bags for everyone. Three of the bags were placed far in the back of the cave, then a folding screen was stretched in front of them. The south-facing entrance of the cave would keep any direct sunlight from coming in, but the Vamps still preferred it as dark as possible.

Howard lit an oil heater, and the cave warmed up a little. They sat and waited for the others to return.

They'd finished off two boxes of donuts before the guys came back, looking exhausted and cold. From the grim looks on their faces, she could tell they hadn't found the third plant.

The Vamps helped themselves to bottled blood from the ice chest. Rajiv guzzled down a bottle of water.

"Sorry." Gregori sat next to her, close to the heater. "We scoured the south side of three mountains, but couldn't find it."

J.L. drank some blood. "It's already daylight in Japan, so it's too late to teleport back. We'll have to wait till tonight. As soon as we wake up, we're outta here."

"I'll hunt for the plant while you guys sleep," Howard offered. "Rajiv and I can take turns."

"Are you sure we'll be safe here?" Abigail asked.

J.L. yawned. "We're hundreds of miles from the last place."

"And that was a vampire army," Russell added. "They can only come after us at nighttime."

J.L. passed his satellite phone to Howard. "Keep calling every two hours. It'll be forwarded to a Vamp who's awake."

Gregori patted Abigail's knee. "When we wake up, I'll take you back to Kyo's place. You can have a long, hot bath."

"Sounds wonderful." She leaned close and whispered, "I need to relieve myself."

"I'll take you." He hefted himself to his feet and grabbed a flashlight.

They didn't venture far from the cave. He turned his back so she wouldn't feel embarrassed, but she was glad to have him nearby in case any wild animals decided she looked tasty.

Back in the cave, she and Gregori washed up in one of the buckets of water the guys had stashed there before her arrival in China.

She yawned. She was too tired and cold to even worry about sleeping next to a dead body. She dragged her sleeping bag to the back of the cave and cuddled up beside Gregori.

It was well past noon when she woke up. This time she didn't freak at the sight of Gregori lying so still beside her. She brushed his hair back from his brow and tucked in his blanket.

Howard was out searching for the plant while Rajiv guarded the cave. He'd heated some water on a kerosene stove to make tea. She ate a breakfast of hot tea and stale donuts.

Three hours later, Howard came back empty-handed and grumpy. He stuffed down six bear claws, guzzled a bottle of water, then decided he should descend the gorge to fill up their wash buckets with fresh water.

"You crazy," Rajiv said. "River long way down. Too hard for a bear."

"You want to bet?" Howard growled. "Just because

it's the Leaping Tiger Gorge doesn't mean it's just for tigers."

Rajiv scoffed. "I'm not going down there. It's too big. River too crazy. Let the Vamps teleport there for water."

Howard grunted. "I'll show you how it's done." He grabbed a bucket and headed for the entrance.

He stopped with a jerk. The bucket fell from his hand and sloshed water on the cave floor.

He ducked down. "Holy crap! I don't believe this."

"What?" Rajiv ran forward.

Howard pulled him down. "Don't let them see you."

"Who?" Abigail's heart pounded as she eased forward. She hunkered down beside the two shifters, and her heart shot up her throat.

On the other side of the gorge, on the crests of the mountains, Master Han's army was gathering. More and more of them lined up along the ridge, all dressed in white. The ends of their red sashes fluttered in the wind.

Her blood ran cold. There had to be a hundred of them! "How—how can they be here in daylight? I thought they were vampires."

"Maybe they different guys," Rajiv suggested. "Maybe Master Han have a vampire army and a human one."

Panic threatened to burst inside her. She fisted her hands and squeezed her eyes shut. *Don't lose it. You'll just make things worse if you lose it.* She opened her eyes, and the army was still standing along the ridge.

"How they find us?" Rajiv asked. "How they get here so fast?"

"I don't know," Howard said softly. "But they're here, and we have to deal with it."

Abigail gasped when some of the soldiers jumped off a cliff. They must be suicidal! But no, they fluttered down the side of the cliff, and landed neatly on a ridge a hundred feet below. Others leaped from rock to rock, even doing somersaults in the air.

"Holy crap," Howard whispered. "They're the same guys. They can move like vampires, but they're mortal."

"How can they be like this?" Abigail wondered out loud. "These guys are supernatural."

"They going to cross the gorge," Rajiv said. "They find us."

Howard sucked in a deep breath. "You need to go. I'll stay here to guard the fort. You can shift and cross the gorge."

"I'm not leaving you and Miss Abby alone," Rajiv hissed.

"You have to!" Howard slipped the sat phone into a zippered case and slipped the cord around Rajiv's neck. "Get out of here and call Angus. He can find us with the tracking chip the Vamps have embedded— Oh shit. That's how those bastards found us."

Rajiv turned to Abigail. "I take you with me?"

She shook her head, her eyes crowding with tears. "I'll slow you down. And I can't get across the gorge."

Howard slapped him on the back. "Go! We're counting on you."

Rajiv knotted the cord so the phone would be secure. "God be with you."

"And with you." Abigail gave him a hug.

He scrambled out of the cave, keeping low.

She whispered a prayer that he would be safe, that he would make it through. She glanced back at the folding screen. The Vamps were behind there, dead and oblivious.

She looked at the sky. The sun was lowering in the west. "How much longer before the sun sets?"

"About an hour," Howard answered. "At the rate their army is moving, they'll be here in fifteen minutes."

So the Vamps wouldn't be awake to teleport them away. Her hands trembled, so she clenched them into fists. "We're outnumbered."

"I can kill maybe thirty or forty of them before they finish me off." Howard regarded her with a grim look. "But then you'll be alone with the rest of them, and they'll be really pissed."

A sick feeling churned in her gut. "We have no choice. We'll have to surrender."

Chapter Twenty-seven

"Careful," Abigail whispered as Howard peered over the ledge. "Can you see the river?"

"Yes." He was flat on his stomach, clutching a nearby bush to keep from plummeting as he eased farther over the cliff.

They no longer worried about the invading army seeing them. It was obvious the soldiers were moving toward them. It was also obvious that even though the soldiers could do amazing physical feats, they lacked the ability to teleport. Otherwise they would simply materialize across the river. Howard described how a few had made incredible leaps across the gorge, and many more were gathered across the river, preparing to jump.

She just hoped Rajiv found a place to cross without the soldiers spotting him.

"I see him." Howard eased out further. "He's downriver. It's wider there, but there are some giant boulders in the river. Yes! He just landed on one."

"He's in tiger form?"

"Oh yeah. He had to strip before shifting, but I'm sure he left the phone tied around his neck. There he goes. He made it to another rock. And yes! He's across. He . . . I can't see him now." Howard scooted back. "Nothing much we can do now. But wait."

She swallowed hard. Wait for what? What did Master Han want with them?

Howard settled by the cave entrance, watching the approaching army. She couldn't do it. It was too nerve-wracking, so she went back into the cave to sit by the heater.

Her mind raced, and foremost among her frantic thoughts was J.L.'s warning about the Demon Herb. *Those who go looking for it are never seen again.*

Why was this happening? It had to be connected to the zombie village and the fields of Demon Herb. What was Master Han up to? From her research, she believed the plant could boost a person's immune system, make him stronger and more impervious to disease. She'd hoped it would help her mother, perhaps even cure her.

But would she ever make it back home? Ever see her family again? Ever enjoy a future with Gregori?

Those who go looking for it are never seen again.

She didn't want to die. She wanted to see her family again. And hold Gregori again.

The sound of crunching gravel echoed in the canyon. The soldiers were getting closer. The sun lowered and the temperature dropped, but she knew the shivers down her back were caused more by fear than by cold.

She glanced at the folding screen. At least there wasn't any sun coming in the cave. If the soldiers tore down the screen, Gregori and the other two Vamps would be fine.

She heard a noise outside and jumped. "Oh God." She pressed her hand to her pounding heart when Howard walked in.

"They're close." He squatted beside her. "The sun has already set in Japan, so when Rajiv calls, Angus will be awake. He'll start gathering every Vamp and shifter he can find. They can track the Vamps, so they'll come for us. We just need to stay together and stall for time."

She nodded, feeling a small measure of relief.

Gravel crunched outside.

Howard stood. "They're here."

Her chest tightened, and she fisted her hands. *Don't lose it.* She had to stay tough. Roll with the punches like Gregori did. She glanced at the screen. The Vamps were helpless right now. She had to be strong and help Howard protect them. She wasn't a warrior, so her best weapon was her mind. She needed to stay sharp and focused.

Four soldiers eased inside with their swords drawn.

Howard raised his hands. "We surrender."

Abigail scrambled to her feet and lifted her hands. *Stall for time.* "We wish to see Master Han."

The soldiers stared at her.

She wasn't sure if any of them understood English, but she had to try. "I'm a scientist. I have a business proposition for Master Han." She didn't know what, but she'd make it up as she went.

The tallest of the four soldiers said something in Chinese, and two of the soldiers sheathed their swords and tied Howard's hands behind his back. They disarmed him, then pushed him down into a sitting position.

More soldiers gathered outside on the ledge. The lowering sun gleamed off their swords.

A huge soldier pushed through them and strode into the cave. She recognized him as the one called Sawat. All the soldiers inclined their heads, so apparently he was their leader. His angry glare passed over Howard and her to the back of the cave. He marched past her and knocked the screen to the floor.

He glanced over the three Vamps. "*Chiang-shih,*" he muttered, then returned to Howard, who was cross-legged on the floor. "Where's the tiger?"

"Glad to see you've learned some English, Sawat." Howard smirked. "But I think your voice has gotten higher."

With a growl, Sawat pulled a knife and pointed it at Howard's throat. "Where's the tiger?"

Howard glared up at him.

Abigail winced when a drop of blood trickled down Howard's neck. "He's not here. He didn't come with us."

Sawat snorted. "He's here. I'll find him." He marched outside and barked orders in Chinese. A group of soldiers took off. Sawat remained on the ledge, scanning the mountains, no doubt looking for Rajiv.

She eased closer to Gregori.

The tall soldier noticed and motioned to the heater. "You sit here. Or we'll have to tie you up."

"You speak English?" she asked as she lowered herself onto the cave floor.

He ignored her and called out something to Sawat. Outside on the ledge, Sawat yelled a command, and two soldiers entered the cave, carrying a black lacquered box with gold metal corners. They went straight to the back of the cave.

She sat up, craning her neck to see what they were taking out of the box. They looked like metal bands linked together with a short, thick chain. The soldiers snapped the cuffs on the Vamps' forearms and locked them. When the bands wouldn't fit around the men's boots, they removed the boots and locked the cuffs around their ankles.

They found knives in the boots and more knives strapped to the Vamps' calves. They gathered them up, along with the rifles and pistols, and stashed them in a pile by the entrance of the cave.

"The cuffs are made of silver," the tall soldier explained. "It will keep them from teleporting away."

"And burn like hell, if they attempt to remove them," a British-accented voice said outside the cave.

She jerked around to the front. A man stood next to Sawat, dressed in black leather pants, a black shirt, and a long black leather coat. Was this Master Han?

His clothes weren't dusty like those of the soldiers who had crossed the gorge and climbed up to the cave. His hair was shoulder-length and black, but he wasn't Asian.

"Lord Darafer," Sawat murmured, bowing low.

The other soldiers also bowed as the newcomer sauntered inside the cave. They kept their eyes downcast, as if afraid to gaze any higher than his knees. He looked around with sparkling green eyes and an amused tilt to his mouth.

"My lord." The tall soldier bowed low.

Darafer crossed his arms and heaved a resigned sigh. "Wu Shen."

"Yes, my lord." The tall soldier bowed again.

"You know how much I hate human error."

The tall soldier turned pale. "Yes, my lord."

"And yet you try my patience. And I have no patience."

Wu Shen bowed. "A thousand pardons, my lord."

Darafer gestured toward Howard. "This one is a were-bear. He could shift and rip your head off."

Wu Shen's eyes widened. He spoke quickly to the soldiers with the black lacquered box. They rushed over to Howard and snapped silver bands around his wrists behind his back. When they moved in front of him to cuff his ankles, he growled at them, and they jumped back.

Darafer chuckled. "Don't be afraid. The bear cannot shift now." His eyes glowed like polished emeralds. "Even if he could, he would be no match for me."

Abigail sucked in a deep breath while the soldiers snapped the cuffs around Howard's ankles. Darafer could defeat a Kodiak bear? He had weird eyes, too, and the soldiers seemed to fear him. She had a sick feeling in her gut that he wasn't human. Then what was he? It was daylight, so he couldn't be a vampire.

He paced toward the back of the cave, then sauntered toward the entrance. "Sawat."

"Yes, my lord." Sawat came in and bowed.

"I count five prisoners."

Sawat grew pale. "Yes, my lord."

"And yet your report claimed there were six sleeping

bags at the other cave. And I count six here. Is someone missing?"

Sawat shifted his feet. "The were-tiger may have escaped."

"Over the Leaping Tiger Gorge?" Darafer chuckled. "That's rich."

Sawat looked relieved. "Yes, my lord."

Darafer's face turned grim. "You screwed up. Go look for him in the gorge." He extended a hand, and a blast of air blew Sawat off his feet, through the air, and over the cliff. His scream echoed in the canyon, then abruptly cut off.

A chill skittered down Abigail's back. Her gut was correct. Darafer was not human.

He turned to the tall soldier and smiled. "Good news, Wu Shen. You've just been promoted."

Wu Shen bowed, his face ashen. "You are most kind, my lord."

"Don't mention it." Darafer gazed about the cave, his green eyes twinkling with amusement. "So . . . we have a shifter who can't shift, three vampires who can't teleport, and . . ." His gaze fell on Abigail. "And a loving daughter who can't save her mother."

She flinched.

He strolled toward her. "How desperate are you, Abigail Tucker? I could save her, you know. It might be fun to have your father indebted to me."

"Don't talk to him," Howard growled.

Darafer glanced at him and smiled. "The bear knows who I am." His gaze shifted back to Abigail and his eyes hardened. "You have something that belongs to me."

She shook her head. "I've never met you before."

He smirked. "I was there six years ago at your father's rally when a man sneaked in with a handgun. Unfortunately he had to brag about it and get himself caught. I hate human error." His eyes suddenly turned black, and she gasped.

He extended a hand toward her backpack. It unzipped on its own, and the plastic bag containing the Demon Herb flew into his hand.

He chuckled, his eyes returning to green. "They don't call it the Demon Herb for nothing."

Demon. She clenched her fists to keep from shaking. How could they escape from a demon? He seemed to know everything. He'd known instantly who Howard was. Who she was. Her chest tightened. He'd tried to use a man to kill her father six years ago.

Darafer removed the Demon Herb and sniffed it. "Best stuff I ever created." He shrugged. "I know. You're thinking only the Big Kahuna can create. That's true to a certain extent."

He twirled the branch of Demon Herb between his thumb and forefinger. "But I can take something He made and distort it, corrupt it. For centuries, I had a jolly good time mutating things into diseases and plagues. Then it occurred to me, instead of making humans weak and useless, why not do the opposite? Why not make something that actually turns humans into supermen? That I control, of course."

He stuffed the Demon Herb into his coat pocket. "Imagine how much pain and despair I can wreak upon the world when I control an army of supermen?"

"I thought it was Master Han's army," Howard grumbled.

"He provides the men. I . . . enhance them. The potion I make with the Demon Herb gives them super powers and a remarkable ability to heal." He waved a dismissive hand. "But I grow bored with the mundane details of gathering and training an army. I leave that to Master Han. You would be amazed how many humans are willing to trade their souls for the chance to be Superman."

He walked over to Howard. "How about you? Want to switch to the winning side?"

"Go back to hell," Howard growled.

Darafer smirked. "Who's going to make me?" He glanced back at Wu Shen. "Master Han can decide what to do with them."

"Yes, my lord." Wu Shen bowed.

"But keep the girl alive. She has good connections." Darafer smiled at Abigail. "Let me know if your father wants to make a deal. I could save your mother."

She lifted her chin, determined to be as brave as Howard. "Go back to hell."

He chuckled. "Actually, I think I'll go visit your mother. Such a shame she's about to take a turn for the worse." He vanished.

Abigail's heart plummeted into her stomach. Would he really hurt her mother? Of course he would. Wasn't that what demons did?

"He killed Sawat," Howard said quietly, looking at Wu Shen. "Next time he gets angry, it could be your turn."

Wu Shen's mouth thinned. "You think to sway me? Our bodies are Master Han's to command. It is an honor to serve and die for him."

"And the demon?" Howard asked.

Wu Shen looked away. "He owns our souls."

Howard snorted. "Then you had better hope you never die."

Wu Shen strode outside and stood on the ledge.

Abigail exchanged a look with Howard and nodded slightly. They might be able to get through to Wu Shen. She sent up a silent prayer that they would all survive. Including her mother.

Wu Shen walked back into the cave. "The sun is setting. The *chiang-shih* will need blood."

"There's bottled blood in the ice chest." She motioned to it. "I could give it to them."

He nodded. "That will be for the best. They would not attempt to attack you."

She hurried to the ice chest and removed three bottles. Then she settled on her sleeping bag next to Gregori.

As the last rays of the sun faded away, torches were set ablaze outside the entrance to the cave. Wu Shen lit the kerosene lamps as he gave more orders. Three soldiers unsheathed their swords and formed a line in front of the Vamps. Two more watched Howard.

The Vamps jerked and their chests suddenly expanded with a gasp for air. Their eyes opened.

"Listen," Abigail whispered.

Gregori reached for her, but the chain pulled tight on his cuffs. "What the—" He sat up, an alarmed look on his face.

J.L. and Russell sat up, and all three Vamps cursed under their breath and pulled at their restraints.

"We've been captured." Abigail unscrewed the top

off Gregori's bottle and placed it into his hands. "Master Han's army arrived during the day."

"How?" J.L. asked, eyeing the soldiers.

"They're mortal." Abigail unscrewed J.L.'s bottle and handed it to him. "But with superhuman powers. They may have enhanced hearing," she added quietly, so the guys would be careful what they said.

"Shit," Gregori whispered, then guzzled down some blood.

"Howard has been captured, too." Abigail passed a bottle to Russell. "They have all *five* of us."

The guys were silent, but she could see a gleam of satisfaction in their eyes that Rajiv had escaped.

"They took all your weapons and put silver cuffs on you so you can't teleport. And Howard can't shift." She glanced at the soldiers. They didn't seem to mind that she was talking. "Master Han isn't working alone. He has a demon helping him."

"A demon?" J.L. asked.

"His name is Darafer. He's mutating the Demon Herb to make a potion that gives humans supernatural powers."

"So a nasty vampire villain has teamed up with a demon." Gregori gulped down more blood. "We're in deep shit."

"Could be worse," J.L. mumbled.

"How do you figure that?" Gregori asked, his eyes narrowed on the soldiers.

J.L. shrugged. "We could be dead."

"He's right." Russell pulled his hands apart, testing the chain. "As long as we're alive, we can fight."

"Exactly." Gregori finished the last of his blood, then

tossed the bottle aside. "It's a shame they took *all* of our weapons." He gave the other Vamps a pointed look.

Russell and J.L. nodded and set their bottles down.

"And a shame they tied up Howard," Gregori said, his voice loud. "He's liable to get really pissed."

Howard roared, rising to his knees, and all the soldiers looked his way. With vampire speed, Gregori, Russell, and J.L. whipped knives out from beneath their sleeping bags. Before Abigail could even see what was happening, three guards were dead on the ground with knives in their chests, and the Vamps had claimed their swords.

"Drop them or he's dead!" Wu Shen held a pistol aimed at Howard's face. The other two guards poked the tips of their swords into his back.

The Vamps froze. When Wu Shen cocked his pistol, they tossed their swords onto the ground.

He gave them a disgusted look. "You think you can escape by killing three guards? I have a hundred more outside. And every one of us considers it an honor to die for Master Han."

"Well said, Wu Shen," a muffled voice announced outside the cave.

"Master Han." He stepped back and inclined his head. "We have the prisoners you wanted."

Chapter Twenty-eight

Shit. He'd killed a man.

Gregori's gaze drifted to the dead body and his knife protruding from the man's chest. Ian had warned him when he'd first begun his lessons in fencing and martial arts. *Once you engage in combat, you have to kill to survive.*

Over the years, Gregori had mentally prepared himself. If a battle occurred with the Malcontents, he wanted to be able to fight alongside his friends. And that meant killing Malcontents. He'd accepted that. After all, Malcontents were vicious vampires who had a long track record of torturing and killing humans. They deserved to die. Skewering them through the heart just made them disintegrate into a pile of dust. One strong gust of wind, and the dust was gone.

No body. No guilt. No remorse.

It had never occurred to him that he might have to kill a human. This body wasn't going to disappear. The dead man lay there in a pool of blood, his eyes wide open, staring but not seeing.

Gregori clenched his fists and looked away. *You're a*

warrior now. Deal with it. He needed to protect Abigail, get her home safely, get them all home safely.

Their first attempt had failed, but he would stay alert and prepared for the next opportunity.

A new group of soldiers dashed inside the cave and retrieved the swords he, Russell, and J.L. had dropped. They even yanked the knives from the dead men's chests, in case Gregori and his friends were tempted to use them again.

Abigail was pale, her hands gripped together, so he gave her an encouraging look. They still had a few aces up their sleeve. Rajiv had escaped. If he made it to his grandfather's tribe, there would be a group of were-tigers ready for battle. Rajiv would manage to call Angus, or the check-in call would be missed—either way, Angus would know they were in trouble. And he could locate them with the tracking chips embedded in their arms.

The soldiers went into a scraping and bowing routine, then moved aside so Master Han could advance into the cave.

He was tall. And slim. That was all Gregori could make out, for his body was covered with black silk robes and topped with a hooded robe of red silk, embroidered in gold. Deep inside the shadow of the hood, his face was hidden behind a mask of gold. No wonder his voice had sounded tinny and muffled.

"Master Han, and the three vampire lords," Wu Shen announced. "Lord Ming, Lord Qing, and Lord Liao."

Three Asian vampires followed Master Han. They were also dressed in flowing silk robes, but their heads were uncovered. Their hair, long and braided, dangled down their backs. Each one clasped his hands together at the waist. Gregori figured they didn't use their hands much, not with fingernails that were about six inches long, curved and yellow.

Gross. From the look on Abigail's face, he could tell she agreed.

It was hard to tell what Master Han was thinking or feeling with the stupid gold mask on his face, but Gregori could see his brown eyes studying Howard before moving slowly toward the back of the cave. His gaze passed over Gregori, lingered on Abigail, then moved on to J.L. and Russell. He stiffened.

"Bastard," Russell muttered.

Lord Ming said something in Chinese, and Lord Qing appeared to agree.

"They want to kill us," J.L. whispered.

"Lords Ming, Qing, and Dingaling can take a flying leap," Russell growled.

Master Han lifted a black-gloved hand and pointed at Russell. "This one is mine. He bears my mark."

The three vampire lords murmured in disbelief.

"Show your mark," Master Han demanded in his muffled voice. "Show you belong to me."

Russell glared back, not moving.

A soldier came forward to grab his right arm, but he pulled away. Master Han motioned to Howard, and a soldier grasped Howard's hair to yank back his head while he pressed a knife to his throat.

"Now, slave." Master Han turned back to Russell. "Show me your mark."

Russell jerked back his sleeve to reveal his tattoo. "It means nothing, asshole."

"On the contrary, it means I will keep you alive until I can reclaim what is mine." Master Han removed three syringes from an embroidered pouch tied to his waist by silken cords. He passed them to a soldier and gave him directions in Chinese.

The soldier came toward them with the syringes.

Gregori assumed a martial arts position, and beside him, Russell and J.L. did the same, although their movements were severely hindered by the damned cuffs.

"Stay behind us," he whispered to Abigail.

Master Han lifted a hand. "Calm yourselves. You must be sedated so we can remove the cuffs and teleport you."

"We don't have to do a damned thing for you," Gregori growled.

"The sedative will not harm you," Master Han replied. "But your refusal will cause your friend great harm." He motioned toward Howard. "I do not care if this one lives."

Gregori fisted his hands. *Shit.* What choice did they have but to cooperate? They needed to keep Howard alive. And they needed to stall for time. Without the ability to teleport, there was no way to escape this cave, not with that crowd of soldiers out front. But if they allowed Master Han to move them to another location, it might be an easier place to escape. And with their imbedded homing devices, Angus would still be able to track them down.

One of the vampire lords murmured in Chinese to Master Han.

"You." Master Han pointed at Abigail. "You will come closer."

Abigail stiffened and gave Gregori an alarmed look.

He turned to Master Han. "Leave her alone, and we'll cooperate."

"You'll cooperate, or we'll kill this one." Master Han gestured to Howard.

Gregori glared back. "If you harm her, I will kill you."

Master Han chuckled, the sound echoing eerily behind his mask. "I have no interest in her. It is Lord Ming who wants her."

Lord Ming said something in Chinese, and Gregori shot a questioning look at J.L.

"He says she has a virgin neck," J.L. whispered. "He wants to be the first to bite her."

"You asshole." Gregori lunged toward Lord Ming at vampire speed, stretched his hands and cuffs apart, and rammed the silver chain against Lord Ming's neck. The silver sizzled against his skin.

Lord Ming jumped back, crying out in pain, while two soldiers knocked Gregori down and pointed their swords at his chest.

Master Han leaned over him. "You do not bear my mark. I would not regret killing you."

"The feeling is mutual," Gregori gritted out, wishing he could rip the golden Frisbee off Han's face and cram it down his throat.

"Gregori." Abigail rushed toward him with tears in her eyes. "Please—"

A soldier grabbed her and pressed a knife to her neck.

"Excellent. I believe everyone will be in a more cooperative mood now." Master Han turned to the soldier with the syringes and gave him an order in Chinese.

The soldier approached Russell and J.L. and motioned for them to sit. After they sat, he stabbed the syringes in their necks, and they both slumped over.

Gregori's eyes met Abigail's. His chest tightened. She looked so pale and scared.

"I love you," he whispered as the syringe plunged into his neck. The cave spun around him, then went black.

Abigail sank up to her chin in the tub of hot water. Maybe if she was real quiet, they would forget about her.

She'd been at Master Han's compound about twenty minutes, she estimated. The three vampire lords had teleported Russell, J.L., and Gregori away after the silver cuffs had been removed from their unconscious bodies. She had no idea where the guys were. She closed her eyes and pictured Gregori's face, remembering the love he had whispered and the worry in his eyes.

The soldiers had knocked Howard on the head so hard, blood had run down his face as he slumped over unconscious. They'd removed his silver cuffs, then Lord Liao had returned to teleport him away.

Lord Ming had returned for her. He'd grasped her arms with his nasty yellow nails, and his breath had smelled foul as he'd pulled her close.

Even now, she shuddered when she recalled it and reached for the soap to lather up her body for the fifth time. Lord Ming had teleported her to a courtyard where about thirty soldiers were practicing martial arts by torchlight. Wu Shen and his hundred soldiers were still by the Yangtze River, she assumed, since they couldn't teleport. Hopefully it would take them a while to travel back to Master Han's compound.

When Master Han materialized in the courtyard, the small group of soldiers stopped and prostrated themselves on the ground. He said nothing, just turned and walked up the steps into what looked like a Buddhist temple.

Lord Ming dragged her inside a one-story building that ran the length of the compound. He steered her down a hall, then shoved her into a room where a group of three women resided. A harem, she figured, since the women were all young and pretty and had bite marks on their necks.

They fussed over her, and although she didn't want to cooperate, the lure of a hot bath was too tempting after a night in a chilly cave.

"You done?" one of the young women approached her, the only one who knew some English.

"Five more minutes." Abigail held up her hand to show five.

"No. We must make ready." The young woman gestured to the other women who came toward her, carrying beautiful teal-colored silk robes and embroidered slippers.

"You will wear these tonight for Lord Ming," the woman explained.

Abigail climbed out of the tub and grabbed a nearby towel. "Look, uh . . . what's your name?"

"I am Mei Li."

"Mei Li, I'm Abby."

"Abby." The ladies all bowed and murmured her name.

"Pleased to meet you. Look, I'll get dressed since I don't want to escape from this place naked. But there's no way I'm going to let that creep bite me."

Mei Li looked confused. "It is an honor to feed Master Han and the vampire lords."

"I think it would be more honorable to let them starve."

Mei Li's eyes widened. "It is an honor to serve Master Han and the vampire lords."

Abigail sighed. "They've done a number on your head, haven't they?"

Mei Li motioned to the silk robes once again. "Come, we help you dress."

Abigail slipped on the white silk slip, then wrapped the teal-colored robe around her and tied the sash. Her mind raced, trying to figure out how to handle this.

"Do not fear." Mei Li adjusted her sash. "Lord Ming will be kind. He does not take as much blood as Master Han."

"You've been with Lord Ming before?"

Mei Li nodded. "But tonight I will go with Ping and Genji. We will feed the American *chiang-shih*."

Abigail's fists clenched. One of these pretty women was going to offer her neck to Gregori? Over her dead body. "To tell you the truth, one of those American *chiang-shih* is my boyfriend. We're in love."

Mei Li tilted her head, her eyes narrowed. "Boy . . . friend?"

"Yes. Lovers. We love each other very much."

Mei Li's eyes took on a distant look. "I . . . remember."

"You had a boyfriend?"

Mei Li nodded slowly. "In Kunming. But I went home to village to see family, and whole village now work in fields for Master Han."

"I've seen that village," Abigail said.

"They bring me here." She stiffened, and her face went blank. "It is an honor to serve Master Han and the vampire lords."

Abigail groaned. Just when she'd thought she was making progress with Mei Li, the vampire mind control had snatched her right back. "Don't you want to escape from here? See your boyfriend again?"

"It is an honor to serve Master Han and the vampire lords."

"Okay. Then why don't you serve the vampire lord? We'll trade places. You can feed Lord Ming and I'll feed the American vampire."

Mei Li hesitated. "Lord Ming will know I am not you."

"Yes, but it is an honor to be bitten by him, right? No honor at all in being bitten by an American." Abigail wrinkled her nose in disgust.

Mei Li shuddered. "I do not wish to feed one of them."

"Great! Then we'll switch places." Abigail felt a twinge of guilt at manipulating someone who wasn't thinking clearly. She was using poor Mei Li as much as the creepy vampires were. But she was desperate to avoid Lord Ming and his nasty nails and fangs. And she had to find Gregori and the guys. They needed to stick together so they could escape.

Five minutes later, Abigail, Ping, and Genji all filed out of the room, dressed in similar robes with identical veils over their heads. Mei Li stayed behind, wearing her robe and veil, awaiting the summons from Lord Ming.

Ping led the way down one hallway after another, then finally emerged outside. Abigail noted they were behind the Buddhist temple now. They crossed to a low building lined with heavy metal doors where three armed soldiers stood in front. The jailhouse, she figured.

Ping spoke to one of the guards. He slid a small window open on the first door, then nodded with a grunt. He unlocked the door and Ping went inside. Abigail caught a glimpse of Russell lying unconscious on a mat before the door was shut and locked.

The guard opened the next door. Abigail spotted J.L. and stepped back so Genji would enter.

The guard unlocked the third door, and Abigail slipped inside. The door slammed behind her.

She hurried over to see if Gregori was all right. He was still unconscious, but his heart was beating strong. The silver cuffs were gone. His boots were missing, since the soldiers had removed them, so his feet were covered with thick woolen socks. His sweater and jacket were still on. He was lying in the middle of the room on a thin mat. There was no floor, just hard dirt.

She straightened to take a look around her. A rectangular fluorescent light fixture glared overhead, making the smooth, metallic walls gleam. Stainless steel? She looked closer. *Silver.* Of course. It was probably the only way to imprison a vampire. Even the ceiling was silver.

Gregori moaned and lifted a hand to his forehead. Then he sat up abruptly and looked around.

His eyes narrowed on her. "Get out. I'm not interested."

Her heart soared at his faithfulness. "Are you sure?" She pulled the veil off her head.

"Abby," he breathed, then leaped toward her and pulled her into his arms. "Oh, thank God, you're all right. And you're with me. I was afraid that asshole Ming would try to get his claws on you."

"I was supposed to go to him, but I talked Mei Li into switching places with me."

"Oh, Scholar, you are so brilliant." Gregori kissed her brow.

"It wasn't all brains, believe me. When I thought about you being locked up with the beautiful Mei Li, I was ready to rip this compound apart with my bare hands."

He laughed and hugged her close.

She gazed up at him and brushed his hair back from his brow. "I'm not sure if Lord Ming is going to accept the trade, since he appears to have a thing for unmarked necks."

"*Virgin* necks," Gregori muttered. "Creepy bastard."

"Well, under the circumstances, I think we'd better get rid of my neck virginity really quick."

His eyes widened. "You mean . . ."

"Yes. I need you to bite me before Lord Ming realizes I pulled a switcheroo on him."

"Abby." Gregori released her and stepped back. "No."

"You have my permission."

"No! We'll just escape from here." His form wavered then solidified again. "Shit. I can't teleport." He paced around the perimeter of the room and examined the walls closely.

"It's solid silver," she said.

He touched the door and jerked his hand back with a grimace. "Even the door is silver."

"We're not getting out of here for a while, and if Lord Ming still wants a virgin—"

"Abby, how can I return you to your family with fang marks on your neck?"

Tears stung her eyes at the thought of her family. For the hundredth time, she hoped her mother was all right. "At this point, I'll be glad to return at all."

"I'll get you out of here. Somehow."

She dragged in a shaky breath. "Gregori, it was terrible. The demon said he could make my mother better if my dad was willing to work with him. I told him to go to hell, and he said he was going to see my mother and make her worse!"

"Sheesh." Gregori pulled her into his arms. "I'm so sorry. This happened while I was in my death-sleep?"

She nodded, her cheek nestled against his chest.

"God, I hate it when I'm not able to protect you."

She glanced up at him. "You can protect me now from Lord Ming."

He winced. "I don't want to bite you, Abby. I've never bitten a mortal before."

"If you don't bite me, he will!" She fisted her hands around the lapels of his jacket. "Please. I can't stand the thought of him touching me. Or sinking his teeth into—"

"Okay." Gregori dragged a hand through his hair. "Shit. I can't stand the thought of him touching you, either."

"You told me at the nightclub that you bit vampire women, and it was somehow pleasurable. Can you do that with me?"

"It's . . . possible."

"Good. Let's do it."

He paused. Shifted his weight.

She lifted her eyebrows. "Well?"

"I don't want you to see me with my fangs out."

"I've seen every other part of you." She huffed with impatience. "Come on, Gregori. I know you have fangs."

He scowled at her. "You haven't seen them extended. They get really long."

"I've seen another extended part of you, and it wasn't too long for me to handle."

He crossed his arms. "You think you can handle it?"

"Yes. Bite me."

His mouth twitched. "You're trying to goad me into it."

"Whatever it takes. I'm not letting that creep touch me." She sat on the mat and arranged her silken robes around her. "So, just how *long* do you get?"

He arched a brow. "Long enough to get the job done."

"Okay, do you prefer the right side?" She tilted her head left. "Or the left side?" She tilted her head right.

He removed his jacket and tossed it on the floor. Then he walked toward her, his eyes glittering with green intensity.

She swallowed hard.

He fell to his knees in front of her. His eyes turned red.

"Right side or left side?" she whispered.

He pulled her onto her knees and into his arms. "Backside," he growled and slapped her rump.

She gasped. "Greg—"

He cut her off with a fierce kiss. Meanwhile, his hands squeezed her buttocks and pressed her against his groin.

She wrapped her arms around his neck and delved her hands into his hair. He nuzzled her neck, and her head dropped back.

He dragged his tongue up her neck, and she shivered.

He did it again, and she gasped. Somehow she'd felt it between her legs. Her knees trembled, and she fell back onto the mat.

"Abby." He untied the sash and opened her robe.

Her nipples hardened under the sheer white silk shift.

"So pretty." He rubbed his fingers over her nipples, then lightly pinched the hardened tips.

She moaned. "Gregori, bite me."

He chuckled. "You really want this, don't you?"

"Yes." She reached for him. "I love you, Gregori. I want to experience every part of you."

His red eyes glowed brighter. "I love you, too." He kissed her, then returned to her neck. He licked and nibbled, and with each move, she felt it between her legs. And she wanted more.

"Oh God, touch me." She rubbed a leg against him.

He pulled up her shift and slipped his hand between her legs. She jolted with pleasure when he touched her clitoris and his fangs scraped the side of her neck.

With a soft pop, his fangs broke through. With each deep suck, it felt as if he was penetrating her deeper and deeper. Her climax hit with a shattering force.

Gregori removed his fangs and held her until the last of the throbs faded away.

He gazed into her eyes. "Are you all right?"

She nodded. His eyes were back to green, and his fangs were retracted. "Make love to me."

"I thought I did."

"Not completely. I want more."

His eyes glinted with humor and he kissed her nose. "I don't want to take you on a dirt floor, Abby."

She smiled. "We could always try the ceiling."

He laughed, then stopped and looked up. "The ceiling."

"It's covered with silver."

"Yeah, but that's a big light fixture." He stood and levitated to the ceiling.

She stood and adjusted her clothes.

"Stand back against the wall. This could get ugly." He ripped the light fixture off the ceiling.

Lights sizzled and popped. He yanked harder. The lights exploded, and the room turned dark.

"Stay put," he told her. "There's broken glass on the floor."

"Can you see?"

"Barely. There's an opening here. I think it's big enough I can levitate through it."

She waited, then heard his muffled voice.

"I can feel the tile roof. I'm going to teleport out. Hang on."

She listened, then heard a thump on the roof. She waited in the dark for what seemed a long time, then the door opened.

Gregori leaned in with a torch in his hand. "Watch your step."

She hurried outside and found the three guards unconscious on the ground and the other doors unlocked. J.L. and Russell were helping themselves to the guards' weapons. They each took a sword and a dagger, and handed Gregori the same. Ping and Genji stood nearby, hugging each other and whispering.

Gregori wrapped an arm around Abigail's shoulders. "I should teleport you straight to Kyo's place."

It was tempting, so tempting. "We can't go until we find Howard."

A roar sounded in the distance. Bearlike, angry and hurt.

"This way," Russell led them quietly around the Buddhist temple.

They stopped behind some pillars.

Abigail gasped.

There in the courtyard was a giant cage, and inside was a huge bear. Blood coated the side of his head. Soldiers stood around the cage, jabbing long spears inside to pierce the bear's skin. The bear circled, swatting and breaking the spears in front of him, but more spears would stab him the back.

Abigail's eyes burned with hot tears. "They're torturing him."

Gregori glanced at the other two Vamps. "Shall we show these assholes how it feels to get stabbed?"

The Vamps teleported behind three soldiers, spun them around, and stabbed them through the chest. With a whooping war cry, they continued fighting and slashing at the guys with spears.

An answering war cry sounded outside the compound, then the courtyard filled with Vamps teleporting in. Abigail cried with joy as she recognized Angus, Robby, and Kyo among them. Another roar filled the air, and tigers leaped over the walls. The Vamps succeeded in opening the cage, and Howard leaped out, roaring and slashing at the men who had tortured him.

Ping and Genji screamed and ran inside the temple. A loud gong sounded, and more soldiers streamed into the courtyard.

Abigail eased up the steps of the temple so she could steer clear of the fight and have a better vantage point. She didn't want to take her eyes off Gregori. He was slashing a path through the enemy, working his way back to her.

Suddenly a hand clapped over her mouth and dragged her back. Lord Ming's sharp nails curled into her skin, and his foul breath filled her nostrils.

She elbowed him hard in the ribs and pulled away. With vampire speed, he was on her again in a second, clutching her by the arms. His eyes narrowed on her neck.

He shrieked with rage and shoved her back. She stumbled on the stairs, banging up her knees, but righted herself quickly. She froze.

He had drawn two long daggers from his belt.

Gregori shouted behind her.

With a growl, Lord Ming threw the daggers.

She ducked just as Gregori teleported in front of her. Two sickening thuds. Gregori's body jerked.

"No," she whispered. He crumpled in front of her.

"No!" she screamed.

Russell ran up the steps and skewered Lord Ming in the chest. He turned to dust.

"Oh God, no!" She fell to her knees beside Gregori. He lay pale and still with two daggers embedded in his back.

She hugged him, turning her head to press her cheek against him. "Gregori."

At the top of the stairs, by the entrance of the Buddhist temple, she saw Master Han.

He stood quietly watching the battle, then vanished.

Chapter Twenty-nine

*H*e's still bleeding!" Abigail cried as she tossed a blood-soaked towel into a plastic tub, then grabbed a fresh one to press against one of the wounds on Gregori's back.

Angus pressed a towel against the other wound. He'd removed both daggers from Gregori's back, but they'd had no luck in stanching the flow of blood.

"Here, we try this." Kyo pushed her hand aside and slathered a paste onto the wound.

"What is it?"

"*Yunnan Baiyao*. Secret medicine to stop bleeding."

"What's in it?"

"If I tell you, it's not a secret!" Kyo smeared more of the paste on the second wound. "But it has some very good things in it—ginseng, myrrh, and dragon's blood."

Instead of streaming from the wounds, the blood slowed to a trickle, then finally stopped.

She collapsed on the floor beside the bed and burst into tears.

"There, lass." Angus patted her shoulder. " 'Twill be all right."

"But he's lost so much blood," she wailed.

"Aye, if comes to, he must drink several bottles."

She nodded. She'd wanted to take him to a hospital in Tokyo, but Angus had forbidden it. Couldn't risk Gregori falling into his death-sleep there, or being put into a room with sunlight.

With a groan, she hefted herself to her feet and sat on the bed next to Gregori. "Don't die on me. We've been through too much together. I don't know how to go on without you."

He lay there still unconscious.

At least Kyo's secret medicine was working. She thought back to that terrifying moment when she realized Gregori had taken the daggers meant for her. She'd clung to him on the temple steps, crying. When Angus had tried to pull her away to teleport her here, she'd actually struggled to keep hold of Gregori.

He'd finally tugged her loose while Robby had picked up Gregori. They had teleported them both to Kyo's estate.

She wasn't sure of all the details of what had happened at the compound. She knew that once Angus had brought her here, all the Vamps had returned. They seemed to be celebrating, so they must have experienced a victory. But she'd seen only about thirty soldiers at the compound. The majority of Han's army was traveling back from the Yangtze River, so they hadn't been there for the battle.

No one, other than Gregori, had been seriously hurt. Howard and Rajiv were brought back. Howard's wounds had mostly healed when he shifted back to human form.

One Vamp did not return with the others. Russell. Angus sent a search party after him when his homing device indicated he'd returned to their first base. A sleeping bag and some bottles of blood were missing, and on the floor in a small pool of blood, they'd found his tracking chip.

J.L. led the search party to the second base. It looked like Russell had been there, since his backpack was missing. J.L. and his team had gathered up everyone's belongings before returning to Kyo's estate. She had her backpack now, but no samples of the Demon Herb or the third plant.

Kyo brought her an ice chest filled with bottled blood and set it beside the bed. "If he wakes up, he must drink."

She nodded. "Thank you, Kyo."

As dawn approached, Angus came in periodically to check on Gregori. And he brought some visitors to meet her. She met Yoshi and Yuki, two of Kyo's friends, who had answered Angus's call to battle.

"I had only an hour to get an army together," Angus explained. "And I had to draw from areas that were in darkness. Luckily, we had a few volunteers from Down Under." He introduced Rick, Steve, and Bryan from Australia.

"Thank you for coming, lads," Angus said.

"No worries, mate," Rick said. "We're always looking for a good fight."

She smiled and shook hands with them. "I'm delighted to meet you. I'm Abigail Tucker."

"Oy, anyone with the name Tucker has got to be good," Steve said.

"Nice place you have here, mate." Bryan rested an arm across Kyo's shoulders. "Have you got any more of that Bleer?"

Kyo laughed. "Come with me. We find it before Yoshi and Yuki drink it all."

Rajiv and Howard dropped in to see her, and she started crying again.

"Don't cry, Miss Abby. We okay, see?" Rajiv smiled, but tears glimmered in his eyes, too. He hugged her, then quickly left, no doubt to keep from crying.

Howard patted her awkwardly on the shoulder, then lumbered from the room.

The room grew silent once more. She sat beside Gregori, and thought about how close and caring the Vamps and shifters were. They were like family.

It was a family she wanted to be a part of.

Shortly before sunrise, Angus and Robby returned to see how Gregori was doing.

"If he makes it to his death-sleep, then he'll be fine," Robby said.

"But what if he really dies?" she whispered. "How would I know the difference?"

"He would turn to dust," Angus said. "Just a few minutes to go, lass. Once he falls into death-sleep, he'll be fine."

They left the room.

"How could death-sleep make you fine?" she asked Gregori, but he just lay there.

It was hard to know exactly when the sun rose, for the thick aluminum shutters on the window blocked out all the sun. But she did notice when he stopped breathing.

"Gregori," she whispered and stroked his hair.

She pulled a blanket up to his shoulders, then lay beside him, wrapped in a comforter. Hours of fear and sheer terror had left her exhausted, so she fell into a deep sleep.

She woke when Gregori's body jolted beside her. He dragged in a deep breath. He'd been lying on his stomach, so when he sat up, he was in the middle of the bed.

She blinked. "You're all right?" She sat up, grinning. "You're all right! Oh, thank God." She threw her arms around his neck and hugged him.

His body trembled. "Stay back." He grabbed her arms and pushed her away. His eyes glimmered an intense green. "*Hungry.*"

"Oh, right." She probably looked like breakfast in bed. She scrambled to the ice chest and pulled out a bottle.

With a groan, his fangs shot out.

She twisted the cap off and handed him the bottle.

He guzzled it down, even though his fangs were in the way, and some of the blood trickled down his chin and neck.

She grabbed another bottle and removed the cap. He was so hungry, he didn't seem to care that the blood was ice-cold. When he tossed the empty bottle aside, she handed him the next one.

She eased around him to check his wounds. The paste was dry and flaking away.

She couldn't find the wounds.

He turned toward her. "I'll need another bottle." His

fangs had retracted, so he finished off the second bottle without drizzling blood down his chin.

She handed him another one. "Are you really okay?"

"Yes. Just hungry." He drank some more.

She went to the bathroom, washed up, then brought a damp towel to clean off his back.

"You don't need to do that," he grumbled.

She ignored him and climbed onto the bed behind him to wipe off the paste. The wounds were gone. As if they had never happened.

She skimmed her hand over the smooth skin. "You're completely healed. How?"

He shrugged. "It happens during our death-sleep."

She recalled how Robby and Angus had said he would be fine if he only made it to his death-sleep. "How can such a miraculous change occur when you're dead?"

"I don't know." He drank more blood. "It's a vampire thing."

"But to have such healing abilities . . ."

"Abby, don't question it. Just be glad we're both alive."

"I'm so grateful for what you did." She wrapped her arms around his waist and hugged him from behind. "It was very brave and noble of you."

He patted her hands. "Any time, sweetheart."

She sat back and eyed his smooth back. It was truly miraculous. "Do vampires always heal during their death-sleep?"

"Pretty much." He upended the bottle and finished it.

She scrambled off the bed and stood in front of him. "I need to study you."

With a wince, he set the empty bottle on the bedside table. "Abby, I am what I am. And you love me, right? So let's leave it alone."

"But you have miraculous healing powers. I need to know how it works. I need a sample of your blood."

He closed his eyes briefly with a pained look. "Don't ask that. Please."

"Why not?"

"You know I have a bunch of Vamps depending on me to keep them safe. If it got out that we have some kind of special blood, none of us would be safe. We would be hunted down by blood collectors and drained dry."

An odd sense of déjà vu flitted through her mind. "I—I wouldn't tell anyone."

"Abby, please. I'm alive. You're alive. We're free to go home and be together. It's perfect now. Don't mess it up."

"It's not perfect! My mother could be dying! And I didn't get any of the Demon Herb or the other plant. I got only the first one, and there's no telling if it'll be of any use to me. But here—" She motioned to him. "We have living proof that you possess amazing healing capabilities. There's no way around it. I need to examine your blood."

"I can't!" He stood up. "I told you that before."

"When?"

His face paled. "Just now."

The sense of déjà vu came back in full force. She rubbed her brow. What was it she was trying to remember?

"I'm . . . really dirty. I'm going to shower." He strode into the bathroom.

She stood there, her mind racing with jumbled thoughts. *It's perfect now. Don't mess it up.* How could she mess things up by asking for his blood? *I told you that before.*

The sense of déjà vu jabbed at her, and she paced about the bedroom, trying to remember. She'd met him at the White House. Then there had been the date at the nightclub and the trip to DVN. No, none of that triggered any forgotten memories.

The next night she'd gone to Romatech. She'd witnessed that scene where Sean Whelan's wife had discovered he'd been messing with her head for years.

She halted. No, it couldn't be possible. Gregori would never do such a thing.

Bits and pieces came back to her. She'd almost fainted. She'd been surprised at dinner that forty-five minutes had gone by. The stress ball had appeared in her pocket without her remembering how it got there. Laszlo had come up to her, acting like he already knew her.

A shudder skittered through her body.

She'd had this conversation with Gregori before.

She walked into the bathroom. He was in the shower stall, his back to her, his back that was smooth without any sign of the wounds he'd suffered.

With a trembling hand, she opened the door.

He turned and smiled. "Want to join me?"

Tears stung her eyes. She was afraid to ask, afraid of the answer. "Did you mess with my mind? Did you erase my memory?"

His smile vanished. "Abby, don't—"

"Did you screw with my mind?"

He grimaced. "We . . . can talk about it."

"No!" She backed away. Her heart plummeted, and a wave of nausea churned her stomach. "You did it, didn't you?"

"Abby, we can talk about it." He turned off the water and stepped out. "I had no choice at the time. And it was only a few minutes."

She pressed a hand to her mouth and ran back into the bedroom.

"Abby." He followed her, dripping wet.

"How could you?" She opened her backpack. Her hands shook as she fumbled inside.

"I told you. I have people I have to protect."

"And what about my mother? I'm trying to protect her!" She found her passport, her emergency cash, and her credit card.

"Oh God." Tears tumbled down her face. She had to leave him. She couldn't stay with someone who would screw with her mind.

She swung the backpack onto her shoulder. "We just went through hell, and we didn't have to! If you had given me a sample of your blood, I might not have needed those damned plants, and we wouldn't have suffered, and I wouldn't have met that demon, and he wouldn't have threatened to make my mother worse!"

She stormed out of the bedroom and down the stairs to the foyer. When she tried to open the front door, an alarm went off. She frantically pushed buttons, trying to get the door to unlock.

"What is wrong?" Kyo asked as he rushed toward her.

She sniffed and wiped the tears from her face. "I'm going home. Can you please call me a cab?"

"Cab?" He looked confused. "Why you crying?"

"Abby!" Gregori ran downstairs, wearing a pair of jeans. "Don't leave like this. We can talk it over."

"There's nothing to say!" she yelled at him. "You don't trust me enough to give me a sample of your blood. And I can't trust you anymore!"

"The devil take it." Angus strode into the foyer, a bottle of blood in his hand. "What is everyone fashed about?"

"I need a cab." Abigail sniffed. "I'm going to the airport."

"No!" Gregori walked toward her. "We'll work this out."

She yanked on the door handle. "I want to go!"

"Miss Tucker," Angus said. "There's no record of you entering this country. If you wait, I can teleport you west. It will take a while—"

"I don't want to wait." She wiped tears from her face.

"I have private jet," Kyo suggested. "Mortal pilot."

"Ye do?" Angus asked.

Kyo nodded. "I like it. I ride in back and sleep in coffin. I don't have to wait for sun to set." He turned to Abigail. "I get you out of Japan. My jet take you to Hawaii. Then you get plane home."

"No!" Gregori shouted. "She's not leaving. We have to talk this out."

"Let her go and think things over," Angus muttered.

"Yuki is my chauffeur," Kyo said. "I have him take you to airport." He punched some buttons on the intercom, then opened the door.

"Thank you, Kyo. You've been very kind." She stepped outside.

A black Town Car drove up, and she climbed into the backseat while Kyo gave the chauffeur instructions. As Yuki drove away, more tears streamed down her face.

She was leaving Gregori. *After he nearly died to save your life.* She pushed that thought aside.

He'd also screwed with her mind. Erased her memory. She might not have gone on the mission if she'd found something useful in his blood. When she thought about all they'd suffered through—Gregori's wounds and Howard's torture—more tears ran down her cheeks.

He refused to give her his blood. Refused to trust her. Refused to help her mother.

But he loves you. You love him. He almost died to save your life.

No. She wouldn't think about that. She couldn't.

He might have saved her life.

But he'd broken her heart.

Chapter Thirty

Gregori paced in his office at Romatech. Desperate times called for desperate measures. And he was desperate.

Time for Plan C.

He squeezed a stress ball. He'd devised the plans on the way back to New York. There'd been several layovers, while he, Angus, and Robby had waited for the sun to set at the next destination. He'd had plenty of time to figure out how to get Abby back. Angus and Robby had offered their advice—beg and grovel—but he hoped to avoid that. After all, he'd saved her life. He deserved some respect, dammit.

But it wasn't going well. Plan A had been a miserable failure. He'd based it on the premise that their squabble had been unimportant in the big scheme of things. They loved each other, so any minor disappointments could be easily smoothed over.

He called to see if she'd arrived home safely. She wouldn't pick up his calls. He left cheerful messages and sent flowers to her at the White House. Sent candy to her office. Sent more flowers and a fruit basket to her mother's room at the hospital. Left more cheerful messages with assurances that he loved her and had every confidence they could weather this minor storm.

He got an inkling that it wasn't working when the flowers were returned ground into mulch.

Undeterred, he moved swiftly on to Plan B—holding her plants hostage until she agreed to meet him. He sent more text messages, reminding her that her Tiger Paw plants were at Romatech. He was taking good care of them. And she could come pick them up some evening. Or he could deliver them to her personally at her lab.

No response.

He'd felt sure Plan B would work. Didn't she want the damned plants? Didn't she want to help her mother? He saw on the news that the first lady was failing fast.

Abigail felt betrayed. He realized that now. And his only hope at winning her back was Plan C.

He dropped the stress ball on his desk, picked up the small package he'd prepared for her, and slipped it inside a coat pocket. He'd waited till it was three in the morning, assuming the hospital would be quiet and free from visitors.

"Good luck," he murmured to himself, and teleported to Belinda Tucker's hospital room.

It was dark, except for the lights of the monitor screens. The first lady lay in her bed asleep, her face pale.

Across the private room, he saw Abigail sleeping on a couch. Dark circles smudged her eyes, and her nose looked red as if she'd been crying too much.

"I'm sorry, Abby," he whispered.

In the corner, a young man was sprawled on an easy chair, also sleeping. Gregori recognized him as Abby's brother, Lincoln.

Sleep. He directed a mental command at both Abby and her brother. He couldn't afford to have them wake up until Plan C was fully implemented.

The door opened and a male nurse walked in. He was a young man, dressed in white, with blond curly hair. He didn't look alarmed at the sight of Gregori.

He smiled. "How may I help you?"

Gregori shot a spurt of mind control at him, but wasn't sure he was getting through. "I want to give blood to her." He motioned to Belinda. "A direct transfusion. My blood type is the same as hers." He'd been drinking nothing but Type O for several nights to make sure he matched up.

The nurse inclined his head. "I will do as you ask."

"Good." He must have the nurse under his control after all. He took off his coat and laid it on the coffee table close to Abigail.

The nurse inserted a needle into Belinda's left arm, since her right arm was connected to an IV. "Bring a chair over here."

Gregori carried a lightweight plastic chair over to the other side of the bed. He sat and rolled up his sleeve.

The nurse rubbed alcohol on the crook of his elbow, then inserted a needle. Soon, blood was streaming through a tube into Belinda.

After about ten minutes, her face took on some color. She opened her eyes, saw the nurse, and smiled. "You ·came back."

"Yes." The nurse nodded, smiling back at her. "And someone else has come to help you."

Her eyes widened when she noticed Gregori. "What are you doing?"

"Trying to help."

Her gaze shifted to the tube inserted in her arm. "You're giving me vampire blood?" She stiffened. "I won't become a vampire, will I?"

"No," Gregori assured her. "It won't harm you in any way."

"You will be fine," the nurse said softly. "Trust me."

"I do," she replied.

The nurse smiled and motioned toward Gregori. "You can trust him, too."

Belinda gave him a curious look.

"This will be enough." The nurse disconnected them, then smoothed a bandage over Belinda's puncture. He stuck another bandage on Gregori's arm.

"Thank you." Gregori rolled down his sleeve.

Belinda looked over at Abigail asleep on the couch, then turned back to Gregori. "You broke her heart."

"I know. I'm . . . trying to mend it."

"By mending me?" She smiled. "I do feel much better."

"I'm glad." He sighed. "I should have helped you earlier. I'm sorry."

"Abby told me you were trying to protect your people, that you feared they would be hunted down for their blood."

He nodded. "I was afraid to trust her."

"I can understand that. I know from being close to my husband that it can be a heavy burden when the safety of so many people depends on your decisions. You must have felt torn between two worlds."

"Abigail is my world. I know that now." He glanced at her on the couch. "I would do anything for her."

Belinda took a deep breath and released it slowly. "I have to admit I wasn't thrilled when I realized she was in love with you. But the more she talked about you, the more I understood why she fell for you."

He felt a surge of hope. "She speaks well of me?"

Belinda smiled. "On and off. She's been very angry, but as much as she fusses about you, she defends you at the same time. She said you saved her life. You stepped in front of her and took two daggers in the back that were meant for her."

Gregori nodded. "I love her."

Belinda reached over and patted his hand. "If you can win her back, you will have my blessing."

"Thank you." He squeezed her hand, then stood. "I have something for Abby. Can you make sure she gets it?" He removed the package from his coat pocket and handed it to Belinda.

"Thank you, Gregori. Thank you for bringing her home safely."

He nodded. "Good night." He put on his coat and noticed the nurse was still there, standing by the door. "Thank you for your help." He started to release him from mind control, then realized it wasn't there.

The nurse inclined his head. "God be with you."

"You too." He glanced at the nurse's name tag. *Buniel.* He stepped back, inhaling sharply. "You—you—"

Buniel's eyes twinkled with humor. "Yes?"

"You're Marielle's friend. She told us about you."

Gregori ran a hand through his hair. "Shit—I mean, sorry." Damn, he'd just cursed in front of an angel. "Aren't you a healing angel?"

"A Healer, yes."

"Well . . . darn." He motioned toward Belinda, who had fallen asleep. "Why haven't you healed her? She was close to death when I got here."

Buniel arched a brow. "I am aware of her condition. I've been keeping her alive."

"But you could have healed her. And then I wouldn't have needed to give my blood."

"But you did need to give it. You needed to learn how to trust." The angel motioned to Abigail. "And she needs to learn how to forgive. It is better this way, don't you think?"

"Well . . . maybe." Gregori looked at Abigail. "You mean she'll forgive me now?" He glanced back at the angel, but he was gone.

Gregori sighed. "Say hello to Father Andrew for me."

Abigail woke at the sound of her mother calling her.

"Mom?" She scrambled off the couch and rushed to the hospital bed. "What's wrong? Shall I call for the nurse? Is it time for more medication?" She glanced at her watch. It was four in the morning.

"Abby, look at me."

She blinked when she realized her mother was sitting up. And her cheeks were rosy. "Mom, what happened?"

Belinda's eyes twinkled. "An angel came to see me."

Oh God, her mom was hallucinating. "It's probably the medication."

"The angel told me everything would be all right, and then, your Gregori came."

"He's not *my* Gregori, Mom. I don't want to ever see him again."

"But he saw you, dear. He told me he loved you and would do anything for you. And he gave me some of his blood."

"*What?*" Abigail's heart lurched.

Belinda touched the bandage on her arm. "I feel so much better."

Abigail ripped off the bandage and saw the puncture mark on her mother's arm. "When did this happen?"

"When the angel gave me a transfusion from Gregori. He was such a handsome man. The angel, not Gregori. Although Gregori is quite handsome, too."

"Gregori was here?"

"Yes. With an angel. He told me his name is Buniel."

Abigail shook her head. She didn't know what to make of this, but one thing was for sure, her mother was looking a hundred percent better. "We'll have to run some tests."

"Later." Belinda waved a dismissive hand. "What's important now is that you find your Gregori before the sun rises. He loves you very much."

"Mom—"

"And he left this for you." Belinda pulled a package out from under her blanket. "It's small. I think it might be an engagement ring."

"Oh my God." This was proof that Gregori had really been here. Her name was scrawled on the package in his handwriting.

"Well, open it! I want to see if it's a ring."

"Mom, are you saying you would approve of me and Gregori?"

"Sweetie, he saved your life. I know that he's . . . different, but he's a good man. He gave us his word that he would protect you on your trip, and he nearly died to keep his word. You don't let a man like that get away."

"He—he messed with my mind."

Belinda snorted. "All men mess with our minds, one way or another. But Gregori is a good man. Even the angel said we should trust him. Will you please open the package?"

"Oh, right." She ripped open one end and pulled out the contents. Underneath a layer of thermal wrap, she found a vial of blood. It was labeled "Gregori Holstein."

Belinda wrinkled her nose. "He gave you blood? That's not very romantic."

Tears came to her eyes. "Oh, it is. It means he trusts me."

"Well, you'd better hurry up and meet him."

Abigail blinked away her tears. "Yes, Mother. Thank you."

She dropped the vial of blood inside her handbag and retrieved her cell phone. After a moment's hesitation, she punched in the number for Angus.

"Miss Tucker?" he answered. "What can I do for you?"

"Could you possibly teleport me to Romatech?"

In one minute she was standing by the side entrance to Romatech. Angus swiped his card, then opened the door for her.

"Thank you." She walked inside.

"Any time, lass." He walked beside her, his kilt swishing around his knees. "I gather Plan C worked."

"Excuse me?"

He chuckled. "Go easy on the lad. He's been lost without you." He opened the door to the security office and went inside.

She took out her phone and sent Gregori a text message. *I would like to pick up my plants. I'll meet you in the foyer at Romatech.*

A message came instantly back. *When?*

She grinned and texted back. *About ten seconds.*

She stepped into the foyer, and in about five seconds, Gregori zoomed in at vampire speed.

He halted abruptly. "Hello."

"Hello." She bit her lip to keep from laughing. He looked so darned nervous. "I came to get my plants."

"Of course. This way."

She walked beside him down a hall.

"How have you been?" he asked.

She shrugged. "Busy."

He nodded and slanted a look her way. "How is your mother?"

"Not bad. She seems a bit better."

"Oh." He frowned. "That's good." He opened a door. "Your plants are in here."

She walked in and looked around. "What a beautiful lab."

"It's yours."

"What?" She spun to face him.

"It's yours, if you want it. Roman wants to hire you. And you can work on whatever you like."

"Like this?" She removed his vial of blood from her handbag.

"Yes." He shifted his weight. "But that is yours to keep, no matter where you work. I trust you."

She set the vial and her handbag down on a table. "I know what you did for my mother. I want to thank you. I can't thank you enough, actually. And I understand that you have a duty to protect your kind. It was wrong of me to judge you when you were trying to do the right thing."

"Then you forgive me?"

She smiled and nodded. "Yes. Can you forgive me?"

He lunged forward and pulled her into his arms. "Oh, Abby, I love you."

She laughed and hugged him tight. "I love you, too."

"Thank God." He kissed her brow. "I have something hard in my pants."

She snorted. "Your phone?"

"No." He reached into his pants pocket and pulled out a large golden disc. "It's a medal of honor. Angus gave it to me."

"Oh, it's beautiful." She took the disc and examined it. "Congratulations."

"There was a big ceremony to thank me for saving the Vamps. And Roman named me his heir apparent. That means I'll be the next Coven Master for the East Coast."

"That's wonderful! You must be thrilled."

He shoved a hand through his hair. "Actually, it doesn't mean much to me if I can't share it with you. I want to be with you, Abby."

"You do?" She set the medal down on the table.

"Yes. And I'll make you happy. You'll see. You can have all the freedom you want. You can work at your old job or here with me. And if you want to live close by, we can buy a house."

"Are you asking me to live with you?"

He stepped back. "Well. Actually, the thing is . . ." He pulled a stress ball from his pocket and squeezed it. "I know how much you value your freedom, but I thought we might have a . . . uh, more binding commitment."

She bit her lip to keep from grinning. "More binding?"

"Yes." He tightened his fist around the stress ball. "Not that I intend to imprison you in any way. I realize a commitment to a vampire could last a really long time, and I don't want you to feel trapped—"

"Are you asking me to marry you?"

The ball exploded in his hand. "Oh God, yes." He tossed the ball on the floor and fell to his knees. "Marry me, Abigail."

She fell to her knees and cradled his face in her hands. "I will."

He grinned. "You'll marry me?"

She laughed. "Yes!"

He levitated them both up onto their feet. "You'll have children with me?"

"Yes."

"And sex on the ceiling?"

She laughed again. "Yes."

"And you'll dance disco with me?"

She feigned a frown. "Now you're pushing it."

He laughed and hugged her tight. "I love you, Scholar. Falling for you was the smartest thing I've ever done."

"I love you, too." She nestled her cheek against his chest. Marry a vampire? It was the craziest thing she'd ever do.

Or maybe not. She glanced up at the ceiling. "Are you thinking what I'm thinking?"

He chuckled. "I'll lock the door."

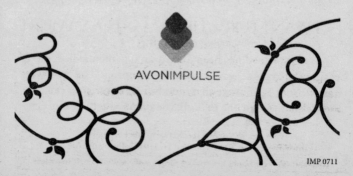

At Avon Books, we know your passion for romance—once you finish one of our novels, you find yourself wanting more.

May we tempt you with . . .

- **Excerpts** from our upcoming releases.

- Entertaining **extras**, including authors' personal photo albums and book lists.

- Behind-the-scenes **scoop** on your favorite characters and series.

- **Sweepstakes** for the chance to win free books, romantic getaways, and other fun prizes.

- Writing **tips** from our authors and editors.

- **Blog** with our authors and find out why they love to write romance.

- **Exclusive content** that's not contained within the pages of our novels.

Join us at
www.avonbooks.com

AVON

An Imprint of HarperCollins*Publishers*
www.avonromance.com